HEALING

NEWEARTH4

Julia Schmeelk

Julia Schmeelk
Salem, MO
www.JuliaSchmeelk.com

Publisher's Note: This is a work of fiction. Names, characters, places, and incidents are a product of the author's imagination. Locales and public names are sometimes used for atmospheric purposes. Any resemblance to actual people, living or dead, or to businesses, companies, events, institutions, or locales is completely coincidental.

Book Layout © 2016 BookDesignTemplates.com

Healing by Julia Schmeelk -- 1st ed.
ISBN-13- 978-1718677241

Thanks Everyone

Cheers...to everyone who has made this book possible. Bryon for tech support, web design, and promotion guidance. Athena for the spectacular visual depictions of my characters and their world. My editor Jo and my fabulous group of beta readers who help me find the worst mistakes and my parents for their unending support. Shawn- you make it all worthwhile.

For Mom, who never gave up.

Happy Mother's Day 2018

Cast of Characters

Trissy- Human, mated to Heron, no companion, 3 youngsters Matti, Jenny and Tonseth.

Hanna- Human, mated to Gordon, no companion, 1 youngster Kenseth.

Mia- Dragon, mated to Pit, no companion, no youngster or youth in her nest.

Jamie- Human, unmated, companion to Janie, no youngster or youth in her nest.

Janie- Human, unmated, companion to Jamie, no youngster or youth in her nest.

Dotty- Human, mated to Tad, no companion, no youngster or youth in her nest.

LeeAnn- Human, mated to Hess, no companion, no youngster or youth in her nest.

Youngster and Youth

Tonseth-Human;   Kenseth-Human

Redseth-Dragon;   Starseth-Dragon;

Jenny-Human;   Matti-Human;

Tria–Dragon; Zack–Human;

Golly-Human

__Foreword__

"It was only a little more than thirty cycles ago when Grabon formed the first bond of communication with a human. To remind everyone, the humans arrived in their flying baskets only two hundred cycles ago, but those who observed them believed them to be incapable of real communication beyond their own species. Upon their arrival a nearby territory dragon approached the strange wingless beings to offer welcome and a fair trade of goods, but the creatures scrambled, panicked and attempted to attack. Another territory dragon was tasked to observe them, and eventually also determined they were not worthy of consideration. Since the past council deemed these newcomers were not a threat to the balance of the planet, or the intelligent inhabitants, they were only observed occasionally. As the designated protectors of the planet, the council decided to wait to see if the planet itself adopted or rejected these newcomers. Over time, most of the territories nearest the humans have become vacant, and no worthy young dragon has been willing to claim a part of the planet where humans reside. This fact should be weighed against the consideration of changing the newcomers from a lower to an upper species."

"An interesting version of our history. Accurate in detail, but a bit accusatory. Your skill for objectivity obviously needs some attention, but we thank you for your contribution." Niggs nodded to the young female before turning to Kessler. *"Your historian reminds me*

of when you were young and eager."

"She is still maturing." Kessler glanced to the side for a moment, a quirk to his lips. The others offered their appreciation for her skills and Kessler's willingness to share them beyond his own clan.

The grey-and-green female adjusted her feet and posture, pleased with the recognition, but there was still more to tell. *"When Grabon reached maturity, he claimed his territory and has included a select group of humans capable of some communication with other species as part of his territory clan. Some council members are curious to see how this will influence his rules and territory structure and have decided to continue to observe. In time, the council might send a designated representative to report on these new developments. According to all reports from other territory dragons, Grabon is a powerful, thoughtful territory holder with unique and interesting ideas. There are no indications, at this time, that his thinking is twisted or wrong."*

<u>Chapter 1</u>

Hess paced back and forth outside the territory dragon's nest, waiting impatiently. What was Grabon thinking? He had to know they were all running off their feet getting everything ready. They were opening the market for the first time at sun-high noon. Whatever he had to say, why couldn't they use mindspeak and get it done? And what was up with these shields? Why was he blocked out of the nest especially when there must be fifteen visitors perched on Grabon's wall? That had never happened before.

Even as he thought it, the shields dropped and he vaulted up the steps and down the other side. What he saw made him freeze. A human was crouched low to the ground brandishing a knife, and Grabon was bleeding. As Hess drew power, preparing to strike, Grabon waved a clawed hand in his direction.

"She is confused. Help me with this."

Hess ran over to him, keeping one eye on the woman, yes, she was female; he just hadn't noticed until now. He ripped off his shirt and used it to help staunch the flow of blood. The cut was deep and it was going to have to be stitched closed before they could do any real healing. Grabon had some healing skill, so did Griss and Gordon. Hess knew his ability was even less.

"What on this good planet happened?" Hess

demanded softly, aware of all the visitors watching.

"Ron, the visiting yellow-and-black, dropped her in the nest. I was surprised she was alive. This wasn't her fault, Hess."

"Wasn't her fault?" His gaze swept over the woman who looked half-crazed as far as he was concerned. "It was her hand on the knife," he accused.

The image of what had happened filled his mind in living color and he gasped, blinking to clear his vision. All right, maybe Grabon had a point. If someone had dropped him from their back claws into an unfamiliar nest, he would have come up fighting too, if he could have gotten up at all.

The woman approached, still looking dazed and shocked, but her knife was tucked in its sheath at her side. She kept flexing her jaw, neck, shoulders, arms, and hands, but he was more concerned about the amount of blood Grabon was losing.

"Get me some water. We need to get this wound closed," Hess told her, doing his best to sound calm and in control.

Keeping one eye on the wall of dragons perched and watching, she dragged up a bucket of water from the pool and hauled it over to them. Hess started to dip his blood-soaked shirt in the water when she brushed his hand away from the wound. Grabon gave a low gasp but caught Hess's arm before he could knock her away. As Hess watched, the wound closed and he felt the vibration of healing energy bouncing all around them, more intense than anything he had ever felt before. It gave off actual heat, and he could not imagine what being hit with such a burst would feel like.

Grabon let out his breath in one huge sigh, and the woman sat down hard on the ground, looking even more dazed and disheveled than she had before.

"Thank you," Grabon offered softly. The female nodded and met his gaze.

"So what happened?" Hess asked impatiently, glancing at her as he cleaned up the blood from Grabon's side. She obviously had enough mindspeaking ability to communicate with Grabon and had some impressive healing skills.

She squinted as she peered up at the wall and pointed at the yellow-and-black dragon who sat with his arms crossed. "He snatched me up off the ground, flew me here, and dropped me. I didn't mean to stab him." She nodded at Grabon, frowning and rubbing her hands together.

"You were understandably confused. I am Grabon, the territory dragon. This is Hess. Who are you?"

"Me? I'm LeeAnn." She looked at the eight dragons remaining on the wall and grimaced, shivered and sighed.

"Don't look at them. Grabon will deal with them. You're a healer?" Hess demanded.

She nodded but was distracted when the yellow-

and-black dragon moved his wings and leaned forward. Standing, she pushed her hair back and straightened her shoulders. "I belong to Sam, the nightmare man with the traveling freak show."

Hess hissed out a breath and looked at Grabon. "Where did he pick you up? Can you throw me a picture?"

When she did, Grabon let out a growl that filled the air as he straightened to his full height and glared up at Ron, who had turned his back on them. *"It is not even close to my territory. He went hunting for a human for the purpose of dropping her in my nest, and he took one from beyond my territory to avoid my judgment."*

"You can deal with him later," Hess reminded Grabon. He had much more immediate concerns, like opening the market for the first time. "What should we do with her? This is opening day, remember."

"She should attend the market. Take her to Heron and have Trissy lend her some clothing."

"Is that the new Dragon Market?" LeeAnn frowned as she rubbed her palms on her legs. They either itched or her palms were sweating. He would bet it was nerves.

"Yes, today is opening day," Hess answered impatiently, tired of correcting people about the name. Was Grabon really suggesting that they offer her a place in the clan? Did he forget the significance of their clothing?

"That's where Sam was bringing us, to the new Dragon Market."

That caught his attention. "No, we would never have a freak show." The very idea offended his sensibilities, and he hadn't even known he had sensibilities.

"How did your Sam hear about our market?" Grabon asked.

"I have no idea; he hears all kinds of things. He was excited about playing to a whole new audience. We're traveling all the way from the fifth colony. That's where we've been lately."

"Are you all right? How is your side?" Hess asked Grabon.

"It is almost completely healed. I know you are in a hurry, but take her down to Heron's. It seems I must deal with Ron."

Hess glanced up at where the yellow-and-black sat with his back to them. Whatever Grabon decided to do with him was fine, but Hess hoped it wouldn't disrupt opening day. "Well come on, we can get you some decent clothing and you can clean up and attend the market. We can figure out what to do with you later."

He was heading for the steps with LeeAnn on his heels when he heard Grabon hiss. *What now?* was all he could think.

"She is injured," Grabon told him.

Hess looked her over twice before he saw what

Grabon had meant. The color and dirt on her shirt hid most of the blood. Now that he was looking for the injury, he could see the holes in the fabric and her blood soaking through the cloth. Cursing under his breath, he yanked the shirt off her shoulder. Her wince and duck to avoid his attention barely registered after he glimpsed so many recently healed injuries and more scars than he could count.

"Let go!" She pulled away and covered her shoulder with the shirt.

Their eyes met and something inside him jerked, causing him to swallow hard. He did not have time to deal with all of this. "Those need to be treated. Can't you heal your own injuries?"

"They'll heal," she muttered, crossing her arms.

He let out a sigh and looked at Grabon. "Heron will take care of her injuries. You really want her in one of Trissy's outfits?"

The dragon nodded, giving him an odd look. *"She is accepted, Hess. The choice of whether she chooses to stay is hers."*

He nodded and took her hand. "Come along, I have to be there to open things up, so we don't have much time. Tad can only cover for so long."

As they left the nest, moving down the log steps, she took a deep breath. "What's going to happen to the one who snatched me?"

Hess glanced at her as they climbed over the rocks.

"First of all it's not my decision. Grabon deals with the dragons, especially the visiting dragons like Ron." She continued down over the rocks, not betraying a hint of pain, but he was sure those punctures had to hurt to the core. "He'll take care of it. Ron broke a territory rule, and Grabon doesn't tolerate that."

"What are these territory rules?" LeeAnn asked, watching her footing, placing each foot deliberately.

"Don't hunt dragons, don't hunt humans, and judgment comes from the territory dragon. Those are the most important ones. Ron snatched you outside the territory but dropped you in Grabon's nest, so he's likely to consider that as hunting humans." They continued down the hill on the easier path, and Hess pointed out Heron's hut. "Heron is Grabon's companion."

When the white-haired man stepped outside the door, she sat down on the path, as if her legs had simply given out beneath her weight.

"We really don't have time for this," Hess told her, trying not to sound too impatient as he tugged on her arm.

"Is she hurt?" Heron asked, coming forward and tossing Hess a shirt.

"No."

"Yes," Hess answered at the same time she did. "Ron's talons pierced her shoulders. We need to clean her up and get her dressed. It's opening day, Heron. I have to get down there."

"Let me look." Heron shifted her shirt and nodded. "You can heal others a lot better than you can yourself. Those are going to scar, just like the others."

"I'm used to it. I don't want to be a bother," she began, but Heron ignored her and lifted her to her feet.

"We need to go inside so we can clean those up. They have quit bleeding at least. I'll get you one of Trissy's outfits while she helps you with a quick wash and gets rid of the blood, before you change."

※ ※ ※

Inside the hut, Trissy introduced herself, and LeeAnn was surprised to see that this woman was rounded with the last stages of pregnancy. She had two white stripes in her hair, but she looked healthy and young, and at least she didn't vibrate the air with power. Heron had all-white hair but looked incredibly fit and not at all old.

The women moved behind a blanket with a bowl of water and some rags, and a very solid shield went up, creating a wall.

Nice trick, she thought as Trissy helped her take off her shirt so she could clean the punctures.

"I'm not prone to infection. My system doesn't tolerate it. We just need to clean off the blood."

"You let me worry about that," Trissy murmured, using the wet rag gently. "Please tell me Ron was not the first dragon you had ever seen."

"To be honest I didn't really see him. He swooped in so fast, I wasn't sure what was happening. When he dropped me in the nest, I suppose I was in shock and that's why I attacked Grabon."

"I can't imagine anything worse than that." Trissy shuddered. "These are healing at an amazing rate, but Heron tells me what you did on Grabon was simply astounding."

"Thanks, but few people can tolerate my kind of healing. I produce a heavy jolt of power in a focused area. It can be excruciating where there is already damage. In my experience, people become angry and scream when I heal them. It's not exactly the reaction I'm looking for when I'm trying to help. That was how I ended up in the freak show to begin with. Nothing is freakier than a healer who accidently hurts people while fixing them and who can heal others ten times faster than herself."

Trissy rinsed out the rag. "I would think they would be grateful not to be injured any longer. Here, put these undergarments on first, then the leggings and tunic. I haven't worn these since I first arrived, so I won't miss them. You can use my brush and I'll look for a tie for your hair."

When LeeAnn joined Heron and Hess, she felt so much steadier. Clean and dressed in better clothes than she had ever owned, even as a child, she felt almost like a real person again. Hess was clearly impatient to go, so she offered a quick word of thanks to Trissy, and Heron followed them outside.

A dark brown dragon was on the roof and nodded to

them as they left.

"His name is Rok. Trissy will join us for an hour or so later," Heron told her, matching her stride as they moved down the hill along the path. "Have you eaten?"

LeeAnn didn't know how to answer, so she settled for "Not today."

They were about to step past the woods when she suddenly stopped walking and scowled at the ground. The energy was distinctive, unmistakable. "I can't go there. That is Farmer land. They have no tolerance for freaks."

Hess sighed impatiently and nudged her forward so she continued to walk. "That's not true. Gordon isn't going to hurt you for walking across his yard. We don't have time for me to elaborate, but Farmers don't have any tolerance for freak shows where humans are exploited by other humans."

She stopped walking and put her hands on her hips. "Someone should tell those Farmers that the freaks have no choice." Even as she scowled, she kept a nervous eye on the house.

"Yes, they do. All they need to do is walk away," Hess answered, nudging her arm to get her moving past the barn to the bridge and across the river.

"Tell me about Sam the Nightmare Man?" Heron asked as they passed what looked like another farmhouse and walked along a path that went by a round structure that held plants. Now that was curious.

"Sam, Sam the Nightmare Man. He visits your mind and makes you think he's inside. He is one creepy man, Sam the Nightmare Man," she sang softly, but kept looking around. She not only noticed Heron's amusement, but Hess's frustration.

Heron grinned again when she stumbled, but caught her arm. "Walking is easier if you focus in front of you. Tell us about Sam. You consider him an enemy?"

"He's the worst kind of enemy." Her eyes met his as she answered and she licked her lips, her expression sober. "At first he seems nice, but he's tricky. He's had two of our people hanged as thieves because they wouldn't do as he said. Others he torments with nightmares because he enjoys their screams."

Hess stopped walking and turned to look at her. "That's how he keeps you in line?"

"That and when I ran away before, he tortured my friend, Golly."

"Did anyone see Ron take you?" Hess asked.

"Golly was there. I was healing his cuts and scratches from running through the brambles when I was snatched. The others weren't far away, so they may have seen it."

"Good, then your friend should be safe. I don't think even a nightmare man would call what happened to you running away. Tonight, when opening day is over, we can talk about what you can do." Hess ran his hand through his hair as they continued walking.

LeeAnn followed, stunned. There was something she could do? Did he think she hadn't tried? Rotating her shoulders, she could tell it was going take a little longer before the injuries were healed enough for her to take on another injury herself. That drop had done a good bit of damage to her insides. It was better to finish healing before she headed back. There was no predicting what might happen along the way.

Heron caught her eye and nodded. His expression made her swallow nervously.

They walked quickly through the tall weeds, following the narrow pathway until it opened up and they were at the back end of the market, only it didn't look like any market LeeAnn had ever seen.

There were booths, all freestanding, round, with space between them. There were benches with tables, and too many things to glance at as they raced through. People called out greetings and Hess waved as he went. As they approached what looked like the entrance, people were waiting, some inside the shields, and many more outside. There were dragons inside, two with wagons and babies or young dragons, she couldn't really tell. Power shimmered around everyone. Hess made a quick introduction, clasped her hand as if for luck and nodded to Pit and Thane, a dark gray and a dark green dragon, to open the shield. Then his voice filled the air, projected by his mind and filled with power.

"Welcome to the opening day of our *Territory Market*. Thank you all for coming. To begin, please notice the statue. This is Grabon, our territory dragon, and his companion of thirty-odd years, Heron." He gestured to Heron in person. "The statue is made of the planet's memory river and holds an important greeting. Please take the time to listen and follow Grabon's rules."

He stepped back, bringing LeeAnn with him to the side of the entrance. "Okay, that's done. Now only a hundred things are on my list for today." He looked down at her and with a slight shrug, tightened his hold on her hand.

"She can stay with us," Janie suggested, glancing at her sister and then Mia. "We're making the tour since we have people running our booths. I thought we'd take Jenny and Matti, but Brom said he would watch them."

Hess released her and ran a hand through his hair, clearly impatient to get on with his list of tasks that had to be done. "That would be great. She hasn't eaten today, so get her some food if you can."

"I am sure we can find something." Jamie took her arm. "You should start at the beginning. Go look at the statue, it's truly magnificent."

Wanting to humor the two sisters and happy to escape the odd feelings that seemed to go with being around Hess, LeeAnn stepped up to the entrance and got her first real look at the statue's workmanship and detail. It was incredible, and clearly a skilled gold crafter had made it. She touched the statue expecting

Grabon's voice. Instead, a heartsinger's voice filled her senses, going over the rules in both Human and what she suspected was Dragon. Then Grabon gave a short welcome and stated the rules once again. How had they trapped the full power of a heartsinger in the gold? She had never seen anything like it.

As she stepped back, she noticed the carving on the pedestal and smiled as she bent to take a closer look.

It, too, was done by a craftsman of extraordinary skill. The Universal Human word *welcome* was carved so cleverly in and among leaves and vines, that it took a moment to see it. As she looked closer, she saw hints of faces in the leaves. She recognized Trissy and Heron, Grabon and Hess right off. After a moment she saw Janie and Jamie and the dark brown dragon from Heron's. As she kept looking she saw Mia and several other dragons, and the faces of a few humans she hadn't met yet. Before she left, she hoped to meet them all.

They were an extraordinary group of people, human and dragon. The heartsong clearly stated that the purpose of the Territory Market was to let humans and dragons learn about each other. The Dragonmen wanted to encourage an honest exchange of goods, ideas, and culture. What a wonderful goal that was. No wonder Hess was so anxious for success.

Jamie and Janie came over and stood by her side. "So what did you think?" Jamie asked, looking almost nervous.

"It's extraordinary. I can't think of a better word.

The statue, heartsong, message, mission, and carving are all incredible, indescribable even. How did they do it?"

With a sigh of relief, Jamie waved Dotty over along with Mia. "She wants to know how they did it?" The women laughed. "Since you're at least dressed as one of us, we'll tell you a few well-known secrets and some that are not as well known," Jamie continued. "Hanna is our gold crafter. Have you met her yet? She's Gordon's mate and out to here with her first pregnancy. They will be here later since Hanna tires easily but she wants to look around. The huge, powerful Farmer by her side is always a clue that Hanna is near. You walked through their farmyard on the way in from Grabon's nest, the house on the other side of the river."

LeeAnn nodded; she remembered it well. The energy had been so strong it had spooked her.

"Trissy is the carver. You met her, didn't you?" Janie asked.

"Yes, she loaned me her clothes. She seems very nice. I hadn't realized she was a carver."

"Next time you're in the hut, take a look at their table. Trissy did the legs and they are amazing. You'll be surprised," Dotty said with a grin.

"I'll have to look at that. Which of the dragons is the heartsinger?" she asked, looking at Mia.

"It is not me; I am the storyteller. We protect our heartsinger because she does not like a large

audience."

Dotty waved her hand low at her waist, and LeeAnn's eyes widened. "What do you do?" she asked the sisters with a smile after she had recovered from the shock.

"Well, let me see. We make candy and goods for sale," Janie answered.

"They design and make all our clothes," Dotty told her, pointing out the women's similar garb.

"These are the finest clothes I have ever worn, so thank you. Even if they are only borrowed, they are wonderful." She meant that with all sincerity. Not only was the style attractive and the fabric evenly woven and carefully cut, but they were comfortable and sturdy.

"Heron mentioned you were an incredible healer," Dotty offered.

"Hmm, more of a freak healer, I'm afraid. What I do works and it is fast, but it's also very painful."

"Really, why is that?" Jamie asked, gesturing for them to walk with her.

"I apply large amounts of healing energy to an open wound in order to close it, or to a broken bone to force it to mend. Most humans have no tolerance for that type of forced energy."

"So you have had trouble keeping clients?" Jamie asked, frowning.

LeeAnn shook her head. "It is much worse than that."

"Here we are; the tea shop. Go find us a place to sit down; Jamie and I will bring them over."

Dotty scouted around and found them a table in a small cove of trees, and the sisters brought over steaming mugs of tea as they all settled around.

"We have a couple of different flavors, all Griss's recipes." Jamie handed one to Mia, Dotty, and LeeAnn, then took one each for herself and Janie. "Now, dear, tell us why you ended up in a freak show."

LeeAnn took a sip of the fragrant, sweetened tea and sighed. "My parents were both healers in the second colony. They did well, and as I matured, they began to teach me healing. I learned brews and sutures and all types of things and I was a good student. The problem is my healing energy is too strong. It was a great disappointment to them, or I was; it's hard to say. They had me working in the clinic with them and I couldn't stop myself from healing people, especially if it was something serious. But the people I helped became irate and then fearful. I had to stop going to the clinic or my parents would have lost all their clients."

Drinking the tea gave her an excuse to pause and collect her thoughts. "When I was seventeen I ran away. A client came to the house instead of the clinic and I healed him. That's when people started calling me a freak, and I couldn't bear to stay."

"What was wrong with him?" Jamie asked suspiciously.

"The short version is he was dying. He had come to plead for stronger medicine to end his life, which he knew my parents wouldn't give him at the clinic."

"You healed him?" Dotty asked softly.

"He was not grateful or happy?" Mia asked, leaning closer.

LeeAnn looked away. "Nobody was happy. Not my parents, not his family who were resigned to his death, and not even the man I cured, because he claimed I had made his insides burn worse than ever before." She took a deep breath. "I ran away and it was hard and lonely. Worse, the only skills I have are healing, so I still healed people and they screamed in agony. So when Sam offered me a place among the freaks, it seemed like a good idea."

"Who is Sam?" Jamie asked gently.

"Sam, Sam, the nightmare man," LeeAnn sang softly. She turned to Dotty. "Sorry, I often end up singing his introduction for the show. He runs it and owns us. He's nice at first, until he has you hooked and either learns something about you or makes it up. The first time I argued with him, he presented me with a list of what I owed him for food, the use of the wagon, even the supplies I had used. In order to pay him back I had to work. In order to keep working I had to eat. It's a vicious cycle. So you run away and that's when the bad stuff starts happening." Clearing her throat, she looked at the other women and smiled. "You don't want to hear this."

"He's coming here?" Janie asked with a gleam in her eye as she looked at Jamie.

A cold shiver seemed to pass over all of them, even Mia.

"That was his plan, but Hess said he'd never allow a freak show to perform in the market."

Janie looked at her thoughtfully before answering. "No, but you have friends there, and someone needs to do something about Sam. You leave him to the rest of us; we'll take care of him for you."

"No, you don't understand. Sam is vicious. He would hurt your people. I'll tell him freaks aren't welcome here and do what I can to direct him away."

"You've been accepted, LeeAnn. Didn't anyone explain you can stay?" Dotty asked.

"Stay?" She looked around and sighed. "If only I could." She drank her tea in a few gulps, now that it had cooled. "I may not be much of a healer, but I don't bring destruction to good people."

Jamie and Janie started to say something, but Dotty had leaned forward, so they waited. Fighting to find the words she wanted, Dotty hesitated.

Mia sat up straighter on her tail. *"They are almost ready. Are you coming to hear this first story?"*

"We wouldn't miss it," Jamie answered. "We'll get

our refills and join you in the storyteller's cove."

A few moments later, they handed LeeAnn a second cup of tea and she followed them out and down the main wooded isle that was filled with people, human and dragon. They found a path through the tall grass that led to a little cleared area that a carved sign proclaimed as the Storyteller's Cove. LeeAnn noticed that moving and breathing was growing easier, so the healing was progressing. They found a place near Mia and sat on the grass. Brom arrived with Jenny, Matti, and Star. The gray-and-white dragon smiled at them as the girls all raced around.

"They have so much energy. I am going to grab some tea if you will watch the girls?" Brom directed the question at Dotty and she nodded with a huge smile.

Griss, a red dragon, arrived next, pulling a wagon with his son, who was anxious to get out and play with the girls. LeeAnn noticed right away that nobody differentiated between the two human girls and the dragons. Griss already had his tea, and he settled beside Jamie, sitting on his tail.

"Trissy and Hanna are on their way, so they are delaying the announcement," Griss told Mia.

Shaking her hands, Mia confessed, *"I can't believe how nervous I am. It's almost as bad as the first time. Isn't that silly?"*

LeeAnn understood completely. She stood and handed the female dragon her cup of tea. "Here, when I'm nervous before a performance, drinking something hot, even if it's just water, can help calm my nerves."

Mia accepted it with a nod and a smile before taking a sip. *"I like this flavor too. Tell us what you perform,"* she invited.

"Well aside from singing the introductions, I'm Golly's target girl: the one he throws knives and hatchets at during the show. Because of all my scars, the audience is always waiting for a show of blood when he misses. Then I have a healing act, where I heal a volunteer from the audience. I fall off the high wire on a regular basis, and anything else crazy Sam the Nightmare Man comes up with for me to do."

Jamie patted her arm. "There is no reason for you to travel back to them when they are headed this way." She gave Brom a meaningful glance. "I am sure someone will be willing to help you rescue your friend."

"I am not putting your people at risk, I already told you." She meant it, too, but she was thoroughly enjoying this time of freedom. They made her feel welcome and she appreciated them more than she could say.

"Keep an open mind," Jamie urged her softly. "We have resources you haven't even met yet."

As if on cue, Hanna and Gordon emerged from the path through the tall grass. LeeAnn recognized them from Trissy's carving and she smiled.

"It's very nice to meet you, LeeAnn. This is my mate, Hanna."

LeeAnn shook their hands and greeted them both, not surprised by the power she sensed in him. As soon as she had seen him, she had known he was the Farmer. Gordon helped Hanna settle comfortably on the ground and sat behind her pregnant form so he could support her back. It was the most loving thing she had ever seen, and she looked away. When they were comfortable, she told Hanna how wonderful the statue was.

Grinning, Hanna leaned in close and whispered, "Keep your eyes open. There are two more hidden in the market."

LeeAnn thought about how clever that was and sighed.

A few minutes later Grabon, Heron, and Trissy emerged from the path. While Heron helped his mate sit on the ground, all the youngsters climbed on Grabon, making themselves comfortable. Brom came back with several mugs of tea and handed them out.

Mia held up a finger and everyone around her seemed to be grinning.

"Pit, did you hear we have a storyteller? She's well known among the dragons for her stories."

"Of course I know that, Thane. Mia is my mate. If you would like to hear a story told in the dragon style, go to the storyteller's cove.

"You can stop by the tea hut first and get a mug of tea, and then look for the tall grass path. It will take you there."

"What a clever announcement," LeeAnn laughed.

Mia was grinning and there were several chuckles. *"Now we will see if anyone comes."*

Pit came down the path and paused to greet his mate. They touched palms and tails for just a moment before he sat near Grabon. People started to come in, grinning and laughing at the announcement. Several asked how many coins the entertainment cost, and Mia gently explained that all stories were freely given. People seemed surprised, but they joined the others and sat in the grass.

As the cove filled up with warm bodies, an air of excitement also filled the space. When Mia stood to begin, LeeAnn immediately recognized the story. It was an Old Earth tale about Little Red and her bad, bad wolf. Some of the characters were different, and there were mind-projected pictures, varying voices, and great drama. That it was told in mindspeak that was so basic even the children could understand, made it even more entertaining.

When Mia finished, the audience's applause was thunderous and several people praised her style. LeeAnn overheard two women planning to bring their children back to hear the next story. As they left, the Dragonmen lingered, congratulating her.

"The next session is a dragon story told in Human. I hope as many people come."

"I don't think you have anything to worry about," LeeAnn said with a grin.

Heron looked over at her, frowning. "Have you eaten yet?"

"We had tea," she answered with a smile.

"Come along, everyone. Trissy will enjoy sitting in a chair to have a meat pie." Heron, Brom and Griss gathered the children and they all moved as a group to a three-sided hut set to the side of the market grounds with tables and chairs. Grabon and the other dragons simply moved the chairs out of the way and sat on their tails. Mia and Pit joined them a few minutes later.

"Thane and I need to go back to work. Don't forget to take LeeAnn to the garden."

As Pit and Thane left, platters of crescent-shaped meat pies arrived. LeeAnn couldn't believe these people's generosity. After she had eaten her first one, Grabon caught her eye.

"You should know that Ron has been banished from my territory. In his misguided attempt to prove how fragile and useless humans were, he disgraced himself by breaking a territory rule. On behalf of all the dragons here, we offer you a sincere apology. Not all of our kind are that cruel or that narrow-minded."

"After having met you and the others, I could never believe that. You have all been so welcoming and kind; words cannot express my gratitude."

"Then consider staying among us. It seems you have need of rescuing and we can do that for you. We will even try to help your friend," Grabon promised.

LeeAnn's heart pounded as she looked at their hopeful expressions. But fear poured through her and she swallowed the bitter taste. "I will consider it, but I cannot make any promises."

Grabon nodded and ate another meat pie. She couldn't help but consider such a generous offer, but what could she contribute? How would she stop herself from healing someone? Could she do something for the market? Worse, what would Sam do? Would he hurt these extraordinary people who were just starting to build something so meaningful and fragile? Did she have the right to ask for their help when she had nothing of value to offer in exchange? What about Golly? Would they welcome him?

A sound jolted her out of her thoughts. It took her a moment to realize it was a low growl vibrating the air. It stopped then, and she couldn't place where it had come from. Nobody around the table seemed concerned, so she picked up another meat pie and took a bite.

When they had finished eating, they went to what everyone referred to as the garden. It was a nest, Jamie explained, domed in a heat shield, and they had planted a garden inside. When they entered, LeeAnn admitted that Jamie's explanation might have been technically correct, but it left a great deal out.

The garden had a pool of water with a bubbling spring. Pathways had been carved through the dense foliage, and so many different kinds of vibrant and fragrant plants and flowers populated the space that the effect was stunning. As they walked through it, LeeAnn found plenty of benches positioned for people to sit and soak up the heat and atmosphere.

LeeAnn caught a glint of gold peeking through the foliage nestled at the back of the pond. Grinning, she had to walk through a shallow pool of water to approach the next statue. Several other visitors followed her, and their sighs of appreciation floated on the fragrant air. The detail on the breathtaking statue was perfect, and it depicted Tad and Pit taking off to share the sky. After a moment, she reached out to see what filled the planet's memory river.

Heartsong floated through her mind, exploding with sound and light. The song was about the birth of the Dragonmen clan and it resounded with power, determination, skill, and love. She blinked back tears and tried not to sniff. No wonder the men called their chosen matches mates; it must be from the song. She went back to her group and they grinned at her.

"That is amazing. I can't wait to find the third one." People must have heard her, because there were murmurs all through the garden about a third statue. Evidently most had not heard that the market had three of them.

LeeAnn and the others spent a little more time exploring the garden before they headed out to see some booths. As she looked around, she carefully stored detailed memories to share with Golly, from the damp heat to the heady fragrance of growing things, because he would love this.

As Hanna and Trissy explored a kitchenware booth, LeeAnn moved to one of the benches. Another flex of her shoulders told her that most of the healing was complete, not that she had been worried. Eventually she always managed to heal herself; sometimes it just took longer.

In that moment of quiet, she realized how profound an impact the market had on its visitors. It provided not only an excellent shopping experience, but entertainment and education. Hess had been right; this was no place for a freak show.

Grabon joined her. He folded his hands and sat on his tail beside her. *"How are you feeling?"*

"I am feeling wonderfully free at the moment."

His large head nodded and he smiled. *"I was referring to your injuries."*

"They are almost completely healed." Her own health and well-being was never very interesting, so she changed the subject. "This is an amazing place you have created."

"It was not my plan; it was Tad, Hess, Pit, and Thane's. It serves our territory well and demonstrates many of our skills and talents." He reached into the pouch he carried across his shoulders. *"So you may make purchases."* He dumped a dragon-sized handful of coins in her hands. Before she could form a reply, he walked away.

LeeAnn stared at the coins in wonder as Jamie came over and grinned. "You should buy a pouch or something to carry those in."

"He just gave me a handful of coins." She indicated Grabon with her head.

"He can be wonderfully sensitive sometimes. Come with me." Jamie led her to a booth that had all manner of bags and pouches. Looking them over, LeeAnn was surprised to see that some had long straps designed for dragons and others had shorter straps for humans. Mia joined them and asked to see a beautifully crafted leather pouch that had flowers stamped into the leather and was delicately stained with several colors. She cooed enthusiastically over the bag and showed LeeAnn the impressive details.

The hairs on the back of LeeAnn's neck stood as a haunting melody of heartsong drifted on the air currents, vibrating and pulsing. Children stopped running, and no one spoke while the music built and crashed. Images of color and light flashed through her mind, as emotions rose to her throat. The song had no words, just music and a beautiful voice rising to pay homage to a wonderful day. As it faded, while most people were still too stunned to speak or move, LeeAnn peeked around to see if she could spot Dotty.

"She is well shielded," Mia told her softly, glancing at LeeAnn with a smile. *"Have you chosen a bag for yourself?"*

LeeAnn looked back at the bags and saw one that matched her borrowed clothing. It had a leather bottom, but was made of cloth and also had a drawstring closure. She pointed at it, and Manny, the man in the booth, handed it to her.

"Consider it a gift," Jamie told her with a grin. "Thank you, Manny. Just write off the two bags for my friends. You are doing an excellent job with the booth."

Manny beamed as he walked off to serve another customer.

"These are yours?" LeeAnn asked, looking even closer at the bag. "Of course, the material matches the clothing." As she stashed her coins and placed the bag over her head to lay by her side, a grinning Dotty joined them.

"That was lovely, dear," Jamie told her.

The women smiled at each other before they moved off to look at something else. All around LeeAnn people were commenting on the heartsinger, and more than one person sniffed back tears or even wiped their eyes. What amazed her most was the dazed look on the faces of the visiting dragons. Soon after arriving at the market, she could tell the difference between the dragons who belonged to the clan and were comfortable here, and those who were visiting the territory and experiencing everything for the first time.

Mia went off to tell another story, and Janie came over and linked her arm through LeeAnn's with a wide grin. "Hanna and Trissy are going back to the farm. Would you like to hear Mia or go see something else?"

"I'd like to hear another story," she answered eagerly.

After saying goodbye to the two pregnant women and their mates, she, Dotty, Jamie, and Janie went back to the storyteller's cove and sat. Rok brought them tea and settled beside them. This time the story was about a young dragon in his first days of awandering and all the amazing things he saw. LeeAnn was fascinated, as were all the humans who had just learned some fundamental facts about dragon culture. Most young dragons began their journey of self-discovery as soon as they could safely fly. They spent many long years awandering from territory to territory, learning and finding out who they were. When they matured, they found their stopping place, searched out their mate, and built their own nest, but not necessarily in that order.

As people left, LeeAnn turned to Rok. "How old are most dragons before they learn to fly?"

"Most are fifteen cycles of seasons before they master flying. However, Grabon has said that all youngsters in his territory are welcome to stay to maturity and beyond."

"How long does it take a dragon to mature?" she asked, fascinated.

Rok eyed her with approval. *"Forty or fifty cycles. Most dragons live as long as two hundred cycles before they return to the planet."*

Holy hell. Their lifespan was more than double a

human's. Her gaze moved immediately to Mia. "That was a great story." She set down her half-filled cup of tea on the ground. "I had no idea about most of that."

"There are many ways to help people learn. Storytelling is a dragon tradition, along with awandering and the hunt for a mate."

"I thought it went very well," Dotty commented, peering down the path. "Brom, Star, Griss, and Red are at the main fountain. Pit is on his way there. Shall we join them?"

As they left the cove, LeeAnn picked up her cup and carried it with her, not knowing what she should do with it. They reached the fountain after passing a number of stalls including a shop that sold wagons. Some were small like the ones Brom and Griss used for their youngsters; another was a large wagon of a new design. She hoped she would have a chance to look them over later. The wagon for the show she was in charge of always needed repairs and adjustments. It also frequently got stuck, especially in mud and snow.

Children were splashing in the fountain while adults supervised and chatted among themselves. She overheard one woman tell Griss that he had a lovely son. He returned the compliment, saying that her children looked very intelligent and capable of fair play. The exchange of compliments struck her as another difference between their cultures. She wondered if dragons ever suffered from vanity.

As Pit greeted Mia, their loving gazes and the way they leaned towards one another clearly showed they were happily committed to each other. They touched palms and their tails crossed as they watched the children play. The sight made LeeAnn sigh, not in envy, but with a longing for something she would probably never experience.

Tad joined them and greeted Dotty with a smile and by tucking a lock of her hair behind her ear. Then he bent and kissed her gently.

Regret filled LeeAnn and she turned to watch the crowd. To her utter shock, a man reached into another man's pouch, right where she could see. When she turned to say something, and relayed the image, Pit and Tad sprang into action. She was so startled by their fast response that she dropped her tea, drenching her front. By the time she looked up, they had isolated the thief from the crowd, away from the youngsters, and had demanded the return of goods.

"I didn't do anything," he protested, looking around as if desperate for someone to blame or someone to save him. "Have mercy."

"You don't want us to call Grabon to pass judgment, or Heron for that matter. Return the goods and be gone from here." Tad's expression was hard as he ignored the man's pleas to let him go.

"I'm telling you, I didn't take anything. There is nothing in my pockets." He dipped his hand into his pocket and came out with a wicked-looking knife. "Back up, both of you," he snarled. His cringing, pleading demeanor had become aggressive and violent.

Tad and Pit didn't look in the least intimidated. Clicking his tongue, Tad shifted to the side. "It would have been so much cleaner if you had just returned the goods you stole."

"Get back, you and your monster." The man's gaze darted from Tad to Pit and back to the human.

Pit hit his hand using a single blast of power and the knife went flying from his grasp, along with a few parts of his fingers. The urge to help burned across LeeAnn's senses, overriding every other concern, even her need to get back to Golly. If she used her energy for another healing session on a stranger, she could deplete what few stores she had regained. Unable to fight the compulsion, she stepped forward only to run into a shield that stood like a wall between her and the action.

"I can stop the bleeding," she called out, clenching and unclenching her hands to keep from pressing against the shield.

Pit shrugged at the struggling thief he held by the throat and looked over at Tad who had retrieved the thief's knife and was collecting the severed parts of his fingers. *"He is bleeding pretty badly,"* he commented blandly, noting the pool of blood forming under the man's hand.

"As long as she retreats if he becomes violent, it should be safe," Brom suggested, stepping forward, having secured Star with Jamie and Janie.

Rok flared his wings. *"Let the thief bleed. Why should one of ours waste her energy? His own people can treat him on his way out of our territory."*

"He may not have any people; he looks like a stranger to me. I say let her treat him. If he becomes violent near one of our females or youngsters we can kill him with Grabon's permission," Griss reminded them.

The crowd gasped in surprise and commented to one another, but nobody protested or offered a defense for the thief.

After a moment of watching the crowd, Tad shook his head. "All right, LeeAnn, you can treat him."

As she passed the shield, Hess arrived out of breath from running. She glanced his way but moved to Pit's prisoner and grasped the injured hand. The man thrashed and screamed his voice hollow from pain before he lost consciousness. When she stepped back, the wound was closed and she stumbled for a moment, weak from using so much energy. Hess's arm went around her waist and he took her back to sit on the side of the fountain.

"Do not fall in the fountain," he warned, his voice rough with impatience. Hess pulled up a bucket of water and returned to Pit's side, where he splashed the man's hand to wash off the blood, then did the same to the ground, diluting the puddle.

Pit slapped the thief's face to bring him around, while Tad searched his pockets and bag. They started returning items he had taken, one at a time. As the thief became aware with a groan, Pit slapped him one more time. *"You will be out of our territory by sunrise or you will be hunted by Grabon. We do not tolerate stealing in our market or territory. Do not return for the remainder of your life."*

To LeeAnn's astonishment, they let him go. There was no call for a hanging; banishment from the territory was enough. If he had not tried to hurt someone, he wouldn't even have been injured. Never had she seen a thief treated so gently. Holy hell, were these people serious?

The man quickly disappeared, and the shields that protected the crowd went down. As she started to stand, Jamie and Janie were beside her, looking concerned.

"I recover quickly," she assured them with what she could feel was a shaky smile, but it was the best she could manage.

"I told you to stay there," Hess snapped, stalking closer while peering into her face and frowning. "You look strained and pale. Are you in pain?"

"I'm fine." She spread her arms to show him her balance had returned.

"Try to stay out of trouble, will you? If you collapse it will be one more thing to add to my list." He stalked off, leaving his friends gaping at his back.

LeeAnn sniffed back her hurt before she shrugged and looked at the sisters. "I can't believe nobody ordered a hanging."

Jamie shrugged. "If he had simply insisted on his innocence, Grabon or Heron would have been called to pass judgment. Even then, he wouldn't have been executed. Grabon only uses execution if a person has killed or intended to kill someone."

"How does judgment work?" she asked, trying to gain some insight from the sisters' guarded expressions.

Sighing, Dotty came over, sat on the edge of the fountain, and motioned for LeeAnn to join her. LeeAnn propped her butt against the edge and stretched her legs in front of her, but the tea-soaked outfit clung to her skin. She picked the material away as Dotty softly explained, "Judgment is when Heron does a reading and pulls the truth from the person's own mind. He shares that truth with Grabon, who decides the punishment. Of course, I suspect Grabon could do the reading independently and so could Heron, but they usually work together."

"They can do that?" she asked, wiping her sweaty palms on her skirt and biting her lip.

"You have nothing to worry about," Tad told her as he approached with Griss. "In order for someone to be accepted among the Dragonmen, they do a reading and both Grabon and Heron have to agree. You've already been accepted," he reminded her. "How are you feeling after the healing? Do you need anything? Food, tea, a brew?"

"I am fine, really," she answered, noticing that Brom was watching them with a smile.

"Maybe she should have some of Griss's wine," Brom suggested, grinning while holding Star steady on his arm as she leaned out to touch one of the tree branches.

"No, but thank you," she answered, smiling at the large red dragon who had a wine skin hanging across his chest. Had she ever had so many people concerned about her health and comfort? She couldn't remember experiencing anything like it.

"I can understand not wanting the wine with your head already swimming and you have to be feeling hollow, but we should take her to see Griss's booth. Not only should she meet Fin and Kev, but Griss makes brews known among dragons for their effectiveness in healing," Jamie said.

"Not to mention lotions that smell really good," Janie added, grinning.

LeeAnn could feel the sisters' energy surrounding her, trying to persuade her to stay in the territory, and while scented lotions and healing brews were tempting, her main concern was Golly.

They left Tad and Pit by the fountain to keep an eye on the crowd as they went to visit Griss's booth. Star rode on her father's arm as he pulled the empty wagon behind them, but she was alert and curious about everything. Occasionally she chortled and squealed to him.

"How old is Star?" she asked Jamie.

"She is six cycles, older then Jenny but younger than

Matti. Her maturity is younger."

"My daughter wants hair pretties like Jenny and Matti have," Brom grumbled.

"As long as she does not want hair like theirs, it is not a problem," Griss answered with a smirk that made everyone laugh. He was pulling Red in his wagon.

"We can find a way for her to wear them, Brom. Let her choose one she likes," Janie suggested.

From the way the youngster was bouncing on his arm, it was obvious she understood their words. Brom made a sharp noise and Star stopped bouncing and patted him instead. Brom gave a great sigh and went to find the booth that had so fascinated his daughter. Janie went along with them with a promise to meet up with everyone at Griss's booth when they were done.

LeeAnn couldn't quit grinning. Such a loving and tolerant relationship between father and daughter was a pleasure to see.

Griss's brew shop turned out to be a busy booth with three solid walls filled with shelves, and a hidden back room for storage and sorting. The boys, Kev and Fin, seemed to be having a good time helping adults find just what they wanted, but they greeted Griss enthusiastically, talking a mile a minute. While the boys filled Griss in on everything that had happened in his absence, Jamie showed LeeAnn some of what Griss made.

"Now his wine is something else. Even though it's often used for different brews, Griss and the others made the decision to sell that brew in a separate booth.

"You can find it down the lane a bit farther. It's a huge booth with tables and benches all around, but this is his healing shop. Look at these."

She showed LeeAnn the different brew packets, then they looked at creams and ointments. Finally, Jamie showed her the liniments and oils, packaged in their interesting bottles. Some were in glass, some in clay, and one was even in a stone jar.

"My parents would have been thrilled with a shop like this nearby," LeeAnn murmured, looking at everything.

"We were amazed to realize that the medicines dragons use also work on humans and vice versa. Griss has collected and tested all the different recipes and only sells the most effective ones. Over here, we have the soaps and lotions, next to the candles. They are very nicely scented."

Sniffing one sample, LeeAnn nodded her agreement, overwhelmed by sheer wonder. There were herb shops in the colonies where each ingredient was separate. Here Griss offered not only what looked like high-quality ingredients, but proven mixtures and alternative recipes. She was sniffing some of the lotion when Griss came over with a jar of cream. He held it out to her with a low gurgle.

"Heron mentioned you had scars. This helps to keep

them supple and fade."

Blinking back tears, she grinned as she took it. "Thank you. How many coins?"

He waved his hand and went back to his conversation with Dotty. She didn't know how many times in one day a person was allowed to be stunned speechless, but she must be near her quota. LeeAnn looked down at the cream in her hand and moved to put it in her bag. Someone grabbed her arm in a hard grip, frightening her to her toes. If she had been wearing her knife she would have pulled it.

"She's stealing something," the stranger snarled in a loud voice.

"No, Griss gave it to me," she protested, her voice squeaky with fright.

"I saw her; she waited until he had his back turned."

"I thank you for your diligence," Griss answered, keeping his mental voice soothing. *"The cream was a gift. Please release her."*

The man let go with a muttered curse about how they protected their own. "I saw her start to put that cream in her bag."

"You did, because I gifted her with the cream for her scars. It is a treatment for deep scaring."

"I don't see any scars," he complained, looking LeeAnn over with an insulting sneer.

With shaking hands, LeeAnn quickly unlaced her tunic and whipped it off over her head. Even with the undergarments covering a part of her back and most of her chest, enough of them would be visible to leave a lasting impression. From the throat up, she had no marks. Sam had insisted that some of the puncture wounds needed to be near the center of her body while others could pin her arms and legs to the boards. Golly always hated throwing the knives into her chest, so her shoulders and arms held the most amount of scars. While her audience gasped, she slowly turned so they could all get a good look.

"Can't you keep your clothes on?" Hess asked from the back of the crowd. He stalked through the crowd, and people seemed to melt out of his way. While some onlookers snickered, she slid the tunic and bag back over her head and adjusted the laces.

"You need to come with me." He held out a hand and waited.

Giving a deep sigh, she put her hand in his and set down the cream, leaving it behind. Hess led her over to a bench and motioned for her to sit. He paced in front of her for a moment before saying, "That was totally unnecessary."

Shrugging, she did her best not to show her own embarrassment and shame. "Being accused of stealing is no small thing."

"No, it's not, but Griss would have handled it. There was no reason to take off your clothes in front of a crowd."

"That man was going to make trouble."

"For himself maybe." His eyes narrowed on her. "This is not a freak show."

She felt like something had slammed into her gut, but nodded. He continued speaking, but she no longer heard him. Her fragile dream of finding a safe haven had just shattered. It was her own fault for letting even a part of herself believe that people such as these could accept and come to value a person such as herself. She knew better, but something inside had begun to hope. As she waited for him to finish, she decided she needed to be gone before morning. If she could leave sooner, that would be better.

Sam would be less angry if she found a way to meet him rather than waiting for him to show up. He was determined to find a new audience at the market, but she would tell him she had been accused of theft and banished. If luck was with her, that would be enough to convince him to head back toward the colonies.

Hess had finally stopped talking. He shook his head and walked off. Taking a few deep breaths, she tried to steady herself.

Jamie came out of the shop and put a comforting hand on her shoulder. "We should go."

LeeAnn stood, more than ready to leave. The market was huge and had such a variety of things it still amazed her. The women walked towards one end, passing more booths as the sisters chatted and Mia and Dotty laughed over something. Brom and Griss had taken their youngsters to the garden, promising to see everyone later. Rok walked beside LeeAnn saying nothing.

When they found a table, they were near the tea shop again, and the sisters brought over mugs of steaming tea. LeeAnn sipped at hers, wondering when would be the best time to leave.

"Sometimes men can be incredibly stupid," Jamie commented, seemingly out of nowhere. "When Janie and I used to trade sex for goods, we learned a great deal about the way a male mind works."

LeeAnn choked on her tea and set her cup down, using her sleeve to wipe her mouth. She quickly looked at the sisters, who nodded.

"Males are not the only ones who can be foolish. I refused Pit for far too long because he was not a territory dragon. My words were not kind as I told him of my dissatisfaction with his choices. As a result I spent too many years alone and so did he," Mia added with a thoughtful frown.

"Mia is right, females can be just as foolish. After I found out that my sister had murdered both my parents and poisoned me, I wondered why I had spent so many years defending her. I even felt guilty for not knowing sooner," Dotty confessed.

LeeAnn couldn't think of a single thing to say. Such revelations were deeply personal. Did they think she was being foolish?

"Not everyone is valued in the beginning. Hanna

was thrown out of her first family and left in the wilderness to die because they couldn't see her value," Janie reminded them.

"Trissy wandered for two years chasing a dream because Heron had accidently formed a bond with her at a distance. That was after the fever killed most of her family and she was left behind by the other survivors," Dotty recalled. "Not everything starts out easy."

"Heron spent thirty years awandering with Grabon after the fire. It left him almost more dragon than human." Rok nodded in emphasis.

"Brom was banished from even visiting his youngster," Mia pointed out.

"Everybody in this new clan of ours has made terrible mistakes, and none of us can afford to judge anyone else's choices or purpose or comitments. If Hess was dumb enough to say something hurtful, please know that he does not speak for the rest of us." Jamie's expression was so serious that LeeAnn offered her a wobbly smile.

"He wasn't hurtful. He simply reminded me of a truth I had been in danger of forgetting. Please don't blame him. Everyone here is building something important. You are all wonderful, highly skilled people. Having a freak would only damage everything you are working toward." She took a deep breath and let it out slowly. "This has been an amazing day for me, truly an experience I will treasure in my heart for as long as I live. But now I have to go back and try again to save my friend Golly. Who knows what Sam did to him while I've been missing."

"What kind of friend is Golly?" Janie asked, leaning forward.

"He's a very special friend, but not what you're thinking. There have been times when Golly did everything but breathe for me while I was in trouble. I can't leave him to suffer Sam's torture alone, not if I can help. If nothing else, I can keep putting him back together."

"What did Golly do before you were there?" Jamie asked.

"Sam was able to make him into the monster that people see. Golly's only act is his knife throwing and he's not very accurate. Otherwise, he's Sam's beast of burden." She shared the image of Golly, the giant man with the split nose, strong, scarred body, limited intelligence, and deformed face.

"Oh dear," Jamie sighed.

Rok eyed LeeAnn as if measuring her determination. *"If you truly want to return for your friend, steer this Sam here so we can help you."*

She blinked back tears and looked down at her tea. "I don't think I have the right to risk all of you in order to save a few freaks who have nothing to offer and no place here. If I can, I will get him to turn back to the colonies. If that doesn't work, remember this. Sam is very clever and inventive and he preys on people's weaknesses. He can project thoughts, images, and fear, but he will not risk his own skin. Every single time I have cut him, even knowing I would feel compelled to heal him before he died, he played on my sympathy and fear for Golly's safety."

She stood and looked at each of them, knowing the time to leave was now. "I cannot express how much this day has meant to me. Please tell everyone how much I appreciated their kindness." She took off the bag and handed it to Jamie, who frowned.

"It is a gift," she protested.

"I will not be allowed to keep it," LeeAnn explained softly.

"Then I will hold it for you, for when you return."

LeeAnn looked at Rok, Dotty, Mia, and Janie. *"Thank you."* She walked away quickly, brushing away a tear and melting into the crowd. When she finally managed to find a path off the market grounds, she followed the territory lines she could sense in the ground. In many places, the lines crossed and intercepted other lines, but she followed Grabon's path all the way to a creek. On the creek bed, she found a sharp rock and meticulously shaped it into her next knife.

Armed, she set out to find the edge of Grabon's territory. What had Sam done to Golly in her absence? Was there a way to gain their freedom without fighting anyone but Sam? The others were content to live under his rules. They would never help her or Golly escape, because they believed that without

Sam's protection, they would have no life at all. She had healed each of them at one time or another, but they called her Sam's special pet and excluded her. At least they were nicer to Golly.

As she walked and thought, she savored the memories of a wonderful day. Soon enough she would need to tuck those thoughts away so they couldn't be used against her.

Chapter 2

Sam was furious, foot-stomping, fit-throwing furious. Tying Golly to the tree and lashing him hadn't even put a dent in his anger. If that little healer had been here screaming, crying, begging him to show mercy, that might have helped. She always pleaded with him in that satisfyingly squeaky, fear-laden voice. Not that he ever showed mercy, but if she were here he would let her heal her disgusting friend before he took his anger out on her. Now that was always thrilling and satisfying, because almost as fast as he could inflict damage, she could fix it when she had to. Also, she screamed, inciting his lust even as he tore her apart.

He spit on the ground and the blood spatter from Golly's lashing mixed with his spit. That's what the freak got for making up such a stupid story. *"A dragon had swooped out of the sky. It wasn't her fault; she didn't run away."* Why would a dragon or any beast want his healing freak? He went over to his wagon and pulled out a jug. He had traded gold beads for the whiskey, brought in by the smugglers from OldEarth.

"Sam?" Brian approached cautiously, staying well out of his reach.

"What?" Sam demanded before taking a big gulp of the heady brew, not caring that some ran down his chin.

"There really was a dragon."

"Really?" he asked sarcastically, sneering at the muscle-bound idiot.

"It was yellow-and-black and we saw it dive down. I guess it could have picked her up." Brian took a step back under Sam's glare. "More likely she ran off." He watched Sam guzzle from the jug.

"Huh, maybe she'll be back." Sam looked out into the distance as if expecting her return.

"Sam, after that lashing, if she doesn't return, Golly is going to be worthless if not dead."

"He'll live through it. A beast that big has extra blood." He drank some more, then rattled the jug to see how much was left.

"How are we going to get the wagons out of the mud?" Brian asked, shifting uncomfortably from foot to foot.

"I guess that's up to you, Brian. We get Golly to do it or I'll be looking at you to get off your lazy ass and pitch in. You can use those muscles to do more than impress the suckers who think they mean something."

Brian backed away slowly and joined the others around their fire. As he and the other freaks murmured among themselves, Sam stumbled over to the tree where Golly was still tied and bleeding. He picked up a stick and poked his giant knife-throwing fool.

"You better not die on me and you better hope she

gets back here before tomorrow or I may just start skinning you next. I could tan your hide and sell little Golly bags. How does that sound? You remember the day I cut off your testicles and fed them to that puton? This is going to be worse than that. If I were you, I'd start calling." He sat on the ground, finished his jug, and threw it at Golly's head. The thing missed and shattered against the bark of the tree, cutting up his ugly head and making him cry out. Sam laughed as he went to get another jug.

***

Golly watched Sam until he was sure he was gone. Then he closed his eyes and called for LeeAnn. That dragon couldn't hurt her for long. She'd find a way to come back; he knew she would. But it might take too long and he didn't want to be made into tiny little bags. Tears mixed with the blood on his face. His arms were tied around the tree and it was a big tree, a really big tree, so there was nothing he could do. He called again, pleading for her to come save him.

***

LeeAnn felt like she had been walking forever when she spotted a dragon flying overhead, heading into Grabon's territory. On a whim, she waved and to her surprise, the dragon flew down and landed. It was Rok.

"Where were you?" she asked with a frown.

"I flew out to see what was happening with your friend."

"You can't do that. What if Sam saw you?"

Rok shook his head and sighed. Then to her utter surprise a series of images flashed through her mind, all of them of Rok fighting other dragons. *"You persist in thinking we are always peaceful; we are not. It is time for you to ask for assistance."*

LeeAnn chewed her lip. "I don't know what you can do, Rok. This is a messy situation."

"No, this is a rescue. Without help, your friend is going to die. You and he cannot stay there any longer."

"I know, but it is not that simple. Finding a place for Golly and me is no easy task."

"You already have a place. We will bring him to Grabon when he has healed enough to travel. If Grabon and Heron accept him, you both have a place with us no matter what Hess has said to you."

"Are you sure? The last thing I want to do is cause a problem for the Dragonmen. You are all good people and Hess has a valid reason for not wanting me around."

Rok snorted and looked to the sky. *"You cannot speak at a distance, can you?"*

It took her a moment to understand what he meant. "No, who are you speaking with?"

Rok stood to his fullest height and slightly flared his wings, looking very impressive. *"Grabon says you should return with your friend. He also says you should listen to reason."*

LeeAnn sighed and put her hands on her hips. "Do you have a plan?"

"Yes, it begins with you riding on my shoulders. We will sneak in. I will take care of the others, and you will save Golly. I believe he is too big to ride on my back, but after you have healed him, we will walk into Grabon's territory and a wagon will meet us."

"There are seven others, not including Sam. I don't know if they will help Sam."

He looked up at the darkening sky, then back at her. *"There is a good chance we can sneak in, rescue Golly, and leave without them even knowing. They stay a good distance away from Golly, around their own fire. Sam has been drinking since he hurt your friend, but he keeps returning to poke him and scare him."*

She took a deep breath. "We'll never get away without Sam knowing. He always finds out because Golly thinks too loud when he's scared. He has no control that way."

Rok nodded and crouched. *"Then I will stop Sam first. Climb on my shoulders. It is time to go."*

She bit her lip and climbed on, doing her best to sit as she had seen the men sitting on the statues. "Is this all right?"

"It is good enough. You must hold on with your knees and give power to me to lift off. From here we use mindspeak. The wind makes it so I cannot hear."

"All right." She gripped with her knees, and when he signaled, she fed him power, hoping it wouldn't hurt him. He did not complain or even comment as he wrapped them in shields and they flew off, his extended dark brown wings extended making him look huge in the sky. *"This is amazing, Rok. Much faster than walking."*

"I am glad you enjoy it. It will not take us long to reach our destination. You must focus on your friend and let me worry about Sam and the others. Trust that I will keep them away from the two of you."

"I can do that."

I can do this, LeeAnn repeated to herself over and over, trying to give herself the courage she needed.

When Rok landed, she could hear Golly begging for help, even though his mental voice had weakened. She had to stay focused if they were going to save him, she reminded herself as she climbed to the ground. Trying to be quiet, she ran over to the tree and began sawing through the rope with her rock knife without telling him she was there. As soon as he knew, he was going to call out her name; he always did. He was quietly sobbing and mentally begging for help. She had to blink back tears to clear her vision.

When she finally got through the rope, Golly sagged to the ground, looking confused at being let go, and immediately LeeAnn hit him hard and fast with healing energy. He cried out in pain, Which did not sound that different from his earlier cries, as long as Sam wasn't paying close attention. Hoping Rok could protect them, she concentrated on the healing, doing as much as she could as fast as she could. Blood loss would slow him, but he should recover enough to walk if they could get some fluids in him. Her head spun from using so much energy and she leaned against the blood-soaked tree.

She looked up in time to see Rok blast the head off Sam's body, splattering it everywhere. The sight shocked her enough that she blinked and glanced back at Golly, but the inside of her head seemed to be filled with plant fluff. Nothing seemed to make any sense.

Some stray sound must have alerted the others because she heard them shouting.

When Rok cried out in pain, holy hell she almost jumped out of her skin. Without a thought for her own safety, she charged in, ripped out the lance protruding from Rok's side, and fell to her knees to heal him.

Her sudden appearance must have shocked Brian and the others because they immediately backed away. Brian recovered first. He ran forward, grabbed the lance, and stabbed her through the leg, pinning her at Rok's feet. Rok roared, pushed Brian toward the others, and drove them back, using fast blasts of energy. She felt him start to move and she shouted at him to remain still while she continued to heal his wound.

When she had the bleeding stopped and the flesh knitted back together, she sat back on her heels only to discover that the lance pinning her lower leg to the ground was still in place. When she looked up, she saw Brian and the others advancing with clubs and other weapons they had collected from their camp.

"Stop, all of you, stop. Rok, please let them go. If they stop fighting will you let them go?"

"If they cause no further harm, but none of them are welcome in Grabon's territory."

She saw Brian reach for another lance. "Drop that before he blows your head off," she shrieked at him. "Didn't you see what he did to Sam? I can't fix that, you fool. Plant your feet and stand still."

Using both hands, she grabbed the lance protruding from her leg and ripped it out of the ground, but her hands were slick with blood and she couldn't get it out of her leg. "Holy hell, this thing is stuck."

Rok backed up to her, put one clawed foot gently on her leg to hold her still, and quickly pulled the lance free. She cried out, but he never took his eyes off the others. *"I am here for LeeAnn, to help her rescue her friend."*

"He's over there, tied to a tree." Brian gestured. "You shouldn't have killed Sam."

"It was the only way to stop him."

Shera let out a sigh and stepped forward. "We all know how he was. Just take them and leave."

"You can give me a minute," LeeAnn protested, looking at her. "As soon as I can move, we'll get out of here."

"You may take as long as you need," Rok told her,

eyeing the others.

Very carefully, she climbed to her feet and hobbled back to Golly, who was regaining consciousness.

"LeeAnn! You came back for me!"

"You knew I would. I brought a friend and we're leaving. You're going to have to help me walk again, Golly."

"That's all right. You healed me all up. I bet you are real tired." He slowly pushed to his feet, tugging his tattered, blood soaked clothes around him.

She gave a short laugh. "You know, I think you're right. Okay, Rok, I think we're mobile." She smiled at Golly. "That means we can move. Golly, Rok is my friend and he's a dragon. If you can get us some skins of water we can get started."

Golly moved to the wagon, frowning at all the blood spatter and the headless corpse as he walked by. He shook his head and brought back the skins. "Something bad happened here."

"That's why we're leaving. Here, I'll carry one of those. You don't have to carry everything."

Golly handed her the skin and she slid the strap over her head.

"Walk out away from the camp and I will join you."

"Could you hear him, Golly?"

"I could. Here, lean on me. Which way do we go?"

"That way." She pointed and they slowly stumbled out the same way she and Rok had come in.

Rok looked at the others and sighed, then slowly backed away, following LeeAnn. *"It would be a mistake for you to go to the new market in Grabon's territory."*

There were some grumbles, but LeeAnn never saw them move. As she and Golly walked, she hoped none of them decided to fight.

It didn't take Rok long to find them; they hadn't made it very far. Rok told her he that he found it disconcerting to meet a human who stood taller than he did, but he looked Golly in the eye and greeted him.

Golly shook his hand and smiled. "I am LeeAnn's friend too."

"That is what she told me."

"Golly, you need to drink that water. Here." She handed the second skin to Rok. "You both need fluids. When we find a stream, we can refill them."

They both drank and Rok handed her the skin. *"Now you drink."*

Instead of arguing, she did as he asked. They walked for a good while before Golly spoke. "Is Sam going to chase us?"

"No, Sam has other things to worry about. He can't

hurt you again."

"That's good. He tied me to a tree."

"I saw that." The energy it took to continue healing her leg was making her head spin. It was a good thing Golly was holding her up.

"I told him you got snatched by a dragon. Are you the dragon that snatched her?" Golly asked Rok.

"No, that was a bad dragon."

LeeAnn suspected Rok was amused, but between the drum of her heart and her spinning senses, she wasn't sure.

They walked until they found a cool stream, and by then she was moving a little easier. After visually checking her leg, she refilled the skins and drank her fill before she washed off the last of the blood. Holy hell she was tired of smelling it. Then she washed Golly's back and had him strip so she could rinse the blood out of his clothes.

Rok looked away from Golly's mutilated body and over at her. Shrugging, she scrubbed out the last of the blood and wrung out the clothes.

"Sam removed his reproductive parts?" Rok snarled.

"He fed my balls to a puton," Golly explained, splashing in the water and chasing a small fish.

When they started walking again, LeeAnn was limping, but walking on her own. Rok moved without difficulty and Golly complained that he had to leave the fish behind, clearly forgetting for a moment what they had escaped. They drank a lot of water as they walked, but they didn't do much talking. LeeAnn was focused on keeping the world right side up while she walked and healing her leg.

Later, it took every ounce of concentration she had to keep walking. After she'd done so much healing, her insides felt hollow. She just had to take one step after another, she reminded herself. They would all need to rest soon and she could stop then.

Between one blink and the next, her feet left the ground and she didn't need to keep moving. Her brain must have been playing tricks because Hess seemed to be carrying her and speaking kindly to Golly.

She woke up, or thought she did, in the bed of a wagon. Hess leaned over her and gave her water, gently touching her head. She gulped down nearly half a skin and then went back to sleep. It was all too confusing.

***

Hess hopped out of the wagon bed to face Rok. "I wish you had told me."

"Grabon did not think it was a good idea."

"He thought it was a better idea that you go in there alone?"

"No, he wanted me to bring her back, but she was worried about her friend. I flew ahead to their

encampment to determine for myself how bad the conditions were and if that worry was justified. I found Golly bleeding to death, tied to a tree."

Hess's jaw flexed and he nodded. He didn't think he was ready to hear any details. He ran a hand through his hair and glanced back at the sleeping healer and her large friend.

"I contacted Grabon and he agreed I should help her perform the rescue, if she agreed to return. If she had not agreed, I would have brought her back to his nest and Thane and I would have rescued Golly."

"She doesn't know that?"

"No, she agreed to return, even if only for a little while. LeeAnn does not understand that she is under our protection. We let her leave today because she was clearly upset and needed time to consider our offer. Grabon monitored her progress through the territory."

He scratched his head. "Why would she refuse to stay?"

"Not all the Dragonmen welcome her and she does not want to cause problems."

Hess considered that, frowning. "Who has a problem with her? It wasn't Heron or Grabon, I know that."

Rok looked over at the wagon where Golly had laid down and LeeAnn slept. *"Someone has behaved strangely to her and made her feel unwelcome."*

"You're not going to tell me who has the problem?"

"Does it matter? It will either work itself out or she will leave."

"So all we've done is buy her some time? From what you said, she has no place to go, and what about her giant friend? He's not going to blend in anywhere."

Sighing, Rok looked back at the wagon. *"I do not know the human words to describe what was done to Golly."* He flashed Hess a picture of Golly's mangled and missing genitalia, scars, and deformities. *"His mind is very simple. There is no aggression in him."*

Hess bent at the waist and took a couple of deep breaths, trying not to be sick. "Did you know he was tortured?"

"She shared some information when she explained why she needed to leave. If she had felt accepted, she might have asked for assistance, which is what Grabon and Heron expected her to do. Her flight took them both by surprise and they objected, strenuously, to her returning to Sam. That's why Grabon sent me to bring her back. He thought I had used poor judgment in allowing her to run away."

"Let's get the wagon rolling, then you can tell me what happened and why she's so exhausted." Hess climbed up to the seat and got the cattle moving. Her condition had scared him, and put a lump in his throat. She hadn't seemed to recognize him. His reaction was confusing, since he hardly spent any time with her.

He was only there with the wagon because Gordon had needed to stay with Hanna. She was having what they were all hoping was false labor since it was too soon for delivery. Otherwise, Gordon had volunteered to drive out and pick up Rok and his charges.

Nobody had even told him LeeAnn had decided to return to the freak show. It was obvious she needed help, so why hadn't she asked? He had been ready to demand answers when she collapsed as if the ground had dropped away. Her friend, so obviously confused, had been very worried. Hess had loaded them both in the wagon, not knowing what to think.

Rok landed on the bench beside him.

"So tell me what happened," Hess invited.

As he listened, he began to realize how impossible her situation had been. "None of them even said goodbye?"

Rok shook his head. *"One stabbed her with the spear, and none of them protested. They stood as if ready to attack her. She managed to pull the spear from the ground, but it was stuck in her leg. I pulled it free for her while I held them off. By the end, they would have been pleased if she had dragged herself away and left."*

Hess frowned, completely confused by his own reactions. "I can't even imagine what that must have been like for her."

"It does explain why she does not want to stay if she

is not wanted. Now that Sam is dead, she is no longer at such risk and she may be more inclined to leave."

"She is at risk," Hess insisted. "Why is she so exhausted?"

"She did three healings in a short span of time, the last on herself. Earlier she healed the thief, and before that Grabon and herself, and even before that, Golly."

Hess didn't need another explanation. What she had done would have killed any other healer, and from what he had heard and seen with his own eyes, she used more energy than most could in a week. Not that she'd had much choice about most of that. "She needs to be protected from herself."

Rok nodded thoughtfully. *"She is not going to walk away from Golly. He depends on her."*

"We can make a place for him. He deserves a chance too. I am sure Grabon will see that." His initial resentment of the tall man had vanished. What Golly had suffered was inconceivable. He was not a threat on any level to anyone. When Rok didn't answer, Hess glanced at him. "What are you thinking?"

"I am trying to reason out what made her decide to leave without asking for help. Was it being accused of stealing or was it something you said to her after that?"

"Me? Why would you think it was something I said?" Hess asked with a frown.

"That is when she decided that she needed to leave.

What did you say?"

"Truthfully I don't even remember. I yelled at her for taking off her shirt in public." He drove a good distance before he continued, his mind spinning and another lump formed in his throat. "It's me. She thinks I don't want her here."

Rok nodded once.

"She seriously thought I wanted her to go back and be tortured? I know I was busy all day, but I couldn't possibly have been that rough on her."

He forced himself to examine what she had been through, and his reaction to her starting with when he had rushed into Grabon's nest. Had he ever been so dismissive of anyone else in his life? He couldn't think of one nice thing he had said to her all day, but he could think of too many things he should never have said. What was wrong with him?

"Why did I treat her like that?" He was mystified.

"She was an unnecessary interruption to your plans."

"Bentar droppings, that's what that is. I am not normally cruel to people."

"Perhaps it was her scars."

Hess looked over at Rok to see if he was serious. "I am not that shallow. There is more to a person then a few scars. Besides, when I first found her I did not know she had scars."

Shrugging, Rok lifted his head to the sky. *"I will fly ahead. Grabon is concerned about Hanna and Gordon and does not want them disturbed with unnecessary communication."*

Hess nodded. Word had reached him that Hanna was finally resting comfortably and it seemed everyone had breathed a sigh of relief. Gordon's shields generally blocked out any unwanted chatter, but none of them wanted the couple disturbed. Rok took off and the quiet night surrounded him, allowing him to think as he drove the team. The light from the two moons lit the path well enough to see. What was it about LeeAnn that had made him annoyed and edgy?

When Hess finally pulled the wagon into Gordon's farmyard, all was quiet. There was no sense in disturbing his passengers until he had to, so he took care of the cattle first. When he got back to the wagon, he found Golly standing in the back staring at the ground as if it might bite him.

"This is Farmer's land. We can't be here," Golly told him, his eyes wide with fright.

"You are invited, Golly." Hess motioned with his hands for the big man to keep his voice down.

"No freaks allowed, no, no, no. Sam told me they would plant me in the dirt and leave me there to rot, to feed their food," Golly whispered with certainty.

Hess took a deep breath and looked around the yard. "This land is Gordon's. He isn't going to hurt you. You can be safe here."

"He isn't going to plant tubers in my eyes?" Golly's plea for assurance was heartbreaking.

The image that flashed from Golly made Hess choke. It was a nightmare, a planted image of his big body being used to grow disgusting things. "That can't happen. Gordon isn't going to hurt you."

"Bring them up to the nest, Hess. I can remove the nightmares from his mind."

Hess sent back a silent agreement, realizing Golly hadn't even caught the exchange. "You can help me get LeeAnn out of the back. We're going to take her up to the nest."

Golly nodded, still looking around suspiciously. "I can carry her. I've done it before."

"We'll do it together. Why don't you hand her to me?"

Golly carefully picked up LeeAnn's limp form. He handed her over, climbed out of the wagon, and stood anxiously waiting for the next instruction.

"Do you want some water? You can bring one of the skins," Hess offered, adjusting her in his arms so her head rested on his shoulder. Something inside him settled and he took a deep breath. Golly grabbed a skin and almost drained it before sliding it over his head.

"You want me to carry her? I'm very strong." He flexed his arm as if to show off his muscles, which the movement did.

"No, I've got her, but you can walk with me."

As they headed toward the path that led up to the nest, Golly kept looking around.

"Do you know where we are?" the big man finally asked.

Hess grinned and nodded. "I know exactly where we are. You're safe in Grabon's territory; nobody is going to hurt you here."

"Is LeeAnn safe too?"

He had to blink back a sudden surge of emotion. "She's safe. You can help us keep her safe. We're going up to Grabon's nest. Rok and Thane live there, too, and we have some visiting dragons, but nobody is going to hurt you or LeeAnn." He hoped if he said it enough times, Golly would believe him.

Golly chewed on his lip as they walked. "Do you want me to carry her?"

"No, I have her. Golly, how long has LeeAnn been with you?"

He continued to chew on his lip. "It was a long time now, ever since Sam brought her. She can heal me all up, so I'm not sick anymore. Did you know a dragon came out of the sky and snatched her gone?"

"I bet that was scary."

Golly nodded and looked up the path. "Sam was very mad. He thought she had run away again." His lip trembled. "I called out for her to come back. Sam was going to sell Golly bags."

Images of Golly being skinned alive bombarded Hess and he took a deep breath as they kept walking. He didn't know what to say. The poor man felt guilty for calling out to her. "She's going to be all right."

"LeeAnn always comes back for me. Sam says she's stupid, but he's wrong."

"Yes, he was wrong. LeeAnn is not stupid. She helped rescue you so you can both be safe."

"I think Rok killed Sam dead," Golly said after a few minutes. He didn't whisper this time, and his voice no longer vibrated on the edge of panic.

Hess glanced at the hut as they passed and wondered why Heron didn't come out to help. "He did, Golly. Sam needed to die so you and LeeAnn could be safe."

"We could never kill him, before. She always healed him, even when she didn't want to. It's hard being a healer."

"I think you're right. I think it's very hard to be a healer." They had gotten to the rocky part of the path. "Let me hand her to you for a minute."

Golly took her, slung her over his shoulder as if he'd done it a hundred times, and over the rocks they went. At the top, Golly stood looking at the nest, his mouth slightly ajar.

"You can hand her back to me now," Hess

suggested, holding out his arms. Golly gently lowered her into place.

"What is that?" He motioned to the nest with his head as he picked up her limp arm and moved it across her waist.

"That is Grabon's nest. Are you ready to go inside?"

"I guess." He didn't sound convinced, but he followed Hess all the same.

Hess slowly walked up the log steps and over the top. Sitting among the visitors were Rok and Thane. Grabon met his gaze as he came down the steps on the other side. *"Is she all right?"*

"She is healing herself and recovering from doing way too much healing. Otherwise, I think she will be fine." Hess walked over and gently placed her on Grabon's bed, then covered her with a light blanket. Before he moved away, he cupped her cheek, absorbing her warmth, reassured by her steady breathing.

Straightening, he saw Golly take his first step inside the nest. He made introductions and sat beside LeeAnn's sleeping form to watch Grabon and Golly.

Golly looked at Grabon with his head tilted. "You're not like the other dragon, Rok."

"No, I am Grabon, the territory dragon. You are the largest human I have ever seen."

Golly nodded and sat on the ground, then crossed his legs. "I kept growing and growing. LeeAnn says it happens sometimes."

Grabon nodded and came closer before sitting on his tail, looking at the odd tortured human with all his senses open. *"She has been a good friend to you."*

"She takes care of me and I take care of her." Golly shrugged and looked at the ground before turning his gaze back to Grabon.

"Sometime in the future, LeeAnn's mate will accept and claim her. It will be his task to take care of her. You will have to share. Can you do that?"

"Is he going to hurt her?" Golly asked, looking confused. He scratched his head with both hands as if something were itching his scalp.

"No, after he has accepted her, he would never hurt her. It is not his way."

Golly gave a small shudder that traveled all through his body. "What is a mate?" he asked, scratching his head again and giving another full-body shudder.

"It is a bond that is stronger than anything. When he has accepted her, he will protect, defend, and love her until the day they die. He is also likely to limit how much healing she does so she does not collapse. This will not always make her happy, but it is important."

Golly nodded and let out a long sigh. "I can share her with anyone who takes care of her."

"That is good. There are many people here who will help to protect her. You will be happy to know

everyone will accept you and treat you kindly. We will find things you can do, and nobody will hurt you again. Do you wish to stay with us, Golly?"

"I can stay? Here?" He looked around the nest.

"Yes, here. Even when LeeAnn is ready to move to a house, you will stay here with me. If you have difficulty with anyone, you will come to me. We will work together, Golly, to make you comfortable and safe."

Golly blinked at the sky and took a deep breath. "I can work hard." Hess could hear tears in his voice.

"Did you eat today?"

Golly looked at Grabon and sighed as though he was reluctant to tell the truth. "Sam said no food for me and LeeAnn."

"We do not withhold food, Golly. You will eat, then you will sleep."

Hess couldn't help himself. "When did Sam say no food?"

Golly shrugged and looked over at LeeAnn. "A few days ago, because I would not throw that hatchet at her chest."

Jaw flexing, Hess nodded. "I'll cook. Please tell me she ate today." He glanced at Grabon as he moved to the fire.

"I believe she ate one or two of the meat pies."

Hess closed his eyes before he fed the fire and

started cutting up some meat. He glanced over at Golly and cut some more. Then he saw that Grabon had a basket with eggs and there were tubers in a bowl. With that he could make a dish that would fill Golly up and have enough left over to feed the little healer if she managed to wake up.

"You will never have to throw knives or hatchets at anyone again," Grabon promised Golly.

"Then what am I going to do?" he asked with a frown.

"We will find something special for you."

Grabon kept the big guy distracted and reassured while Hess cooked. When the food was finally ready, Hess piled a lot of it on a plate and handed it to Golly along with a fork.

 "I can eat all of it? What about LeeAnn? Can I save her some?"

"You don't have to worry about that. I have some over here for her if she wakes up."

Golly looked at the plate and took a big sniff. "I think I like it here."

Hess laughed and handed Grabon a small bowl, then took one over to Grabon's bed and let the scent waft in LeeAnn's direction. When her nose twitched, he did it again. Then he started eating and hoped the smell was enough to cause her to wake. Her stomach rumbled before her eyes opened. Almost immediately, she sat up blinking in confusion.

"Hungry?" Hess asked, getting up to fix her a bowl.

She looked around, spotted Golly sitting with Grabon plowing through a huge plate of food and sagged with relief. "We got away?"

"You did an excellent job," Grabon told her, offering a smile and a nod. *"Your friend here is enjoying Hess's cooking. We have decided he will stay with me from now on. How is your leg?"*

"My leg?"

Rok shifted on the wall and she glanced up at him and grinned. "Thank you so much for all your help. I can't remember if I said that before."

He flew down into the nest and settled beside her. *"You do not need to thank me for killing a monster. It is what the Dragonmen do. It was also my pleasure to help you rescue your friend, LeeAnn. He is a welcome addition to our group."*

"Really?" She glanced over at Hess by the fire before lowering her eyes.

Hess let out an aggravated sigh. He was going to pay for his mistakes, he knew he was.

"You will be surprised, I think, by how everyone reacts to your return," Grabon told her. *"Our people were very upset that you chose to leave."*

"I had to go to Golly," she explained.

"You should have asked for help, and some of us would have gone with you," Hess answered, bringing her a bowl of food and a fork.

"I didn't want to risk anyone else's safety. As it was, Rok was injured. How is your wound?" she asked the dragon.

"Healed, you did an excellent job."

"You risked your own safety by leaving and doing too much healing," Grabon continued.

"Under the circumstances it could not be helped," LeeAnn interrupted.

"It could be helped, and in future it will be. Until you have a mate of your own, like Janie and Jamie you fall under territory care. Which means every male among the Dragonmen will be seeing to your safety, health, and well-being. As the sisters found out when they were sick and did not ask for help, such actions not acceptable."

LeeAnn clutched her hands together, looking from Grabon, to Hess, to Rok and even Thane, who flew down to join the discussion. "What does that mean?"

"It means in the future, you better ask for assistance when you need it," Hess explained.

She shifted on the bed and set her bowl on the floor. "What is the punishment if I don't?" she asked with a frown.

"If you do not, one of the males will be assigned to see to your care." Grabon looked at her and grinned, and Hess could swear he was laughing. *"Until such a*

time as I believe the lesson is well learned."

"That makes no sense. If I don't ask for help someone is assigned to help me? How is that a punishment?"

Hess cleared his throat and shifted so she would look at him. "When the sisters were sick, I was assigned to look after them for almost a month. They complained because I was always in their home and in their way and would not let them do what they wanted, when they wanted, especially if it might risk their health or safety."

"I still don't understand."

"From now on, ask for help if you need it. If you are ill, let us know. If something is too heavy or too hard to do, ask for assistance. If you are hungry, too tired, or injured, you should inform us. It is not our way to refuse help to one another," Grabon explained.

"Who exactly am I supposed to inform?"

The males looked at one another. "You can inform any of us at any time," Hess answered.

"All right, that's not difficult."

Grabon snorted. *"We will see how you do. Eat now, then sleep. I removed Sam's nightmares from Golly's mind. They only served to confuse him and make him fearful."*

"Thank you," she responded softly.

Grabon nodded and looked at Golly. He had finished

eating and was holding his bowl and fork. Grabon showed him where there were skins, stored in a trunk, so he could find a place to sleep and make a pallet. LeeAnn started to get up to wash her bowl, but Hess took it from her and added it to a pile of dirty dishes. She yawned and Thane lifted her blanket and urged her to lie down.

"You need more sleep," he said.

Bemused, she snuggled into the mattress, then told them all good night and went back to sleep.

Golly wasn't far behind. When they were both settled, Grabon, Rok, Thane, and Hess stood around the fire discussing their plans for the following day. Hanna needed additional care, but since Gordon had said he would see to her and call for help if needed, they could focus most of their attention on their two new arrivals. With that in mind, they began to plan.

Chapter 3

When LeeAnn woke the following day, she was horrified to realize she had slept so long. Not only were most of the dragons gone from the nest, but so was Golly. Grabon explained as he fixed her a bowl of porridge and fruit that Golly would be making the rounds with Thane while she spent her day with the territory dragon.

"I wanted to see his face when he went to the garden the first time," LeeAnn muttered.

"We will arrange to be there so you may observe his reaction. Hanna will not be able to join us today. She was ill last night."

"Ill? What's wrong?" LeeAnn frowned.

"We can stop by on our way to the market if you like. It is a pregnancy issue, but I am unclear of the specifics. Human pregnancy is not something I have made a study of before. Have you?"

"I was trained as a healer, so I know a great deal about pregnancy and birth. But Grabon, my energy is too strong."

"Not too strong, but powerful. Healing is not a mild thing, that is true; but how many lives have you saved? How much pain and suffering have you spared your patients? It hurts for a breath or two, but then it is done."

"Humans do not appreciate a painful healing."

"Then they are wrong," Grabon rumbled, crossing his arms and lowering his nose. *"My humans are not so foolish. We will stop and see Hanna."*

LeeAnn ate her porridge and was surprised to see another set of clothes folded on the stool. "Are these for me?"

"Heron brought them. Today at the market we must purchase things to make Golly comfortable in my nest. Tomorrow you will move to a house. We will have to see which one you elect to stay in."

Her attention moved from the clothes to him. "I cannot stay here?"

"You are welcome, but there is no privacy for a human female in a nest. I was told you would prefer the safety of a roof, and privacy for bathing and relieving yourself."

Fighting not to blush, she nodded. "I appreciate that. Yes, human females like privacy for those tasks. Let me wash your dishes at least," she offered.

"Since washing is not a favorite task, I am pleased to let you do this for me."

She found a pot of hot water on the side of the fire, so it did not take long. With that chore done, after a quick change of clothes, they left the nest. As they climbed down the steps, Grabon told her they were stopping first to speak with Heron and Trissy. There, LeeAnn was able to borrow a brush and use their cesshouse, something for which she was grateful.

When she remembered to look more closely at the table, she couldn't quit grinning. What an amazing carving. Trissy offered her tea, so she sat at their table, anticipating a short visit. She was surprised when Grabon and Heron joined them while the girls were running and playing in and out of the hut.

"Grabon tells me your training included birth and pregnancy?" Heron asked as Trissy poured the tea for all of them.

LeeAnn gave Grabon a sharp look, which he ignored, choosing instead to look at the ceiling of the hut. "Yes, it was a pretty big part."

"You are going to visit Hanna to help with whatever was wrong last night?" Heron persisted.

LeeAnn glared at Grabon before giving up with a shrug. "That is what Grabon wants."

"Good. I need you to stop being afraid of being a powerful healer." Heron took a deep breath as though he was going to make a confession. "I know how difficult that is, but we need a healer for our mates, our youngsters, and our people. If your energy burns as it helps, it is a small price to pay. That some people complained and made you feel self-conscious and doubt your own talent is a terrible thing. You should have pride in the strength of your ability and all the skills you have learned. Gordon's sister, Mazy, is a healer. He warned us about the cost of having such a talent and shared many of those concerns with us. We are not going to make impossible demands, but merely ask for your assistance when it is needed. Trissy and Hanna are going to need a healer to attend them when they give birth. This has been on our minds for two full seasons, and we have been unable to locate anyone able to attend them."

"You don't understand," LeeAnn pleaded. "If I use my energy to heal someone, it is actually painful."

Heron grimaced and looked around the table. With a low curse, he pushed to his feet, went to the counter, and came back with a knife. "Show me." He ran the blade across the back of his hand before she could blink.

"Holy hell, are you losing your mind?" LeeAnn grabbed his hand and healed it. Instead of the scream of pain she expected, he laughed at her.

"That was not painful at all. I have cut myself worse shaving and you only used a small amount of energy. That is what I wanted to know."

"What does that prove?"

"That you only use a painful dose of energy if you have no other option. If my mate or children need a full dose of your power, I am pleased to know it's available. However, if the injury is smaller, your energy is much gentler. It was not only important for me to know that, but for you to know it as well."

"Other healers do not hurt their patients," she informed him with a sniff, crossing her arms.

"No, but how many of their patients die because

their *gentle healing touch* is not enough to save them? Do you think we don't know the extent of your ability? We have only to speak to Golly, or read the truths in your own mind. That you don't know your value is a travesty. Trust that we will value you until you can see the value in yourself."

"You would have me be the Dragonmen's healer?" she asked, blinking in surprise, as if she had just realized what they were offering.

"You have already proven you can heal dragons as well as humans. I do not see why we would do otherwise."

She stared at them speechless while Trissy calmly drank her tea. "What if I am forced to hurt one of your children or your mate to heal them?"

"Then I will be grateful to the planet for giving you enough power to save their lives. We are determined men and women, LeeAnn. We do not need a healer who flinches from blood or hesitates to act in an emergency. You do neither and are fast and efficient. Grabon has some small healing talent, as does Gordon, and Griss has a great knowledge of plants and brews, but we need a clan healer."

She swallowed nervously. "I will assist the Dragonmen and their families and friends to the best of my ability," she vowed solemnly.

"Good. Then tell us why Trissy's feet are sore all the time."

Heron and Trissy listened carefully as she explained

and made several suggestions of things that might help.

"Excellent." Grabon stood and nodded to Heron. *"We should go and see Hanna, unless there are more questions?"*

"No, that was very helpful. Thank you, LeeAnn." Trissy offered her a hug and told her to enjoy the market.

"I am looking forward to seeing Golly's reaction to the garden."

Heron grinned and nodded. "I like your friend. I showed him my wagon shop this morning and he was fascinated. Let Gordon know that if he needs anything, he has only to ask. Tad and Hess covered his farm chores this morning so he could be with Hanna."

Grabon nodded and spoke a few private words with Heron. Then they left, and walked down the hill.

"You have a private line of communication with Heron?" LeeAnn asked, curious. She had seen them gesturing to one another without using words.

"It was forged many years ago. Does that disturb you?"

"No, it is just interesting. It seems Heron also has a private path with his mate."

"All mates have a private line. It is part of the bond." Grabon stopped walking. *"Do you know about the mating bond?"*

"I didn't realize it was a mind-to-mind bond."

Grabon shook his head. *"It is a life-to-life bond. Two people merge or twine their power lines."*

LeeAnn gasped and stared at him. "Humans can do this?"

"Humans with sufficient power, yes. At least one of the pair must have a strong power line. The bond is instinct and choice combined. They must be the right pair, or the bond will not form."

Okay, that stunned her. If the two successfully linked their power lines, they not only lived linked to one another, they would die that way. It would affect all types of healing. "I didn't even know that was possible."

"This has been the way of dragons throughout time. Many humans still do not have this ability, but all the Dragonmen are well connected to the planet and have sufficient power to claim a mate."

"That is fascinating. So Gordon and Hanna are mates?" If they shared such a bond, that would make a difference in any healing that they needed, she would need to remember that they shared energy.

"Yes, they are mates." She caught a glimmer of amusement in his eye, but it was obvious he was trying not to offend her.

"So what was wrong with Hanna last night?" LeeAnn asked, not sure if Grabon would know the specifics. No one had been very clear, not when they spoke to her, and not when they spoke to each other.

"She started what seemed like labor in the evening. It continued until the last sun set, but it stopped."

LeeAnn nodded and they continued walking. "That is not unusual in humans. Does it happen among dragons?"

Grabon shrugged. *"I have no mate and no youngsters of my own, so I do not know. Griss is the one you should speak to about that."*

She nodded and they walked up onto the farmhouse porch. Gordon opened the door, looking so relieved to see them that she immediately took his hand. She spoke in the most reassuring tone she could manage and explained that false labor was the body's way of practicing for birth and nothing to be concerned about. He took her in to see Hanna, and LeeAnn repeated the explanation. They spoke for a long while and she made a couple of suggestions on how to sit or rise from a chair, then explained some exercises Hanna could do to prepare for labor when it was time.

She performed a physical exam just to assure everyone that Hanna was progressing normally. Gordon stayed with Hanna in the room, and LeeAnn didn't flinch or hesitate. Back in the colonies, pregnancy was usually not a shared experience like delivery, but if the couple shared a life, power line, and mental bond, nothing was private. When she was done and was able to confirm that the baby was of good size, in position, and active, Hanna and Gordon sagged with relief.

Hanna insisted on getting dressed and making some tea. She also served some cookies, and LeeAnn enjoyed every bite. When LeeAnn was finished, Grabon told them it was time to leave and she suspected the couple was going to go to bed to get some much-needed sleep.

As they crossed the river, she heard Grabon inform all the other Dragonmen that LeeAnn had said Hanna was fine. LeeAnn debated trying to explain to Grabon that Gordon and Hanna should be the ones to spread the news, but in the end, she didn't say anything. As they walked through shields, she realized that perhaps the territory dragon's role was to make announcements that concerned everyone.

As they walked by Dotty and Tad's farmhouse, Dotty came out and greeted them. "I was relieved to hear that Hanna was not in trouble. If you have a minute, I'd like to ask you something."

Dotty blushed as they sat down in her kitchen. "I should offer you some tea."

"No, we had tea at Trissy's and again at Hanna's. You can just ask me your question," LeeAnn assured her.

"Can you tell when poison is out of a person's system and their organs have healed?"

"I am not sure I understand," LeeAnn answered, confused.

"My sister slowly poisoned me, and Tad and I have been drinking one of Griss's brews every morning and every night since I came here. I was hoping you could tell me how it's working and if you could possibly speed up any healing left to be done."

LeeAnn glanced nervously at Grabon. "That would take energy."

Grabon nodded and looked at Dotty. *"It could be painful for LeeAnn to check that. If you wish her to do this for you, Tad must be here because it will affect both of you."*

Dotty nodded and smiled. "He suggested LeeAnn could join us after the market closes and check then."

Grabon nodded his agreement before LeeAnn could make an excuse. She was unwilling to hurt this wonderful heartsinger unless there was no choice. Her mind was racing to form the words she needed to explain this when there was a sudden cry of distress with power behind it. Immediately she looked at Grabon and his eyes narrowed.

"We will return this evening," he informed Dotty. *"It seems Kev has run into some trouble."*

"Is he hurt?" LeeAnn asked. Long-distance communication was not one of her skills.

"No, not that kind of trouble, but we will see to it." Grabon seemed very focused, so she didn't ask for further information. Instead, she followed him down to the market.

"If you need to fly ahead…," LeeAnn suggested softly, walking fast to keep up.

"No, Hess is there. The boy is not in danger or injured. Kev's talent is communicating with animals, humans, and dragons, but he is still learning the skills needed to do this effectively. This sometimes causes him difficulty."

LeeAnn agreed even though she was not sure what he meant. When they finally arrived at the market, she was impressed with the size of the crowd. More dragons were present than the day before, or so it seemed to her. Grabon nodded to them as they passed, returning some sort of ritual greeting.

They didn't go to Griss's shop, as she expected, but to an area off the main market path. There they found Hess, Kev, and a young dragon, less than half Grabon's size. She had distinctive red markings on her dark gray body, and her facial features included yellow, red, and green markings as well as some brown that outlined a bright green mark that went from the underside of her chin to her groin. The young female stared at Kev, her nostrils flaring with each breath, completely ignoring Hess.

Grabon's wings expanded for a moment as he stared at her, his expression one of stern disapproval. The female seemed to deflate before their eyes, her shoulders slumped and head bowed. Several exchanges in Dragon followed and the female let out a sigh before she took off.

Hess chuckled. "My Dragon isn't even half as good as Kev's, but did you just yell at her and tell her to come back again?"

Grabon let out a rough chuckle. *"Young dragons*

need a firm hand. She was curious and came here first before announcing her presence. When she saw Kev communicating with a hopper, she snatched it and ate it."

LeeAnn did her best not to laugh, even as she spotted the small pile of gore left behind.

"I told her it was rude," Kev informed them, still looking indignant. "I was talking with that hopper and she ripped his head off."

Grabon nodded and sighed. *"You also let out a yell, which was appropriate since there is no hunting on this land without permission. A human speaking Dragon startled her and she knew you had to be a member of our clan, and she was caught trespassing."*

LeeAnn had to turn away to keep from laughing. Her gaze caught Hess's and they both grinned before looking away. She bit her upper lip to hide her amusement.

"She was hoping to avoid punishment by ignoring Hess, since he is easily identified as the territory claimer for part of the market grounds. She argued with Kev, instead, hoping that as humans you would not understand her transgressions. Tria will need a guide if she is to experience the market. Youngsters at that age can cause a great deal of trouble for themselves. She will fly over, announce her presence as is proper, and rejoin us shortly."

Kev let out a gusty sigh, rolled his eyes, and looked up at Grabon. "Am I going to get stuck showing the girl around?"

Grabon looked at him thoughtfully. *"Perhaps Fin would be a better choice."*

At the mention of his younger brother, Kev straightened up and all signs of reluctance vanished. "But I speak Dragon more fluently and can explain the rules. It should definitely be me."

Grabon nodded slowly. *"If you insist."*

Tria flew back in looking somewhat sheepish and presented herself first to Grabon, then to Hess. Grabon granted her permission to attend the market only if she accepted Kev as a guide. Her gaze shot to the boy and she nodded and chirped something LeeAnn didn't understand. The startled look he gave her meant it must have been interesting. As the two youths went off, Grabon turned to Hess.

"Let me know if she causes any difficulty."

"I will be sure to do that. How is our healer feeling today? She looks more rested."

"I am right here," LeeAnn protested.

"True, but you didn't greet me, so it would have been rude to speak to you directly." She looked startled and he chuckled. "It is a dragon custom that we have adopted. I thought you should know that."

"Thank you." She frowned slightly. "I am going to have to learn the customs and some Dragon; at the very least some key phrases."

"You will have time," Hess reminded her with a smile. "Have you seen Golly today? He is looking very pleased with himself."

"No, he was gone when I woke up. What has he been doing?"

"He is accompanying Thane as they patrol the market. It is a good way for him to meet everyone and learn the area. They are waiting for you before they go to the garden and then for some food. Would you like me to take you to them?"

She glanced at Grabon and he nodded. *"I believe I will check on our two youths and make sure they stay out of trouble as they explore the market."*

"We will go see the sisters first," Hess said. "Janie said she has your bag. They are at their booth today so Manny can explore the market."

Grinning, LeeAnn followed him into the crowd. When they reached the sisters' booth, Janie came out from behind the counter to give her a hug and handed her the bag.

"We are so glad you returned. If there is anything you need, you have only to ask. It is such a relief for us to have a healer in the territory. I think you will find that there is plenty here to keep you entertained. Oh, we did have an opportunity to meet your friend, Golly. What a sweet fellow. We are going to have such fun making him clothes." She glanced at the customers and shrugged. "I better get back. If you get a chance, can you bring us some tea?" LeeAnn nodded and Janie turned to Hess. "You be nice," she admonished him. Hess held up his hands in a classic sign of surrender.

"I am working on it," he answered with a grin.

Confused by that exchange, LeeAnn turned around, looking for the teashop.

"It's over here." He indicated the left passage as they started walking and she slipped the bag over her shoulder. Funny, it felt heavier than it had the day before.

After they brought two cups of tea back to Jamie and Janie, they went on to the garden. As they stood by the entrance, Hess offered her some tea from his large cup. She declined when she saw Golly far off in the crowd, and her heart lifted to see him grinning. Someone had loaned him some clothes. The tunic was a little tight and the pants inches too short, but the material was excellent and sturdy.

"LeeAnn!" he called when he spotted her. "You won't believe the things we've seen."

Grinning, she nodded and motioned him to come join her. When he reached them, she touched his arm gently. "I am so glad you are having fun."

"Thane said there was something special over here." Golly looked around expectantly. "Do you know what it is?"

"It's inside. Let me show you." She led him through the entrance, and he stopped in awed wonder when he saw the garden. She gently steered him farther inside and let him take in the colors, the smells, the heat and humidity. She was only vaguely aware of Thane and Hess watching them, but she paid them no mind.

Slowly as if in a trance, Golly moved from one flower to another, his eyes bright with excitement. "It is so pretty," he whispered.

"I thought so too," she answered, as a lump rose in her chest. "Did you see the statue out front?"

At his enthusiastic nod, she laughed. "There is another one hidden in here. You have to be careful while you're looking not to step on any flowers. Do you want to look for it?"

"Do I have time?" He glanced over at Thane.

"We can give you some time. If you do not find it today, you will enjoy hunting for it tomorrow."

Golly nodded and started down the first path. She decided to sit on one of the benches and watch.

Hess sat beside her grinning. "He is your child, you know that, right?"

She glanced over at him and shrugged. "He is not a child, not really."

"A part of him is. Do you know how old he is?"

She clasped her hands in front of her. "He cannot be very old, Hess; with a condition like his, people rarely live to see twenty-five cycles."

Hess looked back at Golly and tears rose to his eyes. "I had not realized." He blinked a few times and looked over at Thane.

She nodded and bit her lip, determined not to shed a tear. "It is something I have known since I met him."

"Is he healthy enough now?"

She clenched her jaw, but nodded and wiped away a tear that managed to escape. "I would guess he is sixteen, maybe a cycle or two older."

"Then he still has some time." When he saw the tears in her eyes, he put his arm around her. She flinched but then relaxed. "I did not mean to make you sad."

With a tearful laugh, she wiped her cheeks and sat up straighter. "It is common with his condition to have delays. He does not know much about it and it always seemed cruel to tell him."

Hess nodded and they watched Golly peer through the flowers. "Why did Sam castrate him?"

LeeAnn shuddered and shrugged. She couldn't bear to remember. "He enjoyed his cruelties." She looked up at Hess. "I never told Sam about his condition. I was afraid he would use it as a torment, something to add to his nightmares, visions of death and dying."

"Good for you. So did Sam know how young he was?"

"I don't think so." Sam wouldn't have cared. He just wanted to create a monster to display and torment, but instead of turning cruel, as Sam had intended, Golly had always been sweet.

"How did Golly end up with him?"

"I was only with them for a cycle and the story never came up. He has never spoken of his time before Sam and the show."

Golly let out a squeal of triumph and stomped through the water while LeeAnn laughed. "I think he found it."

Several people looked over at the sound and then smiled as they watched him examine the statue with reverent awe. Three youths joined him on the other side of the pool, and LeeAnn moved to stand, but Hess tightened his arm around her.

"Thane will keep watch. He's safe enough; I doubt those boys will bother him."

Her eyes met his and she relaxed slightly. "I'm used to protecting him."

"Look at it this way: now there are many others to help. Nobody wants to shut you out, but expanding his world and circle of trusted people will help him feel secure."

"I know, it's just hard to let go. Oh, Thane is going over." She let out a sigh of relief.

"I begin to see what Grabon was talking about."

"What do you mean?" she asked, watching as Thane

supervised, standing close and monitoring the situation without involving himself.

"He insists Golly will do better in his nest and that you should have the comfort and privacy of a human home. I thought it would be easier for Golly to stay with you, but Grabon said no. Golly would enjoy some independence and you needed a chance to experience a life of your own."

She frowned and looked back at Hess. "Are you saying I'm overprotective?"

He chuckled and rubbed her back lightly before patting her shoulder. "I'm saying he's doing fine. You are all tense and defensive, afraid he's going to be hurt. Now that you are both safe, it would be easy for you to smother him." His expression grew serious. "Especially when you know he has a very limited time."

LeeAnn swallowed back her sorrow and she took a deep breath. "I try very hard not to think about that."

"So tell me, how old are you?"

She grinned and thought about it. "I must be nineteen by now."

"Nineteen? I would have guessed older; at least twenty, maybe even twenty-two cycles. How did you end up with Sam?"

"I ran away at seventeen. I healed someone who then complained bitterly about my energy causing pain, discrediting my parents' clinic. After that I spent a year working in a clinic as an assistant. I was there when I made the mistake of trusting Sam." She looked down at her hands. "He asked me to come out to their camp to heal one of his actors. It turned out to be one of the freaks from his traveling show. Then he invited me to stay with them. First for the night, then to look after his people." LeeAnn crossed her arms, feeling the chill of memories.

"After I met Golly, I knew he wouldn't have long to live. I thought if I stayed with them, I could help him escape. Sam caught us and publicly accused me of stealing money from the show. We were near a settlement outside the third colony where they have a permanent gallows. He finally agreed to let me work off the sum he said I owed to avoid hanging."

Hess stiffened beside her. "I should not have been annoyed with you yesterday." When she stared at him, wondering what he was talking about, he let out a soft groan. "When you were accused of stealing in Griss's shop. I should not have been upset with you."

"I know the scars are unsightly, but I wanted the man to understand...."

"They are not unsightly." He stood and paced away from the bench. "You were defending yourself; even I understood that. What I objected to was you taking off your clothes."

"Oh, but I thought it was because of the scars, because I'm a freak."

He muttered to himself, sat, took her hands in his

and peered intently into her face. "You are not a freak; you are a very talented healer. For a time you were caught in a very bad situation. We are fortunate you survived, and some scars are a small price to pay for that."

"Thane said we should go eat," Golly cried out as he ran toward them.

LeeAnn nodded and tugged her hands so Hess would let go, but she grinned at Golly. "You found the statue."

"It has a very beautiful song inside. Can we go eat now?"

"That's a good idea," Hess answered, getting to his feet and gently moving them to the exit. "I bet LeeAnn only had porridge for breakfast. It is one of Grabon's favorites."

Thane joined them outside and gestured for them to go right. *"He makes porridge every morning,"* he commented with a shrug. *"Breakfast at Hanna or Trissy's is much more exciting."*

"Hanna's cookies were very good," LeeAnn told them.

"I had porridge with Grabon, then I ate with Heron and his family," Golly told them. "We had biscuits, and I took a bath and got new clothes. Heron is going to make me a bed for the nest."

"Is he?" LeeAnn asked. "That will be fun."

"He said it was time and I shouldn't think about my

old life anymore." He leaned down so he could whisper in her ear. "I didn't even tell him and he knew the big secret. The one I wasn't supposed to tell anyone."

LeeAnn frowned. "What secret is that?"

"That Brian was my father. He said having the strong-man as a father wasn't a bad thing."

She was stunned, but she kept walking. Brian was his father?

"Heron said that everyone has a father and I didn't need to be like him."

"Heron was right," Hess told him. "You don't need to be anyone but Golly. That's more than enough."

"Heron said Brian was a bad father and I didn't need to worry about him anymore or keep his secrets. Even though I kept his secret good because Sam never even guessed, Heron said I should tell you, LeeAnn. I don't know why, but he said you needed to know we used to live normal, but then we had to run away. We joined the show, and Brian made a deal with Sam."

"Can you tell us why you had to run away?" Thane asked.

"Brian got mad and he did a really, really bad thing and we had to run away. Then I had to be Golly the knife-throwing monster and he was Brian the strong-man."

"How long were you with Sam before I came?"

LeeAnn asked, her voice sounding hoarse from holding back questions Golly couldn't answer. She couldn't believe that Brian was his father.

Golly shrugged. "Maybe a season? I would have told you, but it was a really important secret." Golly looked worried and she patted his arm.

"You did a good job keeping the secret. I never would have guessed. Did you used to have a different name?"

"No, but Brian used to be Bertard the blacksmith. I was Goliath, but every one called me Golly. My mother was Sarah, but she got in the way of Brian's plans, so he lost her." Golly frowned. "Do you think we should find her?"

They went into a sitting area and sat at a table.

Hess shook his head. "I don't think we'd have any luck, Golly. Maybe someone who comes to the market will bring us news. If we hear about her, we'll send her a message."

"Okay. Heron said if Brian comes here, he's not even going to be allowed to speak to me. I belong in Grabon's nest now."

"Is that what you want?" Thane asked gently.

Shrugging, Golly looked over at LeeAnn. "He let Sam be mean to us."

She straightened up in her chair. "Yes, he did. Heron is right. He was a bad father and you don't need to see him again."

"Heron said I would be safe here and I don't have to be a monster anymore. He said I could just be a big boy and have a happy life. I could sleep in a bed, eat when I was hungry, live with Grabon and be safe. Grabon will protect me from anyone who wants to hurt me."

"Grabon is an excellent protector," Hess told him.

"LeeAnn was a good protector," Golly told them, his chin set stubbornly.

"LeeAnn took care of you. It's not the same as a protector. Grabon will stop people from hurting you and LeeAnn. She's going to be our healer, and we will all help to protect her," Thane explained.

Plates of food arrived and Golly's eyes widened. "I can eat all of this?"

"As much as you want," Hess answered.

LeeAnn looked up as Grabon walked toward them with Kev and Tria. They joined them at the table with nods all around. LeeAnn now recognized the gesture as an informal dragon greeting of acknowledgment. Grabon introduced Tria to Thane in Dragon and Golly watched, fascinated.

"Tria is visiting the market and Kev is showing her around," LeeAnn explained.

Tria gave a series of garbles and other noises, looking at Thane, tilting her head. Then she turned and nodded more slowly to Golly and he returned the gesture.

"Is she a child dragon?" he asked curiously.

"She is a new youth, not yet mature," Grabon explained with a twinkle in his eyes. *"She is small and still very young. After they eat, Kev and Tria are going to the Storyteller's Cove. Did you wish to join them?"*

Golly looked over at Thane. "Can we go there?"

"We can spare the time. I think you will enjoy Mia's story, even if it is in Dragon. Then we will come back for the one she does in Human, later."

As soon as he finished speaking, a heartsong began and everyone in the crowd stopped moving to better focus on the song. The servers at the booth grinned and set down their trays. Unlike the other heartsongs LeeAnn had heard, this song sounded like random notes before Dotty's voice began to weave the melody together. Images burst out, emotions bled between the sounds, and LeeAnn whole being relaxed into a sigh of relief. The song was a celebration of life, a feeling of victory hard-won, and the triumph of an impossible task finally accomplished.

The song grew and grew until words emerged, as if hidden within. It was a welcome for her and Golly, an offer of safety, friendship, and belonging. The lyrics stressed that nothing was better than being with people who knew the value of survival. Together they would all be able to build something beautiful and lasting that was of value to the planet and the future. As the words faded, the song continued focusing on strength and love, embracing triumph, and letting past failures go.

When it was over, everyone breathed a sigh of satisfaction and wiped at their eyes, and activity slowly resumed. The server brought out food for Grabon and the two youths.

"That was a very special song," Golly said, rubbing his palm on his chest as if massaging his heart. "How can a song do that? It makes you feel all funny inside, like you want to cry and laugh all at the same time."

"That was a heartsinger, Golly. They always have a major effect on everyone. Her talent is that she brings out emotion, which lets you feel better," Hess explained.

"She's very special," Kev agreed, sniffing softly and blinking away tears.

Tria said something to Thane and he answered and shook his head. *"She wants to know who the singer is so she can meet her, but I told her that isn't allowed."*

"Our young guest has much to learn. She doesn't understand why our heartsinger isn't singing among the crowd." Grabon smiled at Tria indulgently.

"She doesn't want people to point at her," Golly answered, glancing up at Tria.

Kev translated, and while Tria responded, Golly ate some more.

"Tria says if she could sing like that, everyone would know who she was," Kev supplied, looking at Tria as though he wasn't sure he agreed.

Golly shook his head and swallowed in a hurry. "Then they would never leave her alone. She could never be who she is; she could only be the singer."

After Kev translated, Tria looked at Golly and nodded, acknowledging his point.

While they ate, Hess leaned over to LeeAnn. "During the story I have some places I need to check on. Did you want to stay with Grabon or go with me?"

"This story is in Dragon?" At his nod, she shrugged. "If you don't mind the company, I'd like to go with you."

"I don't mind your company at all." He nodded to Thane, who looked over at Grabon. In turn, the territory dragon looked from Hess to LeeAnn.

"She has agreed to do a check on Dotty after the market closes. Our healer is concerned she will hurt Tad's mate with her energy because it is so powerful. See if Griss has any advice for her."

"We can do that," Hess answered. "Is there anything else she needs to do?"

"Take her through the food section. She should buy supplies to make dinner." Grabon smiled at LeeAnn and handed her four coins. *"I have meat and eggs, but it would be good if you got whatever else you would like to use."*

"I can do that," she promised, grinning. It looked like she was making dinner.

Hess stood and smiled at the others. "Then we're

going to get moving."

Grinning, she followed him away from the tables. "I think Grabon is expecting me to cook."

Hess chuckled, looking back to where the territory dragon sat. "He enjoys many kinds of human food, but cooking is a challenge for him. We tried to talk him into getting a real stove, but so far we haven't been successful. He says a fire is good enough for his nest."

"We will need to do some shopping, but the fire isn't a problem." She jingled the coins in her hand, patted her bag at her side and again wondered at the added weight. "I had some coins yesterday." She opened the bag and stopped walking. Not only was the cream Griss had given her inside, but so were more coins. Trying not to panic, she grabbed his arm. "Hess, there are more coins. Where did they come from?"

"Five for healing the thief yesterday. Two from the man who accused you of stealing and then embarrassed you." He scratched his head. "I think that was all we added."

"Why would the man at Griss's shop give me coins?"

"He falsely accused you of stealing. You wore the clothes of our clan, even before you were our healer. He should have known better than to do such a thing in public. If he genuinely had a concern, he should have said something to Griss or one of us. Griss fined him after we left."

She add the coins from Grabon, closed the bag, and continued walking, trying not to let her pounding heart show. Nobody was going to accuse her when they had added the coins themselves. "I had no idea you would do that."

"We take attacks on our clan seriously, even if they are only designed to publicly embarrass one of our members. He should be hoping that nobody in his family needs a healer anytime soon."

Chapter 4

"I would never refuse to treat someone if they requested it, Hess. It's against the healer's creed. Even if my energy is too strong and painful for the person I am trying to heal, it is impossible for me to refuse them."

"I was not suggesting you would do the refusing. If someone outside our clan wants a healer, they will need to approach one of the territory holders. While unlike most territories we have multiple holders, we all defer to Grabon, and he is capable of refusing."

"He can't refuse on my behalf," she argued.

Hess raised his eyebrows and grinned. "You should argue that with him. I'm not getting in the middle of it. I will give you a free piece of advice, though: do not give Grabon an order. It is his territory. He stands as protector for all of it, including you."

Somewhat uncomfortable, she frowned and looked away. "Does he listen to reason?"

"He is generally reasonable. We will see what you think after you have gotten used to things." When they reached Griss's shop, it was crowded again with humans and dragons. Fin saw them from his position by a display for cures for common ailments, and waved. Griss had Red on his arm as he dealt with customers, and Brom was there with Star, riding on his tail. It looked like he was sorting something, but she wasn't sure. Griss motioned them over and introduced LeeAnn to a dragon he was speaking with and offered to translate. She nodded and smiled, a little stunned over the title of the clan healer.

Through Griss's translation she learned that the visiting dragon had a persistent boil under his wing that would not heal completely. He was hoping Griss would have something to fix it as it made flying uncomfortable. Now that he knew they had a healer, he asked whom he needed to approach to access her services. Hess and Griss answered together by naming their territory dragon. The visiting dragon nodded in understanding.

"I can at least look at it," LeeAnn told them.

Hess shook his head. "This is not an emergency. You wanted to ask Griss a question?"

"Grabon suggested I ask you for some advice on how not to hurt Dotty when I perform a check on her internal organs."

Griss nodded and gave her a thoughtful look. *"When you heal an open wound in an emergency, you use all of your own energy to knit it closed. It is effective and fast, but the more your energy exceeds the level of your patient's energy, the more painful they will find it. If you can tune your energy to match the pulse and frequency of theirs, it will reduce the amount of pain, but it will also slow the process. Healing is not a gentle craft unless the power of the healer is less than that of those they heal, in which case it is not nearly as effective."*

LeeAnn nodded. When she'd healed Golly's small scratches and cuts, she sometimes managed not to hurt him because she would match his energy pulse. When his wounds were critical, she simply fixed them and let him pass out. "So if I can tune my energy to Dotty's, then it shouldn't hurt as much?"

"It would be uncomfortable, but not painful unless you find extensive damage; a stronger pulse would be needed to fix that. The procedure might be painful, but only for as long as it takes you to complete the healing. The advantage to having a healer of your strength and power is you can work quickly."

"How is it I never learned that part of healing?" she asked, disconcerted.

"You were only seventeen when you left home. Is it possible your parents put off teaching you that lesson until they were sure you could control the pulse of your own power?" Hess asked.

She chewed the inside of her cheek. "It could be possible, but they seemed to think I could never work in their clinic. They were disappointed that my energy was painful for their patients."

Griss shrugged and glanced at the dragon with the boil. *"It is more likely they did not know what to do with your level of power. Gordon's sister, Mazy, is a healer of exceptional skill and power. According to him, human healers rarely have that much power. You might ask him how she learned to change her pulse."*

"I'll do that." LeeAnn glanced at Hess. "Grabon isn't

going to refuse, is he?"

"No, they are negotiating a price and deciding on a private place for you to work. You might want to ask Griss what brews might help after the healing," Hess suggested

"Let me show you what we have," Griss smiled and took her through his shop. Since she didn't yet know what had caused the boil, she couldn't select precisely what he might need, but being familiar with what Griss offered would help. This tour was far different than the one she had taken yesterday. As she asked questions, Griss showed her what he had. She picked out a brew for Trissy that could help her sleep if that became a problem. There was a scented candle, soap and brew that was sold as a set that was supposed to be relaxing. She liked that idea for Hanna and Gordon. Griss also had a skin lotion that would be good for both Trissy and Hanna, to help with their stretch marks. As she collected goods, Hess brought her a basket. By the time she was done, she was surprised she had filled it, and Griss was grinning. She handed him the amount of coins he asked for and promised to be back.

Evidently the negotiations were over, since the visitor was gone and Hess had a location for where they were to meet him. LeeAnn took her basket and followed Hess from the market grounds into a nearby small field.

"I think this visitor is a little embarrassed about his boil. Privacy is not something the dragons generally seek," Hess explained.

Nodding, LeeAnn dug through her basket and took out the supplies she would need to lance and heal a boil.

She looked around chewing on her lip. "What I could really use is hot water."

"I can help with that." He made a fire ring of stones and found some wood. Fin arrived a few minutes later with a tea kettle full of water and a bowl.

"Griss said these would be helpful." He handed her a metal tool she recognized, used for picking small objects from flesh. "Can I stay and watch?"

LeeAnn shook her head. "Not this time." She almost felt guilty for denying the boy, but she was nervous enough.

"Bring her a mug of tea and something sweet. Healing is an exhausting business and drains the healer."

Fin ran off, happy to be of help. Almost as soon as he was gone, the visiting dragon flew in. He settled with a sigh, shifted his ample gray-and-red body, lifted his wing and showed her the boil.

She swallowed, looking at the swollen, painful lump that held a raging infection. It was in a place the poor dragon could hardly reach, but he had managed to drain it with a claw puncture or two to gain some relief. Keeping in mind what Griss had told her, she checked his energy pulse, then cut the boil open and used hot cloths to draw out the infection. Then she applied energy to heal it, drawing out what she hoped was the last bit. Griss was correct: working this way took longer, but her patient didn't scream in pain. He simply gasped and shifted uncomfortably a time or two.

When she was done and had cleaned up the mess, he looked so relieved. She gave him a smile and a pat on the arm. Then she brought out some cream from her basket. Using images, she showed him why the boil had formed. In the future, he needed to use the cream to prevent his wing from rubbing against his body during long flights.

Nodding, the dragon pulled out a handful of coins and took the cream. Startled, LeeAnn looked over at Hess, who nodded. She added the coins to her pouch, and after he left, she turned to Hess. "How much did Grabon charge him? It was a simple boil."

"Grabon agreed to two coins. He added the others because you did it slowly and completed the healing. Among dragons, the healers only perform the critical parts and evidently they charge more. Also, he thought it was bad form to cheat a healer who could one day save his life. You really can't mindspeak at a distance, can you? Grabon was running a translation for you and I didn't realize you couldn't hear him. Next time I'll remember. The dragon was very grateful, not just to you but to Grabon for allowing you to help him. While you were working, Fin brought you the tea and some cookies." He handed her a cup of tea.

She accepted it gratefully and took a few sips. "I never even saw him."

"You were working hard. Wash your hands and we can sit for a bit. I think it's harder for you to change your energy pulse to match your patient's and then get it back to normal when you're done than it is to do the healing."

"That's the truth," she muttered, giving a sigh. She set down the tea, scrubbed her hands clean with a mixture of hot water and leaves, and sat on the ground with her tea. He handed her a cloth bag filled with cookies. Grinning, she opened it and offered him one.

They sat there and ate a few. "You did a good job," he finally offered.

"I was afraid I was going to hurt him. That boil had to be painful to begin with, and the last thing he needed was for me to make it worse."

"I had no idea dragons could get boils like that."

"If he slimmed down a little, his wing wouldn't rub his body and he wouldn't get the boils. None of the dragons I've met in Grabon's territory have any extra flesh, so it would be unusual for them to have that kind of problem."

Hess nodded, grinning. "All of our dragons are at a fighting weight and well-muscled."

"So are the human males." She glanced at him from under her lashes and smiled as she finished her tea. "I guess we should douse the fire. You had some things you needed to check on?"

"We'll meet my brother in a little while. You have a few more minutes to relax." He frowned as he tried to form his next question. "What do you think about Golly's story about Brian and his mother?"

LeeAnn shrugged. "I think Brian killed his match and was being hunted for at least one other murder. He traded his son for sanctuary with Sam but didn't tell Sam that Golly was his child. He felt justified because his son was destined to die young anyway." She paused for a moment. "I think he probably killed the healer who told him about Golly's condition."

Nodding, Hess leaned back on his arms. "That was what I was thinking." He waited until the pulse of her own energy had completely gone back to normal. Then he stood and doused the fire as she collected the last of her supplies, adding the empty kettle and bowl to her basket. "Did you want to contact your parents? We could send a message," he offered, taking the basket.

"I should; if nothing else, to let them know I'm somewhere safe. It's probably been a full cycle. They may not know I'm missing yet, but sooner or later they'll notice. I haven't contacted them since before I joined Sam."

It was hard for him not to comment or make assumptions about her parents, but he tried. There was enough bitterness in her voice when she spoke about them, he didn't need or want to add to it.

They walked back into the market, and Hess led her to a booth she hadn't seen before. It was on the forest side and in the trees, but it was empty. Tad was waiting there and grinning.

"That basket is getting full."

"She healed a dragon's boil. These are all healing supplies. Is this the booth you mentioned? Isn't it a little small?"

"She would only have one person at a time," Tad reminded him.

Hess shook his head. "No, she would need more room and someone to stand as guard and negotiator. She also needs a fire and a table. What else would you need?" he asked, looking at her.

"Me?"

Tad laughed and leaned against the structure. "You don't need to stay at the booth, but you're going to need a secure private place to see visitors and keep supplies. This is private, but Hess is correct, it's not very large. Let me show you some of the others to consider."

As they walked along, LeeAnn realized that parts of the market were like a maze with hidden booths. What kind of merchandise needed to be that private? Before she could ask, Hess whispered, "There are smuggled books, candy, and toy shops where people can purchase gifts in secret. Dragons and humans can also come here to purchase private things they don't want to be seen purchasing." At her blank look he grinned. "Sex objects, LeeAnn. Some of it clothing, scents, or objects that are designed to attract sexual advances or help find satisfaction."

"Oh, well, huh," she stammered. "Dragons too?"

"They have been some of our best customers. Most dragons are highly sexual and enjoy a good romp as much as any human. That's all over when they find a mate, but before then they practice as much as possible with fewer inhibitions than humans have."

She looked at them thoughtfully. "I hadn't realized that."

Tad stopped at another booth, and Hess shook his head. "No, not with that booth next door; if any of the dragons are guarding her they'll be distracted for sure."

LeeAnn looked at the booth he indicated and couldn't resist walking inside. Four dragons were looking around and they each nodded at her. As far as she could see, the booth sold dragon art: Sculptures and paintings that looked impressive with their use of color and form. As she looked closer, she turned red and spun around. Hess and Tad stood near the entrance, biting their lips and trying hard not to laugh at her. Who would have thought that dragons liked pornography.

Hess steered her back outside.

"How did you even get that here?" she asked, looking back over her shoulder.

"I am not even sure whose contacts brought in those specific pieces. Thane has set up some trade arrangements for art. Pit has done the same with other territories. Brom even brought in artistic pelts and tools and has some friends who offered deals on different items. We are always making trades and collecting interesting goods. Some are items for humans, others are better suited to dragons, but many are objects that work for both species. None of the booths are restricted to one species, so if a human wishes to buy a statue of two dragons copulating, he or she can."

She gave a little shiver as they kept walking. "How did you hire humans to run those booths?"

"We told them honestly what they were being hired to sell. Our market has brought a number of new families to the village, while other families have left and gone back to the colonies."

"Are there any restrictions on what you sell?"

Hess grinned and looked around them. "We do not sell weapons. Other than that, no."

"You need to get more dragons to run booths," she told him.

"Heron and Grabon need to accept them first. The restrictions on dragons in a territory are much more stringent than those on humans."

"That hardly seems fair." She and Hess stopped walking when they caught up with Tad, who was leaning against a tree.

"It's cultural, and something we need to respect.

Dragons have reasons for being careful about who resides in a territory." Hess gestured to his brother to continue.

Grinning, Tad showed her the booth behind the trees, but it seemed all wrong to her. "I liked the field where I worked before. Can't we build a shelter there and put up a table? It's near Griss's shop and private."

"All right, show me where it was," Tad invited, looking frustrated.

"Ignore him, he just wanted to populate these booths in this end of the market because we have a bet on what areas will fill up first."

"Really? What is the prize?" she asked with a grin.

"If his end fills in first, I have to help Gordon with a new herd that is coming later this summer. If my end does, he will have that chore."

She looked at him in surprise. "What herd?"

Tad sighed and rubbed the back of his neck. "Old Earth cows. They produce delicious milk, but they do take a lot of work."

"Why can't you simply hire people to look after them?"

"Gordon is our cousin and milking and feeding will be easier with Farmers doing the tending. Not only do we work cheaply for one another, but with Hanna pregnant, he is going to need the reliable help of a family member."

They continued walking and Tad shook his head. "I was tricked into making the bet."

"It is your own fault you were distracted. Besides, we benefit from these cows. We will be selling the milk, butter, and cheeses in the market," Hess added, grinning at his brother.

"We'll be hiring people to make those. The bet was for tending the cows, not making the products," Tad reminded him.

Hess laughed over his protests. "I told you we should see about recruiting other Farmers."

Tad glanced at LeeAnn. "We had a gathering of Farmers here this past winter. Many of them were fascinated by the idea of working with the dragons to build a territory for both species, but none of them were anxious to join us. He is antagonizing me because he thinks he is going to win."

"Why would they not be anxious to join?" LeeAnn asked, truly confused. Now that she knew that the Dragonmen had accepted Golly, this was the best place she had ever seen.

Tad and Hess grinned, walking on either side of her as they moved through the crowd. "The Dragonmen, human and dragon, typically have too much power for others to be comfortable around for very long," Hess explained.

"Grabon says more power and skill are housed in his clan than in any other territory and he still has room for more dragons and humans. For those who enjoy measuring their power against others, we make them uneasy and fearful." Tad shrugged.

LeeAnn could understand how that could happen. Her first impressions had been one of power, too; but she had quickly seen past that to their joint goal and dedication to one another and their cause. When they finally got back to the clearing she had used, Rok was waiting.

"This is a good place for her," he told Hess and Tad before turning to her with a smile. *"I will make the path, and Rigby will make the sign. I have already spoken to him. What type of shelter do you want?"*

"I really don't know. What do you think?"

They shared pictures, making adjustments and changes until they were satisfied.

"It is really more of a hut with a large door. You would use it if it was cold, raining, or if privacy were required," Rok commented.

They started a list of what she would need, and her head was spinning at how quickly these plans were progressing.

"Until the shelter is completed and as long as the weather holds, you can work here with only a few adjustments," Tad told her.

They immediately set about making those adjustments: enlarging the fire pit and gathering wood. Rok blasted and marked the path and then left to get supplies. Before she knew it they had brought in a metal box to contain the brews, lotions, herbs, and bottles Rok was sure she needed. Someone had hauled in water and provided her with a small wagon, a table, and more cloths.

"How many coins?" she asked when they were done.

Tad laughed and patted her shoulder. "You are our healer and are treating my mate. You won't pay coins for this. When you have extra you can add to the market fund. Just give us what you can spare to bring in more goods."

Swallowing, she nodded and sat on the box that was now filled with her supplies. It was the perfect size to be a seat for her, and she wondered if they had planned it that way. Tad left to see to other booths, and Rok settled down on his tail as Hess paced off the space where her hut would be.

"How are you feeling?" Rok asked, looking her over.

"I am feeling amazed at the moment. It is all happening so fast."

Rok nodded and glanced over at Hess, who was ignoring them. *"I do not wish to overtax you, but when you are not busy, my foot needs some attention."*

"Your foot?" She got up to look.

Rok shrugged and showed her the crooked claw on one of his back toes.

"How did that happen?" she asked, touching it gently.

"It happened when we retrieved the youngsters. The claw caught in one of the bundles I tossed in the nest and the weight and force broke the bone. Griss looked at it and we tried to fix it, but it healed crooked. Can it be fixed?"

"Of course it can," she answered, frowning. "It's going to hurt because I have to break the bone again and then heal it in place. Would you rather leave it as it is?"

Rok shook his head adamantly. *"No, I would rather have it fixed. Can we do it now? There is a female visitor here today. If my claw is crooked, it will scratch her and she will not romp with me again. That was why I had to decline her invitation."* His low rumble told her how unhappy that had made him.

She smiled and glanced over at Hess, who was still over by where they were going to build the shelter. "I can do it now, but it really is going to hurt."

Rok shrugged and gave her a sheepish look. *"Only for a minute, and then you will heal it and I can go see the female. It will be well worth it. She is the first female visitor to offer an invitation to me since we have been here."*

LeeAnn cleared her throat and looked down at the toe, checking Rok's energy pulse and adjusting her own. She traced the bone by touch and compared it to the one like it on Rok's other foot. It seemed dragons had two opposable toes on each foot as well as two opposable fingers on each hand. When she was sure of what the structure was supposed to be, she warned him that she was ready to begin. She had to brace herself against his reaction before she got started, but when she was done; the toe and claw were healed perfectly straight. Much to her surprise, she had managed to match his power pulses. Not that it hadn't hurt, but she felt pretty confident that it had hurt less than it could have.

Rok was thrilled and thanked her before he flew off.

Hess came over chuckling and helped her sit on her box. "We'll get you some tea in a few minutes. You made him very happy."

"It's an odd thing to be happy about," she muttered.

"No, being able to have sex is important. He didn't say anything, but I know it bothered him that he hadn't received an invitation from any of the females. Then to have to decline...." Hess shook his head. "How are you? Your face is looking a bit pinched and pale. That energy change thing must be way more stressful than it sounds."

"It is, but it's worth it if I don't hurt anyone. I could use some tea. What about Mia's story, have we missed it?"

"No, she'll wait until you're ready."

LeeAnn climbed off the box and they took the new path back into the market. When they reached the tea shop, it was filled with people, so she waited by the bench while Hess got them two teas, and then they went over to the Storyteller's Cove where it was quiet. Mia and Pit were there and waved them in when LeeAnn and Hess hesitated to approach.

"We were taking a quiet moment, not engaging in intimacy," Pit offered with a shrug, clearly not upset by their interruption.

"The tea shop was crowded, so we thought we'd bring our tea here. LeeAnn was able to fix Rok's toe," Hess told them, sitting on the ground before sipping his tea.

"I am sure he is relieved. It was worrisome." Pit grinned at his mate, then nodded to the two humans. *"I'll be back before the next story. Hess, can you give me a hand with something?"*

Hess handed LeeAnn his tea and followed Pit out of the Storyteller's Cove.

"Do you know what they are up to?" LeeAnn asked.

Mia grinned and nodded. *"Tria and Kev are arguing over by the garden. Grabon has left to check on Hanna and Gordon, and asked Thane to keep track of the two youths. Golly does not like them arguing, so Thane called for help."*

"Maybe I should go as well," LeeAnn suggested, setting down her tea.

"We can go over and watch, but I would not interfere until they ask. Males get annoyed when females do that."

LeeAnn sighed and picked up her tea again. "I better stay here or I won't be able to help myself."

Mia laughed and agreed. After a few minutes, Mia asked what had happened after she left yesterday. As LeeAnn told her, Mia settled down to listen. When she explained how Brian had used the spear on Rok and then on her, Mia flinched, then nodded for her to continue. LeeAnn concluded by telling her Golly's big secret: that Brian, the strong-man, was really his father.

"I know you said Rok warned them not to come here, but a part of me hopes they are foolish enough not to listen. It would be fitting for Grabon to pass judgment on Golly's father."

"They could not be so stupid as to come here." LeeAnn had no idea what Brian and the others would do now that Sam was dead, but she felt certain they wouldn't come to the market. A single dragon had defeated them; they would not wish to engage several of them on unfamiliar ground. Unless they didn't know they had been defeated. She shook her head, denying her fears. "If they did come here what would happen?" she asked with a grimace.

Mia tilted her head and grinned. *"The moment they stepped on Grabon's territory he would know. Likely he would monitor them and alert our males, both dragon and human. They would not inform us, the females, until they were ready to move and had a strategy in place. What that strategy would be, I have no idea. With Hanna and Trissy so close to birth, likely Heron and Gordon would stay close to their nests to keep things safe."*

LeeAnn nodded. "The males are good fighters? Rok said so, but you know how men like to brag."

Mia nodded and looked back at the path. *"Pit, Thane, Brom, Rok, and Griss spent many years moving from territory to territory challenging other males to mock and real combat. Even when they lost, they improved their skills. From what I have heard, the same is true of Tad, Hess, and Gordon. Heron you probably know usually fights dragons in tandem with Grabon. Our males are formidable adversaries against anyone."*

"Not that I would encourage them to fight, but it's good to know that if they need to, they can." LeeAnn let out a huge yawn. "I can't believe how tiring this new method of healing is." As she was about to explain, Mia held up a hand and struck what LeeAnn recognized as a listening pose.

The air suddenly vibrated with music.

Chapter 5

It was a ballad of how two male dragons had lost their youngsters to the same terrible territory dragon. After their fathers joined the great Grabon, he sent in a team to negotiate their release. Rok, who Grabon sent ahead to negotiate, offered a fortune in dragon and human goods. The evil territory holder planned to steal the youngsters back and keep the ransom. But clever Dragonmen had devised a plan to keep the youngsters safe and bring them home for their sires to raise. It was a song of adventure, travel, and triumph.

Mia laughed when it concluded. She explained to LeeAnn that Tad and Hess had driven a heated wagon to bring the goods to the distant territory and to secretly transport the youngsters when negotiations were over. Since dragons almost never travel on the ground, the dragons who pursued Rock, Pit, and Thane had not thought to check for a ground conveyance carrying the youngsters. Instead, they followed Grabon's dragons who flew all the way back to the territory. Grabon and Heron turned the representatives away, but on their flight back, they eventually became suspicious about the movement on the ground and followed the wagon.

After some time, they tried to force the wagon to stop. Dotty had been in the back of the wagon, concealed with the youngsters. To keep the young dragons distracted, she had started to sing, which had not only succeeded in distracting them, but also stopped the fight. That was when the Dragonmen discovered they had rescued a heartsinger from the mountains. The attacking dragons assumed she was the treasure they were guarding so closely and retreated.

LeeAnn laughed over the story. She loved both parts: the adventure the heartsinger sang about, and the triumph the storyteller described. They were an amazing group, and she felt privileged to be a part of them.

Hess returned with Pit and they both sat down with a sigh, then handed Mia and LeeAnn each a fresh cup of tea. Thane announced Mia's next story and the cove began to fill up.

"Can you tell me what happened with Kev and Tria?" LeeAnn asked Hess.

He grinned and shook his head. "Some youths will argue about the color of the sky. They decided to debate whether a particular flower had any purpose other than to decorate the forest floor. Truthfully, they were having fun, but when Thane tried to stop them, Tria hissed at him. Golly told her to stop and the three of them engaged in a free-for-all flower fight that ended with them in the fountain drenching one another. All we did was keep innocent bystanders out of the way. All three of them are trudging up to Grabon's nest to give an accounting of what happened."

"Grabon is at Gordon's," she reminded him, wondering if she should go see about Golly.

"He'll fly up to the nest." He eyed her for a moment. "Do not even think about interfering. Golly was behaving like any youth. Take it as a good sign that he is adjusting and let Grabon do his job. By the time they get to the top of the hill, all three will likely be good friends."

LeeAnn sighed and nodded. "Nobody was hurt?"

Hess chuckled and shook his head. "The worst that happened was they got a fistful of plants in the face or splashed with water. It was a public brawl for fun, not to cause damage." He looked at the crowd forming in the cove. "They managed to entertain a crowd of people, who moved quickly to get out of their way. No one complained until Thane, Pit, and I sent them away, and then people told us we had no sympathy. How they managed to get a sympathetic crowd I do not know. When Tad and I were youths and misbehaved in public, people called on our parents and relatives to use more and harsher discipline."

LeeAnn smiled and looked away. "I cannot imagine the two of you having a public flower-and-water fight."

He shrugged and leaned closer. "We were not well-behaved youths." Then he leaned back and looked at her. "You are a fine one to talk; you ran away at seventeen."

"That was different," she protested, not sure it was something she was ready to be teased about.

A middle-aged woman who was sitting behind them

laughed. "It is always different when it is your misbehavior as opposed to someone else's."

Hess and LeeAnn turned to look at her. "Are you having a good time?" Hess asked.

"Young man, this is the best market I have ever been to. You're one of the Dragonmen, aren't you?"

Hess nodded and introduced LeeAnn. "She is our healer."

"Ah, well you are all doing a fine job. My match, Bert, and I have been trading goods for a long time. We loaded up our wagon and came out for this and missed opening day." Bert joined her and handed over a cup of tea. LeeAnn and Hess nodded to him. "As I was saying, who do we need to speak to about making some trades?"

"You can talk with Thane and me after the story if that works. We'll take you to our favorite food booth, The Office. Have you been there yet?"

"No, we haven't," Bert searched the crowd. "Who is Thane?"

"One of my business partners and fellow Dragonmen. He's the dark green dragon over there." Hess pointed near the entrance.

Bert turned to look and huffed, "He looks like a tough negotiator. Can we choose someone else?"

"Pit. He's the dark gray dragon over by the storyteller. She's his mate, Mia."

Bert looked from Thane to Pit and shrugged. "I guess it doesn't matter. You all look pretty tough."

"We are, but we're also fair. We like return business." Hess grinned.

Mia held up her hand to motion for silence, then began the story. It was an ancient dragon tale about Finas's search for a mate and the final steps of maturation. She spoke the story in Human, and did an excellent job of explaining dragon concepts and culture, including the growth stages all dragons experience from infant to youngster, youth to sexual maturity, and then finally full maturity. Everyone listened with rapt attention, enjoying her pictures, sound effects, and the voices she used for each character. The dragons she built her story around were lovable, imperfect, and behaved similarly to some humans.

The audience watched her in fascination while she described how power lines, emotions, and thoughts merged between mates. When she was done, the applause were overwhelming and Mia clasped her hands together under her chin and grinned. As people rushed to the front, Pit stepped out to block them, and Hess and Thane moved into position to usher everyone back to the market, through the tall grass path. A few people grumbled, wanting to speak to Mia, but for the most part, people understood not to approach Mia directly and obeyed.

For the first time, LeeAnn understood why so many of the clan had turned out for the storytelling. As entertaining as it was, there was also a security concern of having Mia telling her stories to a mixed crowd of humans and dragons. This time it had been mostly humans, but as time went on, that was likely to change. It hadn't even occurred to her before that three out of the four market organizers were here, keeping an eye on the crowd. Bert and his match slowly stood and smiled at them all.

"Very impressive moves; very impressive since nobody was injured, insulted, or even pushed. I am Bert, this is Mable, and we have come from the second colony to trade goods."

"I am Hess, and this is LeeAnn, Pit, Mia and Thane," Hess pointed to each of them as he made introductions. "And we are always happy to do business. Walk with me down to that booth I told you about, The Office. They have excellent food and private tables. Will you mind if LeeAnn joins us?" Hess looked over at her.

"Why would they call it that?" Mable asked, frowning.

"It is a joke. Have you ever read any of the literature from OldEarth? There is a series by that name, where all the characters are working in an office. The owner named his food booth after the books."

LeeAnn shook her head, grinning. "I thought I would go see Jamie and Janie, if you don't mind," LeeAnn suggested. She didn't want to ruin his plans, but a meeting was not going to be very interesting for her.

"I will go with her," Thane told him. *"Pit and Mia can join you."*

"She still has groceries for later to buy too," Hess reminded him.

***

Thane and LeeAnn left together, and Mable turned to grin at Hess, giggling. "Either you are courting her and keeping away all other interested parties, or she's in some kind of danger."

Hess smiled and led them down the path. "I'll leave you to determine which one."

"I love a good romance," Mable warned him.

So did he, but he wasn't exactly romancing the healer. He was helping her acclimate and get settled in her new home. After the way he had treated her yesterday, he was grateful he wasn't attempting to seduce her today. If that turned into a possibility, it was going to be quite a challenge. She was fascinating, talented, and skilled, not to mention protective of and committed to Golly, which he understood, but she was also young and hurt. Whoever decided to pursue her was going to have to get her through all the crap Sam had done to her. A relationship with her was going to take work and he was still debating with himself whether he was interested. Being a single male gave him options. Besides, there were many new women coming into the territory because of the market. There was no need to rush and focus on the first interesting female he saw.

They all sat down in The Office and talked business for an hour. Then while Pit went to see the couple's goods, Hess figured he better make a few rounds, check in with the vendors, and make sure no problems were brewing. He had spent most of his time today with LeeAnn. Not that he had minded; in fact, it had been a fine way to spend the day.

He was at the far end of the market grounds, counting empty booths, checking in with vendors, and keeping an eye on the crowd when Thane contacted him. Grabon was hoping Thane could spend some more time with Golly, so he was leaving LeeAnn to wander the section of the market devoted to fruits and vegetables on her own. She didn't seem nervous about it, Thane reported.

Hess returned to the main aisle and waved at the sisters, hoping to make it past their booth without stopping. They of course waved him over, probably to share some sad tale involving another settler who needed a place in the market. Suppressing a sigh, he went.

"We invited LeeAnn to come and stay with us," Jamie informed him. "She claims she needs to cook up in the nest after she sees Dotty. After that, if she feels up to it, she can come by the house and we'll have a room all set up for her."

"She's not really obligated to cook," he began.

"No, but she's been planning the meal most of the day," Jamie said. "Besides, she needs to make sure Golly is settled in and comfortable, or she won't get any sleep."

"I suppose someone can make sure she gets out to

your place if that's what she wants. I still say it would be a lot more convenient if you two would move closer to the rest of us," he teased.

"It might be more convenient for all of you, but we like our house just fine. No, our concern is whether Grabon, Gordon, or even Heron are likely to object to her being so far away when their mates are so close to delivery. I think that's why she wouldn't give us a firm yes. You might want to discuss it with her when you have a chance."

"I'll be sure to do that when I see her. You wouldn't be matchmaking, would you?"

Jamie looked at him oddly. "Not unless you're her mate. LeeAnn doesn't need a man who would think of her as disposable or interchangeable with another woman."

He straightened his spine, surprised he actually felt offended. "I wouldn't treat her that way."

"Of course you would," Jamie argued. "You enjoy your share of females, just like every other male here who isn't mated. You can all be generous and kind to a point, but the truth is you are all looking for your mates. Until you find her, all women are practice, disposable and interchangeable. It makes sense, but don't do that to her. LeeAnn needs to find her mate, someone who can actually see who she is."

He nodded but was still not happy with her assessment. Grumbling under his breath, he continued his rounds and ran into Tad.

"If I were to get involved with LeeAnn, would you be concerned that I wouldn't treat her right?"

Tad opened his mouth and closed it before he took a step back and stared at Hess. "I'd kick you in the ass so hard you couldn't walk, unless you were her mate. She doesn't need a romp or a bit of a cuddle, Hess. She needs a partner who will stand for her, love her, and accept her, scars and all."

"The sisters basically warned me off and now you're doing the same thing?"

"Why would you even consider her? She's not freeze in your tracks attractive, she has enough scars for ten people inside and out. Don't get me wrong, she's nice and Dotty enjoys her company, and nobody can deny she's a talented and skilled healer and a great addition for the Dragonmen. But for you in a relationship? It doesn't make any sense to me." Tad patted his brother's shoulder. "Not unless she's your mate."

"If she were my mate, I would know by now."

Tad didn't say anything and Hess stared at him, hard. "What aren't you telling me?"

"Have you considered that she could be your mate?"

"What do you mean have I considered it? How much considering is involved?"

"There's a lot if she has power of her own, and our healer has power. All I'm saying is it's possible. Rok said Grabon told Golly that she has a mate and that her mate could claim her, if he accepts her first. Look around you. How many human male bachelors do you see? Now ask yourself how many of them are Dragonmen?"

Hess narrowed his eyes. "I would know. She's been here two days."

"Yesterday you were preoccupied and uncharacteristically mean to her. Today you've treated her well, but the same as you treat Jamie and Janie: with detachment. If she were your mate, you still wouldn't know because you've been on guard and closed off. Grandad used to say if you never look for the spark you'll miss it. All I'm saying is look for the spark, because you'll kick yourself later if you don't."

"Fine, I'll check it out. Is there anything else I need to know? Anything about the market?"

They talked about business for a minute and Hess told him about Bert and Mable. Tad went off to speak with Pit while Hess continued on his rounds. He soon found himself walking through the food market, but he didn't see LeeAnn anywhere. That was probably good because after speaking with Jamie and Tad, he was a little on edge about her. They still had a number of stalls available and he was going to have to consider what else they could use this space for if more vendors didn't show up soon. He'd started to move on when he thought he saw LeeAnn in an empty stall off the main aisle, and he moved closer.

"Look, dragon girl, all I want to know is the identity

of that heartsinger. I got someone who will pay gold coins to know who she is." The creep stood so close to LeeAnn he was breathing on her. Hess frowned and started forward.

"I'm not telling you anything. Who would pay money? What exactly do they want? You need to go away before someone sees you and calls for help."

"What, the little dragon girl can't mindspeak on her own? Maybe I can help myself to some other things before I make you talk."

Hess grabbed him by the back of the neck and pushed his head into the tree he was standing behind. Then he spun around and pointed at her. "You will stay out of this. I know that's hard, but close your eyes or something."

She put her hands over her eyes and turned away. Hess pounded on the man, then he had his own questions to ask about who was offering coins to know the singer's identity. As he expected, the stranger didn't know much and Hess allowed him to escape even before Tad arrived. LeeAnn tried to move, but Hess had used a box shield to keep her safe and contained.

"Someone is after our heartsinger. He has offered a reward for any information, and whoever it is will be at the tavern in the village at sunset. I think we need to be there and have a chat. In the meantime, I have something else to take care of." He reached inside the shield and drew LeeAnn out and the shield collapsed behind her. "I am sorry I had to do that in front of you. Why on this good planet didn't you call for help or scream?"

"I was trying to get information so I could tell you."

"No. That is not how this works." He took her hand, grabbed up her basket, and started walking.

"Where are we going?" When she tried to tug her hand away, he tightened his grip.

"Right now? We are going to my brother's." He walked for another minute before he looked over at her. At the sight of her chalky pallor, he felt like an idiot. He headed for the nearest bench, where she sat down immediately as he placed the basket next to her.

"I'm behaving like an idiot. That man could have hurt you," he said, his voice rough and tense.

"I heal pretty quick," she reminded him.

"That isn't the point. You shouldn't be in any danger, not here, not ever. How did he find you?"

"I was going through the vegetables. I'd already bought a bunch, but they had some I had never seen before, and this man came up and asked if he could speak with me. I followed him to that empty booth and he asked if I knew who the heartsinger was. Naturally, I told him that was private information and she preferred to be anonymous, but wasn't she talented?"

"You followed him?"

"He might have needed a healer for something."

"No, if he needed a healer, he should have talked to one of us. Nobody but us should be approaching you directly about healing. You do not go off with strangers, not ever." He paced back and forth in front of her. "Why are you so pale? Did he hurt you? Were you scared?"

"I'm fine. Why did you let him go? What's going to happen?"

"He's not the person we want. We want the man who offered the reward. That man will either cause another problem some other time or he'll move on. Let's get moving. You can have tea with Dotty until Tad gets home."

"I didn't finish my shopping."

"Yes, you did, and it's the last time you will be alone in the market if I have anything to say about it. Borrow what you need from one of our women or do without."

She stood up to follow, but he took her hand again. "I am not going to run away," she protested.

"I didn't think you would, but I'm also not taking a chance of getting separated in the crowd. Right now I'll feel more secure holding your hand." They walked together for a few minutes.

"I really was just trying to help," she confessed.

He nodded once. "That's why I stopped yelling. We simply have to set some decent rules for you. Number one, nobody should be approaching you for healing when you are on your own, and your first reaction if someone is steering you away from the crowd should be to call for help."

"He might have run away."

"Then he runs away, but you stay safe. That's a win for us." He glanced at her as he continued walking. "We will deal with the threat; we're built for it. Your job is to heal, not to interrogate someone."

"You beat him up," she said, her tone awed.

"He was threatening you, did you think I wouldn't?"

Her steps slowed and he glanced at her again.

"I thought you didn't like me," she finally spit out.

"I like you fine," he answered, walking ahead as the crowd parted around them. "Yesterday I was consumed with opening day, worried about the market, and then I got called up to the nest and find Grabon had been stabbed. You didn't make the best first impression. By the time I found out more about you, you had run away. Last night Grabon needed someone to go out with the wagon, and I volunteered and found you in a state of collapse." He shook his head and tightened his hold on her hand. "Rok told me you thought I didn't want you here, but that's not true."

"I know the Dragonmen need a healer."

"No, LeeAnn, we need you, not just any healer. Trust

us, we know when someone fits in with the rest of us, and you fit just fine and so does Golly. You can relax; nobody is going to ask you to leave."

The crowd thinned and the stalls were farther apart in this section. LeeAnn was beside him, her hand still in his.

"Grabon is probably not going to be happy that our heartsinger is in danger."

Hess snorted. "Grabon has been yelling in my head since I let the creep go. At the moment, he'd like to confine you to his nest for the next cycle. One of the reasons we're going to my brother's is to give our territory dragon a chance to calm down. The idea that someone bothered you hit a nerve."

"Me? Isn't he worried about…?" She paused and looked around. "Isn't he worried about our heartsinger?"

"She has a mate whose job it is to protect her, and if Tad needs help, he knows how to ask. You are the one who is vulnerable, and none of us has forgotten what you have lived through."

"It seems to me every woman here has lived through something."

"That is true, but they either have a mate or don't want one. You haven't found yours yet."

It was her turn to make a rude noise. "He wouldn't want me anyway."

"Yes, he would. He would be thrilled if he found you.

Hold that thought because we will be discussing it again. Grabon wants you to know he will make dinner for everyone in the nest and you should eat with Dotty and Tad. He also said I should bring you up to the nest when you are done. You should not be wandering around alone."

Grabon was right, LeeAnn was better off staying with Dotty until he returned from the tavern. It was obvious she knew he was speaking to someone. "Tad and I are going to the tavern after the healing. Are you still ready to do the healing?"

"Yes, Dotty has probably been thinking about it all day. I wouldn't disappoint her."

"I'm not big on disappointing her either, but you better not collapse. Grabon is already in a bit of a snit over your safety. Now is not the time to push him."

"I'm sure I'll be fine. I haven't done that much today."

He stared at her in shock. "My cousin is a healer. Most healers never see more than three patients a day, even if one or two of them don't require the use of healing energy. How many have you seen today?"

"Not that many, and I can definitely do more than three."

"Good, because by my measure you've already seen four patients: Trissy, Hanna, the visitor with the boil, and Rok's toe. Dotty will make five, and if you don't have any energy left at the end of the day, what are you going to do if we have an emergency?"

"There's plenty energy left under my skin and none of the healings have been especially draining or complex. Changing the energy pulse wears me out, but I recover quickly."

They left the market grounds and walked the path to Tad and Dotty's house. "Whatever you do, I'm telling you, do not end up in the same condition you were in last night."

They walked through a shield and LeeAnn actually turned around as if she could see it.

"It keeps visitors from approaching the house. Dotty needs her privacy. Now I'm going to ask one more time: are you sure you are up to this? Because nobody will be surprised or upset if you wait a day or two."

"I can do this," she assured him.

"All right." He stopped walking and turned to look at her. "We're all a little on edge. I don't want you to think anyone is upset with you if they seem less than friendly."

"I won't. Protecting Dotty is important to everyone."

He nodded and they walked up to the porch, where he knocked on the door. Dotty opened it, wiping her hands on a cloth. She handed the cloth to Hess and she hugged LeeAnn.

"I am so sorry that man bothered you." Dotty motioned them inside, taking back the towel.

"It wasn't that much of a bother. Hess arrived and beat him up, then let him run off. We brought these." She held up the basket of vegetables she had collected in the market. "I was going to cook up in the nest, but Grabon said I should eat here. If it's an inconvenience…."

"Don't be silly. I invited you earlier. Here, let me show you what I'm cooking and you'll understand. It's a meat-and-cheese casserole. The vegetables will go perfectly with it." She glanced at Hess. "Are you staying or going?"

"I'm going to relieve your mate so he can come home. I'll be here for dinner after closing, and then Tad and I are going to the tavern. Rok is on his way, and he's going to keep you both company until everything is done. If you have any trouble, call out."

Dotty rolled her eyes. "Your brother already gave me the lecture."

Hess nodded and smiled. "Good for him. I'd hate to think he had neglected his duty." Hess opened the door, and Rok ducked his head and stepped inside. "Keep them both safe," Hess called out as he went through the door.

***

Rok settled himself in the kitchen with a clear view out the window and watched the women interact. He spoke rarely, keeping his attention on everything around them. He was able to sense all movement large and small a good distance from the dwelling. It was merely a matter of identifying the energy he sensed and choosing to be aware of everything around him. When Dotty said she much preferred Rok the friend to Rok the guard, he grinned, but said nothing.

"Quit tormenting him," LeeAnn told her with a shake of her head.

"They figured out a way for the males to communicate and leave the women out of the loop. I find it highly annoying," Dotty informed her as they finished preparing the vegetables she had brought.

Tad came in not too long after, sat beside his mate at the table and held her hand. LeeAnn took a deep breath and dried her hands. "I know you're both anxious for me to do this, but let me explain what I'm going to do."

Tad nodded, looking grim.

"I spoke with Griss. He explained that matching my energy pulse to Dotty's will make this less painful than I first thought, unless I need to do some major repairs. We're going to try to do this quickly. Then once I know the extent of the damage, I'll talk to you about it before I do anything else."

Tad and Dotty agreed and they moved to the fireplace in the living room.

Closing her eyes, LeeAnn managed to match her energy pulse to Dotty's. At first glance, she could tell there was extensive scaring and some remaining damage, but it wasn't nearly as bad as she had feared.

She moved cautiously from organ to organ, making a mental list of what she was going to have to repair.

When she stopped long enough to share the details, Dotty seemed to be holding up well.

"Unless you are too tired to continue, I'm ready to put this behind us," Dotty told her, gripping Tad's hand so tight his fingers looked a little blue.

Biting her lip, LeeAnn used small pulses of energy to fix one lesion at a time. Progress was slow, the work was precise, but it was much less painful for the couple than it would have been if she had hit it with a stronger pulse over a greater area. Dotty gasped both times LeeAnn had to use a stronger pulse, but the couple urged her to continue the healing. By the time LeeAnn sat back on her heels, her head was swimming with fatigue.

"I think that was the last of the damage. How are you feeling?" She swayed as she looked at Dotty, wrapped in her mate's arms. Rok clasped her shoulders and steadied her.

"She is better than you are," Tad told her with a frown. "Why is she so wobbly?" he demanded of Rok.

"In order to heal with less pain for the patient, she disrupted her own energy flow," Rok explained. *"It takes her some time to reestablish her own rhythm."*

"Isn't that dangerous?" Tad growled, patting his mate's back to comfort her.

"It just takes a minute," LeeAnn said, blinking to

bring her vision into focus.

Tad was quiet for a moment. "Grabon says it is fine to do that occasionally, but not multiple times a day."

She gave a short laugh. "I'll remember that."

Tad looked at her suspiciously. "I think you're worse than Mazy and I didn't think that was possible. She needed a keeper to prevent her from doing too much, especially when she was younger. How many times today, LeeAnn?"

"What?" Her head seemed to be spinning and she didn't understand what he was saying.

"Never mind, it was clearly too many." Tad kissed Dotty's head and moved to steady LeeAnn, but Rok picked her up and laid her on the couch. She swatted at him, which he found amusing if his chuckle was anything to judge by.

"Get her some sweet tea. Griss says she needs to be still and focus on her own rhythm. It won't take her long to recover."

"I can make the tea." Dotty stood and moved to the kitchen, and Tad knelt by where LeeAnn rested on the couch.

"A healer is not supposed to put herself at risk. One day soon you're going to have a mate and he's going to put a stop to this type of thing." He frowned as she tried to bring her own rhythm back to normal. "I guess until then it's up to the rest of us."

"I'm doing fine," she argued, blinking slowly. Her

head felt a little foggy, but it was no longer spinning.

"Do you want to see how well you do with so much shielding around you that you can't sense your own feet? I'm warning you right now, no more healing until tomorrow and no more disrupting your energy flow for a couple of days."

She pushed herself up on the couch. "I can't promise that, Tad. What if Hanna or Trissy need help?"

"All right, but it better be something serious." He stood and glared at her. "How much damage is left?"

"You mean with Dotty? I healed all the lesions. There's nothing I can do about the scars, but everything seems to be working. Whatever brews you had from Griss must have worked because I saw no fresh damage."

He let out a rough sigh. "Then we owe you a debt. I didn't think you could do it in one session."

"I knew both of you were anxious about it, and even doing it slowly, I wanted to get as much done as I could."

"We've been coping for months. Taking a few days to do this so you didn't strain yourself wouldn't have hurt us, but I am grateful."

She nodded and swung her legs over the side of the sofa. Dotty brought her a cup of tea and their eyes met. The look Dotty gave her made her realize all over again how worried the other woman had been.

LeeAnn drank some tea and felt the warmth seep through her. "As I said, all the organs are working. The scaring is extensive, but as long as everything continues to work you shouldn't worry about it. If something goes wrong, if you start to have symptoms, I can make repairs when they're needed."

"So give us the bad news," Tad told her. "What kinds of restrictions and precautions?"

"Nothing. You should both live and enjoy your life together. Conceiving may take longer, but if you do, I think you can tolerate the strain of pregnancy and birth."

"Really?" Dotty asked, looking at her mate with longing.

Tad rocked back on his heels. "The scarring…?"

"It leaves her vulnerable to certain issues. If there are symptoms, we'll make repairs."

"What kinds of issues?" Tad asked, worry lines on his face but a hopeful light in his eyes.

"Kidney infections, heart palpitations; internal scarring can cause those sorts of things. Dotty is perfectly healthy right now. You should both enjoy that."

"You don't know how much of a relief that is." He eased himself into a chair and clasped his mate's hand. Then, he pulled her into his lap and their combined energy swirled around them, locking them together. Rok sighed and let out a pleased coo.

LeeAnn smiled in understanding and sipped her tea. "I am pleased I could help."

"As soon as your brother gets here we can have dinner," Dotty told Tad, her ear over his heart. "I gather you and Hess are going to the village tavern?"

Tad hugged her close. "I want to have a word with the person who is offering money to learn the identity of our heartsinger. Chances are he's an overzealous fan, but just in case, we'll warn him off."

"Who else is going?" Dotty asked, leaning against his chest and picking up her head so they were nose-to-nose.

"Grabon, Heron, and Brom. Rok is staying here with the two of you. None of us frequent the village, much less the tavern, so our presence alone should make a statement."

Dotty sighed and looked at LeeAnn. "I am so sorry that man bothered you."

"He wasn't nearly as scary as Hess. It surprised me when he came out of nowhere and started beating on the man."

"Next time you're going to call for help," Tad told her. "That is, if you ever have an opportunity to be alone. Grabon was pretty vocal on that point."

"Hess didn't tell you he was there?" Dotty asked.

"No, I don't think he was looking for me."

Tad laughed. "He was definitely looking for you, and you can be glad he was too."

"She can only mindspeak at close range. Even if she had called out, we might not have heard her," Rok pointed out.

"Then she can scream and someone who hears her will reach us. There was a crowd nearby and she's easily identifiable as one of us."

"I'm pretty sure your brother already yelled at her," Dotty reminded him.

"Yes, I'm sure he did, but she needs to remember she's not alone anymore."

LeeAnn shrugged and rolled her eyes before she looked at Dotty. "Is every male going to go through this with me?"

"Rok seems pretty understanding," Dotty pointed out, nodding at the dark brown dragon.

"Because she fixed his toe," Tad grumbled. "Otherwise he'd be yelling at her too."

Rok rumbled something at Tad that LeeAnn didn't understand, but it made Tad grin. "I don't blame you and I'm grateful to her too, but she's not going to put herself at risk on a daily basis. Grabon's right, it all comes back to asking for help. She simply doesn't know how."

"Of course I know how," she protested.

"No, you don't. I don't know what kind of parents

raised you, but they obviously left a few things out."

"It has nothing to do with my parents." She sat up straighter, every muscle in her body going tense.

"I think it does. They must not have been supportive or you wouldn't have run away. You knew you couldn't ask them for help coping with an ability and a compulsion to heal that was difficult to control, so you did the best you could on your own."

"They were very focused on their patients and they taught me everything they could. It wasn't their fault my energy was too strong."

"Did they tell you that?" Tad demanded softly, his eyes narrowed.

"No, but they did their best to explain it to everyone who complained that I hurt them."

"They should have contacted another healer with more power and asked them how they managed their ability and avoided causing their patients pain," Tad told her.

LeeAnn just stared at him in shock. She had never realized they could have done that. If they had, she would have learned about matching pulses long ago, and she might never have run away.

"If she had not run away and been caught in Sam's trap, what would have happened to Golly? Everything happens the way it should, Tad. It is impossible to second-guess events that have already happened."

"You are right. Not only for Golly, but for Dotty and myself, your toe, and even the people here in the future who will benefit from her presence. I wouldn't change her past because it brought her here to us. It's the future we need to concern ourselves with."

Rok nodded his approval and grinned. *"Now you are thinking like a dragon."*

"He does that occasionally," Hess offered from the doorway. "Another successful day concluded. Tomorrow the market is closed, a good thing since much of the merchandise needs to be restocked." He smiled at LeeAnn. "Congratulations on healing my brother's mate. Your skill and talent astound me."

LeeAnn grinned and nodded. "Thank you."

"I guess we should eat," Dotty muttered, getting up, and LeeAnn joined her in the kitchen. As they worked, LeeAnn was surprised to learn about some of the demands of the mating bond. Dotty was kind enough to explain the need she and Tad experienced for physical closeness and contact, shared energy and combined emotions.

Soon they had the food set out, and conversation during dinner was light. The primary topics were centered around how people were reacting to shopping alongside another species. Rok reminded them that dragons traditionally did not embrace the idea of having goods collected all in one place. Instead, dragons flew from territory to territory to collect what goods they might need, with each territory specializing in one thing.

The food was very good and she told Dotty that. Flushed with pleasure, the heartsinger accepted the compliment.

After dinner, Tad and Hess left for the tavern, and Rok settled at the table.

"How come you are not on guard anymore?" LeeAnn asked curiously.

"The market grounds have cleared and the only people near are the ones who belong here. If a stranger comes close, I will know."

"You can track people like that?"

Rok nodded and looked out the window. *"We are hunters."*

"What he means is every male here is a hunter and fighter. Not only do they have the skills, they enjoy it," Dotty informed her, shaking her head. "According to Mia, fighters are not in the majority anywhere but here. Grabon is collecting a clan of fighters, and it is a great curiosity to the rest of the dragons."

LeeAnn wrinkled her nose. "We all enjoy doing what we are good at. I just hope nobody gets hurt."

Rok snorted softly. *"They go to talk and intimidate, not fight. Grabon prefers reason these days, as does Heron."*

"You don't have to sound disappointed," Dotty muttered. "You got to fight yesterday and ended up injured."

"I did not anticipate that Brian would use a spear."

"Neither did I, but he did." LeeAnn still had trouble understanding why he had done that.

"I think he did not realize I was there to help rescue Golly. By the time he understood that we only wanted to leave, he had already injured us both."

"It doesn't matter as long as he and the others don't come here." Throughout the day, LeeAnn had thought about Brian and the others and hoped they would listen to Rok's warning.

"I doubt they will come." Dotty scowled. "What possible reason would they have for coming here now?"

The women nagged Rok for updates as time passed, but the stubborn dragon refused to answer beyond assuring them that none of their people were injured. As soon as Tad and Hess returned, Dotty demanded to know "What on this good planet had happened."

Tad chuckled as he put his arm around her. "Didn't Rok tell you everything was fine?"

"That was all he would say. I need details, specific details," Dotty argued.

"Fine, fix us some tea and Hess and I will do our best to recount events. You might even find it amusing."

"I doubt I will," Dotty muttered as she put on the kettle and fixed the leaves while everyone settled at the table.

Hess grinned at LeeAnn. "The best part was when Grabon and Brom couldn't fit through the tavern door." Her eyes grew wide and she covered her mouth to hide her smile. "They were both disappointed and a little upset over being left outside, even though we had no trouble finding the man offering the reward. He was sitting at the bar, sipping on some smuggled ale, when a group of locals gave him up right away. They are enjoying having a heartsinger here in the territory and don't want to lose her, especially not to some stranger. Naturally the people of the village enjoy the debate over whether she's human or dragon, young or old; but they don't really care. The man offering the reward swears he didn't intend her any harm and that he only wanted to meet her."

"Heron called him a liar and explained that he had hoped she was human so he could seduce her. But even if she was a dragon he planned on convincing her to leave with him. That angered the locals almost as much as it did the rest of us." Tad chuckled and caught Dotty's hand. "We tossed him out of the territory and sent him on his way. That's what took so long; we packed his wagon for him."

"Why didn't Rok tell us?" LeeAnn protested.

"There were a few tense moments, mostly when the locals in the bar wanted to hang him. Grabon was stuck outside and decided he needed to intercede. To get in, he ripped off the doorframe and tore out part of the wall. Brom wasn't going to be left out, so he joined in too. Heron and Grabon got into a shouting match and that settled down the rest of them.

Nothing like seeing two powerhouses squared off in a limited space." Hess grinned.

Dotty looked horrified. "What were they arguing about?"

"Most of it was in Dragon, but I believe it had something to do with the respect one should give doorways, walls, and structures. When they ran out of comments to sling at one another, they debated the color of cloth that should be used on a table. It was ridiculous, but they looked very impressive while they effectively distracted the crowd. Almost everyone hid under the tables or behind the bar and all talk of going against Grabon's judgment to banish the visitor disappeared. They all went into appease-the-territory-dragon mode." Tad chuckled and grinned at Rok.

"They staged a scene to stop a hanging?" LeeAnn asked, frowning in disbelief.

Hess nodded and tried to control his laughter. "I think Kev and Tria inspired them with their flower-and-water fight. They threw a few blasts, shattered some glass, spilled drinks, and made a lot of noise, but nobody was hurt. Of course, people think they know what kind of destruction they are both capable of, so they were impressed. When it was over, we loaded the man's wagon and sent him out of the territory under Heron and Grabon's watchful eyes."

"That's when the real fun started, because everyone was pretty stirred up and worried. We explained that they needed to let our heartsinger be a mystery. It was for her protection as well as their own. After we explained what happened to LeeAnn while she was buying vegetables, they all understood what we meant. The next stranger who asks questions about our heartsinger is going to be told by everyone to shut up and enjoy the song."

"With all of that happening, nobody was injured?" LeeAnn couldn't get over that. In her experience, injuries were inevitable when there was a fight, even a fake one.

"Not so much as a scratch, which takes a great deal of skill. Let's hope the villagers don't realize that." Hess held out a hand to LeeAnn. "Since that concludes today's exciting adventure, I'm taking this tired healer back across the river. Then I'm falling into bed. Tomorrow we can rest, recuperate, and get ready for the next two-day run."

LeeAnn took his hand and they left Tad and Dotty's home, then walked across the stream and into Gordon's yard. She was surprised when the big Farmer stepped outside and motioned them over.

"I am glad I caught you, LeeAnn. If you are looking for a comfortable place to stay, we have a spare room up in the house that is free until we set up the nursery. We also have the other side of Hess's. Now that Tad has moved across the river, you might want to consider staying there. Hess was planning on building his own house in the fall, so you can probably have all of it for yourself soon enough."

"I appreciate it, but I haven't made any decisions," she answered, shifting awkwardly.

"Of course, take your time." Gordon nodded to Hess. "You're not taking her to Jamie and Janie's?"

"No," he answered, not offering an explanation.

"Good night, then," Gordon told them and went back inside.

"That was kind of rude," LeeAnn mentioned, looking at the Farmer's back door, where he just passed through.

"Gordon can be that way."

"Not him, you. Why didn't you tell him you were taking me up to the nest?"

"Because I'm not. We have some things to talk about and I'm taking you to the barn."

"What barn?" she asked, looking around at all the different outbuildings.

Hess grinned and pointed. "My house, at least until the other is built. Come with me. We started a conversation earlier and we need to finish it."

Chapter 6

"What conversation are you talking about?" LeeAnn asked with a frown.

"The one where I said you would meet your mate soon and you said he wouldn't want you." He opened the door and let her precede him into the barn.

"This really is a house."

"Yes. So is the other side, and you can explore to your heart's content later. Do you want some tea?"

"No, I feel like my back teeth are floating as it is. I could use your outhouse, though."

He showed her the indoor facilities and she thanked him, marveling over such luxury.

When she rejoined him, he motioned her over to the couches. "Let me tell you something about this mating-bond business from the male perspective. It is the gold bead in a bucket of sand, what every man is looking for. If she happens to be tall, short, fat, thin, scarred, or has an illness or a missing limb, it doesn't matter. She's the woman you are destined to share your life with, to love, live and die with. I always said if I found my mate, I would claim her first and answer questions later. The problem of course is finding her."

"It's probably like that OldEarth story where the

witch turned the prince into a fish, so the princess kissed all those fish hoping to find the man of her dreams. What she found instead was a whole lot of slimy fish."

Hess grinned and nodded. "It does feel like that sometimes. The problem is when I meet a woman, I'm usually half hoping she is my mate. Then I'm disappointed when she isn't."

"So you've had a lot of disappointment?"

"Lately I've been so distracted by the market that I haven't thought about it. Then around five times today someone said your name and the word *mate* in the same sentence and it got me thinking, what if you were my mate? Yesterday I wouldn't have known because I was so distracted. Today you spent all day disrupting your energy flow doing all that healing, so it was impossible to tell. There really is only one test. Do you know what that is?"

"I have no idea," she answered, and he could tell she was humoring him. She didn't even consider them being mates a possibility.

"You bring your power line close to the surface and I do the same and we see if they join. If nothing happens, we're not mates, not destined to be together, and neither of us is hurt. Then I can let the matter drop and get on with the business of looking."

"Sure, and if we are, we can figure out what we want to do about it, right?"

He should have let that go, let her deceive herself

until they knew and it was done, but he couldn't; it was far too serious. "If you happen to be my mate," he managed around the lump in his throat, "there is no figuring anything out." He stared at her intensely. "You would be my mate!"

She stared back, then shook her head, half scowling and half amused. "You're giving me fright bumps. I'll do your little experiment to relieve your mind. How does that sound? Then I really need to get up to the nest and get some sleep."

"Good, that sounds good." He cleared his throat and grabbed the back of the couch, because he had a feeling he was going to need something solid to hang on to. "All you have to do is bring your power line to the surface."

Her brow wrinkled as she struggled to locate and control her power line. "It won't stay still after all the energy fluctuations. Do I bring it to the surface?

"Yes, just like that." His own flexed and responded with an uncomfortable surge and he knew what was going to happen. As soon as he brought his close to the surface, everything was out of their control. She gasped at the same time as it felt like something exploded inside his chest. Their power lines flew around one another as if fighting, entwining so tight no one could tell them apart.

He managed to stay upright only because of his braced position. But LeeAnn pitched forward and collapsed with her head landing hard on his knee. She was probably going to have a bruise from the impact, but that was still better than if she had fallen on the floor. He made himself relax and accept what was happening. One of them needed to be conscious and aware so one day he could describe it to their children.

While his eyes were shut, he felt her move and push up slightly. He turned to watch her, never letting go of his grip on the couch. "You have to relax into it, let your mind float and adjust. If you fight, it will knock you back out."

"So much for your experiment. What did it do? Throw my power line off?" She was squinting as though the room was too bright.

"That's not what happened. Look for yourself and tell me what you see."

"I have a blinding headache," she complained, brushing at a stray hair.

"You hit your head on my knee when you went down." He could see the bruise was already healing. "There's still a bit of a lump. Whatever you do, don't fight it, LeeAnn; you'll hurt yourself."

"What are you talking about?" she moaned and then grew very still, her eyes closed as she focused her mind internally. "Holy hell, what is that?"

He choked back a laugh at her colorful OldEarth curse. "It's us, forming a mating bond."

"No, not a chance. That can't happen to me."

"It already has. Just stay still and let it happen."

She tugged and pushed against the powerlines with her energy and they moved together as one, twisted and twined countless times. "Why would you let this happen?"

"Are you kidding me? What makes you think I would have stopped it if I could?"

"No sane man would want me for a mate. I told you that." She pulled at their joined power lines with more strength and he felt it all through his body.

"If you keep doing that, you're going to knock us both unconscious. Do you want to sleep through this or participate and watch?"

"We can't do this." Her tone was genuinely distressed and he managed to grasp her shoulders, careful not to bruise her.

"No, stop that and talk to me. Tugging and pulling is not going to fix anything." He shook her once and her eyes focused on his. "Talk. To. Me."

"You aren't going to want me." She took a deep breath and shuddered under his hands, and he bought her closer before he scooped her up and put her in his lap, where she was surrounded by his scent and strength.

"Why wouldn't I want you?" he asked curiously.

"Sam did things to me." She winced even as the words came out.

His arm tightened around her. "It doesn't matter.

No, that's not right. It matters like crazy, but it wasn't your fault. Did he rape you?" She nodded and looked away, but he wouldn't let her hide, so he turned her face back to him. "That has nothing to do with this. It's a bad experience and I can guess that it's going to make some things difficult, but it wasn't your fault."

"I've never on purpose...," she tried to explain.

"I can teach you anything you want to know. That's not a problem. What else?"

"I won't like it." She tried to shift away, but he held her hips still so she was trapped in his lap.

"Making love with your mate isn't the same thing as rape, not by any measure. They have nothing in common, and it's my job to make sure you like it when the time comes. We don't have to rush into it, LeeAnn. We just have to get there."

"We don't have to rush?" She looked at him with blind hope in her eyes.

"No, we can take our time. Sex is not the only intimacy mates share. It's not even the most important one." He took a deep breath and she did the same.

"It's not?" She was squinting again and he kissed her forehead.

"No, it's not. We're going to share a million things during our lifetime. You need to calm down, lean against me, and let your mind and your muscles relax. You're giving yourself a headache and we don't need that. Breathe with me and let everything slow down."

"My heart is racing."

"Of course it is; you're scared. My heart is racing too. Nobody who goes through this does it calmly, and if they say they did, they lied or they slept through this part. The trick is to relax into it; don't try to control it or direct it. Poking at our powerlines is not going to help."

"I just wanted to see what would happen."

"Did you figure it out?" He couldn't hide his amusement.

"Sure, they flinch back, but I can't tell what is happening. It would be easier if I understood more."

"You can feel it, can't you?" Hess asked, noting all the odd sensations running through his own body.

"I'm not dead. It feels like everything inside is twisting and turning and changing to something else." She was silent for a moment, then grinned. "Our energy is syncing. That's why it feels like that. It has to create a unified energy base.

"That's good, that's how mates are identified as being mates by strangers. They have the same energy base."

"What if by sharing our energy we lose talents?"

"It's never happened; don't get yourself upset over something that isn't even a possibility. According to the dragons, talents rarely get stronger during a mating either. Usually they stay the same. I've never heard of them diminishing."

"If it were to happen to anyone it would happen to me," she complained.

"You have enough to lose a couple of points on the scale and still be the strongest healer anyone has ever met. I think we can set that worry aside and simply see what happens. How is your headache now?"

"Better. Actually I think it's gone. Who would have thought this would happen to me? What do we do now?"

"We can fix some tea if you think that will help, but then I guess we should get some sleep."

"I can skip the tea and just head up to the nest. I am awfully tired."

"You're going to sleep here, LeeAnn. No matter how you're feeling right this minute, we're mates. You can sleep with me in my bed, or you can sleep in the spare room."

"You said we can wait," she accused.

"I said we can wait to make love. I never said I was going to allow my mate to sleep under a different roof or in a different house." He took a deep breath and forced himself to be reasonable. "You can be safe with me in my bed and under my roof. This is far too important to mess up by trying to push you into making love if you are not ready for that."

"You're telling me I could sleep in your bed and you won't touch me?"

"No, I said we won't make love until you are ready. I didn't say I wouldn't touch you. I'm touching you now and I'll be touching you all the time. Mates crave contact, LeeAnn. They need it."

She shifted on his lap. "I don't mind that kind of contact. It's that other...." She gave a small shiver.

"He hurt you and I am sorrier than I can say about that, but nothing like that is ever going to happen between us."

"I do believe you, but you're right; I'm not ready."

He cupped her cheek and looked in her eyes. "Can you trust me enough to sleep in the same bed, sleep in my arms?"

"I don't know. What if I say yes, but then I can't sleep?"

"Then I'll let you sleep in the guest room. I don't want to deprive you of sleep. I just want to be close: as close as you can let me."

"What about Grabon? Won't he worry?"

"He already knows what happened and he'll explain it to Golly. You're tired. We both are. I have some clothes you can be comfortable in and we'll sleep, all right?"

She chewed on her lip before she nodded. "Your

clothes are going to be ridiculously big."

"They will be comfortable. Come with me and I'll show you." He took her hand and led her into his bedroom, where he pulled out two pairs of lightweight drawstring pants and one soft shirt. "You go change in the washing room and I'll change in here."

"Are you sure this is a good idea?" She took the pants and shirt and held them against her chest.

"I think it's a great idea. Go ahead and change and try to relax."

She got as far as his bedroom doorway. "What about Golly?"

"Grabon will take care of him. You can trust him to do that."

She nodded and disappeared, and he sagged with relief. Holy hell, to use her words, this was so much more than he had even wished for. He quickly changed into the drawstring pants and set aside his regular clothes. Every part of him was aware of her. She was terrified and doing her best to function through her fear. He meticulously wrapped his barn in shielding. If she was going to panic, she might try to run and he couldn't allow her to be at risk.

When she rejoined him dressed in his overlarge clothes, he pulled down a corner of the summer bedding. "You might as well climb in and get comfortable."

She stared at his bed and he could see the debate happening in her mind. "You are going to think I'm a coward," she began.

"No, I don't. I'll show you the spare room."

Swallowing, she nodded and followed. "It's your bad luck to have me for a mate, I know...."

He stopped and stared at her. "You have it all wrong. I am the most fortunate man on the planet. Before you get yourself in a mental rut, let's get this clear." He swallowed and shifted his feet. "We are very lucky to have found one another. No matter what it takes, we will find a way to make this work."

She chewed on her lip as her eyes filled with tears. "You don't feel like you were cheated?"

"Cheated?" He moved closer so he could touch her face, and cupped her cheek. The sensations that moved through him made him tremble. "Honey, you are my reward, my gift. I haven't been cheated." He took a breath and kissed her forehead, then took her hand and led her into the spare room. It was completely dark until he moved the curtain to let in the moon light.

"I don't know how to do this, Hess," she confessed, looking around her with a worried frown.

"Of course you don't. It's something we'll work out together. Climb into the bed and get comfortable." When she did, looking fearful, he smiled to himself. "I don't want you to panic," he said as he sat on the mattress with his back against the headboard. "We're going to talk and cuddle a bit, and after you fall asleep I'll go to my own bed."

"But I thought…."

"I know, you thought I'd treat you like a guest, but you're my mate, LeeAnn. We need this closeness and you want it as much as I do. It scares you down to your toes, and I understand that too." He pressed his back against the headboard and waited.

Little by little she relaxed, and instead of lying there as stiff as a board, she turned toward him, propping a pillow under her head. "What are we talking about?"

"When Gordon claimed Hanna they were strangers. Did you know that?"

"Really?"

"His power line is about six times the size of hers and he overwhelmed her before she even knew what he was doing. The impact knocked her out and she came to confused and disoriented. He brought her home and didn't explain what he had done. He simply claimed her as a family member."

LeeAnn frowned and fiddled with the corner of the sheet. "That was dishonest."

"No, it was simply a part of the truth. She wasn't ready to hear all of it, and he eased her into the knowledge of what their bond was. They slept in separate beds for a few days too."

"Did they?" She was back to chewing on her lip.

"When Tad claimed Dotty, she didn't know anything about men or even her own body. It took my brother awhile to introduce sex into their relationship, and when he did, he left out the intimacy they both needed, which resulted in her panicking and feeling hurt. I don't want to make that mistake."

LeeAnn sniffed and hung on to her pillow. "What are you trying to say?"

"There is no one way to do this. We're probably both going to make mistakes. If things get mixed up we'll work together to make them straight again. We're in this together, and I would never deliberately hurt you, not for any reason."

"I wouldn't hurt you on purpose, either, but this is all very confusing to me."

"We can be confused together. This isn't anything like I thought it would be, but that doesn't mean I'm even close to being disappointed; merely surprised." He lowered one hand onto her shoulder, patted her gently, and left it there. "You should try to sleep. I can feel how tired you are. Hopefully by morning things will feel more settled."

She closed her eyes. "Good night," she whispered.

He pressed his back to the headboard and didn't answer. She really needed to sleep and he had to get a hold of his own thoughts and emotions. Closing his eyes, he let his mind drift over the last few days.

Earlier today he had allowed himself to consider

seducing her. He mentally snorted and cracked his eyes open to glance down at her. Not only would that have been cruel if she wasn't his mate, it probably would have driven her away; possibly out of the territory. After the sisters had warned him, and Tad had all but ordered him to find out if she were his, his thoughts had shifted. Walking her back to Tad's, he'd felt a pull, and instead of assuming it was desire and sexual interest, a part of him had recognized it and he'd been stunned.

There really was a choice for him. As Grabon had told Golly, 'If her mate accepted her,' well he wasn't going to reject her, not when he had finally realized what she was to him. That still didn't make the way clear. She was far too strong to overwhelm, and he knew she would never deliberately walk into a mating, not after everything she had survived. So, while he watched Heron and Grabon tear up the tavern, he'd developed a loosely woven plan. He would lead her into a position where instincts would take over. If they didn't, well, then he would have to think of something else.

It had worked far better than he'd anticipated. Not only had the bond trapped her, but him as well. Never in his life had he felt so out of control. He was used to managing everything and everyone, but this bond was not in the least bit manageable.

He glanced down at her and knew she was on the edge of sleep. It was tempting to try to ease her into it, but she might startle awake and feel betrayed, so he waited. Before he used that kind of mind manipulation, they needed to build some trust between them. Letting her sleep in the guest room was hard enough, but he couldn't simply leave her alone and let her close a door between them. Not holding her when everything inside him wanted her in his arms with nothing between them was difficult.

***

LeeAnn's mind drifted in a warm cocoon of safety. Here she could let herself think about what had happened without being scared. Hess, the rascal, had led her into this. He'd probably suspected she was his mate and instead of telling her that, he'd proposed an experiment to eliminate her as a possibility. Blindly she had participated because she was tired, or perhaps because a secret part of her hoped he was her mate. Ever since Grabon had explained what a mating bond was, she had watched the mated pairs with more than a little envy. Did that happen only this morning? Her life had turned completely around in such a short period of time.

Hess smelled of the forest, and the weight of his hand on her side made her feel safe. She had not felt safe in a long time. Over the past year, she had started to dream of a mysterious prince. It was a foolish mental exercise she performed before she went to sleep, but it kept her calm as she clutched her knife. Her dream prince was strong, reliable, and caring. The awful things Sam had done wouldn't matter to him, and he would help her protect Golly and rescue them both.

Was Hess her prince? It did not seem likely. Her poor dream-man had been dragged out of her imagination, night after night, to do everything she wanted, exactly as she wanted. Hess was more likely to tell her what to do and yell at her if she didn't do it. He was one of the Dragonmen and could keep her and Golly safe. Even if Brian and the others came to Grabon's territory to cause problems, they didn't stand a chance. Sighing, she fell into sleep.

***

Hess kept his hand still by force of will; he had an urgent desire to stroke her back. But if he moved, he was certain she would wake and he didn't want that. She needed to sleep. Her day had been long and draining and that was before the strain of establishing a mating bond. He'd known the second she had dropped off the edge of wakefulness. She had a hard time going to sleep, even when she was exhausted and hovering on the edge. It was a useful piece of information and one he stored in the back of his mind.

The impulse to rub her back grew stronger and he slowly did. Instead of waking, as he feared, she snuggled closer and sighed. His heart clenched, knowing she was seeking comfort, something he would never withhold. If she were awake she might not be able to accept it. He had to find ways to give her what she needed without triggering her fears. Knowing that asleep, she could accept a gentle, comforting touch, he continued to rub her back. Little by little she worked herself closer to him and eventually pressed up against his leg. He closed his eyes and relished the sensation, allowing his hand to sink into her hair.

He knew he should go to his own bed, but he couldn't. Instead, he closed his eyes, absorbed her warmth through his hand, and dropped off to sleep.

His eyes flew open sometime later as she softly screamed. Half-asleep still, he snatched her into his arms, waking her from the nightmare.

"Are you all right?" he croaked.

"It was a dream, only a dream." She snuggled her face into his shoulder, holding on to him and dropped back into sleep.

He held her, almost afraid to breathe. One small shift at a time, he scooted down in the bed until he could lie down with her. She protested the sudden movement but didn't roll away. To his amazement, she held on tight. Wondering if he was dreaming, he rubbed her back and she relaxed against him, boneless and soft. His heart drummed in his chest so loudly, it was a miracle the sound didn't wake her.

As his heart finally slowed, he was able to savor her scent and the way she fit in his arms. Nightmares obviously chased her dreams, and while that didn't please him, this result was too precious to deny. Slowly he let himself fade, comforted by her presence.

***

Hess felt the shift in energy when the first sun hit the ground, just as all Farmers did. His eyes opened and he was more than pleased to find his mate comfortable in his arms and sleeping with abandon. If he hadn't promised to do Gordon's morning chores, he would have stayed right there. He eased from the bed so he wouldn't disturb her and went back to his own room to get dressed. Before he could pour hot water over leaves to make his morning tea, LeeAnn was standing in his kitchen looking dazed.

"Why are you up at the crack of dawn?" she asked with a frown.

"I promised Gordon and Tad I'd do the morning chores. You were sound asleep. What woke you?"

She shrugged and dropped into a chair, slumping with exhaustion. "I do not have a clue. Something didn't seem right, and I woke up needing to find you."

He nodded slowly. "You can come with me and see the animals if you like."

"Is it normal to feel lost if we're not in the same room?"

"Newly mated couples generally have trouble with any distance. The urgency and intensity diminishes after a week or so and small separations become easier."

"This better wear off soon. It's ridiculous to be up this early when I could be sleeping," she muttered as she pushed out of her chair. "Where did I leave my clothes?" He grinned as soon as she had left the room.

He fixed her a cup of tea and set it on the table. LeeAnn returned holding his hairbrush and dressed in the same outfit from yesterday. "Do you mind if I use this?"

"Help yourself to anything you need. We'll start getting you some things of your own, but make yourself comfortable."

"You really got a bad deal. Not only do you get a scarred mate, but one who doesn't own a thing."

"Your scars don't worry me and I own a market filled with goods. I hardly think I can complain when I get the greatest healer and her gentle giant. Golly is on his way down to help me with chores, so brush your hair and let's get moving."

She was smiling as she went to another room to brush her hair. Hess wished he was the reason for that, but he suspected she was happy to be seeing Golly. He sat at the table and sipped his tea, anxious for her to rejoin him. When she did, despite her chewing on her lip, she looked neat and fresh.

"Do you know how easy it would be to surrender everything I am to a man who cares not only about me, but about Golly? He's the most precious person, simply because...." Her eyes filled with tears, and the rest of her words lodged in her throat.

He rose, cupped her cheeks and kissed her forehead. "You don't need an excuse, honey. We're mates, and that means I care about you and everything you care about. That definitely includes Golly." He let her lean against him and he rubbed her back. "Take a breath and calm down. You don't want him to think you're unhappy."

"No, no, I don't and I'm not. I really do try not to think about it."

"Of course you do. So do I, since you told me. Come on, you can talk with me while we collect eggs and milk the cows."

She followed him outside, where she saw Golly running down the hill. He always did enjoy running, and going downhill always made him laugh, even when he fell, which he did regularly. Any rock or root was sure to tangle one of his feet, but someone had been very careful when making the path. He didn't so much as trip. His face was lit up with laughter and she smiled in return.

"That looked like fun," she told him as he ran closer.

"LeeAnn, did you see me? It's almost like I could fly. Grabon said you mated with Hess, but that I could still run down and help with chores. Hanna is going to make breakfast. Did you know that Grabon hasn't found his mate yet, but he's hoping she'll come to the market? Thane said we're going for a walk later to catch fish in the stream; he knows a good spot. I hope I can catch a big one. Tria had to stay on the wall last night because she sassed Grabon, and he hissed at her and sent her to the wall. I didn't have to, so I got to sleep on the bed, but Heron is putting together a bed for me made of wood. I think sleeping on wood is going to be hard, but I don't want to hurt his feelings." He took a breath and Hess whistled to get his attention.

"Eggs, they go in the basket." He handed Golly the basket and pointed to the henhouse before he took

LeeAnn's hand. "When you're done come join us in the barn." He led her there and opened the door.

"Don't you think I should explain about the bed?" LeeAnn asked.

"No, I think he'll see for himself when Heron brings it up to him. Has he always been that cheerful first thing in the morning?"

"No, this is a special kind of cheerful. He's happy, Hess, isn't that wonderful?" Her eyes filled with tears and he wrapped an arm around her shoulders.

"He's safe. Both of you are. It's harder for you to believe it, that's all."

Sniffing, she glanced out the barn door. "He's never collected eggs, at least I don't think so."

"He'll figure it out. Come over here and pet the cow's nose while I milk her."

"Actually," Gordon spoke from beside the barn door, "I can do this with Hess. Why don't you run inside and keep Hanna company. It won't take us long."

"All right." She went past the big Farmer, giving him as much space as possible.

***

Gordon watched as she stopped and spoke with Golly. "I make your mate nervous, Hess. Not when she's the clan healer, but when she's just herself."

Hess sighed and started milking. "I don't know the whole story, but there was a problem with a Farmer and the freak show. When they first felt the vibration of your land, she and Golly both assumed they weren't allowed."

Gordon shook his head and started milking the other cow. "That's a shame because any Farmer worth his land should have helped her." He paused to look at his cousin. "How bad was it? The abuse, I mean?"

"Bad, but we'll cope." Hess frowned and glanced out the barn doors. "The separation woke her while I was still in the house this morning. She hasn't had a full night's sleep and she has nightmares."

"Separation might be hard on her. Go on up to the house. I'll do the milking." Gordon was silent for a moment. "How secure is the bond?"

Hess threw him the image of their entwined powerlines and the big man laughed. Hess could still hear him laughing as he walked by Golly. The legend in their family was the more twists and turns in the bond, the tighter the connection.

"Hess?" he asked, standing next to the hens, his face all scrunched up with concern. "What do I do if the hen wants to keep her egg?"

He took a deep breath and nodded. "That's a good question. Let me show you what I do." As he demonstrated, Golly watched closely and nodded. "Okay, you do the next one and I'll watch."

Golly braced his feet, bent down, and tried to shoo

the hen gently, but she pecked at him and he withdrew his hand. "They don't like me."

"I think maybe we should do this chore together. You hold the basket and I'll get the eggs. After a little while, you'll get the hang of it. You can't let the hens be the boss, Golly."

He collected the eggs and Golly put them carefully in the basket. Then Hess sent him to speak with Gordon and took the basket up to the house.

"There you are," Hanna laughed when he appeared. "Did Golly have trouble with the hens?"

"They were mean to him and pecked his hands. I'll wash the eggs in a minute. Where's LeeAnn?"

"She's looking at the statues."

Hess grinned and walked into his cousin's living room and spotted her staring in wonder at the statues. He put his arm around her shoulders. "Hanna's pretty extraordinary, isn't she?"

"These are exquisite. I've never seen anything that compares. I thought the statues at the market were incredible, but these are so small. Look at this one!" She pointed to the statue of the spring bride.

He grinned. "All of her stuff is incredible. Wait until you taste more of her cooking. Come talk with us as I wash the eggs. Poor Golly got pecked and is afraid of the hens. He didn't say that, mind you, but he thinks they don't like him."

"Aw, those mean old hens."

"I collected the eggs or I would have been here sooner. Did the separation bother you?" She shrugged, but didn't look at him. "No, that's not going to work for us. You have to talk to me. Did it bother you?"

"I felt almost rejected being sent inside, and that's stupid, so I don't know how to answer."

He stroked her hair and kissed the top of her head. "That's an answer. We won't do that again. Gordon sent you in to talk with Hanna so he could ask me if you were all right. He's worried because you're afraid of him and he wants to make that better. Fair warning, he's going to ask you about what happened to make you and Golly afraid of Farmers. I told him what I knew, which is very little, but he's going to ask."

She nodded and touched his chest. "I'm overly sensitive and I don't even know why."

"We are newly mated, so all your emotions are on the surface, and so are mine. Do you want to go back to our house?"

"No, Hanna was looking forward to having people for breakfast. I don't want to hurt her feelings."

"All right, then. Let's go join her. How is she feeling?"

LeeAnn grinned and nodded toward the kitchen. "She's happy and healthy. That was the first thing I asked too."

They walked into the kitchen, where Hanna was leaning against the counter, her eyes wide.

"Are you having pain?" LeeAnn asked, moving forward and supporting her side so she couldn't fall down.

"I don't know," Hanna answered, rubbing her belly. "Everything tightened, it went all around me."

Chapter 7

"Why don't you sit down and I'll make the rest of breakfast. We'll see how good you are at giving directions." LeeAnn helped her to the table as Gordon came through the door, his expression intense. "It's early stages yet. This is going to take hours and hours, and that's if this isn't another false alarm."

"She's in labor?" Gordon's jaw dropped and he extended an arm and leaned against the wall for a second, as if adjusting his thoughts and bracing himself.

"The beginning, only the beginning." LeeAnn moved to see what Hanna had been making while Gordon rushed to his mate's side. Hess came over and kissed LeeAnn's brow.

"I'm going to finish the milking and bring in Golly. Can you reach me in the barn?"

"No, but Gordon can, I'm sure. I'll be all right; he can't very well leave now."

"No, he wouldn't. This won't take me very long."

***

Hanna had been cooking a breakfast pie, and LeeAnn finished preparing Hanna's fried fruit pieces, meat squares, and sauce. Hess brought in the milk and they tried to keep things as normal as possible. They sat at the table, and to everyone's surprise, even between contractions, Hanna managed a few bites of the delicious food.

LeeAnn washed the dishes, and Golly went up the hill to tell the others what was happening.

Gordon sat at the table holding Hanna's hand as another contraction hit, this one a little longer and more powerful. LeeAnn wiped her hands and went over to see what was happening.

She carefully synced her rhythm with Hanna's before checking and was amazed at how much easier it was today, but as she focused on her patient she realized that Hanna's labor was more advanced than she had thought.

"Now we need to get things ready. Gordon, we need a big pot of water on to boil, and Hess, you need to prepare the bed. Birth is a messy business and she isn't going to want to replace the mattress."

"I am sure they have some skins…," Hess stood and left the kitchen.

"I thought we had hours," Gordon commented, filling a big pot from the sink.

"That may not have been accurate. I think she is further along and we need to be ready." LeeAnn bent close to whisper in her ear. "How did you manage to hide the pains for so long?"

Hanna leaned forward, as much as her belly would allow. "I really thought it was gas."

Nodding, LeeAnn patted her hand. "There doesn't seem to be a problem, but I'm glad I did that little check. Everything is in the right place and it shouldn't be too long."

"It better be in the right place," Gordon rumbled.

"I was talking about the baby's head and the cord," she clarified for him.

He shook his head and shrugged. "I think I'm a little unnerved."

"You're allowed; your mate is having a baby. Now here are some things I need you to remember...."

As she instructed the two of them on breathing, pushing, and ignoring the mess to embrace the joy, Hess finished the bed and let everyone know what was happening, including the sisters.

It was still early by most people's standards, but nobody complained. Before Hanna retreated to the bedroom, she stepped out on the porch and gave Grabon a hug. He touched her face with one clawed finger, and Gordon put his arm around her shoulders, then gently turned her back into the house.

LeeAnn brushed away tears at the emotion between the woman and dragon. It wasn't the healer's place to cry. Hess kissed her cheeks and held her close for a few moments.

"The others will be here soon. If she wants any of the women, let us know. Otherwise, we'll keep everyone out of your way."

She sniffed and nodded. "It's all going to go smoothly. There is nothing to indicate a difficulty of any kind. You can tell the others the baby is well positioned, healthy, and strong. Even the cord is in a good place for delivery."

***

Seven labor-intensive hours later, Hanna delivered a baby boy. Although mother and baby were both healthy, the new father was frazzled and relieved it was finally over. During those hours, LeeAnn discovered that mates shared more than power lines, thoughts, and emotions; they also shared sensations. She was going to have to think about that later.

Gordon took his newly born, just-washed and nursed son out to meet his world while LeeAnn cleaned up Hanna and helped her find a comfortable position.

"Three days in bed. I know it's going to seem like forever, and after today you can get up a little, but your body really needs to recover."

"You could speed that up, couldn't you?"

"If it was an emergency, but it isn't and there are plenty of helping hands. You can afford to take the time to let your body heal a little slower. At the end of three days I'll see where we are and make a decision about speeding things up."

"She can follow those directions," Gordon told her. "Hess has the little one. I need a word with my mate if you're done in here."

"I'll go on out." LeeAnn headed for the door.

"Don't go far. We'll need you back in a few minutes."

LeeAnn frowned and went to find Hess. What was left to do? Hess saw her and immediately took her in his arms, bringing her a huge sense of relief. The last seven hours had passed far too slowly for both of them, she suspected. She rubbed her cheek against his chest until she found just the right place and sighed.

"Where's the baby?"

"My brother stole him. I'd rather hold you anyway. How is Hanna?"

"Doing very well and anxious to get up. I told her she needed three days of rest. Can Gordon keep her still for that long?"

"No, but he'll give it one heck of a try." He kissed the top of her head and laid his cheek over the spot. Voices murmured all around them, but she didn't hear them. It was such a relief to lean against him, to be surrounded by him. She sniffed and then sniffed again.

"What have you been doing?"

"Chopping wood mostly, but I also cleaned out the cow barn. Tad and I don't wait well. As it turns out neither do the dragons. They've been digging tubers, fishing, and hunting. The sisters have been cooking and making clothes. Golly will have a new set before morning. They had already put some together for you, and they're in our bedroom. They think it's handy you wear the same size as Trissy did before she got pregnant."

"You've all been so industrious," she answered in awe.

"You haven't exactly been doing nothing. They've all been very patient, but I know they want to speak with you."

"Give me another minute. I could go to sleep right here."

"Soon, sweetheart. You had a rough day and it started very early. I'll get you to bed as soon as I can."

She leaned back to look at him. "You didn't tell me that mates share sensations."

"Didn't I?"

"No. You told me about emotions, thoughts, and the powerline. I didn't know that sensations were part of the bond. This was as hard on Gordon as it was on Hanna."

"They're mates; what happens to one happens to both. That's how it works."

"Well it would have been handy to know that, but next time I can anticipate it." She leaned against him again, making herself comfortable. His arms enclosed her securely and her eyes closed.

"Trissy is next, and from what I know they got

pregnant right around the same time," he murmured low.

"Hanna was a few weeks early, so we probably have some time with Trissy."

"I hate to interrupt," Tad spoke from the side. Hess growled low and opened his eyes to glare at his brother. "I know, you've been separated for long hours, but Hanna is asking for LeeAnn."

That stopped Hess's growl, but LeeAnn patted his chest while he slowly released her. "Don't be long," he warned, turning to Tad.

LeeAnn ran back inside to the bedroom and slid to a halt when Gordon and Hanna greeted her, both looking undisturbed. Someone had brought them the baby, and Hanna held her infant with such care, LeeAnn grinned.

"You wanted to see me?"

"We wanted to thank you," Gordon answered, motioning her closer to the bed. "This was probably the smoothest delivery I've ever heard of, and that was in large part due to your knowledge and skill. I honestly don't know what we would have done without you. Being newly mated, I am sure this put an undue strain on both you and Hess. For that we are both sorry. Is there something we can do for you?"

LeeAnn smiled at Hanna. "When Hanna is fully recovered I'd love a statue of Golly. I'd pay, of course, but if you could do that for me…." She blinked back tears.

Hess hurried to her side from the doorway and wrapped an arm around her. "It's all right. They know what that would mean to you."

"I'm so sorry," she muttered, trying to swallow back the emotion that rose to her throat.

"There's no reason to be sorry," Hess murmured.

"I would be honored to make a statue of Golly," Hanna told her, looking baffled. Gordon didn't seem to understand either, and LeeAnn realized that nobody understood they would have Golly for only a short time. It wasn't something she would tell them now, not with a new birth to celebrate, but she would explain his condition soon.

***

Not long after that, Hess led LeeAnn outside, but before they headed to his barn he connected with Grabon while she spoke with Jamie and Janie.

"What do you know about Golly's condition?"

"I know he is destined for a very short life and every day is a gift."

"Good, I was afraid you didn't know."

"I knew before she ran away. It is often uppermost in her mind."

"He doesn't have very much longer, does he?" Hess asked.

"A few days, weeks, or months. It is impossible to say."

"It's going to break her heart to lose him."

"Loss is inevitable; there is nothing we can do to change it. Our best option is to embrace each moment. As a couple you will find your way through that too."

Hess went to collect his mate and found Golly spinning fish tales for her and the sisters. "I didn't catch it, but it was this big." He held out his arms to show a distance longer than the length of his arm.

"That is a big fish," Jamie agreed. "It's a shame you didn't catch him."

"I tried but he swam too fast. Thane caught all the ones we brought for supper, and we took some up to Heron and Trissy. I only caught two, and Thane said we could cook them later."

"I need to go," LeeAnn told Golly with a grin. "I need a nap and so does Hess. I'll see you later, all right?"

"That's good, Rok is taking me to visit Brom's nest. I can tell you all about it."

She gave him a hug and moved to Hess's side. "I am so ready to get some sleep."

"So am I. He took her hand and waved to the others as they walked to the barn. They were barely inside when a knock sounded on the large door. Hess opened it quickly to find Pit standing there. The dragon handed him a large bag.

"What is this?"

"Human items we thought LeeAnn might need. Mia and I picked them out."

"That was very kind, thank you." Hess stubbornly stood in the doorway, but LeeAnn ducked around him.

"You can come in," she told the dark gray dragon.

"No, you both need to sleep. We simply wanted to drop off the package for you," he told LeeAnn.

After Pit left, Hess set the bag on the table. "Do you want to look now or later?"

"I want to look now. What did they bring me?" She opened the toggle holding the bag closed and peered inside. She first pulled out a huge sleeping shirt that would brush the ground on her. LeeAnn laughed and held it up to her shoulders, and he grinned. Next, she pulled out a hairbrush and mirror tied with a ribbon. LeeAnn hugged them to her chest for a moment before setting them gently on the table. Then she found hair ribbons and combs, a special cream for her face and hands, shoes, a tin of flavored tea, three different spices, and a bundle of something she couldn't identify. When she unrolled it, she found socks and undergarments.

"I can't believe they got me all of this."

"They wanted to gift you with something, so they did their best to find things a human woman would want. It looks like they did very well. Do you think the shoes will fit? We can always exchange them if they don't."

She tried them on and to their surprise they fit.

"That must have been a lucky guess." LeeAnn looked at the shoes and grinned. They were made of soft leather. "These are a lot nicer than my old ones."

Yawning, he looked at all her new things and smiled. "I suppose you want to sleep in the new sleep shirt?"

"I do, and I'm going to brush my hair with my own brush, and when we wake up, I'm going to take a bath and put on the creams. I still have the one from Griss for my scars. Maybe it really will help them fade."

That stirred his interest. "I can help with the cream."

"Maybe. We'll have to see what I can reach on my own. I'll go change."

"Good idea. Here, take these." He handed her the hair accessories, then gathered the kitchen items and put them on the counter. As she scampered away, he connected with Pit and let him know how much she valued the gifts.

"Good. Mia was sure LeeAnn would need some things of her own that didn't come from you."

"She was correct, so thank her for me. Now I bid you a good afternoon."

"And we bid you good sleep. We'll see you both at dinner."

He went into the bedroom and changed into his

drawstring pants, then climbed into his bed. She came to the door and with a determined stride walked to the side and climbed in beside him.

"I don't know why this is so hard," she muttered.

"It doesn't matter, but I'm glad you could join me. Now cuddle in so we can go to sleep."

She quickly found a comfortable spot beside him and dropped off into sleep. He was amazed at how much trust he felt coming from her. Careful not to risk losing ground, he closed his eyes and joined her in sleep. Little by little they moved together until they were two bodies occupying the same space. Shielded and at peace, they knew nothing of what was happening beyond their dreams.

***

Grabon noticed the wagons crossing into his territory shortly after Hanna had given birth. He assumed they were more humans coming for the market. After Hess and LeeAnn had retired for the afternoon, he took a moment to check on the newcomers. It pleased him that these people had crossed into his territory, but their presence also made him suspicious and angry. Instead of informing the others of their presence, he flew down to the hut to consult with his companion.

Heron scowled even before he finished sharing the news. "Who would think Brian and the others were so twisted and foolish that they would invade our territory after being warned to stay away?"

"What do we do about Golly?" Grabon asked with a frown. He didn't want the boy upset if they could help it.

"We don't tell him," Heron decided. "Brian is his father, a connection to his past. With such a short time left to him, he doesn't need to know about their presence or intentions."

Grabon could see the wisdom of that. However, they needed something or someone to keep Golly occupied and happy while they dealt with whatever this proved to be. Who did they have who was deceptive enough to fool the surprisingly sensitive youth?

Grinning, Grabon contacted Jamie. She was more than willing to help and immediately enlisted her sister. They would take Golly to Brom's nest as planned and watch Star while Brom helped with these unexpected visitors. Griss could bring Red as well, giving the busy fathers a chance to assist their territory dragon.

Golly was thrilled to go visiting and rode with the sisters in the bentar wagon, admiring their large green birds. Brom and Griss greeted them kindly before they flew off to join Grabon, Heron, Tad, Pit, and Thane.

After making sure Hanna and the baby were sleeping, they let Gordon know what was going on, but told him they would make do without his great strength. He suggested that Heron bring Trissy and the children down to the farm if he was going to be gone for very long. Not only did that provide protection for Trissy, but the other woman could keep Hanna company when she woke.

"I could do this without you," Grabon told Heron, knowing that leaving his mate when she was close to giving birth was difficult for his companion.

"No, this is something I need to see done," Heron informed him. "The idea of humans hunting dragons is a personal nightmare of mine. After Benny tried to convince the Farmers to kill you and the others while you were sleeping, the concern has only gotten worse. Even knowing that Brian and the others are not hunters, but confused enough...." Heron frowned. "They are here for a twisted purpose after being warned away," he reminded Grabon.

Understanding completely, Grabon nodded. It took some time for arrangements, including for him to settle the curious visitors on the edge of his nest. Finally, he signaled the others to take to the sky.

From the air, he could see movement on the bridge. Mia, according to Pit, was visiting Dotty, and they were crossing the river to visit with Trissy and the girls at Gordon's. The dragons swooped down one after another, offering a greeting before heading in the direction of the wagons that had crossed into the territory.

Knowing that the freaks had been able to sense the energy in the ground as a claimed territory, much as humans were able to identify Farmer land, Grabon had no doubt that they had come with an agenda of their own. Since they knew nothing about dragons or their customs and rules, Grabon thought they would anticipate an attack from the sky. To confuse them and catch them by surprise, Heron and Grabon planted themselves on the ground in the wagon's path while the others positioned themselves to surround the other wagons at the same time.

Brian was driving the lead wagon, and when the large green dragon did not move from in front of his bentars, Brian pulled his birds to a halt.

"We don't want any trouble," Brian called, shifting on the bench seat.

"Then you shouldn't have crossed into our territory," Heron told him from the side of the path.

Brian spun to face him, while reaching for something under the seat, and Grabon blasted him in the shoulder, knocking him off the wagon. The blast broke Brian's shield, and also gave him and Heron the opportunity to do a fast reading and sense his motivations and intentions.

"Stop, wait, what are you doing?" Brian pleaded from the dirt, trying to scramble to his feet and rebuild his shields.

"Defending our territory. You were warned not to come here," Heron snapped. "Rok told you we would not welcome any of you."

"That dragon exploded Sam's head," Brian groaned, clutching his shoulder.

"We'll do the same to you before we're done. Why did you come here after you were warned?" Heron's voice was loud and fierce.

"We need that healer-" Brian clutched his shoulder and groaned again, finally gaining his feet.

"You do not need LeeAnn. You do not care about her or Golly. You chose to come here to hunt dragons and collect and sell parts." Grabon's words echoed in the tense moment.

Brian looked at Grabon and sneered, dropping his arm and no longer pretending to be injured. "The others will get you."

"Your friends? From the other wagons? They're all dead," Heron informed him. "Did you think we came alone? You came into our territory to die. Golly and LeeAnn are both safe from you, as they should have been all along." Heron stepped close, but stayed well out of reach. "What we needed from you were the truths in your mind. Now we can end your life as easily as we would extinguish a flame."

Brian scowled and took a step toward him. "I'm not telling you anything."

Heron used energy to push him back and send him stumbling.

"We wouldn't believe your words anyway." Grabon nodded at Heron and waited for him to nod back and move out of the way. Then Grabon blasted Brian's head. Fortunately the spatter missed them both as the body collapsed.

When they connected to the others, Griss showed

them the arrows and spears the freaks had brought with them. He warned them that they had prepared the tips with a fast-acting poison. Griss wanted their recipe and he collected some samples as the others gathered the bodies. After unhitching the bentars and setting them free, they made a pile of bodies, wagons, and goods and set it all aflame. Fed by their anger and the power of the planet, it burned quickly.

They returned to Gordon's yard after everything had turned to ash and there was no risk of the fire spreading. Grabon gave the all-clear to his visiting dragons as well as his people. Trissy had been anxiously waiting at Gordon's back door and ran into Heron's arms as fast as a woman in her condition could.

"Was anyone hurt?" she demanded.

"None of our people got a scratch. It's not good for you to get so worked up. You'll bring on labor."

"I won't, but I was worried." She touched his face and peered into his eyes. "They were really planning to hunt our people?"

He nodded and wrapped his arms around her. "They really were," he murmured.

"Why? What would make them decide to do that?"

Heron sighed and tightened the embrace. "We'll sit down and I'll explain. We didn't want to tell Golly about this because we didn't want him upset, but it doesn't look like that will be possible."

They gathered everyone in Gordon's yard so he and Hanna could be part of the discussion. Hess and LeeAnn joined them looking sleepy and slightly confused. The newly mated pair had recently woken, and Tad had invited them to join the rest.

The sisters brought the youngsters and Golly to the farmhouse. In order not to strain the bentars, the humans had walked part of the way and Golly had directed the birds. Mia and Dotty had followed Trissy from the house and had gone immediately to their mates. Kev and Fin, as soon as Grabon gave the all-clear, ran up from their parents' home. Tria and several other visiting dragons were drawn to watch the two species gathering in the Farmer's yard. After gaining Grabon's permission, they perched on rooftops or stood at a distance to watch.

Gordon carried out Hanna and the baby and settled her on a chair. She had wanted to walk, but Gordon had refused to allow it, so they argued the whole time. Grabon realized it was the first time LeeAnn had seen them all gathered in one place. The amount of power, talent, and skill in his clan must have surprised her. He watched as she looked from face to face. Hess took her hand, but she did not seem upset, only interested.

The large outside table was set up and food would come out later, but for now, they had things to discuss.

Grabon stepped forward and it pleased him when everyone turned to listen. *"Today we saw the birth of Gordon and Hanna's child. We gather to congratulate* them and celebrate this new addition to our unified clan. Hanna safely delivered a healthy male youngster. LeeAnn, our healer, assisted and minimized her and Gordon's pain. We welcome LeeAnn and Golly, our large youth, as well as this new youngster."

Applause, whistles, tail thumps, and roars of approval followed his words. When the racket died down, Grabon continued, his tone far less jovial.

"Unfortunately, we also need to share news of an attempt by unwelcome humans to hunt dragons. Everyone involved in it is dead, their goods and bodies burned to ash and returned to the planet. It was a deliberate act of aggression. Rok warned these same humans not to enter our territory due to crimes they committed against LeeAnn, mate to Hess, and the youth, Golly. They chose to come here armed with poisoned weapons. Heron read the truth in their leader's mind before he, too, was extinguished."

Silence greeted that announcement. LeeAnn looked like she might need to be sick as she checked to see if anyone was injured.

"This is not the first time humans or dragons have broken the territory rule about hunting. Recently, a dragon named Ron hunted and delivered LeeAnn to my nest. I chose to banish him instead of extinguishing him solely because he had unknowingly rescued her. Let it be known," Grabon's voice resonated with his powerlines deep in the ground so everyone in the territory could hear him. *"There is no hunting of humans or dragons in my territory. My Dragonmen will extinguish any persons involved in such hunting.*

They will act swiftly and with little warning if the need arises." Grabon looked at his people and nodded.

"Define hunting for us," Tad suggested, glancing at his mate. "We'll spread the word among the humans, but it would help if we know your thoughts on the matter."

Nodding, Grabon answered thoughtfully. *"Hunting is the search for an individual or group with the intent to do them permanent harm. Are there any other questions?"*

There were plenty of comments, but no questions. Grabon had a feeling it would be the same among the humans throughout the territory.

Golly sat down and rubbed his chest, drawing a few concerned glances. LeeAnn went to his side with Hess and hugged the youth, murmuring reassurances.

"They are all gone?" Golly asked.

"Yes," Hess answered swiftly. "They are no longer a threat to you and LeeAnn or anyone else."

"That's good. Then they can't take us back."

Hess looked down him and smiled sadly. "No, they can't."

"We can stay here?" His eyes were pleading.

"You belong here now," Heron answered. "We're going to bring out the food. Why don't you help me?" He extended a hand and helped Golly to his feet.

He followed Heron into the house to get the platters of food the sisters had prepared while Hanna was giving birth.

***

Frowning, Tad caught Hess's eye and motioned him to the side of the group. "What is happening with Golly?"

Hess let out a breath and glanced back at his mate. "The condition that makes him so large also substantially reduces his life span."

Tad jerked with surprise and glanced at Grabon. It was clear he was wondering if this was information their territory dragon needed to be told. "How long does he have?"

Their eyes finally met and Hess let out a sigh. "Not much longer."

Tad cursed loudly in Dragon and turned away for a moment. When he turned back he nodded to Hess and patted his shoulder before walking over to join his mate.

Little by little as the celebration unfolded, Hess could almost see the difficult news travel through the males of their group. They had finished eating and the table was being cleared when Gordon returned Hanna and his sleeping son to their bedroom. When he emerged from the house, Heron pulled Gordon aside. Hess took a few steps closer so he could hear the exchange.

"I would not ruin your pleasure of the day with sad news, but there is something you probably need to know before Hanna hears it from one of the women."

"What is it?" Gordon frowned.

"It concerns Golly, and LeeAnn in a different way. The condition that keeps him growing has severely shortened his life. Eventually his size will put too much strain on his organs and he will die."

Gordon stared at Heron and let out a loud sigh. "I should have thought of that."

"It is not something that is easy to contemplate. LeeAnn of course knows. The news is slowly spreading through our clan and I thought you might want to prepare Hanna."

Gordon shook his head and glanced at Golly. "His time is very short now, isn't it?"

Heron nodded. "I don't know how he has survived as long as he has. LeeAnn has done all she can."

Gordon nodded and took a deep breath. "She saw him rescued. Let us hope that will be some comfort to her when the time comes to say goodbye."

"I do not envy Hess at all. At the best of times it is difficult to claim a mate."

Hess took a step closer, hoping to catch a word of advice. If there was something either of these men thought he could do to ease LeeAnn's mind, he wanted to know what it was.

"He will see her through this, Heron. My cousin has depths that few can see, but his mate will be able to draw strength from him. We will not grieve the living, but celebrate each day he has. I will prepare Hanna as best I can."

Heron nodded and patted his friend's shoulder. "So you still do not have a name for the boy?"

Hess's shoulders sagged and he looked back at LeeAnn sitting with Golly. At the moment they were both content.

Gordon shrugged and glanced back at the house with a grin. "Hanna is reluctant to name him aloud. I am respecting her wishes."

"How long does she intend to wait?" Heron asked curiously.

"Until she is allowed to walk outside on her own and make the announcement on her feet."

Heron laughed and punched his arm. "Feisty, as always. Grabon will greatly enjoy this story."

"Feel free to share it. I told her everyone would be pleased to wait until she is recovered before learning the name of our son."

"You are correct, but they will be curious." Heron walked off laughing. Gordon's gaze met his and he nodded toward the table. Tad joined them as they broke it down.

"I noticed we have plenty of stove and fire wood," Gordon commented as they placed the boards in the barn.

"Our gift for the birth of your son. We do not idly wait well," Hess told him with a grin.

"I know well how that is. So tell me, cousin, what can we do to help LeeAnn?"

Hess shifted on his feet. "We make Golly's last days full of joy. When the time to say goodbye arrives, it will not drag on her heart for years. She is a strong woman, not just in power and talent, but in character."

"We will of course do all we can to make that happen. Is there nothing else we can do?"

Hess thought about it for a minute. "Can we send a message through the Farmers to find her parents?"

Gordon looked startled, but nodded. "That is an excellent idea."

"I have an even better idea," Tad offered, looking at his brother. "Bert and Mable are from the second colony. Isn't that where her parents are? We can pass a message through them at the end of the season. They may even know one another."

"Do we meet with them tomorrow?" Hess asked, having lost track.

"Pit and I do. We can ask about her parents then. We are helping them set up two different booths in the morning."

"Excellent," Hess answered.

"It still does not tell me what I can do," Gordon complained.

"Talk to her about the Farmer who terrified her and Golly and get to the bottom of that," Hess suggested.

"I can do that with pleasure." Gordon headed off and Hess shook his head.

"He is going to be persistent."

"Gordon? When is he anything else? It will do them both good." Tad shifted his feet and looked over at Dotty. "When I told you to look for a spark, I was not sure you would act immediately."

Hess felt himself frown. "I did not. I waited until we had returned from the tavern and we could be private."

Tad nodded and leaned against the tree at his back. "When did you make the decision to accept her? You never even reached out to me."

Hess sighed. Gordon was not the only one in their family who was persistent. "Did you really think I would reject my mate?"

"No, but she is obviously equally as powerful as you and she... this past year must have been…. I did think it would have taken you a few weeks to not just accept her, but convince her to accept you."

"It was no impulse, easily regretted, if that is your concern. I spent the day with her and was already contemplating a relationship of some sort. She is appealing in a way I cannot describe. In the garden yesterday, she confided in me about Golly's condition. You were right, I was not looking to see if she was my mate. Yet, even before that drew us closer, I admired her skill and dedication to healing. Her character shines through her actions."

"There is no denying that she is a worthy mate, Hess. What I can sense of your bond seems incredibly strong, but I was surprised by how quickly you accomplished it."

Hess smirked and glanced about him. "I tricked her."

Tad coughed in surprise. "You did not!"

"I did. You can ask her how I did it."

Tad glanced over to where Gordon was speaking to LeeAnn. "I think it will be better if you tell me."

Hess saw the intense conversation and grinned as LeeAnn reached out a comforting hand to Gordon. He would bet that most people couldn't sense that Gordon's fiercest scowls revealed his emotional distress and not anger. He looked back at his brother. "I told her I wanted to eliminate her as a possible mate. She agreed to participate in an experiment to do that." Hess shrugged and glanced back at his mate and saw her grinning at his cousin.

"An experiment?" Tad's eyes widened.

"She brought her power line to the surface to see if mine would reject it." Hess shrugged again and grinned at him.

"I knew you could be devious, but that was brilliant."

Hess rubbed the back of his neck. "She assumed that even if we were mates I would reject her. I disabused her of that notion before we had our experiment. Devious is one thing, dishonest is another. I am going over to rescue my mate. It seems our cousin is trying to intimidate her."

***

Grinning, Tad watched Hess leave as Dotty came over and took his hand.

"Why is Gordon looking at LeeAnn like that?" she asked.

"He is trying to get to the bottom of the mystery of why LeeAnn and Golly are afraid of Farmers."

"Oh, well Gordon was going to find out sooner or later. I hope he takes action against the Farmer responsible."

"You know the story?" Tad asked.

"She shared it while you were playing in town last night. She and Golly once escaped by drugging Sam's drink and making him sleep soundly, a very clever and effective plan. They were cutting across a Farmer's field when he came out of his home to confront them. The man seemed especially large and intimidating late at night to two escaping fugitives. She explained their situation and begged for his help. Instead of lending aide, he held them prisoner all night locked in a meat shed and returned them to Sam the next morning. He issued a warning to Sam's group that if he ever sensed or saw any of them on his land or any other Farmer's land, he would blast them to pieces."

"Who was this Farmer?" Tad growled.

"I am sure she will give the image to Gordon."

***

Hess grinned at Gordon as he put his arm around LeeAnn. "Are you trying to intimidate our healer or my mate?"

Gordon took a deep breath and forced the tension out of his expression. "Either one, but it would be helpful if you could explain to your mate that when she is asked a question is it polite if she answers."

Hess laughed and kissed the top of LeeAnn's head. "I do not think explaining will help. She enjoys being evasive. What is it you want to know?"

"I want the location of this Farm where the Farmer not only denied her and Golly assistance, but told them that all freaks were banned from all Farmers' land."

"She didn't give you a location?"

"Holy hell, Hess. How am I supposed to know exactly where we were?"

Gordon's expression further relaxed. "I had not

considered that."

"You might have if she hadn't been entertained by your attempt to intimidate her."

"It's not the best image because it was a cloudy night." LeeAnn interrupted, giving him a bit of elbow in his side. "Do you recognize him?" she asked Gordon.

His jaw firmed. "I know him and I can do something about this. Benny has lost all respect among the Farmers. He attended the gathering this past winter and tried to recruit others to sneak up to Grabon's nest and attack the dragons."

LeeAnn's eyes widened. "Why would he do that?"

"He is a stupid man with a small mind," Gordon answered with a snarl. "I will let it be known that he did not honor a request for aid. If nothing else, he can lose his land if the others agree. On behalf of all Farmers, I apologize. Such a thing should never have happened. It has always been our way to lend aid when requested."

"I had always heard that. It was why we ran in that direction. I am relieved to know that my parents did not raise me with a false trust in the guardians of the ground."

Gordon grinned. "I have not heard a Farmer referred to that way in a long time. Have we addressed your unreasonable fear of me at last?"

"I believe so, although watching you and Hanna in

labor together took care of most of that." She took a deep breath and released it slowly. "I may still be nervous crossing another Farmer's land. Your cousin, or whoever he was, scared Golly and me badly that night."

"You have no need to be nervous. All our future travels will be together. I am a Farmer by birth and still in good standing even though Gordon, Tad, and I elected to be Dragonmen," Hess reminded her.

"How did your families react to such a choice?" LeeAnn asked.

Hess grinned and patted her shoulder. "My parents were actually pleased. They think it is a reasonable choice for us and an ambitious cause, to introduce and integrate the two species. We will see what Gordon's parents think when they arrive. His sister, Mazy, gave birth in the spring, and his parents plan to travel here in midsummer."

"No doubt they will bring goods for your market. I am looking forward to showing my father what I have accomplished and having them both meet Hanna and the baby."

"I am sure they are very proud of you. How is it your father can leave his crops during the summer?" LeeAnn asked.

"I have many cousins who will see to the land in his absence. No doubt some will come with him to make the trip easier. They may even bring a few others who are curious about what we are doing. Tad and Hess have three other siblings, all much younger. My parents only had Mazy and me, but my uncle Eldon and my father have seven other siblings, all of whom had at least five children, many of whom are now adults. There is never a lack of helping hands."

LeeAnn looked around, took a deep breath, and grinned. "I begin to see why you decided to claim land so distant from your family. You were expanding their claim while giving yourself the space you need."

Gordon nodded and looked at Hess. "She is perceptive. I am the most powerful Farmer, followed not too distantly by Hess and Tad. The others found it uncomfortable to be around me. As my cousins matured and their power and connections grew, they faced the same problem. That was the reason they chose to come out here and join the Dragonmen. Most of us know how it feels to have people think we are too powerful."

"Even our dragons have faced similar problems in other territories," Hess explained. "We are all too powerful or too different, yet together, as Grabon says, we make a united force."

LeeAnn leaned forward and kept her voice low. "The sisters must have faced similar problems because of the unusual nature of their talents."

Gordon and Hess nodded and grinned. "You read them well if you can sense any power from them at all. It is difficult because they keep their power well masked. They are unusual women and came to us because they befriended Hanna when she was alone. It wouldn't have mattered if they had no talent. Their acceptance was based on their kindness, but of course that is not the case."

"No, they are a wonderful addition to this clan. I was so pleased to see that they were valued and treasured," LeeAnn said.

"Who is valued?" Jamie asked, coming up to join them.

"I was telling them it was wonderful that the Dragonmen value and treasure you and Janie for yourselves as well as your talents and skills," LeeAnn explained with a grin.

Jamie grinned back and looked at Gordon and Hess. "It took us a long time to believe they were sincere in their offer of acceptance. As you can imagine, we make most people who know of our talent nervous. Most people do not want anyone to know what they need or desire. They certainly do not want their thoughts manipulated by someone else. In truth as much as we have benefitted from joining the Dragonmen, we have been able to employ and assist that many more people."

"As the market grows and expands and draws in larger crowds, there will be more people to help," Hess promised.

"That is the most valuable aspect of our new clan; that we are all free to be who we are," she said, looking intently at LeeAnn.

"I can appreciate that." LeeAnn met the older

woman's stare with a curious half-smile. "What part of myself do you think I am denying?"

"Not denying, only hiding from. I think we can trust your mate to help you accept the woman inside who yearns desperately for love and affection. What Sam did to you was a crime, but it might be time to consider healing the damage he did to your body."

Hess looked at her with raised brows. "Which damage is she referring to?"

LeeAnn sighed and shook her head. "It's not as easy as she makes it sounds. The scars have already formed."

"You can heal your scars?" Gordon asked.

"They do not matter," Hess told her in frustration.

Jamie shook her head. "They do matter, because they matter to her. LeeAnn allowed them to form, and hopefully after she has the courage to show them to you, she will have the strength to heal them."

"You allowed them to form?" Gordon asked, frowning.

"This is a conversation for the two of us to share, not for everyone to participate in," Hess protested.

LeeAnn squeezed his hand. "It takes more focused energy to heal myself as completely as I heal others," she explained to them. "Since Sam, well, I didn't bother and I needed that energy to survive and to keep Golly safe."

Gordon shrugged and turned to his cousin. "You are correct. This is between the two of you. I think I need to find someone to see the sisters home."

"Rok has volunteered," Jamie said. "That's actually what I came over to tell you and to congratulate you one last time." She turned to LeeAnn and gave an apologetic smile. "I probably should have spoken privately with you."

"No, Jamie, you were trying to help and we know that," Hess spoke for both of them.

"Then I'll bid you all a good night."

LeeAnn caught her in a hug and whispered in her ear, "We'll talk about it later."

Hess chuckled and winked at his mate as she wrinkled her nose. Evidently she had thought he would not hear her.

Jamie nodded and left to find Janie and head for home. Hess looked down at his mate, grinning. "Since we all have the market tomorrow, I think we will head home as well."

"I need to say good night to Golly."

As LeeAnn ran off, Hess and Gordon watched her. "Does she worry about him staying with Grabon?"

"No, she simply worries about him," Hess answered.

Gordon nodded and watched the giant youth embrace the young healer and had to clear the lump from his throat. "It must be hard for her."

"Most of the time she is able to push thoughts of his death aside."

"Good. Let us know if we can do anything."

Hess smiled sadly. "I will do that." He held out his hand as LeeAnn returned to his side, and she took it with a grin. "Heron has promised him a wooden bed for tomorrow night. He's still puzzled about how that will work."

"What is he puzzled about?" Gordon asked with a slight frown.

Hess chuckled. "Golly hasn't figured out that a wooden bed comes with a mattress. He's envisioning sleeping on the wood frame. We decided not to clue him in since he's enjoying the puzzle."

Gordon walked off shaking his head and chuckling. Hess and LeeAnn headed back to the barn, where they shut the door and closed out the crowd.

Chapter 8

When they were inside, LeeAnn put on the teakettle and looked around the kitchen. "Maybe tomorrow I should pick out a few things for the house."

"I'd appreciate that." Hess looked at the stark counters and sighed. "I didn't do any decorating and resisted Trissy and Hanna's suggestions."

"Why would you do that?" LeeAnn asked, getting out the flavored tea Mia and Pit had given her.

Hess pulled out a chair and sat with a sigh. "I didn't want to get too comfortable without my mate." He shook his head. "I would have done better to prepare our home, but every time I tried to pick something out, I worried that you might not like it. Tad let Hanna and Trissy set up his side, and I spent most of my time there until Dotty joined him. Even then, I still had meals with them."

"You really won't mind if I choose a few things?"

"No, you can choose anything you like. As you might have guessed, I have limited domestic skills. I enjoy comfort as much as the next man, but I don't have any talent in putting things together beyond the visual appeal."

"I can probably make things more comfortable with a little help." She looked at Hess, tilting her head. "Are you going to ask me about the scars?"

"If you want to talk about them, I'm listening."

LeeAnn swallowed nervously. "I'll have to tell you the whole story and I don't know how much you already know." She poured the tea and tried to keep her hand from trembling.

"Our thoughts aren't fully connected yet. That can take weeks or months to form between mates. Tell me what you think I should know," Hess suggested, accepting the tea she handed him.

"After I ran away, I was working in a clinic just outside the second colony. Gregor was the healer in that area, and I helped him as much as I could. Sam came in needing help for one of his crew, but they were a good distance away. I elected to go with him to do what I could. Gregor warned me to be on guard and return as quickly as possible." She chewed her lip and stirred her tea.

"When we were outside the village, Sam stopped the wagon to pick up Brian. He had been waiting on the side of the road. After seeing his tattoos and the way he was dressed, I figured out that Sam ran some kind of freak show. He had said they were traveling entertainers, but I hadn't asked what kind. Brian made me uncomfortable, but Sam had been nice, so I stayed close to him.

"When we finally got to their camp, things didn't feel right, but I set my worries aside. I did the healing they needed as fast as I could, thinking I needed to get back to Gregor. The woman had an infected knife wound in her shoulder and was unconscious anyway, so a stronger dose of power didn't make all that much difference. When they saw what I could do, Sam grew very excited. He said he could provide me with many opportunities to heal people who really wanted and needed my help." She let out a rough breath and took a sip of her cooling tea.

"I was stupid enough to fall for his praise and agreed to stay the night and at least think about it. I woke up tied to stakes stuck in the ground." She shook her head and took a deep breath. "He had drugged me, so my mind was slow, but I remember every sickening thing he did. Golly untied me before morning, and instead of running as Golly urged, I curled in a ball and wept like a child."

"You were still drugged," Hess soothed, his voice hoarse.

"Maybe, probably; but I still should have run. Sam beat Golly bloody when he discovered I was untied. Before we traveled the first time, he finally let me heal him.

"After we tried to escape the first time, Sam dragged me into the nearest village and presented 'proof' that I had attempted to steal from him." She gave a shudder. "He proved his power, they were anxious to hang someone, but he put on a show, pled for leniency, promising he would keep me confined and allow me to work off the debt as Golly's target girl. Since Golly was known for his poor aim, they thought that was funny."

She paused to wipe away her tears and collect herself. "He used mind manipulation on them, an entire crowd of people all at once. I was terrified and didn't know what to do. Golly did his best not to hit me with his knives and hatchets, but Sam insisted that the audience wanted to see some gore. He would beat Golly badly if he didn't hit my chest or stomach at least once. After a few times, I quit worrying about doing a complete healing on myself. What did it matter anyway?" She couldn't look at him and took some deep breaths.

"We tried again to run, but the others caught us. After that, Sam was more careful and changed my act so I had to heal several people from the audience as well as myself, leaving me tired and drained. When he was angry, he would torment me and Golly, forcing me to do even more healing."

She took the cloth he handed her and blew her nose with a trembling hand. "I tried not to heal myself, but it wouldn't work. My own body and talent wouldn't let me die. I knew that was cowardly, but you have only to look at Golly to know the extent of Sam's cruelty. We did our best to escape."

"You aren't going to get an argument from me. I am merely grateful you survived." Hess took her hand.

"We tried to escape again, using a drug to knock Sam out, but that Farmer caught us. The punishments were worse after that and Golly was running out of time. We tried to keep Sam happy, maybe lull him into a false sense of security. Golly told me to leave him behind so many times, but I couldn't, not after everything he had done to help me."

Hess nodded and held on to her hand, hoping the contact would be comforting.

"After I started really scarring, Sam seemed to lose interest in using my body to satisfy his needs."

"The scars protected you," Hess muttered.

"In a way they were my only defense, but now I'm stuck with them unless the cream Griss gave me and my own healing energy can make them fade. There is one other way, but it would take more energy."

"What is that?" Hess asked, still fighting off images of her abuse.

"I could cut out each scar and start over."

Hess was so stunned, he didn't think he had heard her correctly. "No," he stated, leaning forward so their eyes met. "That is not an option we're going to consider."

"It would be messy," she admitted.

He managed to stop himself from reacting. "If you can fix damaged flesh and scars, why haven't you fixed Golly's nose?"

"I don't see the point in causing him that kind of pain. Sam did the damage before I was there and tried to get it to heal so he would look grotesque. His plan didn't work, but in order to rebuild it, I would have to rebreak it and cut it open to force the healing. Why would I hurt him like that?"

"Exactly, the same is true of your scars. Let's try the cream and some focused healing. It's not worth the pain of cutting them out."

"You haven't seen how disfiguring they are," she said, looking away.

"There is an easy solution to that. You can show me the scars, let me put on the cream, and we can discuss this healing in more depth. Let me remind you that we are mates, not merely matched or lovers, or even just friends with passion between us. As mates there is no part of you that is private any more than a part of me would be to you."

"I don't want you to be disgusted by me, Hess."

His teeth clenched and he had to force himself not to squeeze her hand to the point of pain. "There is nothing about you that I could ever find disgusting. I can't promise not to react to the sight of what Sam did to your body, because I probably will. That doesn't mean I find your scars or body repulsive, it means I want to kill Sam all over again."

"You're not going to blame Golly?" she asked with a tremble in her voice.

"No, he would no more deliberately hurt you than you would deliberately hurt him. Sam is to blame and he's dead. Show me and let me get over the first shock so we can talk about this rationally."

Making a face, she stood and took off her tunic. He

had seen these a few days ago, so they weren't a surprise.

"These are not the worst ones," she warned.

"These are bad enough," he answered, staring at what must be at least a hundred scars that covered her arms, shoulders, and the part of her chest her underwear didn't conceal. Many of the marks were raised and puckered while others looked more like faded lines etched into her skin. She turned and moved her hair out of the way, revealing the claw marks Ron had left. She slid the material down farther, displaying a number of scar lines crisscrossing her back.

"He used a whip?"

"Sometimes," she answered with a shiver. "I have some lower down, but the ones on my back are the worst."

"Don't do this in stages, LeeAnn. It's too hard for both of us. Just take off all of your clothes and let me see."

When she did, he bit his lip, clenched his fist, and took a deep breath, his nostrils flaring. The hatchet scars were the worst, cutting into her breast and one into her belly. There were more on her legs and one impressive one on her side. The rest were from knife wounds, leaving smaller finer scars. He motioned her forward to look more closely.

"I told you they were bad."

His eyes met hers. "Where is the cream Griss gave you?"

"I put it in the washing room."

"Go and get it. It's a wonder you lived through all of that."

"That's all you have to say?" Her tone was harsh, as if she were challenging him to reject her.

He slowly leaned back in his chair. "You're an amazing healer even when you're exhausted and overworked. I don't know anyone else who could have survived this type of torture. Go and get the cream so we can get started."

She padded slowly away and he let out a shaky breath. He had felt her exploring his emotional reaction and he'd been afraid to move, to shift his focus. He knew she didn't understand that new connection, but he did. If he'd been disgusted or shocked, she would have felt his reaction and it might have driven a wedge between them. Fortunately he had not felt that way.

"It's a good thing you can't kill someone twice," she said as she returned with the cream.

"You would deprive me of the satisfaction?"

"Rok did an excellent job. He even made it look easy, exploding his head like an overripe melon. I'd never seen anything like it."

"Flesh tends to burst when you blast it with hard power. Let me start on your back. Hold your hair out of the way." He opened the jar and began to apply the cream. "I would have killed him slowly."

"No, this was better; very final, and over so quickly that I never felt compelled to heal him. It's hard being a healer when you have to repair the damage you cause."

"I bet you didn't even leave him any scars," Hess muttered.

LeeAnn shifted as he used the cream across her butt. "Shouldn't we just put the cream on the scars?"

"No, this is easier and more efficient. I'm sure Griss can make us more." He worked it all down her legs. It quickly soaked into the skin and he asked her to turn. "How much energy is it going to take to heal with the cream?"

"I don't know. I've never even heard of a cream like this."

"It's similar to what they used on Dotty. She had open blast marks and scars on her face, another gift from her sister. That stuff worked miracles. You'd never know, looking at her today." Hess shared the image.

"Her sister blasted her face?" LeeAnn gasped.

"Yes, leaving her vulnerable to infection and all manner of other complications." He was done with her shoulders and arms, but hesitated before applying the cream to her chest. "Are any of these still sensitive? I don't want to hurt you."

"No, not at all. The cream feels good, sort of tingling on my skin."

"I like the way it smells all fresh and new. It absorbs almost instantly into your skin. It sat more on the surface with Dotty."

"Maybe it's a completely different cream."

"I'll have to ask Griss. How often did he say we should apply this?"

LeeAnn thought for a moment, then shrugged. A second later, she gasped as he started on her belly. He put one large, warm hand her back and their eyes met. "Did I hurt you?"

"No, I was thinking and you startled me. I don't think he said how often, Griss that is, about the cream. That was a crazy time."

He managed not to smile as he continued applying it. "I can ask him that too. Tomorrow first thing, you'll probably want to check on Hanna, but is there anything else on your list of things to do?"

"I should check in with Trissy before we get too busy. Then I would prefer to see Golly if that's not a problem."

"Golly is never a problem. If he doesn't come down the hill, we can go up to the nest. Then after we pick up groceries for us and whatever Hanna and Trissy want, we should make the rounds of the market grounds and make sure every booth is restocked and staffed, including the healing corner." He put the lid back on the jar and handed it to her. "Go put on that sleeping gown. It's hard not to notice that my mate is standing here naked."

"You really don't think the marks are disgusting?"

"No, I really don't. Before I prove that and push us both too far, go put some clothes on."

She snatched up the clothes she'd taken off and moved from the room as he rubbed what was left of the cream into his hands. His mate was warm and soft and the scars didn't dim his desire. He dumped out their cold tea and brewed some fresh.

"I think that cream is already working." LeeAnn sounded puzzled and he turned to look at her. She was dressed in the too-long gown and let out a sigh.

"What do you mean?"

She bared her shoulder and showed him. The scars were already less visible, and he smiled. "Isn't that amazing?"

"I need to know what's in that cream."

Snorting, he poured her some fresh tea. "He's not going to give you the ingredients."

She took the teacup and sat at the table. "Maybe not, but it's still worth asking. This stuff is miraculous."

"I'm glad it's working." He poured some tea for himself. "Especially because I am not in favor of your other option. In fact, you might say I am violently opposed to it."

LeeAnn shrugged and glanced out the window. "I wasn't looking forward to it, either. Truthfully, I thought you would agree with the idea after you saw how bad they are."

"No, I would rather us both live with them." His brows went up as he spoke, and she grinned.

"You really mean that."

"I do, and I can tell how much that surprises you. Our bond is expanding and we're starting to share emotions. That should make things easier, although I should warn you that I do have some violent feelings."

"Really? About what?"

"Any number of things, most recently about what Sam did to you and Golly."

She gave a slight shiver and looked at the table. "I should never have gone with Sam in the first place."

"No, you're a healer and I understand why you felt the need to go. Don't take on any of his blame. From now on, anyone requesting your help has to go through Grabon or me, and one of us will always be close. It's not our way to leave our women vulnerable."

"Are you going to be overprotective?"

Grinning, he sipped his tea. "I'll let you be the judge of that. Drink your tea so we can get some sleep."

Chapter 9

Gordon held the baby, trying to calm him. "You better hand him to me," Hanna said.

She took the precious bundle in her arms and managed to hold him just right so he could nurse. "You're getting to be an expert at that," Gordon commented, sitting beside her on the bed.

"I think I'm going to get plenty of practice." She stuck her finger in her ear. "He can sure make a lot of noise."

"He wanted his mama and his milk. He's entitled to complain when something isn't right. Are you going to tell me my son's name?"

"Can I get up in the morning and make breakfast?" Hanna countered with a smile.

"No, but I'll let you walk slowly into the kitchen and sit in a chair."

"Then you can wait to call your son by his name."

Gordon laughed and kissed her soundly before stroking his son's head. "I think we can both be patient for his mother's sake. You be as stubborn as you want, Hanna, just as long as you heal fast, recover quickly, and don't put me through something like that again anytime soon."

She touched the side of his face. "I am sorry it was so hard on you."

"It's only fair. We both had the pleasure of making him, so we might as well both suffer through the birth. I am just grateful LeeAnn was here to help."

Hanna nodded and touched the baby's face. "Did you find out why she fears Farmers?"

"Benny caught her and Golly escaping, and instead of helping, he returned them to Sam." His expression was so grim that Hanna stroked his jaw.

"The circumstances must have been very bad for her and Golly."

Gordon sighed and kissed her palm. "It was, though I don't know many details. Sweetheart, Golly isn't going to last very long."

"I know; he's too big for his heart. Grabon is pretty sad about it."

"Ahhh, I wish you had told me that you knew." He stroked her hair back away from her face as she watched the baby nurse.

"I picked up on it as they were leaving and I was hoping I was wrong. Poor LeeAnn, that's such a burden on a healer and a friend."

"We'll all help her. It's the least we can do." He wiped a tear from her cheek. "Do you want me to fix you anything?"

"No, just sit with us. When we put him down in the cradle, you can hold me."

"I'd love to."

***

Grabon watched Golly get cleaned up for bed. The youth rubbed his chest again, and Grabon had to stop himself from asking if something hurt. Years ago, he and Heron had met a young dragon who was almost twice the size he should have been. They traveled with him until he no longer had the strength to fly. Three days later, he had passed in his sleep. It was the first grief he and Heron had shared. From the vantage point of maturity, he finally understood Heron's blind outrage at whoever had allowed the young dragon to wander alone. No youngster of his who was sick would stray far from home.

"Grabon?" Golly asked softly from his pallet.

"Yes?"

"Are you going to let Tria and Kev go to the market tomorrow?"

Grabon gave a soft sigh. *"Kev has to help Brom tomorrow, and Tria has to stay on this side of the river until the next day. Maybe Fin, Jenny, and Matti will go with us to the market. Would that be all right?"*

"Can't we take Star and Red too?" Golly asked. "Then you could make Tria help us with the little ones. That would be a kind of punishment."

"Did she ask you to speak to me?"

"No, but it will be more fun if she goes too. Otherwise, she'll be here all alone. Being alone can be scary."

"I will think about it. Now go to sleep or you will be too tired to attend the market and have fun."

Golly stretched, yawned, and then grew still. Tria stirred on the wall and Grabon asked her if she was all right. Her mental voice was choked with emotion when she asked if Golly was sick. In soft rumbling Dragon, Grabon explained Golly's condition and the inevitable result. Every dragon's head on the wall bowed low and Tria flew down to stand next to Grabon. He extended one large wing over her head in a gesture of comfort.

"Why would someone mutilate him if he was already sick?"

Grabon looked up at the visiting dragons, and Rok and Thane joined them. *"Dragons and humans have the same capacity to be cruel. Golly's tormentor enjoyed what he did to Golly partially because Golly was so large."*

"Dragons are never that cruel," Tria responded with confidence.

Thane ruffled his wings. *"As a young wanderer I saw a dragon deliberately drop a youngster off a cliff."*

Tria stared at him in disbelief.

Rok glanced down toward the farm. *"Ron, a visitor Grabon banished before you arrived, snatched LeeAnn in a back claw, then flew across several territories and dropped her into this nest. She still has the scars. She only survived because she is a healer of extraordinary talent."*

"But she is human…." Tria glanced at the others in the nest.

"I have seen cruel territory dragons," Nat offered from the wall. *"They have denied visitors the right to hunt in their territory, then called their place forfeit on the nest edge if they left to hunt. It is starve while you wait, or seek assistance elsewhere."*

"I have seen dragons intent on earning a reputation for fighting who would attack any other dragon in the sky," Dane offered from the edge.

"Dragons can be cruel, and a sick, twisted dragon is as dangerous as a sick, twisted human," Grabon explained.

"I have not yet met a cruel dragon," Tria told them.

"You should consider staying in Grabon's territory because he will protect you. If you go awandering for long you will see cruelty among dragons in many different forms," Dane warned her.

"Would you consider staying?" Tria asked boldly.

"I am considering it if Grabon offers me a place, as are many of the others. You are not yet old enough to understand, but this is a unique territory with a

distinctive leader. Residing here would be an honor for any dragon."

Grabon bowed his head in acknowledgment of the praise.

Rok ruffled his wings. *"Beware, if you truly intend to join the Dragonmen, Grabon will set you a task and give you only one cycle to complete it."*

"A task?" Dane asked, tilting his head in curiosity.

"I set a task for each of you. I might not do the same with the next applicant," Grabon warned Rok. *"First I must consider if an applicant can work well with the rest of my people and give him or her a chance to prove their worth. Then I might consider setting a task for them."*

"I have worked with Rok before," Dane informed Grabon.

"I have worked with Brom and Griss," Nat mentioned.

"My people includes the humans: male, female, and youngsters. If you cannot work and play with them, you would forever be an outsider. We are a social clan, gather often, and help one another with a variety of tasks," Thane explained.

"I do not speak Human," Dane complained, frowning.

"Kev can teach you," Rok informed him. *"To live here you have to be fluent. Many of the humans are*

learning Dragon. Are you less intelligent than the humans in our clan or simply less willing to cooperate?"

"I am neither. I was simply stating a fact. Do not attempt to twist my words," Dane snapped.

"I can learn Human," Nat stated. *"I have already picked up a few words."*

"Good, if you are serious and interested, you may accompany me tomorrow as we take all the youngsters to the market. We will see how social you can be." Grabon smiled and settled back on his tail, extending his hands to the fire. *"Golly asked if I will permit you to attend the market tomorrow with him."* He looked at Tria. *"Have you learned how to behave?"*

"I would be honored to go with Golly," Tria answered, avoiding Grabon's question.

He was amused, but then grew serious. *"You must be cautious. Golly is unaware of what his condition is doing to him. Because of the damage to his head, he is not an advanced thinker. There is no reason to scare him."*

"I can be cautious, Grabon. It would be a cruelty to hurt Golly."

"Yes, it would. It is his task to enjoy what time he has left and explore a little of this world. I am inclined to let him try anything that is not dangerous or harmful. You may help me steer him toward fun that will not be too much for him."

"I can do this." Tria nodded and shifted her feet.

"Good, then I suggest you sleep. You may stay in the nest if you do not cause a problem."

Tria glanced up at the wall and tossed her head slightly as if pleased by the invitation. After a few moments of looking around, she found a good spot perched beside the sleeping Golly and settled down to sleep.

Thane chuckled softly as Grabon signaled to Nat and Dane to join them. *"Do you choose to accompany me with all the youngsters tomorrow?"* Grabon asked.

"I am willing, but I know nothing of human youngsters other than what I have observed," Nat confessed.

"They are fragile, even more so than dragon youngsters and just as adventurous and dangerous to themselves," Rok informed him.

"I think I am up to the challenge," Dane told Grabon with confidence.

"Then I will be sure to introduce you to my people tomorrow. We will see how you perform."

***

Dotty and Tad sang a duet at the end of the day, something she had been working on for days. It was a song about the mysteries of life and the wonders of the unknown. Soft drums, which beat like a heart, accompanied the haunting melody. Many of the

Dragonmen found themselves fighting tears as they listened. It was a tribute and welcoming to the new child. He was a treasure that was still unknown, but they would see him grow to manhood and become something wondrous.

***

First thing in the morning, Hess left LeeAnn to her bath as he went to help Gordon with morning chores. He returned faster than he had expected because Tad had decided to help as well. When he walked by the washing room, LeeAnn showed him the healing scars in disbelief.

"That is excellent. I'll put on a fresh coat for you now and we can do another tonight before bed." As he put on the cream, he tried desperately to think of something besides his mate's body. As soon as he was done, she dressed, giving him a slight frown.

"I am trying hard not to be sexual, so why are you frowning at me?"

"Perhaps you are trying a little too hard. I cannot tell if you will find me attractive when the scars heal."

Hess rattled his head and let out a frustrated growl. "Woman, it takes every ounce of my willpower not to stroke your skin with pleasure and you are not sure if I find you attractive?"

"All I can feel from you is controlled frustration. It's not like you have said anything."

"I did not want to scare you. Of course I find you

attractive, more attractive and desirable than any woman I have ever seen. You are my mate. You find me attractive, don't you?"

She glared at him. "I'm not dead, Hess. Any woman would find you attractive."

He grinned and stroked her hair. "No, you are not dead, but I appreciate your viewpoint. We are so attractive to one another because we are mates. Now go make some tea so I can bathe and get ready for the day."

When he stepped out of the washing room, he realized she had done much more than make the tea.

"You cooked?"

"I thought having something here might be nice before we check on Trissy and then Hanna. They are probably better cooks…."

"No, this is perfect. Let's eat."

They dug into the food, had a second cup of tea, and quickly washed up before they left.

Trissy was feeling good and was up and about and grinning. "Heron is out in the barn. The girls are going to the market with Grabon, Golly, Tria, and two of the visitors, Dane and Nat. Both are interested in staying, or at least considering the possibility. Wouldn't that be nice? I told Heron we needed more dragons and he simply laughed."

"I don't think we need to worry about that," Hess

muttered.

"Why not?" LeeAnn asked.

"As word spreads we are going to have plenty of dragons coming to visit. Many of them will be applying for clan status and many, I am sure, Grabon will decline."

Trissy nodded and rubbed her belly. "I suppose he can afford to be choosy."

"He can, just as he and Heron are choosy about which humans are accepted. Dozens of people have applied and Grabon has only accepted LeeAnn and Golly."

"I... I didn't know that," LeeAnn stammered.

"Heron and Grabon know what they are looking for." Hess touched LeeAnn's arm. "I'll go out and greet Heron and give you a few minutes alone with Trissy."

***

As soon as he left, Trissy grabbed her hand. "I am so glad Hanna had an easy delivery. Can you tell if mine is going to be difficult?"

LeeAnn squeezed her hand. "It is almost impossible to predict. As soon as you feel a contraction call for me and I will do everything I can to help you through it as fast and smoothly as possible."

"You don't have to worry about that; you will hear Heron."

LeeAnn grinned. "I would, except I don't have much range. I really don't get anything unless I am face-to-face with someone."

Trissy shook her head. "You will hear Heron. He is a mind-to-mind communicator. He connects to each mind separately over long distances. I have no doubt he will make himself heard."

"Well if that doesn't work he can contact Hess. It seems my mate is not intending to be far from my side."

"That is normal, so do not fight it. Once the bond is more secure, he might be gone for short periods."

LeeAnn grimaced. "I think he is worried about leaving me alone at the market."

Laughing, Trissy patted her arm. "I don't think that was supposed to happen the first time. You will get used to them. They are all protective, arrogant, and overbearing, but you will come to appreciate it. When that doesn't work, stand up and yell. It may not change their minds, but you will feel better."

LeeAnn laughed, then did a quick examination of Trissy and the baby, being sure to sync her energy with Trissy's. "He looks very healthy."

Trissy stared at her, stunned. "It's a boy?"

LeeAnn nodded and grinned. "You already have two girls, although not from your body."

"Jenny is my sister by my father's second wife. Matti

we adopted from a Farmer and his wife. She was in a difficult situation in her first family. Living here is much healthier for her and she is settling in very well."

"You and Heron are amazingly generous. I know many children who would benefit from two such skilled parents."

"That is a very kind compliment. We believe love and acceptance make a family, not blood alone. Take you and Golly: he is very much yours. Even now that he is staying with Grabon and exploring his independence, you can tell it whenever he speaks your name."

"I'm going to see him next and then Hanna and the baby."

"The last time I checked, he was in the barn with Heron and the girls. We'll join them. Just let me pack this sack for you to take to Hanna. I thought having some cookies might please her, and I made a few other things."

"When did you find the time?" LeeAnn asked, impressed.

"I was awake for part of the night and decided to bake. Heron is always helpful at times like that. He doesn't complain, which always surprises me."

"He loves you dearly and must know that this final stage of pregnancy is very uncomfortable for the mother."

"Not only does he know, he shares it with me. There

is great comfort in that."

LeeAnn glanced at the door. "We have not yet shared sensations, but some emotions are coming through."

"Just wait, it only gets better. Trust in the bond and your mate. Hess is a good man, and he will make an excellent mate with a little practice."

"I think so too. Although I seem to need him a great deal more than he needs me."

Trissy shook her head. "No, I think you are mistaken about that. Wait until your emotions are more connected. Hess had a difficult time when Tad found Dotty. They have always been connected and done everything together. When he was excluded from their bond, he was lonely and somewhat adrift. Trust me when I tell you that he needs you, his mate, in order for him to stay connected to everything and everyone else."

"I had not considered that."

"Let's go out to the barn. I want to see Golly's reaction to his bed."

"Is it finished?"

"Almost. Heron was up early stuffing the mattress so Golly could see how it would work."

Hess, Heron, and Grabon were comparing comments Golly had made about sleeping on wood and laughing as LeeAnn and Trissy walked into the barn.

"LeeAnn, look! It's my bed! Heron made a skin mattress stuffed with fresh bedstraw, and other herbs so it smells nice. I even fit on it."

"That's wonderful. It must be the longest bed in the whole territory."

"It must be. Did you know that Grabon is taller than I am? Isn't that amazing? He stretched his neck to show me."

Grinning, she patted his arm. "How are you feeling this morning? Do you need me to fix anything?"

"No, everything is working; no infections and I am peeing fine. I had an itch on my back but I scratched it on Grabon's wall. Did I tell you Tria gets to come with us to the market? That will be fun."

"I am sure it will, but don't get into trouble and get sent back to the nest. You better listen to Grabon."

"I listen good! Grabon, don't I always listen to you?"

"You have been very well behaved," Grabon answered, grinning.

"See, I told you I could be good. Did I tell you about Dane and Nat? They are visiting dragons who might want to stay. We get to introduce them to everyone today. Rok is making porridge, and then we'll go visiting before the market opens. What are you going to be doing?"

"Hess and I are going to check on Hanna and then

help get the market ready. We have some shopping to do. Is there anything you need?"

He looked over at Grabon, then bent down to whisper, "Can you get me one of those really soft blankets? I saw a red-and-blue one."

"I'll see if I can find it along with some other surprises. Are you sure nothing hurts?"

"No hurting, not today. I like it here a lot. All the people are so nice and we can go to the market. I can see the garden almost every day and touch the statues and even walk in the fountain. This is a very special place. I am glad Rok rescued us and Hess drove the wagon and we came here."

"So am I, Golly, so am I. Give me a hug, and then you better go."

He hugged LeeAnn, almost lifting her from the ground. Then he let her go and went with Grabon back up the hill.

"How are you going to get that bed up the hill to the nest?" LeeAnn asked Heron.

He laughed and nodded toward the barn door. Thane and Rok stuck their heads inside. "He's gone with Grabon. Come and get it. It's ready; all it needs is bedding."

"I'll get that for him while we're shopping. Is there anything you need?" LeeAnn asked.

Heron and Trissy talked about it, but agreed that

they had enough for now. She and Hess were all the way down in Gordon's yard when Heron spoke in her head. *"The only person I have difficulty connecting with is Hanna because she has no mindspeak ability at all. She is only an emotional communicator."*

"That is amazing, and you can hear me?"

"I can hear you very clearly. If anyone needs your help, they have only to contact Hess or me and we can make sure you get where you need to be. Your inability to communicate over distance will not be a problem; we will ensure that."

LeeAnn sighed and Hess put his arm around her shoulders. "I didn't know you were even worried about that."

"I can't do anything to change it, but I was afraid people would think I was less competent than everyone else."

"Nobody is ever going to think that. Come on, let's visit with Hanna and Gordon."

***

Gordon grimaced as he let them in. "Good, you can convince her that she *just had a baby and she should rest*," he called back into the house.

LeeAnn grinned and Hess chuckled as they followed Gordon inside.

"How are you and the baby?" LeeAnn asked Hanna after following Gordon all the way into the bedroom.

"We are fine. It seems ridiculous to stay in bed when I am not feeling weak or sick," she complained.

"That is good. Let me check your son first, and then I'll see how much healing you have done."

Hanna handed her the baby with a sigh and watched closely as LeeAnn examined him.

"He looks good to me," Gordon told her.

"He needs sunlight, just a bit, and to lie on the ground." She glanced up at Gordon. "Your son is trying to connect to the ground already."

Gordon grinned and touched Hanna's shoulder. "He's far too young."

"He can't do it, but he's trying. Find a good spot for him and Hanna outside. They'll both be happier, which in turn will relieve your worry."

After handing the baby to Gordon, LeeAnn examined Hanna and was amazed at how much she had healed. "You recover very quickly," LeeAnn told her.

"All mates heal quickly when they are together. Is it safe for her to be up and about?" Gordon asked, frowning.

"Yes, but she should rest when she grows tired. Some women find nursing exhausting."

"I am not overtired. Do not put ideas in his head," Hanna protested.

LeeAnn checked her balance, which could be off after birth, as well as the temperature of her feet. "If the feet are different temperatures, it can indicate a circulation problem, but you do seem to be doing well," LeeAnn murmured.

"Excellent." Hanna beamed at her.

"Trissy sent a sack full of things for you. If you have any problems or questions don't hesitate to send for me."

"We won't. I am so glad you were here to reassure him," Hanna said, clutching her hands. "If you hadn't been here he would have kept me in bed for a week, and I was sure that was unnecessary."

"I am not risking my mate because she does not like to sit still," Gordon told her with a scowl.

Hess cleared his throat. "We are not getting into the middle of your argument. If you have no questions for LeeAnn, we should get over to the market. We have a number of things to do."

"One of them is shopping," LeeAnn told Hanna. "Do you need anything?"

Hanna gave her a quick list, mostly things for the baby and a few things for Gordon, which she whispered to LeeAnn. After promising to get everything, they managed to escape across the river. They were laughing over Gordon's fierce glare, when they heard Dotty start singing. They waited until she was done, then found her in the private garden.

"That was beautiful, but I am surprised Tad left you here alone," Hess told her.

"We planned that I would meet with both of you and walk in with you and LeeAnn. I must have lost track of time."

"You are welcome to join us." LeeAnn grinned.

"Good, I have some shopping we need done."

***

Dotty brought out a wooden handcart and they walked through the tall grass, following the path into the market grounds and moved directly to the food stalls. That part of the market opened early at the vendors' insistence. Hess didn't think that would last long since few shoppers were here first thing in the morning. Unlike at other markets, their crowd came closer to lunch where they could enjoy a cup of tea or even a meal. Vendors called out greetings, and the women visited and shopped while Hess checked that everything was running smoothly.

He was moving several baskets of vegetables for one of the vendors when he felt a disturbance. He turned slowly and saw a man watching Dotty and LeeAnn. Without hesitation, Hess walked up to him, noting that he radiated power.

"Can I help you?" Hess asked, blocking the man's view of them.

"Actually I am hoping you can. My name is Porter and I heard about this Dragon Market from some

Farmers. Are you one of the Dragonmen?"

"Yes, and the women you were staring at are ours."

"I wasn't staring with disrespect, I was examining their garb. It's unusual and I was curious. Anyway, I was hoping to learn more about this new clan."

"What is your reason for wanting this information?" Hess asked cautiously.

Porter looked around, shifting as if with some internal discomfort. "I am a news carrier for the five original colonies. Generally I do not announce that, but I was warned the Dragonmen would be more receptive if I simply stated my intentions."

"That was good advice since we have a number of people who would simply pluck the truth from your mind. At the moment, we are setting up the market, but you are welcome to observe and ask questions. Did you find the statue outside the main gate?"

"I did. It is an incredible piece of art. That alone sparked my interest about your unusual clan. What artisan did you commission? I did not recognize the work."

Hess grinned. "I am pleased you appreciated it; then you already know the rules. Come, I'll introduce you to Dotty and LeeAnn."

After introductions, Hess finished moving the vegetables, allowing Porter to help. They moved to a different area and one of the fruit vendors caught LeeAnn and Dotty's interest. As they stepped away,

Thane flew in and Hess introduced Porter.

"It is always good to meet someone interested in what we are doing," Thane told him with a nod.

Porter smiled even as he looked around. "This part is not so very different from other markets."

Thane snorted, then wiped some spit from the man's shirt. *"A dragon expression of disagreement. Some humans find it offensive, so I should apologize. However, even this part is very different; look at how large the booths are and how distant they are from one another. In addition, they sell a larger variety of goods."*

"I did notice some different foods. I assumed they were common to this area."

"They grow here, but have not always been looked at as food. Many are gathered and provided for the market, some are from gardens, still others are grown as crops. You have only to ask a vendor for a recipe and preparation instructions."

"So they don't merely sell them?"

"No, this market is an opportunity to learn as well as to buy and experience things people have never seen before."

"Thane?" Dotty called, standing a small distance away. When the dark green dragon turned to her, she motioned him over. "I know Trissy cooks these scold fruits. Do you know if Tad enjoys them?"

Thane grinned. *"Hanna cooks them as well, and yes, they are greatly enjoyed."*

"Who is Tad?" Porter asked Thane as he approached.

"He is mate to Dotty, just as Hess is mate to LeeAnn. We have many couples among our people."

Hess took the handcart from Dotty with a few murmured words. "Colony Boy thinks the market is not so different from other markets." While his words made both women laugh, they continued on their way. They finally found the booth both LeeAnn and Dotty wanted, and Hess motioned them forward. They quickly collected what they needed and paid the vendor. When they finished with their final two stops a little later, Thane took the cart, promising to leave it at Dotty's and flew off with it in his back claws.

"He is making the delivery?" Porter asked, sounding baffled.

"We have other things to do and he is saving us time. Flying is much faster than walking," Hess explained.

The news carrier nodded and proceeded to watch what they did with great curiosity. The man did not seem inclined to make trouble, so even though Hess watched him closely, he was not worried.

They met with vendors, then checked on the sisters, who greeted Porter with friendly smiles but a reserved manner.

When Griss and Brom flew in from dropping off their youngsters, LeeAnn pulled Griss aside while Hess introduced Brom to Porter.

"You say you are here to learn about the Dragonmen?" Brom asked, keeping his neck extended rather than relaxing.

Porter looked startled by the question, and Hess's brows lifted in amusement. "That is what I am here for."

"Then I will take you to meet Heron." Brom's manner was not discourteous, merely direct.

"I am happy to meet all of the Dragonmen," Porter told them, looking faintly worried.

"Good, then we will see you when the market is open," Hess told him. "LeeAnn picked up groceries for Hanna and Trissy this morning, Brom. Thane took them back to Tad and Dotty's. Would it be convenient for you to deliver them?"

"I am pleased to do that." Brom grinned, leading Porter away.

Hess watched with satisfaction as they left. He was interested in seeing what Heron and then Grabon thought of this *news carrier*. Either he was going to be joining them, or he was here to cause trouble. Porter had far too much power to be a simple news carrier, and if he spent much time in the first five colonies, he was not well accepted. Hess knew well how nervous people were around those who carried so much power.

LeeAnn came to stand beside him with an irritated huff. "You were correct; he will not tell me the ingredients. However, he is especially pleased with how well the cream is working with my own healing energy. What did you do with Porter?" she asked, looking around.

"I sent him off with Brom to meet with Heron."

LeeAnn's eyes widened. "Really? Why Heron?"

"Because Heron can determine why a man of such power would be a news carrier for the five original colonies. It is far more likely he is looking for a place where he can fit in."

"What if Heron decides he would make a good addition?"

"Then he will meet with Grabon and be invited to join us. We will see what they decide. If you are done with Griss for the moment, we need to meet with Tad and Pit over at the greenhouse. We are hiding the statue in a new location."

"I never even found the third statue," LeeAnn complained.

Hess grinned and took her hand. "We hid that one a little better. I imagine it will be discovered today or tomorrow."

As it was, she didn't get to see where they moved it to. She and Mia watched from the entrance as lookouts to keep other vendors from being nosy as Pit,

Tad, and Hess changed its location. When they returned, they went to help Mable and Bert set up their new booths.

LeeAnn was pleased to see several handmade goods, many of which looked familiar from her own childhood. "Why didn't they sell these in the second colony? Why cart them all the way out here? These are wonderful pieces," She asked as she and Hess carried crates from the wagon as the older couple uncrated the pottery.

Hess jerked his head toward Mable and Bert. "I think they wanted the adventure; selling goods was the excuse. I imagine we'll get more of the story as time goes by."

"Do you think they would let me pick out a few pieces and set them aside? Just look at that teapot and those matching mugs. Hanna would love that tray, and Trissy could use a big mixing bowl."

"I am sure they can help you out. I'll handle the crates while you speak to them."

Hess watched as LeeAnn walked over to Mable, who stopped uncrating pottery and porcelain to talk with her. Her grin spoke for itself and he carried over another two crates.

"I really appreciate the help, Hess. It seems your courtship is going well." Bert darted a glance at LeeAnn and his match, who were speaking animatedly.

"Are you familiar with a mating bond?" Hess asked, setting a crate on the wooden bench.

Bert quickly looked up and smiled. "Ah, you are one of those Farmers. I have heard stories."

"Now a Dragonmen, but yes, so is my brother, Tad, and cousin, Gordon. LeeAnn is my mate. It seems all the Dragonmen have the ability to initiate such a bond, as do the dragons."

"All dragons?" Bert asked.

"All that find their mate. They make a great search of it between sexual maturity and mental maturity. According to what they have told me, most still do not find the female that matches them perfectly until after they have passed full maturity."

Bert shook his head and looked back at LeeAnn. "Then I suppose courtship is not needed after all."

Hess grinned at him. "Oh, we still court our women; we just do a much better job of it after the bond is started. It can take a long time to establish." He went off to get some more crates, leaving Bert to continue unpacking.

When Hess had unloaded all the crates, Mable came over to add her thanks to her husband's. "This has been a great help. LeeAnn asked me to set aside a few things. Is that all right?"

"Absolutely, she can purchase whatever she likes. We are just starting to furnish our home and I know she is fond of your merchandise."

"That is because it all looks familiar and I recognize the markings of the Craftsmen. I grew up in the second colony," LeeAnn explained, holding up a large bowl. "We can add this to my pile."

"Tad mentioned that your parents are healers. We have never heard of them. What part of the colony are you from?" Mable asked.

LeeAnn smiled and patted her shoulder. "The east end near the river. My parents have a clinic, just beyond the boundary. Many of their clients are fishermen and their families."

"So they are not within the walls of the original second colony? Most of our clients have their family's original home."

"Of course." LeeAnn grinned, knowing that in those colonies having the original home was a point of pride. "Your shop, kiln, and pottery are well established. My mother owned a piece and so did one of our neighbors."

Mable glanced nervously at Hess. "I suppose you would like an explanation?"

"Do I need to know why two well-established Craftsmen have come to my market out on the frontier? No. You are more than welcome to sell your excellent wares. There is even a group of people able to afford them."

Bert let out a heavy sigh and glanced at his match. "We might as well explain now; later it will only be more difficult. When we heard about your new clan and your plan to open a market, we strongly encouraged our family to send someone to represent our pottery. In case you didn't notice, we're on the old side for such an adventure. Objections arose among the senior set because any of the younger men or women we sent might well find frontier life too appealing. After dozens of discussions Mable and I volunteered to make this first trip and pave the way.

"We were astounded by what we saw yesterday. This place has an established feel for something so new. It would indeed be appealing to many of our younger family members. Bert and I don't believe in keeping them close and losing opportunities, but some of the others are far more conservative. When we return we'll select someone to take our place who we think will not only do well, but thrive here," Mable explained.

"I thought you two were runaways." Hess raised his brows and grinned.

Bert laughed heartily. "No." He glanced at Mable and they both flushed slightly. "It really wasn't like that, but when you have as many siblings as we do, it did feel somewhat like a mad escape plan."

"Are you going to be here for the full season?" LeeAnn asked.

"We are expected back in mid-fall at the latest," Bert answered with a shrug.

"You might let the younger generation cover the harsher seasons and simply make the trip once a year to supervise," Hess suggested.

"What a lovely idea," Mable answered. "All we really need to be comfortable is a decent place to stay. We're a bit stiff from sleeping on the ground. Do you happen to know of one?"

"We'll ask around and get back to you. Let me know how much we owe you for our purchases. We'll be by later to pay and pick them up. For now we better continue our rounds."

As they walked farther into the market, Hess took LeeAnn's hand. "What do you think about asking the sisters?"

"I am sure Jamie and Janie would be pleased. However, I don't know how Bert and Mable would react to them. Jamie and Janie make no secret of what they used to do for coins, and many people find that... off-putting."

"There's only one way to find out."

They headed to the sisters' booth and stopped to chat with a vendor who had some concerns about Grabon's announcement about hunting. They explained that his announcement had nothing to do with hunting game. As soon as he understood that humans had come into Grabon's territory hunting dragons, he seemed to understand. By the time they left, Rafet was feeling supportive of the territory dragon's rules.

Janie and Jamie were thrilled at the prospect of

helping the older couple and rushed off to make an offer of hospitality. Hess shook his head as he and LeeAnn went to check on LeeAnn's booth area. When they arrived, Brom had already started a fire and brought in water.

"Is something wrong, Brom? Do you need help?" LeeAnn asked, shooing Hess away.

Hess leaned against a tree and crossed his arms. He trusted Brom, but with the bond so new, leaving her alone did not feel like a good idea.

"I am concerned that Star is not eating enough. When she first came here, she ate good portions. I thought that meant she was happy and adjusting."

"Human children sometimes eat in fits and starts. The same is probably true of young dragons. Why don't you bring her to see me and we'll make sure she's healthy. How long has this been going on?"

"It started yesterday morning. I know she prefers cooked food, and I made her porridge with some berries. My daughter picked out the berries and refused to eat the porridge. She used to eat it every day."

"What did you fix this morning?"

"She ate pan biscuits with meat strips cooked on the fire and cut to fit the bread, but only two."

Hess cleared his throat and stepped away from the tree. "Did she know she was coming to the market with Grabon?"

"I told her before we ate," Brom admitted.

"Is it possible she's eating less at home when she knows she's going somewhere exciting where there will be good food?"

Brom wrinkled his nose and snorted, but fortunately, he turned his head away from them. *"She had me worried about her health!"*

"You should really consider that it's a good sign," Hess suggested, trying not to grin. "She's feeling secure enough to be a little naughty. I know you were concerned because she has been so very well behaved."

Brom used some words in Dragon that LeeAnn was certain she had never heard, and Hess was laughing. The gray-and-white dragon nodded to LeeAnn. *"I will find out more about this before I bring her to see you."*

"I am available whenever you need me," LeeAnn assured him.

Brom walked by Hess and punched his arm. *"Porter is talking with Heron in the barn. Porter said he was born a Woodsmen and travels between the colonies."*

"Interesting," Hess answered, grinning at LeeAnn. "It would be hilarious if he turns out to be a relative of Heron's."

"Why would that be funny?"

"Heron has completely lost touch with what was left of his line. Several of us have offered to help him reconnect and he has always refused. It would be funny if they found him anyway. Porter carries enough power to be related to our Heron."

"Power is only one measure of a male's character," Brom reminded him as he walked down the path back into the market.

"I hate it when he does that. He drops some profound piece of wisdom and walks away," Hess snarled in frustration.

"He is not as good at it as Grabon," LeeAnn remarked. "You should have seen it when he gave me coins. Trying to argue or disagree is not effective when he simply walks away."

"No, arguing does not work with Grabon, not if he is determined. Do you know why he gave you those coins?"

"Why?"

"You were brought here against your will. Before he banished Ron, he fined him. He thought it fitting that you should get the fine. Only he did not want to make you uncomfortable with too many coins to carry, so he only gave you a few. He has more, so be warned he is likely to hand you them or stuff them in your bag."

LeeAnn laughed and shook her head. "Then I will not feel guilty for asking for the teapot and matching mugs."

"You should not feel guilty about asking for anything. Do I need to remind you yet again that we are mates? What is mine is yours. I doubt we will lack for anything during our life together."

"Maybe not, but I need not be extravagant, either." She frowned. "My parents were not extravagant, but they lived very well compared to the others on the east end."

"I am sure we can send a message through Bert and Mable. Perhaps your parents would even consider a visit."

She shook her head. "No, I doubt they would want to visit, but a message might be welcome. I didn't live very far from them after I ran away and they never bothered to visit then. My relationship with them is difficult to define."

Hess nodded and gently touched her cheek with the backs of his fingers. "We can buy you a sheet of paper and you can send a written message if you think that would please them. One of the stalls has a supply."

"Paper? Holy hell, Hess. They would think I had riches coming out of my… well, leaking out of me. No, that almost invites them to ask me to send coins. I'll manage fine with a bead, like a normal person. I cannot imagine how they would react to a paper message." She grinned at the image and rubbed her hands together. "As long as we're here and Brom was kind enough to start my fire, would you like a cup of tea?"

"We can pause long enough for that. Then I am afraid we're back to making rounds."

She set up the kettle and found the two cups in her box, along with tea leaves. As she made the tea, she glanced at the cloudy, darkening sky. "I hope it doesn't rain."

He took the mug she handed him and smiled. "If it does, we'll make sure you don't get wet. We have shielding all over the market to keep our shoppers dry."

"You can do that for such a large area?"

"We can when we work together. It will be interesting to see people's reactions when the rain starts."

"It certainly amounts to a show of strength, doesn't it?"

He nodded and drank some of the tea. "Most of what our visitors see, if they pause long enough to think about it, is a show of strength, skill, and power. Not many heartsingers can project over so much distance. Few people have the power or connection to maintain a garden like ours, especially in winter. Our visitors need to know that Dragonmen have an abundance of power and skill. We want them to be impressed, to notice all the details that highlight our abilities and strength, and to absorb the notion that humans and dragons can work cooperatively and share many of the same interests."

"Let us hope that most people respect what they see and embrace it. You all make much better allies than enemies."

"*You* are definitely one of us, LeeAnn. Even before we started the bond, Grabon accepted you based on your own strength, talent, and skill."

"I still find that amazing," she murmured before finishing her tea. "What do we do next?"

***

They spent hours helping vendors set things up and arranging stock, clearing the way for wagons to get in and out of the market, and generally calming people's nerves over Grabon's announcement. LeeAnn soon realized that people were genuinely worried Grabon would blame all humans for those who had tried to hunt him. She found that notion ridiculous. Their territory dragon was far too intelligent to make that kind of mistake, but then most of these people in the market didn't know him.

They were headed to the front gate, for noon-high opening, when someone behind them cried out in pain. LeeAnn pivoted and ran with Hess beside her toward the sound. The woman on the ground cradling her arm, and the over-turned table were all the clues LeeAnn and Hess needed.

"She must have fallen off the table," someone said in a rush.

Her arm sat at an odd angle and tears streamed from her eyes as she rocked in pain on the ground.

LeeAnn crouched at her side and took the injured arm in her hands. "Clench your teeth. This is going to hurt." Using muscle and power, she put the bones back together and hit the break with energy to seal it in place. As soon as the bones was secure she synced her energy to the woman's and began the much slower process of mending the muscles, tendons, and ligaments that had been ripped and twisted. The delicate work of repairing circulation was last. It was precise, concentrated work, but the bones were knit solid when she released the arm. The woman let out a relieved sigh and collapsed against LeeAnn.

"Thank you, oh thank you. It stopped hurting." The woman looked at her arm, moved her fingers, and looked back at the healer. Her eyes wide, she gasped. "It works." She moved her arm to show herself and the others.

"It will likely be tender for a few days, but the bone is healed," LeeAnn told her, feeling her own head spin.

Gasps came from the crowd and a low murmur spread. The woman on the ground grasped LeeAnn's hand. "You fixed it? I thought you were deadening the pain. It was broken; I broke my arm. That is amazing." She opened and closed her hand. "What do I owe?" She looked up at Hess. "She fixed my arm."

"Here, let me help you up." Hess brought the woman to her feet, then put an arm around LeeAnn. "Are you ready to stand?"

"Not yet. She should baby the arm for a day or two. It's going to be sore."

"You'll explain in a little while." He picked her up and set her in a chair. "Someone get me a cup of tea."

"I have it," Janie answered, plowing through the crowd. "How is she?"

"Recovering fast. Drink it, LeeAnn. No, don't try to get up." He kept an arm around her and looked at the crowd. "Get to your own booths. They'll open the main gate in a minute and people will be streaming in." He looked at the woman who had fallen. "You will meet with LeeAnn in an hour so she can check you again, over in her healing booth. Will it bother you if we sit here for a minute?"

"No, it must take a lot out of her."

"I am recovered." LeeAnn pushed at his arm, which he ignored.

"A few more moments," he told them, keeping his grip solid and warm on her. "LeeAnn, this is Vira. Vira, my mate, LeeAnn; who is also the healer for the Dragonmen."

"You have a remarkable talent," Vira told her, her voice still soft with disbelief.

"I tried not to hurt you too much," LeeAnn said.

"The broken arm hurt worse than anything you did. Goodness, people are coming in. You take all the time you need. I'll find your booth after the first rush." She moved away and Hess looked in LeeAnn's eyes.

"Finish your tea. We have a crowd waiting for us." The next sip went down the wrong way, and he tapped her back a few times as she coughed. When she was breathing normally again, he grinned. "I bet that got your blood flowing."

She got to her feet and found they were steady under her. "I didn't have Grabon's permission to heal her."

"You did and I was beside you. If I had wanted to stop you, I could have." They moved out of the back of the booth to find Janie and Griss waiting for her.

"Is she all right?" Griss asked.

"I am fine," she told the red dragon with a smile. "Syncing energy is taxing."

Griss nodded and glanced at Vira, who was in the booth. *"You did an excellent job. I think I will explain to her that she should not be climbing on tables when there are people who are tall enough to reach the top of her booth."*

"Good idea, go yell at Vira," Janie told him, grinning. Then she turned to LeeAnn. "Now that people know what you can do, you are going to be overrun with patients. Be cautious with your own energy. We don't want you worn out all the time."

"Oh she's not attending anyone else today, not unless it's Trissy. You can pass the word that anyone who needs a healer will go through Grabon or me. If anyone approaches her directly they will not receive any service, not here."

"Good, I'll make sure people understand. There is one other thing. Porter, the man whom we met this morning? He was at the main gate and asking questions. Have you heard anything from Heron?"

Grinning, he nodded. "Treat him like one of the family and let him make up his own mind, Janie. If he can find a place for himself, he may join us."

"All right, but I am sensing that he's looking for something specific."

"I am sure Heron knows what that is."

Nodding, she patted LeeAnn's arm and went back to her booth.

"What is Janie worried about?" LeeAnn asked.

Hess took a deep breath. "I think she gets nervous when we accept new human males. Male or female dragons she has no trouble with and women she embraces, but any time Grabon and Heron consider a new human male, she and Jamie are uncomfortable."

"Don't they know they are protected?"

"I am not sure they are worried about their protection. They are over thirty years old, yet still very attractive. Maybe they are concerned a new male will try to stake a claim?"

"More likely they are afraid of being judged harshly. Among many people their talent is considered somewhat shameful."

"Only because most people find any form of mind manipulation threatening. There is nothing wrong with their talent, or how they choose to use it. They help people."

"I agree, and they help a great *many* people." LeeAnn sighed and looked around at the crowd. "What do we do next?"

"We return to your healing booth after we pick out something to eat." He took her hand and they went in search of the perfect snack.

Vira came by after the first rush and listened carefully to LeeAnn's instructions and cautions. As she left she handed over four coins to LeeAnn. Before she could argue or give the coins back, Vira left with a few muttered words to Hess.

"Why are you reluctant to accept payment for healing?" he asked curiously.

"I am not, but four coins could leave her or her children hungry."

"No, she is making a tidy profit on her booth. If her arm was still broken, she would need to hire someone to help her. As it is, you saved her that expense."

"Four coins still seems excessive to me," she complained.

"Then when she brings you four more at the end of the day, you can argue with her about the value of two working arms. In the meantime we have other things to see to."

"Like what?" she asked, moving with him into the market.

"I believe we have some purchases of our own that need to be made," he reminded her.

Chapter 10

They were examining some fine blankets, wonderfully soft and colorful, when Hess touched her arm. "You keep looking for Golly's blanket. Porter wants to speak with me, and I'll be right over there." He indicated where the other man waited.

"I'll be fine on my own," she murmured, motioning him away. "You should take him to get some tea."

Hess's jaw clenched. "We're waiting for you."

Sighing, she looked back at the piles in front of her. "It won't take me very long."

"No hurry, we'll be waiting." He turned to leave, then stopped and ran an impatient hand through his hair. "I mean that too. There is no reason to rush. Finding the right blankets and bedding for Golly is important to you. I find myself impatient with interruptions, but not with you and not with Golly."

Nodding, she gave him a smile that she struggled to hold. It was hard enough knowing Golly that would spend his last days in the wonderful bed Heron had made. She was determined to make it as comfy and cozy as possible, but talking about it was beyond her. If she was forced to do that, she'd spend the day in tears and that wouldn't help anyone.

***

Hess rubbed her arm for a moment and left her to find the perfect blanket as he stalked just behind the crowd. Porter stood with his legs braced and his hands behind his back.

"Sorry to bother you."

Hess shrugged and glanced back at LeeAnn. Buying the bedding wasn't easy on her and he wasn't feeling generous about being pulled away when he knew she was fighting to maintain her composure. "I'm sure you have a reason."

"Heron pretty much insisted, and when I spoke to Tad, he warned me that if I didn't talk to you on my own he would drag my ass over here. Since I'm not anxious to see who would help him, I thought I'd take care of this as peacefully as possible."

"You have my attention," Hess said, his brows lowered.

"I am a news carrier, but I am also a hunter, and I track down family members who have gone missing. There are people looking for LeeAnn."

"One would hope it's her parents, seeing as how they haven't heard from her in a cycle or two."

Porter shrugged and nodded toward LeeAnn. "I can confirm it with her, but his name is Gregor and he claims she worked in his clinic as an assistant. Why a gifted healer would be working as an assistant I can't explain. He hired me to find her and report back. He did not mention family or parents but he did seem genuinely worried. I followed her trail and what I heard left me feeling pretty sick."

"I would hope so, or we would have tossed you out of the territory. Sam and all the rest of his people are dead, all except LeeAnn and Golly."

"Golly? The giant man who buried a hatchet in her chest?"

Shaking his head, Hess looked over at LeeAnn to make sure she was undisturbed. "Golly is a youth, not a man. He's been tortured and maimed and he hasn't long to live. More important, he is like her child. Do not make the mistake of being judgmental of him. Golly is no more to blame for anything that happened than LeeAnn is." He shared the image of what Sam had done to Golly that could never be fixed. Porter turned green and looked away.

"My mate is a healer. She stayed with Sam to save Golly and got trapped. None of what happened is their fault."

"I can see you believe that."

Hess stared at him and slowly grinned. "Let this Gregor know she escaped and has now made a life for herself. He doesn't need to know the details."

"I'll send a message. Are you going to tell her?" Porter indicated LeeAnn with a nod.

"Yes, it's important she knows that someone cared enough to go looking. I'll pay your fee, because you don't need to feel obligated to return to the colonies."

Porter looked oddly in her direction. "Why is she having such a hard time choosing a blanket?"

Sighing, Hess shifted his feet. "It's for Golly's new bed. He's beginning to weaken and he rubs his chest from time to time. She has cataloged the symptoms and knows this is the blanket he will die under. Would you have her choose it on a whim?"

Porter frowned and looked at his feet. "Ripper guts, no wonder you weren't thrilled to leave her side."

"It looks like she's made her selection. We'll go get some tea and you can explain all this to her." Hess stood at attention and watched as she paid for the blanket and smoothed it gently with her hand. She then stepped outside the stall and headed toward them.

"I think I found the one he wanted," she told him as she approached.

"Good. If not we'll look tomorrow and take him with us. I'm ready for tea and so is Porter." He gently took the blanket and her hand.

When they were sitting at a small table in the tea shop with three mugs, she inhaled the fragrant tea.

"I like this one." She took a sip and nodded. "Did you want to taste it?" she asked Hess, passing over her mug.

He turned the cup, placed his lips where hers had been, and tasted the brew. "Mmmm, very sweet."

Porter shifted uncomfortably and sighed. "Try courting her when you don't have an audience," he muttered.

"I'm not missing an opportunity, and you can just look away and pretend you're not here instead of interrupting us next time."

"We're already mates. He doesn't need to court me," LeeAnn protested.

"Need has nothing to do with it," Hess told her, taking her hand and squeezing gently. "You remember when I said I thought Porter had an agenda, and Janie was sure he was here for a specific reason? It turns out we were right. Gregor from the clinic outside the second colony hired Porter to find you and report back. He was worried."

Blinking in shock, she held on to Hess's hand. "Gregor was worried?"

Porter looked at her oddly. "Is that surprising?"

"I guess not. I did work for him, but he never displayed any interest in, or concern about me."

Porter scratched his chin and looked at Hess. "Why was she an assistant?"

"LeeAnn ran away from home at seventeen and worked for Gregor for a year before she went with Sam to heal one of his people."

Porter sat back in his chair and took a deep breath. "You're only nineteen?" he asked in shock.

LeeAnn winced and looked away. "I probably look older."

"Not really," Hess said, squeezing her hand. "Your level of training and talent has him confused. Your parents were skilled healers but probably didn't have much talent. When you displayed real power, they were horrified and didn't know how to help you. Instead of taking pride in what you could do, they let the people in the east end chase you away and barely stayed in touch afterwards. Gregor got a fully trained healer with raw talent for assistant wages." Hess glanced at Porter. "He didn't help her cope or get her the information she needed, either. After one conversation with Griss about syncing her energy with her patients' to prevent causing them pain, she's been using the new technique. By any standard, she's done an amazing job."

Porter let out a growly sigh. "I could twist his head off."

Hess tried hard to suppress his amusement. "So what did Gregor tell you?"

"He said she had some raw talent, but no training, and no known family. Gregor claimed he took her in, provided housing, and out of the kindness of his heart was giving her what training he could. She'd gone missing after accompanying Sam the Nightmare Man to see about one of his players. In retrospect, he felt bad about letting her go unaccompanied, but no one had seen where she'd gone. When I asked why he waited so long to make inquiries, he said he'd heard some bad things about Sam and his freak show and had felt guilty for not looking for her. Originally he'd assumed she'd run off with one of Sam's employees, but later he became worried. It sounded plausible, but I didn't really believe him."

Porter shook his head and grimaced. "As soon as I heard about her act, I knew he'd told me a bald-faced lie about her talent. Then as I followed the trail, I heard about some of the cruelties Sam practiced against her that people witnessed." He shook his head, not willing to explain.

"I am very grateful to have escaped," LeeAnn told him quietly.

"I am sure you are," Porter answered before sipping his tea. "I'll let Gregor know you survived, but not much more."

She looked from Hess to Porter and sighed. "I can tell you are both having similar thoughts and they are unpleasant. Why did he really send you to look for me, Porter?"

Porter held up his hands and shook his head, and Hess let out a deep breath. "He's either hoping to blackmail you or possibly your parents. Let us deal with Gregor in our own way. You should contact your parents as you planned. As you said, it's important to let them know you're safe. Other than that, we really don't owe them an explanation."

Porter nodded.

"So that was your big secret mission?" LeeAnn asked, sounding disappointed.

Porter choked on his tea.

"I was really counting on something more dramatic. How did you ever trace me here?"

He flushed. "That was a complete accident. I had heard that Sam was heading this way and thought I'd intercept him. Then I saw you this morning and could not believe my luck."

"Heron told you what happened?" Hess asked.

"Yes, in excruciating detail, along with Rok." He glanced briefly at LeeAnn and shook his head. "I really am interested in staying, but I don't know what I could do here."

"There's no question you have the power needed to fit in. I'd suggest giving yourself a season or two to see how things work and then figuring it out. Where are you staying?" Hess asked.

"At the moment, I have my bag hidden near where you found me. Heron said in a pinch I could sleep in his barn."

"You might be more comfortable next door to us. I'll take you by to meet Gordon later. If you pick up your bag it can go with our purchases back to our barn."

"You live in a barn?" Porter looked like he might well believe it.

LeeAnn shook her head. "It's a house that looks like a barn. It's very comfortable and the other side is empty. You'd have privacy and room of your own complete with water inside and a stove."

"A very comfortable barn it sounds like." Porter smirked at Hess. "I would have thought a Farmer like you could rough it a little more."

"I can, that doesn't mean I would enjoy it. You are welcome to make the rounds with us, wander on your own, or meet up with Grabon and all the youngsters."

"I'll skip the kiddie parade for now. If you really don't mind, I'd be glad to accompany the two of you. I think I'll gain a different perspective than if I tour by myself."

"You are more than welcome," LeeAnn said with a smile. "All I have left to buy is some sheeting for Golly. Then I want to find Hanna's other two statues."

As they stood to leave, they could hear Dotty starting a song. Porter looked so shocked that they sat back down so he could focus on it. This one was all heart and music to spin out a dream. There were no words, just a melody moving through a maze of notes. It was beautiful, uplifting, and filled with glorious hope. When it ended, there was a collective sigh from everyone, and Hess stood and collected their purchases, then LeeAnn and Porter followed him from the tea house.

"That's our heartsinger," Hess explained, grinning.

"We have to take him to hear one of Mia's stories after I find the sheeting I need."

As they expected, Porter was enthralled with the

story, a dragon tale told in Human about a newly mature dragon's attempts to build his first nest. It was a hilarious story about poor planning, and the dangers of taking shortcuts and not heeding well-meant advice. In the end, the dragon's labors went sliding down the mountain in the rain as he flew after them.

LeeAnn laughed herself silly along with the rest of the audience, including the dragons. Porter sat perfectly still through the whole story listening intently, but never laughing aloud.

"What do you think?" Hess asked when the audience had left.

"When is she telling the next story? Does she ever repeat a story? You must realize you have a heartsinger, storyteller, sculptor, carver, and healer all in the same clan."

"We noticed, but that isn't all. Wait, you'll see the rest of it," Hess promised.

The garden made Porter's jaw drop, and he walked through with a glazed look of wonder. Then they went to the far end where Thane and Pit had games and challenges set up for humans and dragons to try. The game area was mostly empty, but the idea had been that the two species might benefit from competing against one another.

When LeeAnn spied the third statue, she shrieked in triumph. As she raced by a small crowd of people toward an isolated gazebo, they watched, utterly confused until they, too, caught a glint of gold. The statue was behind the gazebo in a small pool of water crowded with fish. She simply stood admiring the statue of Hess and Thane perched on a carved pedestal that looked like a flat-topped tree with spreading branches and dangling leaves. It was every bit as detailed and spectacular as the others, and LeeAnn moved with care as she approached it so she didn't step on any of the fish.

After circling the statue, she gently placed her palm on it. Power resonating with sound, light, and images exploded with Dotty's voice in her mind. Their heartsinger invited people to celebrate the differences between dragon and human, and to also seek out the similarities and learn from one another. She sang about the ancient race of dragons and the recent arrival of humans and the planet's acceptance of both species.

A dragon tale about trade followed the song, Mia told it first in Dragon and then in Human. All dragons make tools, but one perfected the skill. His metals were harder, his handles were smoother, and his edges were sharper. His friends and clan mates admired his skill, but one young clan member saw an opportunity to trade knives, pokers, scrapers, and skinsewing tools with other clans. The others in the clan thought the idea was ridiculous and a waste of time until they saw the result. The trader was able to bring back the best skins, the best meat, and the best wine. He shared his newfound bounty with the toolmaker. The other clan members begged to be allowed even a small share in these fine skins, meats, and wines, but the trader said they had nothing of value to exchange. When they began to perfect their own crafts, their clan rose to be the most distinguished and prosperous territory, and their territory dragon the most powerful. Leadership does not always come from the old and wise, the tale concluded: sometimes it comes from a new idea that sparks a change.

LeeAnn went back to Hess grinning. "I enjoyed that story very much."

"I thought you might. There are not many trade stories among the dragons. Mia had to search hard to find that one."

***

Porter intended to go look at the sculpture, but first he decided to explore a few of the challenges. They had rock pitching, which sounded a lot easier than it was because the rocks were larger than his fist.

Another challenge involved markings on the ground. Hess explained that the goal was to move three rocks together from one location to the next and then the next by only setting them down in specific locations and never retracing your steps. It was obviously a strategy game.

Another challenge was horseshoe throwing, something he had seen and played before. It was a holdover from OldEarth and it involved tossing metal half circles at a metal target in the ground for points.

The last one, according to Hess, was called fishing, but he didn't see where it was.

"If you are looking for fishing, it is over by the statue," Brom told him. *"I'll show you, but you have to be prepared to get wet."*

"I'll dry," Porter told Brom as he followed him to the pool. His gaze was immediately drawn to the golden statue, and Brom smiled.

Nodding, Brom stood on the edge of the raised pool and hooked in his claws. With two opposable toes and three forward with thick talons on each, Porter suspected their foot grips were very strong.

"This is a dragon challenge, but you are free to try," he told Porter. Then with his arms crossed, he leaned down into the pool, picked up a fish in his teeth, then spit it back into the pool unharmed. He slowly came back to an upright position and let out a deep sigh. *"Heron, Tad, and Hess developed a human adaptation of hooking your feet under the rim of the pool. Would you like to see Hess do it?"* The gleam in his eyes was unmistakable. Especially when he looked over and saw Hess speaking tenderly with LeeAnn, stroking her hair and leaning close.

"He's not going to leave that to demonstrate a game," Porter predicted.

"Hess, this human does not think it's possible for his species to fish like a dragon."

"I didn't say that," Porter denied, glaring at Brom.

"You wanted him to show you?"

"Not if he's going to want to fight me over it."

"Hess would not be violent over something so petty."

"He's trying to court his mate."

Brom snorted and gave him a sideways look. *"That is going to take a cycle or more. He can spare us the time it takes to demonstrate a new skill."*

"You just want to see me get all wet. I saw you showing off. Did you tell him we managed to dunk Pit six times before he finally got the hang of it?"

"I would not brag on my friend's failures. Instead, I told him you could show him a human way."

"Thanks." Hess took off his bag and shirt and handed both to LeeAnn to hold, along with their small purchases. Then he spent a couple of minutes stretching as people gathered to watch. "I'll do best of two out of three and we'll make Porter judge."

Brom shook his head and looked over their audience. *"I choose the nice lady with the red tunic. Will you judge for us?"*

The woman pointed to herself, and at Brom's nod she came over. "I don't know the rules."

"It counts against you one point if you get wet, three points if you fall in the water, and you forfeit if you use your hands or tail for anything but air balance."

Porter stepped back to stand by LeeAnn. "I didn't realize this was such a serious game."

"Neither did I," she commented.

Brom went first and lost one point because the fish splashed him. Then Hess did it perfectly, grabbing the fish by the top fin and releasing it slowly enough that it did not splash. It all worked until he tried to stand, but he regained his balance by waving his arms like a madman and didn't lose any points.

Brom's second turn went perfectly and he had the crowd cheering as he danced around. Hess took his turn and the fish splashed going back in the water. He managed to get out of the way but lost his balance and landed on his shoulder in the pool. Fortunately he was well shielded, so his dignity took the worst bruising. LeeAnn handed him his shirt to dry off with and he sighed.

"I'll never make up two points," he muttered.

"Wait and see. No sense in losing before you lose. Brom is really good at this," Porter muttered.

"You're next, so pay attention," Hess warned.

Brom stepped up onto the rim and dug in with his claws. He slowly lowered his body, chose his fish, and then fell in with a tremendous splash when a child screamed with glee. He came up sputtering and laughing, and Brom and Hess ran around and put back the three fish that had jumped out to avoid the dragon invading their pool. Then they looked at their judge.

"Was that a forfeited match?" Hess asked.

The woman looked startled, then apparently remembered her job. "Oh, no, he didn't use his hands, but he didn't get a fish. Doesn't he need to do it again?"

Brom gave a big sigh and looked around as though to make sure no other child was going to break his concentration. Fortunately Brom had no other loss of points, just the four. Hess stepped up, hooked his feet under the rim, and slowly lowered himeself over the pool. When he caught his fish, it splashed him and he spit it out and stood, laughing.

Their judge declared a tie and they both turned to Porter.

"Who do you want to go against?" Hess asked.

"I don't want a full game, I just want to try it," Porter said.

"It's more fun as a competition, but suit yourself." Hess put on his shirt and slid his bag over his shoulder and head before he took their purchases from LeeAnn.

Porter stripped off his shirt and hooked his feet under the rim. Suddenly what hadn't looked so very difficult was a feat of strength and endurance. He managed to get his face near the water and got his teeth on a fin, but he felt half-drowned when he spit it out and stood. Despite that, people cheered and a couple of other men gladly stripped off their shirts to try.

"Are you ready to try something else?" Hess asked

with a grin.

Porter rubbed his abs and slipped on his shirt. "Are any of these games less strenuous?"

Hess looked around grinning. "The human horseshoe throwing," Hess suggested, a challenge in his eyes.

"Fine, show me something else." Porter gave a resigned sigh that was also filled with anticipation. They heard a splash behind them and saw one of the men climb out of the pool amid calls that he had used his hands.

"I don't know how they fell in and didn't get hurt," the man protested.

Hess walked over and explained that a player had two options. One was to shield their body before they started to prevent injury, the second was to fall and roll from one shoulder to the other. The man nodded and went back to try again.

Porter enjoyed trying the pitching-stones game by himself until Mia came into the area to meet Porter. It was not long after Brom had returned to the market, where he was setting up a booth to sell skins and tools. She watched with LeeAnn before she walked over, carefully took position, and out-pitched his farthest stone.

"Dragons are physically stronger. Don't ever pitch stones against one for money. The only human who wins consistently is Heron," Hess warned him.

"Heron can outpitch a dragon?" Porter asked in disbelief.

"He has been known to outpitch Grabon," Hess said, his tone seriousness.

"What about Gordon?" LeeAnn asked.

"I haven't enticed him into a game yet. I'm hoping to match him myself. The trick is to use power as well as muscle. I know that much and I can get a good distance, but not like Heron."

"Heron is an impressive dragon," Mia told them with a nod.

Porter blinked at that but didn't comment. "I haven't been using power," he admitted.

"Do you want me to demonstrate?" Hess asked.

"No, let me try it first." When he tossed the next stone, he definitely improved his distance. In fact, he passed Mia's stone. Then he signaled Hess.

Hess stepped up to the line, took one of the rounded stones, and got in position. He took a deep breath and let it fly. The power around him was so strong, Porter swore he could taste it. He blinked and shook his head, looking at the distance between both stones.

"I need more practice," he admitted.

Hess shrugged and shook out his arm. "I'll admit, I've put in some time at it. I spent a lifetime putting out energy in dribs and drabs so I wouldn't scare the pants off everyone. It has taken work to learn how to really access it and use it. One day it was simply there and I finally got to see what I could do, but each skill still requires practice."

The crowd had come to watch, but they said very little.

"I can see that your clan members not only use their power, but play with it. That's got to be healthier than hiding it all the time."

"That's the truth, and it sets us up as protectors for the territory. We're all aware that most people and even dragons don't have the same degree of power as the Dragonmen, but our abilities are to everyone's benefit, because aside from play we use them to work for the good of the territory."

"Like making this market," Porter clarified.

"Growing food as Gordon does, or hunting and providing for those in need. Before a big winter storm, Grabon provided a fresh carcass for each household."

"That's impressive."

"Heron's been known to shield a few houses during storms, and Grabon performs judgments to settle conflicts for humans as well as dragons. Having a territory dragon is an asset, especially if someone who is twisted hurts people. Territory dragons are trained to be impartial judges and carry out executions. There's no risk of punishing the innocent because they take their proof from the accused person's mind. If they are guilty of murder, or intended murder, the dragon executes them. Of course, you have the same problems of corruption and self-serving among territory and clan dragons as you do among humans. Some enjoy killing. Luckily Grabon is a good leader and impartial judge.

"We are fortunate here to have other territory holders who work with Grabon and Heron to secure the larger territory claim. Grabon, Heron, Gordon, Tad, Pit, and myself all hold territory, claimed through the planet, but we all yield to Grabon's judgment and larger claim."

Porter nodded and set down the stones in a row. "I think I'm ready to see something else."

"I'm ready to get some tea and food," LeeAnn suggested and Mia agreed.

Chapter 11

They went over to a booth that had skewers of meat and vegetables with bowls of rice. They placed their orders and got comfortable with their tea, and when Tad, Dotty, and Pit joined them, they moved to a bigger table.

"The youngsters are having a good time with Dane and Nat, and Grabon is enjoying their comparisons to a 'normal' territory. How was your morning after the healing?" Tad asked LeeAnn.

"Good. I think Vira will be recovered by tomorrow. I managed to find some nice bedding for Golly and some fine pottery pieces for us. I watched Hess fishing against Brom; it was a draw, and then Hess played at pitching stones. I found the third statue, and it's wonderful, like all the others."

Porter looked stunned. "I was so involved with the games I completely forgot to read the messages inside."

"I'm sure you'll be able to find it again," Hess said while LeeAnn giggled.

"They move them every couple of days. Isn't that clever?"

"They move the statues?" Porter frowned and looked at Hess, then Tad. "Why would you do that?"

"It keeps everyone entertained. We started the tradition during setup, and everyone was on the hunt all the time. When the thrill wears off, we'll probably stop. At least until Hanna makes more. I know she and Trissy have been scheming, but I don't know who they'll make a statue or carving of next."

"I'm looking forward to meeting Hanna," Porter mentioned.

"She might be about as early as tomorrow. Yesterday she had her first child, and I gave her the all clear this morning for gentle activity. Together she and Gordon heal quickly."

"Mates have that effect on one another. Add that to what you did during and after delivery and she should be doing exceptionally well." Tad grinned.

"You delivered a baby yesterday and did a healing this morning?" Porter frowned.

"One of our merchants fell off a table and broke her arm just before the market opened. I'm sure that sort of thing doesn't happen often. Besides, do I look like I am suffering?"

Porter shook his head and looked away, causing the rest of them to grin.

Their food arrived and Tad looked at Hess. "Is she up for one more patient this afternoon?"

Hess took her hand before she could answer. "What is it?"

"It was supposedly an accident, but we have very few details. Bernard from the mercantile in the village." Tad curled his lip and shifted. "He hurt his back this morning, or his back is just hurting. Someone brought the matter to Grabon and asked if we had someone with healing ability."

Hess let out a sigh. "We can hook up a wagon and I'll take her into the village." Squeezing her hand, he tried to explain his reluctance. "We've had some problems with Bernard. He's not always a nice man."

"He hunted Trissy and terrified her and Jenny," Tad reminded him.

"I haven't forgotten, but Heron dealt with it. She's a healer, Tad. Nothing can stand in the way of that, unless it's her own safety and well-being."

"I'd at least make him wait," Tad muttered.

"We are. We're going to eat lunch first," Hess answered and looked at his mate. "I know you want to go right away, but Gordon will get the wagon ready and we'll leave after you finish eating. You were hungry and wanted some tea, and your needs come first unless it's an emergency."

"Are we certain it's not an emergency?" she demanded.

"Yes, because Grabon would have told us."

"Then I suppose eating is not unreasonable." Her gaze shifted to Tad. "When did you find out about this?"

"Right before we came in. There is no need to glare at me, LeeAnn. I didn't delay giving you the message. I wouldn't do that."

"Would you like some company when you go into the village?" Porter asked Hess.

"How is your tolerance for fools?"

"Pretty low, why?"

"Then you'd be better off staying here. Bernard is not known for his intelligence."

"Neither is Golly, that doesn't mean he has less feelings than others," LeeAnn protested.

"Not that kind of intelligence, sweetheart. We are talking about the kind of intelligence that should kick in when a person is asking for a service. Bernard is likely to be rude. He was not in favor of us creating this market."

"That has nothing to do with him being injured."

He grinned at her sharp tone and nodded toward her full plate. "You worry about eating."

As she started to eat, Porter nodded to Hess. "I'd still like to go."

"You are more than welcome. My job will be to get her whatever she needs and attend to her afterward. Have you ever worked with a healer?"

"No, but I saw one once for an injury. A woman

named Mazy. She was very talented."

Hess nodded. "She's a cousin, Gordon's sister. You're right, she's very talented and skilled." He turned to LeeAnn. "Do you want to stop by Griss's shop before we go?"

"Yes, I think I better see what he has available and bring some options. Do we know if Bernard was running a fever? Did his tongue change color?"

Hess held up a finger, stalling Tad's answer as he communicated with Griss over distance. "He'll bring your supplies here and a bag to carry it in." He ran through a list of things Griss had suggested. She agreed to all of them and asked for a few more items besides. By the time Griss brought over the bag stuffed with treatment packets, they were ready to leave. Tad would make sure their purchases made it to their house.

"I'm sure I'll be fine to come back," LeeAnn protested.

"We'll see." Hess nodded to Porter.

LeeAnn, Porter, and Hess left the market grounds and headed across the river. Gordon was waiting in his yard, holding the two cattle hooked to the wagon. The big Farmer grinned and shook Porter's hand.

"It's good to meet you. I hitched up the big wagon just in case she needed to bring a patient back here. Instead it is transporting three of you." He looked over at Hess and their eyes met. "Make sure she gets plenty of fluids if she has to do a second healing today."

"I am sure I'll be fine," she protested.

"Griss stuffed some regular tea leaves in her bag, but can you grab me a couple of blankets?"

"They're already in the back along with a wineskin, mugs, and a few other snacks."

"Thanks, Gordon. I never saw myself as a healer's assistant before."

LeeAnn opened her mouth to protest, but Gordon was faster.

"Manager and mate, Hess. Your healing skills are abysmal. Thankfully you just manage the situation, her transportation, and recovery. She can use the wagon whenever she needs it. Heron was already planning one for her to use. We'll keep this one loaded in the barn until the other is ready. It's the least I can do. Now you better get moving before she chews on us."

"I would never chew on you, but Bernard is hurting and we need to go. If you see Golly, ask him about his bed."

Hess lifted LeeAnn into the seat and vaulted up as Porter went up the other side. The large wagon had a long wide seat and the three of them fit comfortably. Hess noticed that Porter wasn't saying much, but he was watching.

They were almost in town when Porter finally asked, "Dotty is the heartsinger, isn't she?"

"Yes, but she doesn't enjoy crowds staring at her," LeeAnn offered quietly.

Porter nodded and held on to the seat back. "I can see that she's a bit shy."

"Her parents wanted her to be a gold crafter. Singing wasn't practical to them." Hess tried to sound objective but failed miserably. He was still baffled by how that could have happened.

Porter made a face of disgust. "That would have been a waste. How did she convince them?"

"She didn't," LeeAnn answered. "After her mother died, her father took Dotty and her sister into the mountains, where they eked out a living in isolation until he died. Later on, Dotty learned her sister murdered both her parents and poisoned her."

Porter raised his brows. "I bet that's one heck of a story."

"All of us have one," Hess commented. "I bet yours is just as interesting. This is where the sisters live." He pointed out their house before he pulled the wagon in front of the mercantile.

Inside, a young man showed them to the stairs leading to Bernard's private quarters. "There won't be room for all of you," he warned.

"We'll make room," Hess informed him with a grim smile.

The young man shrugged and they went up the stairs. LeeAnn inhaled sharply at the crammed mess of goods on the stairs and filling the loft. She found her patient lying down, speaking to another man through clenched teeth, in pain.

"I thought you went to the stupid dragon and requested help?"

"I did. He said they had someone with healing skill and as soon as she was available she'd make the trip, hopefully today."

"Well I hope she's at least decent to look at. I hate having an ugly woman seeing to my needs."

LeeAnn took a deep breath and cleared her throat. "You sent for a healer?"

"About time," Bernard groaned shifting in bed so he could see her.

"What are they doing up here?" he demanded, glaring at Hess and Porter.

"We're guarding our healer, Bernard," Hess answered. "It looks like you really hurt yourself."

"My legs are week and it hurts like a fire stick in the back. I could barely stand up to piss."

"If you can lie on your stomach, I'll do an internal check and find out what the problem is. It may hurt. I'm sorry about that."

"If you can fix it so it doesn't hurt, I'll be grateful. Then you can see about cleaning up the mess up here and cook me some food."

Hess let out a low snarl but LeeAnn held up a hand.

"Umm, Bernard. I'm not a nurse or a household helper. I'm a healer. Lie on your stomach so I can see what is wrong."

He grumbled as he slowly moved, muttering all manner of complaints. She synced her energy with his and ran her check, then sat back chewing her lip. "How exactly did you hurt your back?"

"I don't see how that matters," Bernard barked. "It's your job to fix it, so get about that."

Hess and Porter shifted and LeeAnn waved a hand at them, telling them to stay quiet. "Sometimes these things are embarrassing, but can you tell me if you fell?"

"I fell down when the pain hit," he snapped. "It took me down like one of those great old trees, or whatever the Woodsmen call them."

"Was there pain anywhere else?"

"I told you it's in my back."

"I heard you and there's a good reason why your back hurts so much. We have a couple of issues going on. One of the discs in your back is out of place, but you also have an infection in your kidneys."

"In my kidneys?" Bernard muttered, glancing at his friend with a frown.

"Your kidneys are an internal organ around your lower back. An infection there would make it burn like fire when you relieve yourself. You also have some stones built up in your gallbladder. That would explain why your stomach burns after you eat, which is probably making you pretty cranky. Does that about sum up all your symptoms?"

His grumble was too low for her to understand, but she figured she was correct. "I'll heal the disk in your spine first, Bernard. It's going to hurt some, but then you'll feel great relief. Then we'll put some energy into the infection and then the stones. I'll leave you with a couple of brews that you need to drink for a week to clear things out."

"Get to it already instead of talking about it," he demanded.

She took a deep breath before getting started. He screamed loud and long when she slid the disk back in place, but then he sighed in relief. Then she started on the rest. Infections were not so easy to cure, but between the brews and healing energy, he would be able to fight it off. The stones were a different matter. Blasting energy to break them up so they could pass was a delicate and time-consuming process. By the time she refocused outside his body, Hess was at her back, keeping her upright.

"Which brew does he need for tonight? He can come to the market and see you when you're recovered tomorrow."

She pulled out the two brew packets he needed. One for tonight and another for in the morning before she closed her eyes. Vaguely she heard Bernard complaining and Porter telling him to shut his mouth. Hess must have been carrying her and she snuggled closer. Having people she could depend on felt wonderful. He kissed her on the mouth and told her to sleep.

Later, soft warm blankets were around her, and Hess was urging her to drink. The tea was good and she opened her eyes, or thought she did. The space around her was pitch black and she was confused.

"Are we at home?"

"No, you're in the back of the wagon, LeeAnn. Drink the tea and I'll take you home and put you to bed," Hess answered.

She took a few sips. "I'll be better in a minute."

"You'll be better tomorrow."

"No, I'm not missing one of Golly's days." She suddenly sounded almost coherent as she struggled to sit up.

He cursed in Dragon and she grinned. "I'm going to learn those words."

"No, you're not." He helped her sit up more. "Drink the rest of it and then sleep for a while. I'll make sure you're awake to see Golly when he gets back and help him make up his bed."

"O...kay," she sighed as she fell back into sleep.

***

Hess laid her down and covered her up, then climbed over the bed and seat divider onto the wagon seat and glanced at Porter. The man was looking at him strangely. "You have something to say?"

"I'm very glad I'm not a healer."

"Me too." Hess got the cattle moving toward home.

"Why did you let her do it?"

"Fix that nasty man with the bad attitude? He was sick, feverish, and in pain. Even if he was a terrible human intent on causing harm, she still would have needed to help if she could. Healers have an amazing compulsion to fix everyone all the time. They can't help it, and frankly they'll kill themselves pushing too hard, unless someone stops them."

"When she told us how serious it was, why didn't you tell her she could only heal one of the problems today and save the rest for later?"

"She would have done it anyway and we would have been at odds. I need her to trust me and rely on me. We're newly mated and are just building our relationship. Until our bond is stronger, I am not making any demands so when I finally do, she will know it is for her own safety. That may not stop her, but it will slow her down, and I'll use a shield to keep her away from a patient if I think it's necessary."

"Why does healing exhaust her so much? Shouldn't she have a better tolerance for it? She did a lot of it with Sam and the show."

Hess let out a groan and looked at Porter. "The healing takes a different toll on her, but what knocks her silly is syncing her energy. In order not to cause pain while she's healing, she has to alter her own energy rhythm to match her patient's."

"Why would that exhaust her?"

"If I altered the beat of your heart and the flow of your blood, even for ten or twenty minutes, it would knock you on your ass for hours if not days. That's what happens to her. It's better since the mating bond, but it still affects her when she does it."

"These probably seem like foolish questions to you, but I don't know anything about healing and healers. It's not a subject I've had cause to research or think about."

"They're not foolish, but not many people know or even question how healing works. You're a news carrier; it's your nature to ask questions and be curious. Most people aren't interested in anything beyond themselves and their immediate group of people. Feel free to ask us questions about anything that interests you. When we know nothing about a subject, we'll tell you that too."

Porter looked at him thoughtfully. "Why did Mia refer to Heron as a dragon and not a human?"

"Heron traveled with Grabon for thirty years and lived among the dragons. In some ways, he's more dragon than human in his thinking. The dragons see him as one of their own. Are you a relative of his?"

Porter shrugged and shifted. "Yes, and of course we have stories of him that are shared among the family. He's not a regular Woodsman, they always said. I always wanted to know what that meant."

"Did meeting him satisfy that curiosity or make it worse?"

"I'm definitely more interested. Why did Bernard hunt Heron's mate and why did Heron allow him to survive?"

"When Trissy arrived here, news spread of a woman wandering alone in the woods. Bernard and a few visiting Miners went looking for her, claiming she was a thief, but they were unable to find her. Heron also went looking and found Trissy and Jenny. Jenny is actually Trissy's sister, and they walked for almost two years searching for him. Heron claimed Trissy before he had Grabon fly them up to his nest. I believe the reason he didn't kill Bernard for hunting his mate was that if word of the hunt hadn't reached him, he might not have found her. Bernard gives Trissy a respectful distance."

"You know that Sam accused LeeAnn of being a thief?"

"She told me. It seems to be a common practice among humans in order to strip a person of their rights."

They pulled into Gordon's yard, and Hanna came out with the baby with Gordon at her back.

"You were gone a long time," Hanna told Hess, looking worried.

"Bernard was pretty sick. I'm going to put LeeAnn to bed for a few hours and I'll come tell you about it."

"All right." She watched as Hess collected LeeAnn from the back of the wagon, then looked at Porter. "You must be Porter. I'm Hanna." She held out a hand and shook his. "This little guy will be named this evening. So tell me what you think of us so far?"

"I think this place houses some extraordinary people," Porter answered with a smile.

Gordon laughed at his mate. "He wouldn't tell us even if he thought we were crazier than a gibber that ate coocoo berries."

"Maybe not, but he'd be thinking it and I'd catch the emotions." She grinned at Gordon. "If you hold the baby, I'll put on the kettle and put together some snacks."

"There's still some in the wagon," Porter volunteered, moving to get the bag. "We stopped so Hess could feed her some tea, but she was pretty out of it."

"I thought it was just a back injury." Gordon adjusted the baby in the crook of his arm.

"According to what LeeAnn said, it was a slipped disk, kidney infection, and gallstones," Porter informed them.

Gordon emitted a string of garbled sounds and

Hanna laughed. "That hardly sounded like Dragon," she told him, laughing.

"It wasn't," he growled. "That's a lot of healing for one day."

"She fixed a broken arm this morning at the market," Porter told him with a wince.

Gordon let out a sound of frustration that vibrated the air. "She's going to wear herself out. Then Hess is going to start refusing to let her work and she's going to have a fit."

"I can't picture LeeAnn having a fit," Hanna said defensively. "Besides, we all know she's done more than this before."

"Yes, but not while disrupting her own energy. The healing she did before was safer."

Hess walked up to them looking grim. "If one more person is sick or injured today, I'm going to be tempted to blast them to pieces. She agreed to sleep for a little while. Remind me, how does Karn manage Mazy?"

Gordon shrugged and looked at Porter. "Karn is my sister's match. He lets Mazy work and then insists on periods of recovery." Hanna went inside to fix the tea and bring out a plate of food. "He also tries to limit her to no more than three healings a day."

"LeeAnn is now at four since Bernard alone should count as three. I know in time she'll adjust to shifting her energy, but how long does that take?"

Gordon firmed his jaw. "Mazy was twenty or twenty-one before she was able to shift her energy easily."

"LeeAnn is only nineteen," Hess complained.

"She started younger," Gordon reminded him. "You could always keep her in bed for a few days, locked in shielding."

"I can't do that, not with Trissy close to delivery and Golly…." He glanced back at the barn.

Hanna returned with tea and some cookies and little round cakes. Porter and Hess set up the short table and she set them down, took the baby from Gordon, and returned to the house to get cups.

"We've been playing pass the baby all day. She's still figuring out what she can do with him in her arms." Gordon looked both pleased and amused.

"She's taking to it well," Hess said, helping himself to one of Hanna's exceptional cookies.

"I knew she would. My Hanna is the motherly type, very domestic and careful."

Porter took a bite of his cookie and looked at the confection oddly. "She made these?"

Grinning, Gordon slapped the newcomer on the back. "Hanna can cook and she loves to feed people. Feel free to stop by at mealtimes; everyone else does."

Hess was laughing at him when Hanna came back

out. She set the cups on the table and sat down. "Porter, tell us about being a news carrier. Is it exciting?"

Porter poured them all tea and gave the first cup to Hanna. "There have been moments. I've done a lot of traveling and I have an excuse to ask questions. Other than that it can be disappointing. Too many people expect me to pass on gossip or a story instead of the truth. I rarely oblige them."

"How many of them take your truth and then invent the story they wanted anyway?" Hess asked.

"Too many. It's one of the reasons I'm looking for a change. This would definitely be a place I'd consider staying, but I don't know what I could do here. It's not like you don't have plenty of power and skill."

Gordon looked out over the land and sighed. "We can always use more. Let your mind consider the possibilities and connect to your heart, and your purpose will come to you. Grabon and Heron are better at giving this kind of advice, but be who and what you are, not what people have expected. Most of the men here are hunters, territorial and dangerous. I think you are the same, but maybe I'm seeing the façade?"

"No, that's what I work to hide." Porter gave Hanna an apologetic look. "As I discovered playing with Hess earlier, I might need some help letting that side of my nature free, but I've always known it was there."

"We can help you with that," Gordon said. "Finish

your old life first, then we can help you start a new one as one of the Dragonmen. Heron is convinced you'll take to it well and he's never wrong, not about things like this."

Hanna laughed softly and looked up at Porter with a wince. "Sorry, it just occurred to me that if you were a news carrier for us, it would be a very different job. Grabon would want the facts, all of them, and your impressions; so would Heron. Gordon would want the weather and what crops you had seen. Hess and Tad would want to know about trade opportunities and business ideas you may have seen or heard about. Mia might want a story or two. Griss would be looking for recipes for everything non-food-related. Brom and Rok would be looking for information about how dragons work with human ideas and goods. Dotty would want songs and music. Pit and Thane would be looking for dragon application of human ideas and goods. Trissy and I would be looking for crafting and carving inspiration and ideas as well as recipes. LeeAnn, I imagine, would want to hear about healing techniques and medicines; and the children and youngsters would want to know about games, toys and whatever other interests they have."

"Don't leave out Jamie and Janie looking for fashion tips, materials, and special sewing supplies." Hess grinned and nodded at Hanna. "She has a good point. If you were our news carrier you would be in charge of developing and maintaining trade relationships, passing messages, gathering information, picking up supplies, and acting as our territory's ambassador. We'd probably pair you up with a dragon and really complicate your world."

Instead of looking appalled, Porter looked intrigued. "You could use someone to do all that?"

Gordon cleared his throat. "This is up to Grabon and Heron, but they'll want a human-and-dragon pair. I always assumed it would be Hess and Thane, until my cousin met LeeAnn."

"No chance of doing it now. A healer needs a solid base," Hess admitted. "Besides, I'm up to my neck in the market. You should talk to Thane; he might be interested. Unless he chooses to stay with the market. He certainly spent enough time awandering and may not want to venture too far, now that he has found his stopping place."

"It is certainly an interesting idea, but one I need to think about before I start looking for that partner. It seems to me talking to Heron would be the best way to start."

"Do you need some gold beads to record your thoughts or send messages back to the colonies?" Hanna asked.

"I'm sure I can get them at the market," Porter answered.

"I'll give you a few." Hanna handed the sleeping baby to Gordon before going into the house. She came back with a handful of beads. "It's always best to finish your old business before starting something new."

Porter went with Hess to look at the other side of

the barn and immediately agreed to stay there. It was sparsely furnished but it had a bed, a stove, and a few pieces of furniture. Hess left him alone and went to check on LeeAnn.

She sat up and blinked a few times when he came into the bedroom. "Is the market closed for the day?"

"No, you can sleep for another hour."

"I seem to be awake again," she answered, rubbing her eyes. "Did I remember to make an appointment with Bernard? He needs to drink those brews and I need to see if that infection is responding."

"He's coming to see you at the market. I took care of it. This can't keep happening, LeeAnn. We either have to get your system accustomed to needing to change the pulse of your energy for each patient or you're going to have to accept a limit on how much you can do in a day."

"I keep thinking I'm adjusting," she admitted.

"You probably are, just not as fast as you need to for as far as you push yourself. Come and get some tea and we'll talk about it. I don't need to ambush you when you first wake up."

After she had half a cup of tea and was considerably more coherent, she let out a sigh. "What would I have done if Golly or Trissy needed me?"

"Exactly," Hess answered as he put together some food for them. "No matter what is happening, you have to have a reserve for the odd emergency. What you were able to do for Bernard was amazing, but next time, work it over three days so you can rest. Vira was an emergency this morning, but you rested afterward. In time, your system will adjust to what you're doing, but you'll still need to be careful. Healers can utterly drain their reserves and endanger their own health. I will not stand aside and let that happen."

LeeAnn covered her mouth to hide her smile.

"What is so funny? I can feel you wanting to giggle at me," Hess demanded.

She took a deep breath and tried to keep a straight face. "You really want to yell at me. I can feel that, but you also are trying very hard to be reasonable."

"You're laughing because I'm trying to control myself? Would you like to guess what is going to happen if I decide that isn't working?"

Her smile vanished and she shifted in the chair. "I'm sorry."

"I don't want you to be sorry or upset. What I want is for you to work with me to find a solution we can both live with; otherwise, I'm going to make the decision that is good for us."

"I'll work with you. Maybe I can make my body adjust faster."

Hess let out a tense sigh. "We aren't going to force your body to accept anything. If you hadn't synced your energy with Bernard, what would have happened?"

"He would have screamed with pain, fainted more than likely, and I would have worked faster."

"You wouldn't have collapsed or used as much energy, right?"

"No, but it would have hurt him."

"But he would have been healed and complaining, the same as he was when we left, and you wouldn't have been wiped out. If you can't slow down the pace of the healing, only sync your energy if it's someone who can't take any more pain."

"I don't like hurting people as I heal," she informed him with a scowl.

"You won't like being wrapped in such thick shielding you are forced to stand there helpless like everyone else." He crossed his arms and glared at her.

"How would you suggest I decide who gets synced energy and who doesn't?"

"Most men can tolerate the pain; so can many women. For children and youngsters I would think you should sync your energy unless the illness is so bad you're going to need every ounce of your strength. If you're easing pain, sync the energy. But if it's going to hurt anyway, why bother?"

"That seems so cold," she muttered.

"Then come up with a different guideline." He leaned down so their eyes met. "If you want to do more than three healings a day, we need a solution. Otherwise, you're forcing me to protect you from yourself, and I will. My mate will not collapse for hours after performing a healing. She will only need a few moments to recover and some tea, maybe even some food. On a bad day she might be tired and feel hollow, but she will not lose consciousness for hours at a time."

"She might when it's time to ease someone's final hours," she warned him.

"That's a whole different matter. When it's time to ease Golly at the end, I'll help. As long as you remember not to endanger our lives to ease his way, I'll assist any way I can. When it's over I'll make sure you recover, that's a promise."

"I guess that is a compromise. I notice that you didn't seem affected by the healing."

"It doesn't seem to knock me out, but I can feel it from you. I doubt you'll ever be able to hide it from me."

"If I pushed too far, would you be affected?"

Hess stared at her thoughtfully for a moment before he answered. "Yes, I think so, but I am not anxious to try that. If you actually depleted your strength, I'm sure we would both be incapacitated. I don't know why disrupting your natural rhythms doesn't affect me even while I sense it."

"I may have an idea. According to what Griss said,

most healers shift their energy, but it takes practice to perfect the skill. Over time syncing my energy probably won't affect me at all; so why would it affect you?"

"That seems about right. Now, we need to eat and you, my dear mate, are going to get that message ready for your parents because Porter will make sure it gets delivered. He's our new neighbor, on the other side of the barn. Thanks to Hanna, he may have figured a few things out today."

"Really? Tell me what happened?"

Hess explained while they ate, and they were both clearing the table when someone knocked on the door. LeeAnn let Porter in and he stood, staring at her.

"You look much better," Porter muttered.

"Thank you. I just needed a little sleep."

"I'm surprised you recovered so fast. That was a lot of healing you did today."

"She isn't fully recovered. Her energy is still disrupted. If she were to try another healing right now, she'd knock herself unconscious."

With her hands on her hips, she narrowed her eyes at Hess. "How do you know that?"

"I can feel it. We have the same base energy and we are mates. Go make some tea instead of challenging me and then get that message done and give it to Porter. Since he's got a messenger going to the second colony anyway, it should be simple to include one small bead."

"How do you know I have a messenger?" Porter asked suspiously.

"You said you would send word to Gregor. That means you plan to use a messenger, and unless you have a partner who happens to be a Woodsman who speaks with animals, I'm assuming your messenger is human and can carry and deliver a bead."

Porter sighed and sat at the table. "He's human, and yes, I can include a message to your parents. You said they were outside the second colony? I'm also including a resignation with a final news report on the new clan of Dragonmen. I wanted to show you the report so you can make sure it's accurate, but that I didn't include any details best left out. My messenger is not going to be happy when he realizes I intend to stay."

"Is he someone Grabon and Heron would consider?"

Porter looked at him thoughtfully. "He doesn't have a large power base, but he's clever. I really don't know if he would even be interested."

"When you tell him your plan, ask him," Hess suggested. "We're looking for new clan members, but they need to be the right ones."

Porter nodded thoughtfully. "I'll ask, but I doubt he'd consider it."

"Why wouldn't he consider it? This is a wonderful territory," LeeAnn asked.

"I agree since I'm joining all of you, but Denny is going to be uncomfortable around so much power, or at least I think so."

LeeAnn shrugged and asked about a bead. Hess gave her one and she went into the living room. He then reviewed Porter's last news report and nodded. "It sounds good to me. You left out a lot of details, but it's clear, concise, and factual."

"I didn't want it to read like an advertisement for the market or the territory. That made it especially hard. You should have seen the first few attempts."

Grinning, he patted Porter's back. "We're all gathering this evening since Hanna refused to announce the baby's name yesterday. That will give you a chance to see everyone together. Hopefully that won't scare you off."

"I don't scare that easily. What do you do at a clan gathering?"

"Eat, play with the youngsters, harass one another, and offer support and opinions. If something serious comes up, we hash it out. Otherwise, it's mostly for fun."

"Are you expecting anything serious?"

"Not tonight, but you never know."

LeeAnn returned with the bead and handed it to Hess. He shook his head over the cool tone of her message, but handed it to Porter. He added that bead to his own in the bag and went in search of his messenger.

After Porter left, LeeAnn chewed on her lip. "Should I have included more details?"

"Not unless you think they would be interested. Someday I'd like to meet your parents, but not until we've had a few happy years and we're both ready to face them."

"I'm pretty sure we'd have to go there. It would take too much effort for them to travel all the way here. I just hope they reply to the message."

"Let's not focus on your parents. Let me tell you something about mine." Hess told her about his father, Eldon, and how he and Tad had gotten him to ride a dragon during the recent gathering. He was pretty sure that was never going to happen again. Then he told her about his mother, Sarah. She was a powerhouse, but also loving and supportive.

Chapter 12

Golly knocked on LeeAnn's door, full of news and excitement. When she opened it Thane brought in a couple of boxes of goods, things they had bought at the market. Golly talked to her the whole time she was unpacking, washing and setting things in place.

According to Golly, Tria, Dane, and Nat were joining them for dinner along with everyone else. "What are you making to bring?" he asked.

"I haven't even thought about it. Would you like to help me cook something?"

"Yes, but I don't know how to cook on a stove like that."

"Did you see all the berries on the path to the stream? Can you get me some of the red ones?"

"I can do that," he promised, taking the basket she handed him.

While he was gone she quickly put together a simple cake batter. When he brought the berries back, she cleaned them and added them to it, letting Golly gently fold them in. Then she let him spoon the batter into the cake pan and lick the bowl and spoon as she put it in the oven. While it baked, Hess taught Golly a simple game called hide the button. They were on round six when Porter knocked and LeeAnn let him in. His eyes widened at the sight of Golly, but he was polite.

"We are playing hide the button. Would you like to play?" Golly asked, grinning.

"All right, what should I do?" Porter frowned at the button on the table.

"Hide the button," Golly answered, laughing.

Golly covered his eyes and started counting and Hess took the button from in front of Porter and placed it in one of LeeAnn's new cups.

"Okay, it's hidden," Hess said.

"Good, I was almost out of numbers. So where is it?" He looked around the kitchen and scrunched up his face. "Is it in this room?"

"Yes," Porter answered, glancing at LeeAnn.

Golly hunted for a few minutes and asked for a clue.

Porter looked at Hess, who shrugged. "It's in something new."

"It's in something new," Golly repeated. "I have new shoes." He sat and checked them. Then he made LeeAnn check her shoes. Then he checked his pockets and had LeeAnn check hers. Then he looked at Porter, and his expression turned horrified. "Did you eat the button?"

"No, why would I eat the button?" Porter laughed.

"You're new. How else would it get inside you?"

"It's not inside me," he laughed again.

"I'll give you a new clue," Hess said, chuckling. "It's inside something you drink out of."

It took Golly a few minutes to find the button, but he did and even Porter cheered. The cake was finished then and Golly helped LeeAnn decorate it with frosting. The uneven layer of frosting looked a little odd, but also very precious. They went outside to join the gathering crowd, and Thane let Hess know that the bedding was all up in the nest.

"I appreciate it." Hess nodded.

As the food was set out, Grabon, Heron, Porter, and Hess stood off to one side.

After looking around to be sure their words would not be overheard, Porter leaned closer to Hess. "When you said Golly was no more to blame than LeeAnn for what happened to her, I really didn't know what you meant. It became clear as we were playing hide the button."

"I told you he was simple. Aside from his growth condition and the torture, I think he was hit in the head. LeeAnn hasn't explained and I don't know if she knows why or how that happened."

"It doesn't really matter," Heron said, moving closer.

"No, it doesn't. He's a sweet boy, that's what matters," Hess responded.

Porter frowned and looked at Grabon. "You told me he was innocent of anything malicious. I should have believed you."

"You wanted to blame him because of how he was described to you. It is an important lesson that description can breed hatred or sympathy, fear, or even understanding. When you describe us to others, it is important to remember that."

"I will," Porter told him as he reached into his pocket and pulled out a bead. "This is my description of the Dragonmen that I am sending back."

Grabon took the bead, listened, and nodded. "Good," Then he handed it to Heron, who listened and scowled.

"We have a variety of skills and talents? I would have put it in grander terms, but it is true, we do have variety."

"I was trying not to incite jealousy and an inclination to challenge any of you for control of your resources. Anyone who comes here will know instantly how much talent and power is in this territory. The ground vibrates with it. My messenger, Denny, said he would die here because he would be on the bottom rung of the power chain."

"Yet he didn't mind working with you?" Heron asked, mystified.

"No, because he wasn't surrounded on all sides by that kind of power. That's what he told me. He claims this is an interesting place to visit, but he would never be comfortable living here. He joked and said I would probably fit in better here than any other place we had been."

Heron gave him a smirk. "Imagine that, and he doesn't even know how much power you really have, but he knows you fit in better here. It will be interesting to see what happens when you finally discover how much power is under your skin."

"I am not that unaware, Heron. I just haven't had an opportunity to use it."

Snorting, Heron turned to Grabon. "Tomorrow, we should take him gaming. Let's see if he can learn to pitch stones with something more than a little muscle."

"*I think Gordon is ready to make his announcement,*" Grabon told them, nodding toward the large Farmer. Hess moved to stand by LeeAnn while Heron went to Trissy's side.

"My mate, Hanna, chose a name for our new son and we wanted everyone to know at the same time. His name is Kenseth. We welcome Kenseth to life, our family, and our clan."

The cheers of course caused Kenseth to cry, which made everyone laugh. Gordon signaled that he wasn't done. "Hanna would like to propose a tradition of naming our children with names that end the same way, or in such a way that will be identifiable to outsiders as Dragonmen."

Silence greeted the proposal and then discussion broke out. Grabon gave a whistle drawing everyone's attention. *"It is a good proposal and has much value. I think we should welcome Kenseth, eat, and discuss possibilities."*

There was general agreement as people found their place at the large table. Porter sat beside Hess, Dane sat by the sisters, and Nat was over by Brom and Star. Tria sat by Golly, who sat with LeeAnn. Grabon welcomed Porter and let everyone know that Dane and Nat were interested in becoming Dragonmen, and Tria was Golly's guest. Everyone smiled at the young female, who did a good imitation of a dragon blush.

They passed the food around as they discussed ways to make distinguishing names. Ideas were proposed, talked about, shelved, added to, and modified. Dinner was halfway over when Hanna finally asked what sounds humans and dragons had in common.

Brom answered that very few were the same because of the different structures of their mouths.

"Well having heard a few words spoken in Dragon, since the men find it convenient to curse in it, I've caught a few sounds. The sounds I hear are S—E—Th, so I named our son Kenseth. Add that to any name and you would conceivably have a Dragonmen name." Hanna grinned and folded her hands together.

Janie laughed and started converting everyone's names with Jenny and Matti helping. Grabonseth, Heronseth, Trissyseth, Gordonseth, Hannaseth, and as people listened, they realized it worked.

"I am too old to change my name," Jamie protested.

"You wouldn't have to," Heron answered thoughtfully. "Not here among us. To outsiders you would be Jamieseth."

"We deal with outsiders all the time at the market," she reminded them.

"We could call it Marketseth," Pit suggested with a laugh.

"Territory Market, Human Market, Dragon Market, or even The Market seems to work just fine," Tad reminded him with a grin.

"I wasn't suggesting we change our names," Hanna clarified, laughing. "I was thinking about the children."

"It is a good idea for dragons as well as humans," Griss admitted.

"I think it is a wonderful idea, Hanna," Trissy agreed. "After a few generations, it will allow descendants from this time to identify kinsmen easily."

"What about our youngsters now?" Brom asked, one hand on Star's shoulder.

"Would you change your daughter's name?" Grabon asked.

"I would, because it adds to her security and tells other dragons immediately that she comes from a strong territory with a good leader."

"Then we will call her Starseth," Grabon answered.

"I would have my son called Redseth for the same

reason," Griss said.

Heron looked at his children and at Trissy. "We will make a decision by morning."

"But with this new child we can follow this tradition," Trissy added.

"When we have a child, we'll follow it as well," Dotty promised.

"So will LeeAnn and I," Hess said with a grin at his mate. She was still stunned at the idea of having a child of her own. Until that moment, it hadn't even occurred to her, but of course they would follow the naming tradition.

"I think it's safe to say Janie and I won't have any children unless we adopt, but if we did, we'd rename them to give them the full protection of the clan. That's really what we're talking about, right?"

"That is what you are all talking about," Porter told them, frowning. "It's even more powerful than a shared last name. It would be part of their inner identity."

"They would have the shared last name as well, but yes, this is more powerful," Gordon confirmed, looking pleased.

With the new tradition agreed to, the focus turned to the food. Everyone greatly enjoyed it and admired Golly and LeeAnn's berry cake, much to Golly's delight. With dinner being done, many of them trooped or flew up to the nest to see Golly's new bed.

Golly started to run up the hill, but then stopped.

"What's wrong?" LeeAnn asked gently.

"Nothing. Running up hill isn't as much fun as running down. I'd rather walk with you and Hess. I told Grabon that sometimes my chest feels funny when I run too hard. Do you know what he told me? He said, 'Don't run so hard.' Isn't that funny?"

Hess laughed and put his arm around LeeAnn. "That is funny. What else did he say?"

"He said I was a good boy. That I didn't need to be scared because he, LeeAnn, and everyone else would take care of me when my heart got too weak. I didn't think he knew, but he does."

"Everyone knows, Golly, but you're still feeling good now," LeeAnn reminded him.

"I am most of the time. Grabon says when I'm tired to sit down. That it was okay to be tired or even to be sick with something you can't fix. The end comes to all things and they go back to the planet and nourish something new. I kind of like that part."

"So do I," LeeAnn told him, blinking away tears.

"Do you think I can nourish a baby tree and make it grow really tall?"

"I think you can," Hess said with a smile. "It will be the tallest tree in the woods."

"Good, then you can remember me."

"I'm not ever going to forget you, Golly. You don't forget your friends."

"No, you don't forget your friends." He stopped for a moment and took a deep breath, then kept walking. "I wish Sam didn't make me look so funny."

"Why?" Hess asked, holding LeeAnn's hand as they climbed over the rocks.

"If I looked like other people I could be a statue in the garden," Golly said.

"You don't look that funny. You could still have a statue," LeeAnn told him.

"Oh, Tria flew up fast." He went up to the dragon and they went off for a minute.

Hess paused beside LeeAnn and squeezed her hands. "I guess he knows."

Sniffing, she nodded. "I would have told him, but it was probably better coming from Grabon."

"I am glad you are not upset that we spoke of it," Grabon told her softly, shifting his wings. *"He asked at the market if I knew he would die soon. It seemed a good time to reassure him."*

"You did a good job," LeeAnn said as they came over the last rocks and approached the nest.

"Let's take a good look at this bed," Hess suggested with determined cheerfulness.

LeeAnn gave a choked laugh as they entered the nest.

Tria kept Golly busy while everyone made up the bed. When it was done, LeeAnn looked at Grabon. "What are they doing?"

"They are watching the birds fly. Golly much enjoys this activity."

Tria and Golly finally joined them, and Golly looked at his bed with wide-eyed wonder. "Look, I even have a pillow. LeeAnn, you found the exact blanket."

She laughed and shook her head. She had spent so much time looking that Furd, who ran that stall, asked if he could help. When she told him she was looking for the blanket Golly had admired, he had pulled it out from under the counter. He had anticipated that someone would come looking for it for their giant friend.

"It was the best one there," Golly told her with a pleased grin. He sat on the bed and bounced a little. "Heron said he made it extra strong."

"I did, and extra long. Go ahead and try it out," Heron urged.

Golly lay down with an exaggerated sigh of pleasure. Everyone laughed a little and he sat back up grinning. "I thank everyone for a wonderful bed; Heron especially for not forgetting the mattress."

"Well, we have Bert and Mable staying with us, so we should get home," Jamie told them. "You sleep nice and sweet in that new bed, Golly. I'm sure we'll see you at the market tomorrow."

After that, everyone started to leave. LeeAnn gave Golly a warm hug and touched his face. "Are you still having fun staying here?"

"Oh yes, and no nightmares. Grabon took them all away. I want to stay here."

"You can stay. I was just checking. Come and see me in the morning," she told him with a grin.

After he promised, Hess led her out of the nest and helped her back onto the trail. She was still fighting tears when they reached the hut.

"Come inside for some tea," Heron invited. "I can't imagine anything harder for a healer than what you're doing for Golly, but it's so good for him. He knows that you love him. That he is supported during this final time of his life. Now let us support you, LeeAnn, because we know this is breaking your heart."

"I'll be all right," she told him, following as he took her into the hut. The girls were getting ready for bed, arguing and making noise and running around.

Trissy saw them and laughed. "Welcome to bedtime mania. I'll be out in a minute." She disappeared behind a blanket, and Heron grinned as he filled and put on the kettle.

"They are a little wound up," Hess commented with a laugh over the giggles coming from the other side of the blanket.

"We are fortunate; they are both happy and healthy. Soon we will be adding another voice to the confusion. I am looking forward to that, if not the labor that comes first. Tell me, LeeAnn, is there anything we can do to make this easier for you?"

Smiling sadly, she shook her head. "Most of the time I can set the concerns and heartache aside and enjoy the moment."

"Good, that's important. We were all hoping your parents would be a comfort, but it does not seem like you have any faith in their interest or concern. Being a parent, I find that hard to accept, but I know it happens." He poured the hot water over the tea leaves. "Who comforted you when you were a child?"

LeeAnn grinned and glanced at Hess. "My grandmother lived with us, and she was wonderful. She passed not long before everything went wrong."

Heron sighed and looked directly as Hess. "You have a difficult task ahead. She needs to anchor her emotions, yet she is afraid."

"I know very well what needs to happen, Heron. But knowing and seeing it done are two different things. We make progress every day. It's only been a short time since we started the bond."

"You should have taken him out to the barn if you're going to have a private discussion," Trissy told him, moving to the table. "Poor LeeAnn is sitting there not knowing what to think."

"She is not the least confused; she is stubborn,"

Heron informed his mate. "LeeAnn knows full well that she needs an emotional anchor, someone to love and trust. Hess is the obvious choice, but she fears trusting a man. After her experiences, she is entitled to her fears, but she needs to move past them."

"I am not going to push her, Heron." Hess scowled, his voice rough with emotion. "She will allow what is between us to grow in her own time. The rest of you need to stay out of it."

"We are simply concerned," Trissy said, rubbing her belly as she accepted a cup of tea from Heron.

"You are concerned; he is meddling," Hess informed her with a nod toward Heron.

"Actually they are distracting me," LeeAnn said. "It took me a minute, but I finally realized what he was doing. He completely pulled my focus and thoughts from Golly and my grief and refocused them on you and our bond."

"Good, then it was successful. Do not let your mind dwell too long in grief. It is not good for either of you," Heron warned.

"I will work on that," LeeAnn answered with a confused smile.

"Good, then enjoy your tea. I have to finish our bedtime ritual." Heron walked off, letting his fingers trail over Trissy's shoulder and brush her hair as he walked by.

"Your mate is devious. I hadn't realized that,"

LeeAnn told Trissy.

She giggled, covering her mouth. "He lived with Grabon. They are both tricky when it suits their purposes. Tell me honestly how much time Golly has and what we can expect," she invited.

"It is very difficult to predict. I am hoping he will simply pass in his sleep, not linger, and have no pain. Unfortunately it can go the other way and take months of him slowing down and then languishing, unable to do for himself."

"That is why you do not encourage him to slow down?"

LeeAnn sighed and looked at Hess. "He should not stop living. I want him to enjoy as much as he can, for as long as he can. More time does not mean a better life."

Trissy nodded and drank her tea. "I can agree with that with my whole heart. Tell me, what do you think of changing the children's names?"

LeeAnn blinked at the change in topic. It took her a few moments to formulate her response. "I think Jenny and Matti need all the protection they can get. If adding some extra letters to their names can make them safer, I would do it."

Trissy nodded. "The problem is remembering it," she sighed and leaned back in her chair.

Hess put his arm around LeeAnn. "I think they'll remind you. They seemed anxious enough to embrace the idea."

Grinning, Trissy patted her belly. "They did seem to like the changes. I can't imagine what Porter must think of us all."

Heron returned to the table. "At the moment, he thinks we are unaware of how different we are from the other human clans. Worse, he is not sure we know the repercussions of what we are creating."

Hess chuckled softly. "Give him some time. He'll come to understand that all those differences are deliberate. We know exactly what kind of responses to expect from humans and dragons and how to manipulate those responses to promote peaceful coexistence."

"That will happen sooner than you think. He's really quite brilliant. Our welcoming him took him by surprise, but I expect him to gain some understanding of the situation within a day or two."

"Why would he underestimate us?" Trissy asked, her brows drawn together.

"He is accustomed to gathering news and gossip for those who want it. When necessary he reports on real problems or concerns, which are often dismissed in favor of more trivial information. Porter is used to being the smartest man in any group, the most farsighted and aware of consequences."

"Is Porter going to be permanently damaged when he realizes that Grabon, a dragon, can lead him in intellectual circles?" Hess asked bluntly.

Shrugging, Heron set down his cup. "If he is, it's his own fault. I warned him not to underestimate the intelligence of the dragons, and not just Grabon. His own arrogance is preventing him from seeing what is in front of him. When he gets past that false belief that humans are superior, he will be an asset to all of us."

"Are you expecting a problem first?"

"I am always expecting trouble. We will see what he decides. Truthfully I expected him to be less spontaneous and wait a week or two before making a decision. Something happened today that made him decide impulsively, but I do not know what that was."

"I do," LeeAnn answered. "I saw it happen. It was the lure of being able to really access his own power to work, help, and play without fear."

Heron nodded and looked at Hess. "That does explain it. Porter has spent his whole life repressing his power to blend in."

"So the attraction of finally being himself was too much to resist," Hess concluded.

Chapter 13

LeeAnn and Hess soon left the hut and walked slowly down the hill, holding hands and talking quietly. Porter stood outside the barn watching them. LeeAnn waved and he returned the gesture.

When they got closer, Hess could see that something was on his mind. "Is something wrong?"

Porter's jaw tensed. "There are shields everywhere."

Hess nodded and motioned for LeeAnn to go inside. "To ensure privacy in a community of strong mindspeakers, we each use our own kind of shielding."

"This is on my side of the barn," Porter explained.

Hess frowned slightly and followed him inside, considering that he or Tad could have left some residual power behind. Instead, he found a solid wall of shielding blocking off the bedroom.

"You didn't do this?" Hess asked.

"Why would I block myself off from my own bedroom?"

"I don't know, but this is odd." Using power to enhance his voice, Hess called out to anyone inside the bedroom. A moment later the door opened and a sleepy-looking face with strong features and curly brown hair peered around it.

"Sorry, I thought the place was empty." He disappeared for a moment, then returned, dressed like a Farmer and looking considerably more awake. "I just needed a few hours to close things down. This is my cousin's farm and I came ahead of the wagons."

"Josiah, you idiot, someone could have killed you," Hess complained.

Grinning, Josiah held out a hand to Hess, recognition in his eyes. "Nah, I was careful and sailed over the energy lines. I thought I'd surprise Gordon in the morning and do his chores. There was no shielding, Hess. So I thought this side of the barn must be empty."

"We let Porter stay here this evening. He didn't have a chance to put up any shielding." Hess introduced the two men and shook his head. "I'll get my cousin out of your place," He promised. "He can sleep on the floor on my side."

"I didn't recognize you right away. It's almost as if your energy has changed," Josiah muttered.

"That's because I found my mate. You can meet her, come on." Hess led the way to the connecting door, but Josiah paused.

"I'm sorry about invading your space, Porter. I really didn't mean any harm."

"No, I understand, and I'll get some shielding up. It's nice to meet you."

"I hear Hanna is a good cook, is that true?" he asked Hess.

"You'll get to see for yourself," Hess said, grabbing his cousin by the back of his neck and shoving him toward the door. He nodded to Porter. "Have a good night and sorry about that."

***

Porter waited until the door closed and took a deep breath. Then he put up some shields of his own, the strongest he knew how to create. It was almost funny the way his world had flipped upside down, except a part of him was furious with himself. He had spent his whole life trying to mask his strength and repress his predatory nature while these men embraced theirs. Even the cousin who was so obviously a Farmer wasn't surprised that Hess had been primed to strike at him. Instead, he had sheepishly apologized and explained his trespass in terms the territorial crowd here would understand. Porter's side of the barn couldn't be occupied, there were no detectible shields in place. Well, he would never make that mistake again. Porter found his bag, hidden in a small spot of shielding in a corner. With a savage wave of his hand he tore down the weak shield so he could unpack his few possessions. This was his side of the barn. Gordon had said he could stay here until he decided to build a place of his own, and he intended to do just that.

As he unpacked and moved into the kitchen to set the kettle to boil, he realized he felt more like himself. In fact, he felt good about being himself. Whether that came from using his own shields or letting loose a little temper didn't matter. He was able to relax with his tea and as his mind reviewed the day, he began to put pieces of information together. He had the time to examine conversations from various angles, catalogue different observations, and make a list of things about the Dragonmen that he still didn't understand. At the top of that list was the human acceptance of a territory dragon whose authority superseded their claim on the land. It just didn't make sense. He could see Heron or even Gordon as the leader here, but why Grabon? Not that he had anything against the dragon, he seemed like a fine dragon, but why didn't Heron or Gordon challenge his leadership?

***

Hess introduced LeeAnn and Josiah.

"Is it something in the water? You are all dropping like flies. I heard Tad found his mate as well," Josiah said.

"We were lucky," Hess told him, accepting the tea from LeeAnn with a smile. "How did you manage to sneak in?"

"I didn't get past the dragon, but I managed to step over Gordon's lines. I don't think he realized I was even close. Your Grabon makes an interesting conversationalist. He probably asked a hundred questions. Shouldn't he have warned me not to stay on that side of your barn? There are other barns here, but they're all shielded."

"He pretty much set you up. I'm glad Porter waited for us to come down the hill before confronting you, or you would be one dead Farmer. When did you get here anyway?"

Josiah shrugged and put his elbows on the table, looking dejected. "According to Grabon you were all up in the nest. He invited me to join in, but I was tired. The rest of the family should arrive tomorrow sometime." He dropped that bomb and continued, as though hoping to distract Hess. "How is Hanna?"

"She had the baby, a boy named Kenseth, and they're both healthy," LeeAnn answered before Hess could explode.

"That foils our plan to be here in time for the birth. There will be plenty of disappointment over that one. How did Gordon take it?"

Hess gritted his teeth and decided to let Gordon eat this cousin of theirs alive. "He did not break down and weep, if that's what you're implying."

"He was amazingly supportive of Hanna," LeeAnn added. "Why did you come ahead of everyone?"

Josiah glanced briefly at Hess, doing his best to look innocent. "We're a larger group than expected, so I came ahead to warn Gordon."

Hess sat up straight. "How large?"

"There are four wagons. It's your own fault. You started a market. Something new and interesting, and there are plenty of stray Farmers; some young, some older with little need to stand around and watch their crops grow in high summer. Besides, a bunch of us missed the gathering."

"You couldn't send word ahead?"

"I came out in front to let you know."

Hess let out a ragged sigh. "A day ahead is not much warning!"

"I know there are extra barns; we'll simply stay there. The cows will be the challenge. There are twenty of them and the bull of course. The wagons can go to your market, since the majority of the weight is goods for trade or sale with a few gifts thrown in for you, Tad, and Gordon. Where is Tad?"

"He is across the stream, in his own house with his mate. He claimed some land and so did I, but I haven't built the house yet. How many people, Josiah? You said four wagons, but how many people?"

"Including Gordon's parents? I think there must be twenty of us. Don't look ill, we won't be much in the way."

Hess mumbled certain curses in Dragon and LeeAnn laughed. "Don't mind him. He's having trouble adjusting to the news."

Josiah smirked and drank his tea. "If you show me where I can sleep, I'll get out of your hair."

LeeAnn showed him to the spare room and closed the door.

"Don't feel sorry for him," Hess warned. "He was sent ahead, probably days ago, maybe as much as a week, and he got distracted. Now he arrives dead tired, sneaks into Porter's space, and I almost blow off his head. Then he sits here and acts like it's no big deal to have twenty guests show up. We knew Gordon's parents were hoping to make the trip this summer, but at most we were expecting half this number or less."

"Not to mention four wagons full of goods, and twenty cows."

"Yes, and one bull who needs to be housed separately. Gordon is going to kill him, which is why he wanted to sleep before seeing him. He's lucky Grabon didn't blow his cover."

LeeAnn grinned and squeezed his shoulder. "He did let him get surprised in Porter's half of the barn."

"He did. I wonder if Porter has figured out that our territory dragon is testing him?"

LeeAnn shook her head. "Men are strange creatures whether they are human or dragon. I think I'm ready to take a bath and go to bed. Are you still willing to help me with the cream?"

Hess's eyes narrowed on her smiling face. "I am never going to refuse an opportunity to touch you, especially not when you're naked. Until you're ready to find out what making love with your mate is going to feel like, it's as close as we can get."

"I was sort of hoping you felt that way. How would you feel about taking a bath with me? I noticed that the tub is large enough to accommodate two if we sit close."

His smile developed slowly and he stood and held out a hand. "I would be delighted."

When they were in the washing room, he lifted her chin so he could see her eyes. "I know you are pushing the boundaries of your fears. A man's body doesn't hide his desire, so I don't want you to be afraid of me when I take my clothes off."

"I won't be. There is a vast difference between you and any other man."

He grunted and kissed her softly. "Remember that, because we are all built with the same parts." Before she could change her mind, he quickly stripped and climbed in the tub, hoping to spare her embarrassment. When she followed, he helped her sit between his up-drawn knees. "Lean back against me and we'll wash you first."

"You know I just needed an excuse to see you naked."

"Hmmm, I am not complaining, am I?" He used the soap on the soft cloth and washed her from the neck down, marveling over how much healing had happened. Then he had her sit forward and did her back. He carefully washed between her legs and kissed her gently when she didn't flinch away. Then he handed her the cloth and soap, then leaned back and gripped the side of the tub. "Now it is your turn."

He didn't move or speak, but simply watched her as

she slowly soaped the rag. She turned slowly so she was facing him and came up on her knees. In her sudsy exploration of his body, she found small scars and one larger one. As her hand hovered above the waterline, there was a knock on the washingroom door and she screeched and covered herself.

"I swear I am going to kill you, Josiah!" Hess snarled, tenderly wrapping an arm around LeeAnn's shoulders and drawing her against him.

"How was I supposed to know you had your woman in the washingroom?"

Hess closed his eyes, trying to calm his racing heart. "Go away!"

"Fine, but there's a dragon in your living room, waiting. He says his name is Rok."

"Make him a cup of tea, be polite, and tell him we'll be out soon."

There was muttering and the sound of footsteps. LeeAnn pushed back from Hess's chest with a hand over her heart. "He scared me."

"I am seriously going to kill him one of these days. Give me your hand and stand up." She did and he helped her out of the tub, then he stood up himself and wrapped some toweling around his waist. "It's not an emergency," he said, stopping her from dressing. "Hand me the cream. Rok won't mind waiting a few minutes."

He applied it carefully before they slowly dressed

and went to the living room. Rok was sitting on his tail drinking tea while Josiah sat on one of the couches looking utterly confused.

"What brings you to our door?" Hess asked, his arm around LeeAnn. He would not have her embarrassed in her own home.

"Grabon thought you would want to know that the Farmers are still two, maybe even three days out. It seems your father is traveling with them, and Grabon was able to connect with him."

Hess looked at Josiah, who didn't meet his gaze. "Is everyone all right?"

"They are all healthy and looking forward to a visit. Traveling with cows is slow, but not too difficult. Eldon assured Grabon they have plenty of help. Some of your relatives have come along to attend the market and brought goods to trade. They will find their own accommodations, so do not be concerned. The four parents are hoping Mazy's old house in the village is still available. Grabon told them it was and they would be welcome to join the clan while they were here."

"Good, Gordon and Hanna do not need to be overwhelmed. They already have a new baby to contend with." He glared at his cousin.

"I am sorry to interrupt, Hess. Please accept my apologies."

"I am not annoyed with you, Rok. My cousin is responsible for my bad mood. We were taking a bath and he knocked on the door."

Rok shook his head, looking at the visitor. *"He does not look especially simple."*

Josiah sat up and glared at Rok. "I am not simple. What was I supposed to do? There was a dragon at the door."

"You should have told me they were in the bath. My message could have waited."

Josiah started to speak, then closed his mouth. "You did know that many of our friends and clansmen were dragons," Hess reminded him.

"Of course I knew, but I hadn't seen them. I rarely saw Grabon when he came with Heron to the farm."

Rok snorted softly, glaring at Josiah. *"Grabon and Heron traveled together, not one leading the other. If Grabon stayed out of sight, it was because he was not as welcome as his companion."*

"I understand the same thing happened to Heron in different territories. It's one of the things we're fighting to get rid of in our own territory. Here people are people whether they are dragon or human. Go to bed, Josiah, before the urge to beat on you overwhelms me."

"You have lost your sense of humor," Josiah complained.

"More likely yours has strayed into dangerous territory."

Rok snickered as Josiah left the room.

Hess shook his head. "What an idiot. I'm glad you set the record straight. Extend my thanks to Grabon. Holding a connection for all that distance couldn't have been easy."

Rok shrugged. *"Territory dragons have a capacity to communicate over distance. I do not believe it placed him under undue strain."*

"Thank him anyway. Hess was worried and now he can relax," LeeAnn told the brown dragon. "How was Golly?"

"He was sleeping." He shared the image, including Tria sleeping perched on his new headboard.

LeeAnn laughed and stood. "I am making more tea," she offered as she headed into the kitchen.

"I am going back to the nest. I have all the youngsters tomorrow," Rok explained.

"Good luck," Hess said.

After Rok left, Hess joined LeeAnn in the kitchen.

"I seriously considered burning your cousin's breakfast, but instead decided you need to challenge him to stone pitching with Porter, and fishing. How many times can a person get soaked fishing?"

"I'll do that. Maybe we can get Brom or Griss to play."

"Just as long as he's beaten so soundly he never forgets. I can't believe he was going to spring all these visitors on Hanna."

Hess shook his head. "No, I think he was trying to fool me and maybe Tad, get us upset and occupied with unneeded preparations and plans. I don't think it was aimed at Gordon and definitely not Hanna. He probably wouldn't have tried to mess with Gordon."

LeeAnn sat with her tea, swishing the liquid gently in the cup. "He lied to Grabon."

Hess smirked. "I am sure he didn't fool him, but he'll have reason to regret the attempt. Josiah hasn't figured out what is happening here. In his mind it's all fun and games with a little business on the side. We'll see what he thinks after a few hours at the market."

Chapter 14

That night, LeeAnn snuggled into Hess's arms and sighed as he tucked the blanket around them.

"I am very proud of you, did you know that?"

She lifted her head and looked at him. "Of me? Why?"

"You are doing an amazing job of fighting your fears and allowing the bond between us to grow and expand."

"I am trying," she admitted softly. "Sometimes I feel like I am not succeeding very well."

He touched her chin with his thumb. "You are doing more than I expected. Kiss me so we can go to sleep," he invited.

His lips met hers softly and he licked his lips as she pulled back. "Try that again and linger so I can taste you," he coaxed. When she did, he nipped her lip and she pulled back with a gasp. "I wouldn't hurt you, LeeAnn. Not for any reason. Do you believe that?"

"I think so."

"Will you let me teach you this much? There is a way a mate kisses that is very tender and carnal. It will feel good and make you warm and if I do it right, aroused."

She pulled back a little farther so she could see him

more clearly. "What if I can't respond?"

"Then we will try again later," he promised. "If I didn't think you would be receptive to this, I wouldn't suggest it."

"What do I have to do?"

A warm light entered his eyes. "You put your arms around my neck and let me put you under me. Then I am going to kiss you with my mouth open on yours and I am going to put my tongue in your mouth against your tongue."

"Really?" she asked faintly.

"Oh yes, and then we are going to play with one another. You'll see, it's very intimate and warm. At the same time we will share emotions so you can feel my arousal as I feel yours. We feed one another."

"This is going to lead to more than kissing, I can feel that already."

"Maybe. It will depend on how you respond. If you get scared, I will stop or slow down. Trust me that I never want what we do together to hurt you."

"Your cousin is in the next room," she reminded him.

"The room is shielded; he is not going to hear anything."

She slowly put her arms around his neck. "Like this?"

"Just that easy."

Her heart beat against his as he moved her slowly so her back was on the bed as he guided her hips to his. He kept his weight off her but let her feel his warmth. "Now I'm going to kiss you. Are you ready?"

"I don't know." Her heart was racing, but she wasn't sure it was with fear.

"I'll kiss you softly at first while you decide." He did, then he licked her bottom lip and nipped her upper lip and then kissed her and took her mouth, just as he had warned her he would. Arousal hit and made her gasp and her heart drum hard. Slowly he pressed his body down on hers and kept kissing her, letting her move against him as arousal grew between them. Hess pulled back panting and her arms tightened.

"I know," he told her as she groaned. "If we keep doing this we're going to make love," he warned in a growl.

"I don't care. Kiss me again," she demanded, tugging at his neck.

He took her mouth again, letting her feel his arousal in his mind as well as his body. She didn't pull back or react with fear. Her arousal had taken over and he encouraged it, fed it, and nurtured it until she was panting, breathless, and close to begging. Then he slipped out of his clothing and helped her do the same before kissing her again. As soon as her arousal came back up to match his own, he joined their bodies. She gasped at the sudden invasion, then softened all around him, connected to his own need, and the storm took them both, moving their minds and bodies closer together.

Afterward, she lay against him, her mind blank and her body limp as her heart slowed to its normal rhythm. His large hand on her back kept her close. Her eyes closed and she drifted into a light sleep as Hess dragged over the blanket, enveloping them in warmth. He kissed her softly and tucked her head into his chest so she could hear his heart. Together they slept, emotions still linked.

LeeAnn's eyes opened and she knew immediately that something was different.

"You're fine," Hess told her, his voice warm and reassuring in her mind.

"Where are you?" She spoke aloud because she was still half-asleep and she didn't normally have the ability to mindspeak unless she was face-to-face with someone.

"We're in the kitchen. Do you need me?"

"No, I don't think so." She rubbed her eyes and looked around the room. She could feel his amusement at her sleepy confusion.

"When you're ready to put on the cream, let me know and I'll help you."

"Who is here?" she was finally awake enough to ask.

"Josiah and Golly. There's no rush, so take your time."

She took a bath, but before she dressed, she called to him, wondering if he would hear her. He must have because he came in with a smile.

"Good morning," he offered before kissing her softly. He gently applied the cream. "You're very quiet," he commented softly, then kissed the back of her neck.

"I'm still half-asleep," she told him, avoiding his gaze.

"As well as feeling a little shy," he added with an understanding smile.

"We really are more connected," she muttered.

"Yes, we really are. If my cousin and Golly weren't here, I'd still be in bed with you, possibly inside you."

"Stop that," she demanded, turning red as a slight shiver moved inside her and she reached for her clothes.

"I can behave, for a little while. You better get dressed and join us for breakfast."

When she came out, Golly was sitting at the table looking well rested and happy. "LeeAnn, Hess is going to make pancakes, and I gathered berries to put inside. We were waiting for you."

"That was very nice of you, but I thought you didn't like pancakes." She forced her expression into a frown.

"I love pancakes, you know that." He grinned and

looked at Hess. "She knows that."

"I am sure she does. So since Golly really likes pancakes, do you think he'd like the first one, or should that be yours?"

LeeAnn pretended to consider before grinning and telling him to give the first one to Golly. Josiah drank his tea and watched the exchange with open curiosity.

"I see Gordon didn't kill you," LeeAnn commented to their guest.

"No, but it was close. It seems I owe Grabon an apology."

"Should I ask Porter to join us?" LeeAnn asked.

"No, he's having breakfast with Gordon and Hanna." Hess slid the first pancake onto Golly's plate. The berries were arranged into eyes and a smile, and Golly laughed as he picked up his fork. Hess grinned at LeeAnn and started the second pancake as she drank her tea.

"Hess tells me you're a healer?" Josiah began.

"Yes, for the Dragonmen and anyone who applies to Grabon or Hess for assistance. Did you need something?"

"No, not me," he answered quickly. "I have a friend with a bit of a rash. It's just little bumps, like blisters only smaller."

"Where is this rash on your friend?"

"It's on his palms, his feet, and under his arms. You know, all the places he gets sweaty." Josiah glanced over at Hess and shrugged.

"I'd tell your friend to go to Griss's stall at the market and get a healing cream, the one with green swentar, and it'll take the itch out and stop the rash. Then I'd warn him that he needs to quit eating a particular spice that's coming out in his sweat, because he's allergic to it."

"How is he supposed to know which spice that is?"

"There are two ways, really: he can smell his sweat and probably identify which spice is coming through, or he can burst a few small blisters and taste it."

Josiah shuddered and frowned. "I'm sure a sniff would work."

"That's usually the better choice," LeeAnn admitted.

Hess slid a pancake onto her plate and grinned. "You have to love a healer; they're even earthier than a Farmer. Nothing at all fazes her."

Josiah nodded and sighed. "I can see that. So, what is on the agenda today?"

"LeeAnn has a patient she's following up with today at the healing-corner booth. Golly is going with Rok to the market, and you are going with us as we make rounds and supervise. I may enlist you to help with a few games and other demonstrations." She could feel his amusement and anticipation, and she stuffed a bite of pancake in her mouth so she wouldn't smile.

Josiah agreed and they ate and enjoyed Golly's excitement. He had a list of what he planned to do when he was at the market.

After breakfast, Golly went back up the hill. Heron had made him promise to stop by, so that was next on his list. LeeAnn stood in the doorway and watched until he was out of sight. When she joined the men, Josiah looked faintly ill.

"What's wrong?" she asked immediately.

"I explained Golly's physical condition and what Sam did to him."

"Oh, but he's having a good day. I just want to enjoy that. Let me clean up since you did the cooking, and then we can take off. I probably should check on Hanna. Can you find out if Heron or Trissy need to see me?"

"Everyone is fine, including Hanna. She says if you get tired later, you can stop by and visit, but she and Kenseth are doing very well."

"She was up that early?" LeeAnn felt a faint stirring of guilt. Should she have been up? It seems she was the last one awake.

"Yes, Hanna and Trissy were both awake, and you shouldn't feel guilty. I'd rather you slept when you need to. Hanna will sleep during the day when Kenseth naps."

"I suppose," she answered softly.

"I'm sure of it because Gordon will insist. If you start getting up at the crack of dawn, you'll be napping too."

"Don't get bossy with me," she warned.

"I don't have to get bossy. Our minds are connected and if need be I can send you to sleep if I think you need it."

"That is so unfair," she complained.

"Maybe, but I won't have you overtired and strained when what you do can be so draining. As it is, I wasn't out doing chores first thing this morning. I joined them when they were done."

"That makes me feel better."

Hess grinned and touched the side of her face. "I didn't want to get out of bed at all."

"I am in the room," Josiah reminded them.

"Ignore him, he's a bit sensitive."

LeeAnn laughed and patted Hess's chest, rubbing over his heart with her thumb.

"Here, let me show you." He drew her closer and let her put her ear over his heart, and she sighed softly as he rubbed her back. "You've probably seen Hanna do this a dozen times. It allows the connection to seal us in."

"It really does. Your energy wraps around me, and mine does the same to you." She took a deep breath and let out a soft sigh.

"How long have you been mated?" Josiah asked with a frown.

"Just a few days," Hess answered absently, as immersed in the bond as LeeAnn was.

Josiah stood speechless for a moment. "A couple of days?" he finally demanded.

Hess focused on him and frowned. "Shut your mouth and wait outside."

Josiah left them in peace to wrap around one another.

LeeAnn barely even noticed his departure. After a few minutes, she rubbed Hess's chest. "I can see why Hanna does this so often. It's so safe and comforting, better than a warm, soft blanket over your emotions."

"Now I know why Gordon stands still sometimes and opens his arms for her. This has to be the best feeling in the world."

She lifted her head and looked at Hess with a smile. "I guess we better get going."

"I suppose, but we're going to do that again today."

"That won't bother me at all," she answered with a grin.

They found Josiah speaking with Gordon, looking utterly shocked. "They didn't say anything," he protested.

"What would you have them say?" Gordon growled.

"Holy hell, he told your cousin," LeeAnn whispered.

Hess laughed and hugged her close. "Yes, I think he did. Where did you learn that curse?"

"It's OldEarth. My grandmother used to say it."

"It sounds very funny. I've read it, but I've never heard anyone in our time say it, other than you."

"I like it," she muttered defensively.

"So do I, but it makes me laugh."

"What are you two whispering about?" Gordon asked curiously.

"LeeAnn uses an OldEarth curse when she's surprised. I wanted to know where she learned it."

"What is it?" Gordon asked.

"Holy hell," Hess said with a grin.

"Huh, I don't think I've heard that one in use." Gordon was trying not to smile.

"You will," Hess warned him. "So you told Josiah how LeeAnn came to be here?"

"I did, and I warned him not to interfere or get in the way. It's a delicate time and you're entitled to your privacy."

"We are," he agreed softly. LeeAnn slipped her head onto his shoulder, and his arms closed around her, adjusting her position so her ear was over his heart. She instantly felt better and could tell he did too.

"If you chose to spend the day alone with each other nobody would blame you," Gordon told them.

"No, she has Bernard coming in and I should make some rounds. We may come home early. We'll see."

"Is Josiah still welcome to come with you?"

"Sure, have you seen Porter?" Hess asked as LeeAnn moved away to look around after patting his chest. His arm caught her before she could move too far.

"Not since breakfast. You might want to knock on his door," Gordon suggested.

Hess nodded and looked at Josiah, his eyes narrowed. "Can you knock on his door without causing a problem?"

"Yes, I swear, I'm done. I had no idea what was going on."

***

Hess let out a low, level growl as Josiah headed for the other side of the barn and walked too close to LeeAnn. "Is he more annoying than usual?"

Gordon shook his head. "No. You're newly mated and ready to fight. It takes a few weeks to calm that down."

"All right, I just have to remember that I like him."

"He's going to find someplace else to stay tonight. That should help."

"I hope so." Hess frowned until he looked at his mate. LeeAnn was frowning too. "Hey, it's not your fault. This is a symptom I have to deal with." He brought her close, and she put her ear over his heart and sighed as his arms closed around her. He closed his eyes so he could absorb the feeling.

***

Gordon left them standing there and went to find Hanna. She greeted him and came in close to lay her head on his chest.

"You need to see LeeAnn and Hess. They're in the yard."

"What are they doing?" Hanna asked, not moving.

"This," Gordon told her, his hand on her back.

"Ah, that's good, then."

"I think so." He rubbed her back and she lifted her head. "You'll want to see this."

They stepped onto the porch where they could see them, and Hanna sighed.

"That's a statue, right there," she told him with a grin.

"I think you need to do Golly first," Gordon warned

her, his expression solemn.

She looked up at him. "I'm going to need a lot of gold to make Golly's in proportion with the others. Can we go down to the stream?"

"We'll take Kenseth and let him lie on the ground out there. I think he'll enjoy that."

"I think we all will."

***

LeeAnn picked up her head and patted Hess's chest. "I think we have an audience."

"Who?" Hess asked, scowling and looking around until he saw Hanna and Gordon. "We're going," he called, and they walked toward the bridge to cross the stream.

Josiah and Porter were waiting by the bridge.

"Did you have a good night, Porter?" Hess asked.

"I did, and your cousin apologized again. Hanna is probably the best cook in the known universe. You know that, right?"

"She is talented in all the domestic arts. You should see her use energy to get dirt out of clothes and then drain all the water. It's like magic, but most of us agree, the only thing that beats her cooking is her gold crafting."

"I can agree with that. I've never seen anything like

her sculptures."

"We had berry pancakes with Golly," LeeAnn told him, grinning. "Hess made one for Golly with a smile." She shared the image.

Porter laughed and looked over at Hess. "I bet he loved that."

"He did. Then he ate it with enthusiasm. I bet he ate at Trissy's table and he'll stop and get something from Hanna as well." Hess shook his head. "I would be too fat to walk."

"Don't forget Grabon's porridge," LeeAnn reminded him.

"That's right, he ate before he came to see us."

"All boys need their food," Porter answered softly, trying not to grin.

"LeeAnn and I haven't had a chance yet to eat with Hanna in the morning. When we do, I hope she makes her morning bread. The smell alone makes my mouth water."

"I wish I was a great cook. Maybe Hanna could teach me," LeeAnn suggested.

"We'll see. We manage all right and we're likely to be too busy to do much cooking. I'd rather grab the occasional meal over there. Josiah should join them for dinner if he gets a chance."

"I was thinking about that." Josiah nodded. "Gordon probably won't mind my company tonight. But your conversation is making me hungry right now and I ate three pancakes."

"Wait, don't eat too much at the market. If you are taking a meal with Gordon later you'll want to be hungry," Porter warned him, grinning.

Hess walked up and knocked on Tad and Dotty's door, and Tad came out with a grin. "Come on in. Hey, Josiah, my brother tells me we should probably kill you dead this morning."

"I'm an idiot," Josiah confessed softly.

"Well you're family, so you can be temporarily excused. Hess, why don't you show LeeAnn Dotty's garden. She has a nice group of flowers growing by the pool."

Hess grinned and tugged on her hand. "Call when you're ready to leave." He led her into the private garden and pulled her close. She placed her ear over his heart and sighed. "I think we're addicted," Hess rumbled, his hand on her back.

She laughed softly. "I think we might be."

"This is going to be one long day," he sighed and held her.

"Not if everyone keeps sending us off to be alone," she giggled.

"You're not going to believe this, but I was not as sensitive as I should have been when Tad was going through this with Dotty."

She looked up at him. "What did you do?"

"I hung around, said the wrong thing sometimes. One time I was trying to tease Dotty about the women Tad had known and she started to cry. My stupid brother hadn't linked emotions with her yet. Instead of bowing out, I yelled at him. Do you know what I would do to someone who made you cry today?"

"You'd make me heal them," she muttered and he laughed.

"Probably. Although if it were my fault, I'd feel so guilty it would hurt us both. This bond is even stranger than I thought and better, so much better."

"At least you know something about it. The whole thing still seems unreal to me."

He rubbed her back and she looked up at him. "I'll explain what I can," he promised, taking her hand and they walked over to the warm flower-scented pool and sat on the bench. He faced her and held her hands. "First, we link our power lines. That joins our lives and makes it difficult to be apart. Then as the bond grows, it links emotions and our bodies so we can share sensations as well as our feelings. Later, it will link our thoughts and our dreams. I have no idea how long that will take."

"You connected to my thoughts earlier," Leeann told him.

"No, that was mindspeaking. I can reach you at a distance, just as I can reach Tad or Gordon, but now with you, I can hold the connection open indefinitely.

This is more than mindspeaking. It's a window into your thoughts just as it's a window into mine. It allows us to share memories."

She shuddered, clutched his hands, and looked away as though she was afraid to look at him. "I do not want to share certain memories."

"There is nothing in your mind you need to worry about, LeeAnn. Now aside from that, there are a few other benefits, like healing faster when you sleep in my arms and sharing energy. We can also help each other through heart pain and grief. The saying in my family is 'skin to skin and heart to heart.' Meaning if either of us has a heart pain or an injury, we lie naked together with our hearts pressed against each other's and we can ease the hurt and help it heal."

"All through the mating bond," LeeAnn muttered.

"From that bond comes love, affection, acceptance, loyalty, and all the rest of what we need. There's no way to lie, no chance of one of us being unfaithful or separating. We can't get lost or injured without the other knowing. If you're afraid or hurting I'll know and I'll do whatever it takes to make it stop."

"This bond is huge, isn't it?" she asked in wonder.

"It is huge; it totally links two people. That's why it takes time to forge the link properly. Mistakes can happen, such as one partner trying to control one aspect of the bond, and that throws everything out of whack. It messes things up until the pair reconnect properly. That happened to Heron. He tried to keep his emotions private. I wasn't here for that, but I heard about it. Tad and Dotty rushed the bond, missed steps, and had to back up a couple of times. That was to help her deal with the poison and because she was fragile."

"I can't imagine rushing it." She cringed. "It takes everything in me not to fight it, but can you imagine trying to make it go faster?"

"No, I'm not letting myself fight it either, or get as territorial as it pushes me to be, but I can't imagine what would happen if we tried to hurry it along."

LeeAnn grinned. "You're not letting it make you territorial?"

"Not really," he answered defensively.

"You growled at Josiah because he walked close to me, and we're now isolated in a private garden."

"I didn't hit him, blast him, or even yell. I think I'm being reasonable."

"Maybe from your perspective," she said with a grin.

"My perspective is the only one that counts besides yours. Everyone else needs to give us a little space."

She put her ear to his chest and he held her close. "At least Golly didn't bother you."

"No, Golly doesn't bother me. It's men, mature males, who are close to you. I don't even know if it would be the dragons, but maybe." He frowned at the thought.

"Hess?" Tad called from the entrance. Hess sighed. "I'll contact you when Bernard shows up so she can see him. Don't be an idiot; take your mate home."

"Are you sure?" Hess frowned as he thought of all the things at the market that needed to be seen to and checked on.

"I am certain that if the two of you go out there, you will have someone by the throat before we even open. Spend the day with LeeAnn; share secrets, interests, talk to one another. If you feel like company, visit Heron and Trissy or Gordon and Hanna. Mated couples aren't going to bother either of you."

"It's a lot of work," Hess reminded him. "I don't want to stick you with it all."

"There are three of us, as well as Brom and Griss. Porter will even help as needed, I'm sure. Go home."

"All right," he conceded, knowing that his brother was most likely correct. If he could turn on Josiah, whom he liked, he was feeling too dangerous to be around a crowd.

"What are we going to do?" LeeAnn asked, still against him.

Hess grinned. "We're going to spend some time alone, learn about one another, and furnish the rest of the house out of the stores in the barns so it feels like home."

Chapter 15

Porter had greatly enjoyed his breakfast with Hanna and Gordon. It had been an education in mate dynamics and communication watching the two of them pass the infant. Hanna cooked and made a delicious breakfast while Gordon checked on Josiah, brought in milk, then eggs, and gathered from the garden. They had sat down to eat and any questions he had planned to ask were suspended in favor of savoring every bite. The food had been like nothing he had ever tasted.

After the table was clear, he'd gone back to his side of the barn to make notes of his observations. When he'd rejoined the others, he'd seen how edgy Hess was and had kept a careful distance. Tad had sent the pair off and let out a relieved sigh.

"Instinct must be riding him hard," Tad told them. "He needs to be alone with her without interruption."

Josiah had immediately agreed, and when he finally asked, Tad had explained exactly what a mating bond was and how it affected males. Porter had heard about it among the Farmers but hadn't understood it. Evidently the dragons had some experience with it and had been a great help to Tad when he met Dotty in getting the bond started. They were able to offer a different perspective and more information on how they could speed up the process and how to repair any missteps.

Porter accompanied Tad and his cousin into the market, still puzzled about a great many things. They left Josiah at the main entrance, gaping at Grabon and Heron's statue with the rules and heartsong imbedded, sitting on the stand Trissy had carved. Tad moved through the market quickly, checking each stall to see who needed assistance.

"We are moving a lot faster than Hess did yesterday," Porter commented.

Tad grinned. "Hess had LeeAnn with him. She's still meeting everyone and he didn't want to rush her. My brother rarely moves at less than a slow run, unless his mate is by his side."

Tad met with Pit and Thane for a few moments to adjusting patrol areas, and then they were off again.

They entered what looked like a maze of stalls that Porter hadn't known were there. They had tools he had never seen before, rare skins, objects made of clay, art and metal items that were completely unfamiliar to him.

"What is this?" Porter finally asked, gesturing to the area and a particular display.

"Over there are old and rare tools and skins. These are dragon porn and sex toys. These paintings are done by well-known dragon artists, but not for public display among humans. Farther down are more artisan goods, including cups, utensils, and mats. Across the way"-Tad pointed to a stall shaded by a tree-"we have music and literature in Dragon that if you understood, would make you blush. There's human porn over here." He gestured to another stall up ahead.

They kept walking and Porter looked around with interest. One of the stalls even proudly displayed printed books.

"Dragons don't have the same reservations about sex that humans do, but it seemed in bad taste to mix this in with the rest of the goods, so we created a special section. They do a brisk business among dragons as well as humans."

"I imagine they do," Porter muttered.

"We still have some open stalls in this section. I'm hoping to fill them in before our next season."

Porter followed Tad as they moved back into the main section. "You aren't worried about attracting the wrong element?" he asked.

Tad looked at him oddly. "This is Grabon's territory. If the wrong element comes here, he'll get rid of them. He's very efficient. As far as humans are concerned, we caught one thief already. He lost a couple of fingers due to his own stupidity and we banished him. If he ever returns, Grabon will hunt him."

Porter swallowed and looked around. "I thought Grabon was more of a figurehead."

Tad stared at him and then laughed. "You have some mixed-up ideas. Let's get Josiah and I'll fill you in on our great territory dragon and why all this is possible."

He led the way and they found Josiah wandering and looking lost.

"We're going to get some tea. Do you want to join us?" Tad asked. "Porter needs a lesson on what a territory dragon is and does."

"Sure, I'm anxious for tea," Josiah said, looking around as if unsure what planet he was on.

They went over to Tad's favorite tea stand, took a table, and got three cups of fragrant tea. Dotty joined them with a grin and sat with her own cup. Tad kissed her softly and put his hand on the back of her chair.

"Territory dragons are different from clan dragons. Sometime during their awandering, a young territory dragon becomes self-aware and begins to hunt for his or her territory. When they are fully mature, they claim the land that is meant to be theirs and send their power into the ground, planting roots that connect to the planet. The land responds and sends more power back. This works the same as a Farmer claiming land." He glanced at Josiah, who nodded. "Only, a territory dragon claims from the highest point on their land in all directions as far as they can see. They don't own this land but assumes a kind of stewardship over it. They protect the water, animals, and plants in their territory. Anyone willing to follow this territory dragon can then apply to him for acceptance. If you don't accept the territory dragon, you move out of the territory. If they don't accept you, you move out of the territory. Any people, human or dragon they accept, becomes clan and lives under the territory dragon's protection while others, if allowed, merely reside there. They monitor all activity, set the rules, render judgment, lend aide, and settle disputes. Any children or youngsters unclaimed by a mated pair go to the territory dragon, and all visiting dragons apply to the territory dragon and are required to announce their presence and intentions upon arrival."

Tad took a breath and looked at Porter. "Are you getting the idea? No human would think to assume responsibility for so much." He looked at his mate and smiled. "I wouldn't want the job and neither would Hess. Gordon was here for ten cycles and was more than willing to accept Grabon's leadership. His solution to the people who settled around the farm was to help them occasionally and ignore most of them. They could survive or not by their choice, skill, and talent. Our territory dragon takes an active interest in everything in his territory. He accepts our Farmers' claims on our land, Heron's claim on the woods, and even Pit's claim. He allowed Brom and Griss to raise their own youngsters even without mates, which is against all dragon tradition. During storms he lends support and help as needed. In short, he is the responsible party, the judge, the caretaker."

Tad glanced at Josiah and sighed. "I don't know how to describe Grabon's strength and endurance. From what Heron has said, he's still growing in power. He's stronger than the average territory dragon, more capable, less corrupt, and despite his young age for a mature dragon, educated and reasonable."

Porter felt somewhat sick. Impulsively he had decided to stay without building an understanding first. Had he based the decision on a message embedded in a statue and a feeling? Apparently he had built a false idea of how the territory worked based on fragments of information. "I really didn't understand."

Tad shrugged and sipped his tea. "You thought he was an elected official, chosen mostly because he was a dragon."

Porter nodded and looked around. "As much land as he can see from his highest perch?"

"That's where he built his nest, and Grabon has excellent vision." He sat back and pulled Dotty close. "Last night you saw his management style with those of us who he accepts and who have accepted him. It's very different with outsiders, visitors, and the general population of his territory. He has offered you acceptance, but you need to choose if you accept him; the rest of us too, but him specifically. If you were a dragon, he'd set you a task with a time limit, and until you accomplished that task, you would live in his nest under his supervision. If you accomplished it, he would grant you acceptance. Then you could choose a place for your nest and either build it yourself or ask for assistance from the rest of us. If you didn't accomplish your task, he would ask you to leave and you could never be more than a visitor in his territory."

"Instead, since I'm a human, what happens?" Porter asked, frowning slightly.

"Grabon took your measure when you crossed into his territory. You carry enough power to be of interest. Hess met you and assessed your strength. Brom brought you to Heron so he could determine your level of threat to everyone else. Heron not only spoke to you but did a reading and gave a recommendation to Grabon. Grabon accepted his recommendation. Hess then showed you around and further assessed your strength. You were able to see all of us together last night, and if you think Josiah really got into your place under Grabon's radar, think again."

"No, he talked to me all the way through the territory and even helped me avoid Gordon's energy lines in the yard so I could surprise him. I told Grabon I was bedding down in the barn. I was being cagey about which one."

"What would Grabon have done if I had blasted Josiah?" Porter demanded.

Tad looked at Josiah and grinned. "Grabon would have understood. He was invading your territory without permission. Do you think any of us would accept that? Of course, it was your fault; you had no real shields in place."

Porter narrowed his eyes and his jaw tensed. "I now have my shields in place. The rules here are confusing. I'm not expected to be civilized and tame?"

"No, and if you were, he wouldn't have made the offer. You'd be useless to yourself and the rest of us. Look around you; none of us are tame. It's why we don't fit in, in other places. We're all under control, but not tame. Thane was thrown out of more territories than the others were, but they each caused their fair share of trouble and then some. Hess and I were accused more than once of using intimidation as a tool during negotiations. Nobody has ever thought of Gordon as tame, and I'll let you judge Heron."

Porter shook his head and sighed. "It's going to take me some time to adjust."

Dotty laughed lightly and grinned at him. "It's going to amaze you how easily you adjust when you have all the facts straight. The thing to remember about Grabon is he can see into you, all the way past everything, all the lies we tell ourselves, to find the truth."

"Speaking of the big guy." Josiah nodded toward something in the market.

Tad stood up to see what was happening and Dotty followed. Porter wasn't far behind.

"What is happening?" he asked.

Grabon had swooped down and was walking with purpose.

"What is going on?" Tad asked him.

"I am looking for a youth who likes to throw rocks," Grabon informed him, sharing the image of a human boy of fifteen or sixteen.

"We'll help you look," Tad said.

"What did he do?" Josiah asked as they left the table.

"He must have thrown rocks at somebody or something," Dotty answered, looking around.

Grabon let out a piercing whistle that had everyone flinching and stepping aside to let him move quickly through the crowd. The next thing they knew he had the young man by the shoulder.

"Let me go!" The youth struggled.

"Stand still, you idiot, or he'll use his claws to keep you still," Tad warned with a snarl.

Thane and Pit materialized from the growing crowd and began moving people back until a ring had formed around Grabon and the youth.

"Explain to everyone why I came looking for you," Grabon instructed.

"I have no idea. I didn't do anything," the boy protested, trying to duck away. His expression was defiant and surly.

Grabon tightened his hold and shook the boy. *"Explain,"* he insisted.

"I didn't do it," the boy wailed, pleading with his audience.

"Explain," Grabon urged, his voice hard and firm.

"It was someone else!"

"EXPLAIN!" Power resonated in his voice and the air around them.

"Someone was throwing rocks."

"What did those rocks hit?" Grabon insisted.

"They might have hit a sheep." The boy tried to duck away again, but there was no give in the dragon's grip, only the bite of claws.

"Whose sheep were they?" Grabon demanded.

"The Tailor. He keeps a whole herd of the smelly beasts." The boy wiped his face on his sleeve.

"You were practicing using power while throwing stones. Your aim is poor and you never anticipated hitting the sheep," Grabon announced. *"When you hit one, it was exciting because it reacted and ran, upsetting all the other sheep. Then you saw the woman out feeding the sheep. She was even farther away."*

"I didn't hit her," the boy screamed, looking around wildly.

"You threw the stone!" Grabon bellowed.

"I missed. It didn't hit her!" he insisted.

"You threw the stone! Then you ran away and came here to hide."

"It was a mistake."

"You and your parents will meet with me and the

Tailors in my nest at midday. Do not make me hunt you." He released the youth.

No one seemed surprised when the boy ran, and they had no trouble getting out of his way. Grabon watched until he was gone, then nodded in satisfaction.

"Did the Tailors complain?" one woman asked curiously.

His gaze level, Grabon turned to look at her. *"There was no complaint. Kimmi was the boy's target, but he missed. The sheep was uninjured except for a bruise; it had not been shorn recently. But that does not excuse his actions."*

Sweat slid down Porter's back and he swallowed nervously. "What is he going to do?"

Tad grinned and nodded toward Grabon. "Ask him."

"What kind of penalty are you planning?" One of the vendors asked before Porter had a chance.

"There was no injury," Grabon answered, reminding them of the facts. *"The boy needs training and supervision after he accepts responsibility for his actions."*

People nodded and moved off and Grabon headed toward Porter followed by Thane and Pit. Mia came from the back of the crowd as visitors and vendors dispersed. "Nothing like a little excitement. Why did you let him run from the Tailors?" Tad asked.

"I had some hope he would speak to his parents or

some other guiding influence. Zack was disturbed by the impulse to throw a rock at Kimmi and knew what might have happened, had his aim and power been more developed. Yet instead of seeking an adult he ran and hid here." Grabon shook his head. *"He needs guidance, an example to follow."*

"Human boys of that age can be secretive about their misdeeds," Tad offered quietly.

"It sounds like the boy needs more influence and meaningful tasks to perform, with less time on his own," Mia offered with a sniff.

"Such were my thoughts," Grabon agreed. *"I think the market would benefit from an assistant in the gaming area to demonstrate the skills needed to play the games. Porter would be a good influence for the boy and could provide him with supervision."* Grabon looked directly at their newest applicant and smiled. *"Consider it your task to improve your own skills as well as Zack's."*

Porter groaned. "You're going to stick me with the boy?" Disbelief colored his tone.

Looking at him, Grabon shifted his wings, flexed his claws, and lifted his head. *"Only if you choose to join us."*

"So my first task is babysitting a misbehaving adolescent?" Porter grimaced.

"If you choose to consider it that, I will not argue."

"Fine, but I am not going easy on the boy. Your idea

of punishment is a bit backward."

"You will do as you think best. Please attend the meeting at midday so you can decide for yourself if I am wise or foolish." With a nod to the others, Grabon took off toward his nest.

Thane and Pit snickered as they left, and Mia let out a soft sigh. *"I am glad Kimmi was not injured. It would greatly upset Kev and Fin if she were, especially when tending her own sheep."*

Agreeing, Tad looked at Josiah. "The boys, while born Tailors, are ours. Assigning Zack to Porter was a good choice, since he wouldn't take the attempt as personally as the rest of us."

"I am very glad I did not have Grabon looking over my shoulder when I was a youth," Josiah muttered.

Dotty chuckled and they returned to the table and their tea. Porter was quiet until they were walking through some other stalls checking with vendors and helping move goods.

"If I am going to be teaching Zack games, I had better figure them out," he finally said.

Setting down the last crate, Tad nodded. "I'd get Brom or Griss to show you, and don't forget to be at the nest at midday. That's during opening."

Porter didn't have to do much to persuade Brom to demonstrate the games and give him a few pointers. His mind raced as he thought of a few others he could add, stick fighting on a log being one of them. When he mentioned the idea to Brom, the gray-and-white dragon shook his head.

"You need to speak to Tad and Pit. They deliberately avoided combat games."

Looking around at the games they had, Porter realized how true that was. Every one was a test of strength, coordination, or strategy. None in any way promoted violence, and he had yet to see anything resembling a weapon sold in the market.

"I had not realized." He looked at them again and smiled. "Interesting."

"Our goal is to peacefully integrate dragons and humans. Among ourselves we enjoy many combat games, pitting human strength and strategy against dragon, but not at the market."

"That makes perfect sense. I'll come up with something else. So what do you think of Zack helping me demonstrate the games?"

Brom let out a growl that resounded all around them and turned his head away. *"The boy could have harmed Kimmi."*

Raising his brows, Porter sighed. "He didn't cause any harm, and really it probably wasn't even his intention to get close. Zack is young and didn't consider his own strength."

"He should have," Brom answered with a sniff. *"It is good that he was not assigned to me."*

Porter was forced to agree. Any of the others would have been harder on the boy. He looked up at the sky and decided it was time to head for the nest. Brom agreed and walked with him as far as his stall. Porter waved to Griss as he passed and Griss immediately acknowledged him. The sisters called to him and told him to bring that boy around so they could tell him what they thought. Porter seriously doubted he would do that first.

On the walk out of the market, plenty of vendors and workers nodded to him. When he was off the market grounds and had passed the shielding for Tad and Dotty's private land, he sensed something out of place. Stopping, he took a careful look around and saw a man standing by the bridge. Recognizing Denny, he walked toward him.

"Why are you over here?" Porter asked.

"Shielding wouldn't let me go any farther. I couldn't back up, couldn't move forward. It's like a solid wall and a snare," Denny muttered.

"The shields are protecting Tad and Dotty's home. Were you looking for me?"

"I was before I got trapped. I'm heading out of here and thought I'd give you a last chance to change your mind." Porter shook his head, but Denny held up a hand. "You don't need to say it. As I was standing there, I could see more than trees. It looks like you shed a cloak of shields yourself. This land suits you, as do the dragons and all that power. For a couple of cycles, I've enjoyed our travels. Having a Woodsman on long treks has been convenient. You always did the most work and I've let you, because for the most part I'm lazy." He laughed at himself. "Those days are over, I guess, but I wanted to let you know I appreciated it."

Porter shook his hand after they made it over the bridge and onto Gordon's land. The shielding didn't stop Porter; he could push through it. "We had some fun."

Denny nodded and shifted his feet. "I don't know how all this is going to work out." He waved his hand around. "Too many people like to think they're the superior species, simply because they are... human. It could very well put you smack in the middle of a species conflict."

Porter shifted and nodded, remembering how guilty he was of that kind of thinking. "I'm well aware of that."

"Good luck, then, Dragonman." Denny walked away as Porter watched, even as he realized Gordon was watching too.

"Problem?" Gordon asked, moving to stand beside him.

"No, he was just taking off. Got himself trapped on the other side of the bridge in the shields. I'm heading up to Grabon's."

"Yeah, that stupid kid. Kev and Fin stopped by with Golly a little while ago, all fired up. Why are you going?"

Porter let out a sigh. "Grabon wants me to work

with Zack. Teach him the games in the market and be a mentor, I think."

Grinning, Gordon slapped him on the back and chuckled. "Good luck!"

"You do know that nobody was hurt, right? He was just a dumb kid throwing rocks."

Gordon sighed before he faced him. "Kimmi heard that rock whiz by her head. She thought it was a stinger and ducked. The boys came to see me about a defensive shield for their mother. If his aim had been better, they would be planning her burial. They have cause to be upset."

Okay, that surprised Porter, but it didn't change the basic facts. The boy had power; it simply needed to be trained properly, channeled, and challenged. "I better get up there." He nodded up the hill.

"Do a good job defending him; it's what Grabon expects. We may all be irritated, but nobody will doubt Grabon's judgment."

"I'll remember that." Porter grinned and started toward the trail. "Tell Hanna thanks again for breakfast."

Grinning, Gordon waved. "You're expected for dinner. If you're bringing that scrappy boy, let us know. Young men eat twice what you or I do, but not as much as Golly."

Porter chuckled as he went up the hill. Trissy stopped him as he passed the hut. She was rubbing her belly and any complaint over the delay died long before it reached his lips. "Are you all right?"

"I'm fine, just feeling overburdened. Can you move something for me?"

"Of course." He followed her inside the hut, which was cool. "What do you need?"

Trissy pointed to a small log by the chair. "I was going to do some carving, but I need that on the table. Heron put it over here for me, and then after he left I realized I can't get to it."

Porter looked at the log and looked at her. *"Heron?"*

"You're late!"

"I'm at the hut. Trissy wants this log on the table so she can carve. She's rubbing her belly and looks uncomfortable."

"I'm on my way. Do not leave her alone."

"You called him." Trissy gave him a hard glare.

"Yes, I did. Go sit down," he said, hefting the log, bringing it to the table, and laying it on its side.

"He's going to yell at me."

"Maybe not." He put the kettle on because he didn't know what else to do. "Are you in labor?"

"I don't know. Everything feels funny and I have these pains in my back."

Heron came in the door, looking fierce. "LeeAnn and Hess are on their way. You tried to move that log, didn't you?" he accused.

"No, I tried to slide it on the floor and ended up on my knees. Then I had to climb to my feet."

"Why didn't you call?" Heron bellowed. "Rok is on the roof!"

"I didn't need him watching every breath I take. He's worse than you and that's saying something!"

Porter fixed the tea and tried to stay out of it, but Heron turned to him. "Go up and deal with this Zack boy. I'm staying here with my stubborn mate." He walked over and cupped her cheek. "I shouldn't have left. I knew you were uncomfortable."

"I was just moving the log. It's not even that big," she wailed, clutching her belly.

"You're fine, you're both fine." He wrapped his arms around her as Porter slipped out of the hut. He signaled Rok and smiled as the dragon made a comment about females. As he headed up to the nest, Grabon asked him if Trissy was all right.

"LeeAnn and Hess are on their way and I'm heading up. I think she just scared herself, but it could be early labor."

Grabon muttered and Porter smiled as he climbed up the last rocky part. Zack stood with his mother inside the nest, while Kimmi, her match, and her boys were on Grabon's other side.

"I was delayed, sorry about that," Porter offered.

"It was more important that you help Trissy as requested," Grabon answered with a nod. *"It seems Zack's father has declined to make an appearance."* Grabon made the introductions and looked each of them in the eye. *"Here are the facts. Zack was about very early, without proper nourishment due to an outburst that occurred in his home. He climbed to the area overlooking the Tailor's while seeking solitude. Emotions released power he had not been able to tap into previously. While throwing rocks he unexpectedly hit a sheep. This surprised and pleased him in his current mood. Then he threw his next rock toward a distant human target with more power, but without any intent to do harm.*

"Fortunately his aim was poor. This near miss distressed him when he realized what he had done, and he ran. Instead of running home, because of the outburst that morning, he went into the market to hide. When confronted he attempted to deny responsibility." Grabon looked at the different parties involved.

"I have concerns." He looked at Kimmi first and then at Thorne. *"Your match should not be out feeding sheep without shielding. If she cannot form and maintain her own, you or one of the boys should see to this."*

Thorne acknowledged that with a nod and a sideways look at Kimmi. "That is something we will resolve. It will not happen again."

Grabon nodded and turned to Zack. *"You should not throw rocks at someone else's sheep. You should not throw rocks at a human target. You should accept responsibility for your actions even when you know they are wrong."*

Grabon looked at Zack's mother. The woman looked terrible, as though she had been up half the night crying. *"You are having a difficult time. Your male is angry, drinks too much wine, and is physically confrontational with your son. This has made your house an uncomfortable and unsafe place for you and for Zack. I have several choices for you. I can offer you shelter away from them both. I can provide a safe place to live with your son, or if you choose, you may remain where you are and I can simply remove the boy. What is your choice?"* Grabon sat back on his tail and waited, crossing his arms.

Zack stared at his mother, eyes wide. "Mother?"

"Let me think?" she snapped, rubbing her head. "You could make sure Zack is safe?"

"He will be safe no matter your choice and will not return to that house. The boy has too much power and no training. If left unchecked he would become dangerous."

Zack started to protest and Porter put a hand out and shook his head. "Don't speak. Let your mother make her decision."

"Rick isn't bad, he's just having a hard time. Getting Zack out of there would help. The two of them don't get along and never have. Zack is my first husband's child."

Grabon didn't say anything for a minute and then nodded. *"I will assume responsibility for Zack from this day until he is determined mature enough to live independently. You may return to your home. I thank you for attending and standing beside my boy."*

She nodded, looked at Zack and shrugged. "You shouldn't have provoked him, Zack. This is better than waiting for one of you to kill the other. I can't keep stepping between you."

"But Mom, you know that's not what happened." The boy looked stunned.

His mother sniffed as she walked toward the steps leading out of the nest. "He's really not a bad boy," she told them as she left. "He'll have a better chance here."

Zack stared after her, as if expecting her to return. Thorne cleared his throat. "I'll take everyone home, if you don't need us for anything."

Grabon nodded and looked at Kev and Fin. *"You learned some shielding from Gordon?"*

"We did. We'll make sure our mother is shielded," Kev said.

"There are puton and other predators, but I do not believe she needs to worry about more stones. We will see you at the market."

The boys nodded and got their parents out of the

nest quickly. Grabon focused his full attention on the boy. Zack looked as if someone had pulled out his insides and shown them to him.

"I didn't provoke him," he muttered.

"No, you are a young man and in need of someone to pit your strength against. Rick is not that man. He could not be a father to you because he does not have the physical, mental, or intellectual strength needed. Your mother does not have the skill to manage both of you."

"She threw me out," Zack complained, anger edging his voice.

"No, she gave you to me," Grabon corrected. *"I have the strength needed to help you grow into a powerful and good male. Hopefully the next time Rick hits her she will remember our conversation and will ask for assistance."*

"You know about that?" Zack asked, clearly shocked. He must not have been listening closely earlier.

Chapter 16

"I am Grabon, the territory dragon. I will always know. Do not run or hide from a problem, simply come and explain the difficulty. We are Dragonmen, we do not duck responsibility. We embrace it, even when we are wrong."

Zack looked at Porter, who nodded. The boy swallowed and took a deep breath. "What about my things?"

"You will have no need of them. Porter will see to your needs for now." Grabon looked around his nest and smiled. *"We will make room for you here."* Porter raised his brows as images of clothing, a trunk, and other items flashed in his mind. *"After you have shopped and carried everything here, Porter will begin to teach you. By dinner, you will be tired. After dinner, we will play a game, and you will show me what you have learned. Let us hope it is sufficient and I do not think you need more practice."*

With those ominous words hovering over them, Grabon handed Porter two handfuls of coins. *"Make sure he eats well,"* Grabon whispered in his mind.

Porter nodded, stuffed the coins in his pouch, and got the boy out of there. "We need to stop at the hut and see how Trissy is doing." He looked at Zack. "Do I need to tell you to mind your manners?"

"No," Zack answered quickly. "I'm in enough trouble, I think." He glanced up at the nest, where Grabon perched on the edge watching them. "How long is this going to last?"

Porter looked at the boy. "I'll let you think that one out for yourself." He walked fast down to the hut, where Heron was standing outside looking up at Grabon. "Well?"

"She's fine, mostly scared. I'd offer you tea, but it sounds like you're going to be busy. Bring Grabon's boy back later and we'll talk," he told Porter.

Porter nodded and they continued down the hill, Zack at his heels. "Why did he call me Grabon's boy?"

"You can think that one out too. We better hurry because Grabon gave me a list for you and it's not short."

Hess and LeeAnn were talking with Gordon and Hanna in Gordon's yard.

Hess grinned and glanced at Zack only briefly. "It sounds like Grabon's boy is going to be running up and down the hill all day. You might want to warn him about Golly and then educate him a little on dragon etiquette. An introduction is necessary for an exchange. Sooner or later he's going to want to ask questions, so he might as well know how to begin."

"Zack, this is Hess, LeeAnn, Gordon, and Hanna. Bow your head and repeat their names; that's how it's done." Porter waited for the boy to finish. "Now we better get moving. Hanna, is that dinner invitation still open?"

"Yes, and Zack is invited too if he's not required up in the nest," Hanna answered.

"He'll need to get permission from Grabon. He's being tested after dinner in the nest."

She made a sympathetic face as they raced off. "Tested?" Zack asked as they moved quickly across the bridge.

"What did you think he meant when he said he'd play after dinner? He's going to test your skills. Let's hope you are a fast learner and that I'm a half-decent teacher."

Zack was almost jogging to keep up until he lengthened his stride as they passed the shields and moved onto the market grounds. "We better practice a lot," Zack told him with a frown.

"It's all going to depend on how much you can carry and how fast you can run up and down the hill. First we go to Brom's for the skins you're going to need."

"Skins?"

"To make up a bed; Grabon has a bed of his own, as does Golly. You're not going to sleep on the wall with the dragons, are you?"

"No, but that other bed was huge," Zack told him.

"It belongs to Golly and it's private. Golly is another one of Grabon's boys." Porter found himself searching for words. He stopped abruptly and looked at Zack. "Food first and I'll tell you about Golly. Have you eaten here before?" Porter indicated the stall in front of them.

Zack looked at the booth and shook his head. "Other than this morning, I haven't been here."

"Does Rick work at the market?"

"No, but he's been getting the wine here." Zack's jaw flexed a few times.

"That's his problem. I bet the food is good." Porter led the way and saw Brom at a table with a couple of other dragons. Brom made introductions, referring to Zack as Grabon's boy again, and Zack and Porter brought over chairs and sat with them.

"What should we get?" Porter asked Brom.

"The fish is good today, very fresh; I caught it this morning. Tell them you want it cooked."

Porter ordered two cooked fish. The woman smiled and left them to their conversation after bringing them tea that smelled different than Porter was used to.

"What kind of tea?"

"It's good," Zack told him, earning grins from the other dragons.

"It is a special blend. Not many humans drink it."

Porter tried it and nodded. "It's not bad. When did

you fish?"

"I took Starseth as the first sun rose. She likes the water, especially splashing her father. I left her with Griss, to come and speak to these two." He indicated his companions. *"They are surprised Grabon has allowed us access to our youngsters. I was explaining that Grabon believes in family, even when a male is unmated. They believe Grabon is foolish this way."*

Porter cleared his throat. "There is nothing foolish about Grabon."

Brom grinned and nodded slowly. *"I agree, and I will tell them you and I both see this the same way."* As he did so in Dragon, their cooked fish arrived and Porter was able to see Zack's look of surprise as a huge platter of fish was put in front of him. He knew there was a reason the dragons were eating here. The portions were huge.

Zack wasted no time digging in. Porter took a little longer to start eating, but he enjoyed it just as much. Of course, it was his second meal of the day and the youth had not eaten at all.

"I need to tell you about Golly," Porter began softly. Brom nodded and looked at the others, who stood and bowed before they left. "Golly was tortured, his body mutilated, so he looks different. He's also unbelievably tall, but he's about your age and he's simple."

Zack looked up and nodded while chewing. "You mean dumb simple?"

"I suppose, but nobody would say that out loud; it's mean. He's just simple and kind." Porter swallowed and looked at Brom.

"Golly is dying. He has only a short time before all his organs fail. We all protect Golly," Brom told him.

Zack looked stunned, but he nodded. "Okay."

"He is sensitive and scared. It is his job to find some joy before he dies. You understand?"

"I understand, but there's nothing a healer can do?"

"We have the best healer and she helps him every day. There's nothing else that can be done," Porter explained.

"Well what's wrong with him?" Zack demanded.

Porter looked at Brom, who shrugged. "We'll ask LeeAnn and she can explain it to you. She's the healer and Golly's special friend."

Zack shrugged and went back to eating. "You'd think a real healer could fix him."

Brom laughed and patted Porter's back. *"Let us hope he does not say that to Hess or LeeAnn."*

Porter gave a groaning sigh. "Listen up, kid, before you get yourself in real trouble. LeeAnn is an exceptional healer and she's a Dragonman. There are things that can go wrong with a person that a healer cannot fix. That's a fact you might as well accept."

"Is she the lady we met in the Farmer's yard?" Zack

asked, looking thoughtful.

"Yes, she's Hess's mate."

The boy nodded and ate some more fish. "She seems to have some power."

Brom snorted softly. *"When you are ready to shop, let me know. I will be in my booth."*

Porter watched Brom escape so he could laugh, he was sure. "It's a good thing you are Grabon's boy. It might be the only thing that saves you. Finish eating so we can get started. We have a lot to do."

Brom loaded the boy down with skins and tools he might need, and Porter went with him as he took that all the way up to the nest. Several dragons there watched, including Grabon as Zack dropped off that load. Then back at the market, the sisters made sure he had a pouch and several changes of clothes and handed Porter some as well. Zack was sure he could handle more than that, so they stopped by Griss's shop and picked up tea and some brews, especially for sore muscles and a liniment the red dragon recommended. While Zack took those up to the nest, Porter put away his own clothes.

The next load was a wooden trunk with carved gaming stones inside. Zack about died carrying that across the bridge and up the hill, and they stopped and drank some water before they continued. The last load consisted of blankets and linens Grabon thought he should have, along with new shoes. By the time they were done, Zack was drenched in sweat, and

Porter wasn't much better. They found a tea booth and fell into chairs, grateful to sit still for a few minutes.

"You still have to practice, so don't get too comfortable," Porter warned.

Zack grunted and sulked into his tea. Porter looked up and saw Rok come in with all the youngsters and he nudged Zack with his foot. "Don't be a baby. Help me put some of these tables together. Rok just brought in the nursery."

Mia entered and joined them, followed by Pit.

Zack glanced at Golly and smiled. "I'm Zack."

Golly helped move the tables, returning his grin. "I'm Golly. Rok said we can come and watch you train with Porter and maybe play some games. We were late because Trissy was upset, but she's feeling better."

As everyone settled at the table, Zack stared at the dragon youngsters for a moment too long. Matti gave him a hard look. "Why are you staring at Red-seth and Star-seth?" she emphasized their new names as she spoke.

Zack cleared his throat. "I'm sorry, I've never seen a young dragon before."

"We are all young dragons," Jenny told him. "We're Dragonmen and so are you."

Zack looked at Rok, who was grinning. *"Jennyseth is correct. You are all dragon youngsters, but Zack is older and more mature. I am sure he meant no offense."*

"I didn't," he answered, looking somewhat bewildered.

"You should change your name like we did," Matti told him.

"Why would I do that?" Zack asked, holding on to his teacup as if the planet might tip him over.

"If you were Zackseth, everyone would quit calling you Grabon's boy. You could just be one of us," Matti explained.

"I don't think he's ready for that, Mattiseth. He's still adjusting," Porter explained.

Matti nodded wisely. "When I left my old family, I was afraid and cried a lot. Did you run away too?"

Swallowing, Zack looked at Porter. "Sort of?"

Matti grimaced. "Did Grabon spank you? When I ran away in the winter, Heron spanked me."

Zack shot a sharp look at Rok and Porter. "No, he didn't spank me," he answered, looking worried.

"Zack did not endanger himself in the cold," Rok reminded Matti. *"I believe that is why Heron spanked you."*

Matti shifted in her seat. "I remember."

Their tea arrived and Porter thought Zack had been

tortured enough for the moment. "I think we better go and practice. Enjoy your tea and we'll see you out at the games." He patted Golly's back.

"Make sure to teach Grabon's boy how to fish. I will challenge him to a game so the youngsters can watch." Rok grinned as they left.

"Fishing?" Zack asked.

"It's not as easy as it sounds. I'll show you, and know that we'll be attracting an audience, so no sulking. It just makes you look younger and less mature. Something tells me as Grabon's boy, you don't want to be considered one of the youngsters."

Zack glanced back toward the tea stand, frowning. "No, but I guess Golly is and happy to be so."

Porter searched his expression. "Golly is happy to not be tortured. You're going to find out anyway, but let me show you what someone did to him." He shared the image that Hess had shared with him of Golly's mutilated genitalia and scars. "Sam fed his balls to a puton while he bled."

Zack gagged and swallowed hard. "I... I... ungh."

"So you understand why Golly is a youngster?" Porter asked, looking at the youth with a piercing gaze. Zack nodded, as if not trusting his own voice. "Good, and I'll tell you this: everyone responsible is dead. Grabon and the others killed them before I arrived."

Zack smiled a little as they reached the gaming end

of the market. He stood looking around at the deserted area. "Why isn't anyone here?"

"Because they don't know how to play these games. That's why we're going to be demonstrating and honing your skills and mine at the same time. These are not combat games, but they take tremendous strength, balance, power, and endurance; you'll need all of that to be a Dragonman."

"Are they going to teach me how to fight?" Zack asked, amazed at the possibility.

"You're Grabon's boy; you'll have to know how to fight. I'm hoping to be a full Dragonmen; to do that, I need to practice. Let me tell you about fishing."

As Porter explained the rules, people walked by, looked in, and left. Soon enough they were stripping off their shirts, and Porter secured the pouch. He made sure Zack was shielded and they took turns falling into the water. They were catching their breath when Dotty started singing, and they both froze. By the time the song ended, Zack was openly weeping and Porter choked down his own emotions.

Dotty had created a song about setting loved ones free. He didn't know if the song had been aimed at Zack or if it was for LeeAnn or even little Matti, who had spoken so bravely about her first family. But it had touched his own heart as he thought of all those he had lost, not only through death, but because they had left him, afraid of his level of power and not trusting his control.

After a few moments, they resumed practice and were both doing considerably better. Zack was even crowing over a round where he didn't lose points. Then a man stumbled into the gaming area and Zack took a clumsy step back, as if in fear. Every repressed instinct rose in Porter as he moved between the boy and man.

"Can I help you?" Porter asked, even as he sent out a warning that there might be trouble brewing.

"It's Rick," Zack supplied, softly.

"What is that kid doing here?" Rick's tone slurred with drink, and his stance was aggressive.

"Grabon's boy," Porter emphasized the title, "and I are practicing."

"He's here playing games?" Rick demanded.

"He's learning. Do not come any closer," Porter warned as the man lowered his head and charged forward, causing Porter and Zack to move. "We are not looking for a conflict with you. Why don't you leave?"

"I could kick your ass," Rick sneered. "I kicked his often enough."

Zack started to step around Porter, but Porter waved him back. "You really need to leave. There is no fighting in the market, but I will defend Grabon's boy."

"How will you do that?" On the last word Rick charged again, and Porter sent a blast at the man's knee.

His reasoning seemed sound, a man with a damaged knee didn't run and couldn't fight, but Porter certainly hadn't meant to burst it open down to the bone. Zack stepped farther back as Tad arrived on Pit, but Porter stood still, staring down at Rick's leg.

Tad hopped down and ran over to check on the fallen man. "Hess and LeeAnn will be here shortly. He'll live that long. Any other injuries?" Tad's tone was calm.

"No, I imagine Zack is upset." Porter turned to see the boy retching in the bushes.

"It's probably the first blast injury he's seen. He's entitled to puke it up. Grabon is on his way and it looks like LeeAnn has arrived." Tad stepped aside.

LeeAnn didn't spare a glance for anyone but her patient. Rick screamed and fainted as she applied energy directly to the wound. Hess stood at her back, prepared to catch her. Within ten minutes the wound was healed over with no scar, but some pieces of flesh and bone were gone. "In time the flesh will fill in, but his knee will never be the same. He lost some significant bone."

"He should not have been threatening my boy," Grabon told them, patting Zack's head with a kind of rough affection. *"Porter did tell him to leave. I find no fault with his actions. Let Rick recover and send him home."*

"I think it's reasonable to banish him for a week for causing trouble," Tad suggested.

Grabon nodded his agreement, and Hess and Thane dragged the man away to a corner so they could clean up the gore. They used buckets of water drawn from the fountain and soon all evidence of violence was washed away. Someone brought LeeAnn a cup of tea and she sat quietly drinking.

"Show me what you have learned so far," Grabon invited Zack. While the boy demonstrated, Hess put his arm around his mate.

"You didn't sync your energy. I am very pleased."

She gave him a faint smile. "I was afraid if I tried you would let him bleed to death."

"Hmmm, that might have occurred to me," he answered softly.

LeeAnn grimaced and looked around. "He didn't deserve the consideration of a painless healing. Why did he come in here?"

Porter stepped toward them. "Zack had just had a perfect round, not a point lost, and we were celebrating. Rick must have recognized his voice. He was set to hurt the boy and I stepped in his way."

"Good for you," Hess answered.

"Are you hurt anywhere?" LeeAnn asked, looking him over.

"No, he never touched either of us. I thought one decisive blow was better than engaging in a brawl."

"Always a better choice than open combat. I'm

almost sorry you didn't go for the head," Thane said.

Chuckling, Porter glanced at Zack, who was showing off for Grabon. "As it is, Zack puked. He would have been traumatized if I had killed his mother's match while he watched."

"It would have saved the boy's mother, which is what he has been trying to do."

"She wasn't willing to save herself. Grabon gave her a choice."

"Not every woman can make that choice the first time it's offered," LeeAnn told them. "She did save her son; she gave him to Grabon."

Porter had to acknowledge that, but he didn't think Grabon had intended to let the boy return to that house no matter what the mother had said.

"Look, Porter, you have to see this," Zack called, catching their attention.

Grabon was fishing and they all went over to watch. He completed the first round with no loss of points, and Zack was to go next, beginning the second round. He managed to lose only one point and Grabon beamed at him proudly. Then after his second round with no point loss, Zack went again. This time he spread his feet wider as he saw Grabon doing and used his arms behind him as Grabon used his tail for balance. He didn't lose a single point and he was cheering. The noise disturbed Rick, who came awake cursing.

Grabon put a hand on Zack's shoulder and turned him back to the pool. *"He is not your concern. My men will send him away. I believe it is my turn."* While they finished their game, LeeAnn spoke with Rick.

"I healed as much as I could, but with a blast that results in so much missing muscle and bone, there is not much more to be done. Some of the muscle will regrow in time and you must continue to use the knee, but the bone that is missing is permanent. You might find it helpful to use a stick for walking."

Rick did his share of ranting and cursing, which LeeAnn ignored. Tad put up shields then, so nobody could hear him, including Zack. As LeeAnn stepped back, Tad and Hess stepped forward. They fined him for drunken brawling in the market and banished him for the week. One coin went into their fund, and the rest went to LeeAnn for the healing. Then Thane escorted him to the main gate.

By the time he was gone, Grabon had won the game and needed to return to his nest. *"I will see you for dinner,"* he told Zack, messing up his hair with his hand and claws. *"We are having ripper steaks, so do not eat too many meat pies."* He looked over at Porter. *"Get him some food and tea. It will settle his stomach even more. Then teach him the stones."*

"Rok has challenged him to a fishing game," Porter told him.

"One more game before the stones, but make sure he is shielded properly." Grabon took off and flew up toward the nest.

"It looks like you get a break for food and tea," Porter said.

"I can't believe he flew down here," Zack muttered.

Tad snorted and so did Pit. "You were upset and puking, what did you expect? Of course he came down. He sure didn't come down for the rest of us. Come on, we'll make sure you only eat four or five of those meat pies."

***

The men and dragons surrounded the boy as they walked out with LeeAnn and Hess. She and Hess went to see if anyone had seen Bernard while the others took Zack to get some food.

"I am glad Porter didn't blow up the man's head," LeeAnn whispered as they walked along.

"So am I, but I hope Zack's mother doesn't pay for his injuries with her own flesh. It all could have been avoided if he had just left the boy alone."

Sighing, she leaned into his side. "Some men can't. Maybe Rick is like Sam."

Hess shook his head. "No, Grabon would have killed him long ago if that were the case. Rick's problem is the wine."

They found Bernard asking for her over by the sisters' booth, and he followed them into the healing corner, away from prying eyes.

"I want to apologize for my behavior yesterday," he began, looking genuinely embarrassed.

"You were sick with pain and fever," LeeAnn answered dismissively.

Bernard nodded, obviously relieved she didn't hold it against him. "I feel so much better. I really can't thank you enough."

"You can pay her," Hess reminded him. "Then follow her directions so you don't get sick again."

Bernard had no trouble handing over payment and didn't argue about the brews or where he needed to purchase them. "I would like a word with Hess before I leave," he told LeeAnn in a respectful tone.

"She's my mate and she's not going anywhere without me. Why do you need to speak to me?"

"We got off on the wrong foot. I'm losing business because of the market and that's made me less than cooperative. I don't want to pack up my shop and go elsewhere. Before you opened the market, you had an idea of what I could do, but I wouldn't listen. Well, now I'm listening."

Hess looked at Bernard closely, but he seemed genuine. "All we wanted to suggest is that you carry some of the items we don't sell and won't sell at the market. Then we can refer interested parties to you."

Bernard nodded. "What kind of items?"

"You want the whole list? Start with building supplies, sinks, stoves, counters, and cold boxes.

Nobody here is selling bathing tubs, buckets, or laundry tubs. We will not allow the sale of any weapon in the market and that includes knives, even those for cooking. We are looking to put in a booth for sewing, but so far, we don't have a seller or much in the way of supplies. If I were you I'd stock materials and trims, needles and pins. If you want to open a booth for tubs and buckets, you'd probably do well, or simply have them in your store so we can send people there."

"That is very helpful," Bernard said, sounding shocked.

"We told you our goal was not to drive you out but to increase what people could buy. Walk around, take a look at what's available. Decide if you want to run a booth in addition to your store or simply carry things we don't have. Then let us know."

"I'll do that. Thank you." He looked over at LeeAnn and nodded. "I'll stop and get those brews."

After he left, she looked at Hess oddly. "He's a completely different person today."

"After you fell unconscious we had a little chat. He's decided he doesn't want to be an enemy of the Dragonmen, not and stay here."

"I suppose that was necessary?"

Hess grinned. "It was if he wanted to survive. I have more patience than some of the others. Now that we've completed your healing duties for the day, let's get out of here."

She laughed as he took her hand. "Where are we going now?"

"Home, where I can have you in my bed. I think we've both waited as long as we possibly can."

Chapter 17

Stuffed with meat pies, Zack returned to the gaming area to find Rok with the youngsters. They were all playing games of one kind or another. Porter grinned and raised his brows at Zack. "Don't forget what you have learned and make sure your shield is good."

Rok stepped up grinning. *"I heard you played well with Grabon. We will see how you do against me now that you have eaten and are feeling lazy."*

Zack laughed and stripped off his shirt. He hooked his feet under the rim of the pool and Porter and Rok both stopped him. *"You are not getting injured in a game. Step back and shield properly."*

Zack rolled his eyes. "I haven't fallen into the pool since the first rounds."

"It does not matter," Rok informed him with a growl. *"You do not play this game without proper shielding. If you even attempt it again I will inform Grabon."*

Feeling put upon, Zack shielded and then stepped up to the pool. Rok nodded and agreed to three rounds allowing the boy to go first. Zack made a good showing with only a small splash, so he only lost one point. Rok, who used a completely different style of standing on one foot, lost no points. Zack stepped up again to take his turn, and as he leaned over the pool, he lost his balance. The boy fell with enough force that he sat in the water shaking his head as Porter and Rok checked him for injuries. Golly joined the children scrambling to pick up the fish and toss them back in the pool. Zack climbed out feeling foolish, but all in one piece thanks to the shielding.

"You did not use your hands, so the game can continue if you are not rattled," Rok offered.

Zack agreed and took his turn, this time completing it with only the three-point loss. In the end, Rok lost one point and Zack lost four, but he had played well and wasn't hurt. The dark brown dragon slapped him on the back. *"You did well. Grabon will be proud. What do you work on next?"*

"The stones," Zack answered, looking at the game.

"Would you like me to demonstrate?" Rok asked, glancing at Porter.

"It's not going to hurt my feelings, go ahead." Porter nodded at the game stand and field.

Rok stepped up to the bucket, selected the five stones he wanted, and set them down at the throwing line. Two stones weighed as much as a bucket of water, Rok explained. The trick was to choose stones you could grip and release. There were three lines drawn down the game field. The first line was longer than the second, which was longer than the third. The goal was to get each stone past the third line and land it in the small square, and stop. It had to stay there, not roll or bounce away.

"As a beginner, just try to get it past the first line,"

Rok encouraged.

"Can you get it past the third?" Zack asked, measuring the distance with his eyes and figuring it was impossible.

"Of course, but I am a little out of practice. We will see how I do."

Rok threw one stone after another in quick succession until all five were past the third line and the air was scented with his energy. Zack stared at him in awe.

"It is an important skill to use power and muscle together. Not all of them are in line with the target; as I said, I am a little out of practice."

Zack ran down to bring back the stones and saw one was outside the lines. He shook his head and collected them, realizing just how heavy they were.

When he got them back, Golly asked if he could try and Rok nodded stepping back. *"Do not drop one on your foot,"* the dragon warned.

Golly picked up the stone, stepped back, and flung it past the second line. Porter grinned and patted his back. "That was great." Golly tried a few more times and always got the stones past the first line, but never to the third, but they could feel the power he used in the air around him.

"This is much better than throwing knives."

"I am sure it is," Porter told him.

Rok held out a stone to Porter and he took it, but Rok didn't let go. *"Muscle and a blast of power to send it flying."*

Porter nodded, took the stone, gathered his own energy, and flung the rock. Unfortunately, it blasted into small pebbles.

"That didn't work right." Porter scowled.

Rok laughed and patted his back. *"That is a different game and not for the market."*

Zack looked at Porter thoughtfully. "Your pebbles made it past the third line."

"I don't think that counts. Here, you give it a try." He handed another stone to Zack.

Zack didn't come close to the first line with five different stones. Then he and Golly ran down and collected them and brought them back. The large boy was out of breath and sat down for a minute, rubbing his chest. When he seemed recovered, Rok gathered the youngsters and they left to catch one of Mia's stories.

"I shouldn't have invited him to bring back the stones with me," Zack said softly as they left.

"From what I have seen, Golly likes to run and play. Sometimes it hits him hard, and he has to sit down and recover. There is nothing else that can be done."

"She could fix Rick's knee," the boy accused.

"But she couldn't replace what is now missing.

Golly's problem isn't fixable, or she would have already fixed it."

"Maybe she doesn't like him because he's big and sort of ugly."

"No, Zack. LeeAnn loves Golly with her whole heart. He's been with her for more than a year while they were both tortured, and she healed everything she could for him. LeeAnn helped him escape and she always heals him first. When that boy dies, it's going to break her heart. If there was a way to extend his life and make him happy, she would do it."

"It's not right that he should die after everything he's been through," Zack protested.

"No, it's not, but unfortunately, that's the way it is."

Zack picked up another stone, and power crackled around him as he threw it past the third line. They smiled at one another and Zack reached for another stone. After he had thrown five, he raced down to bring them back. Then Porter took a turn, and soon he got the stone to fly past the third line intact. As they continued, people came in to watch, among them the two visiting dragons they had met earlier with Brom.

Porter smiled, nodded, and held out a stone in invitation. The gray dragon looked at his companion, shrugged, took the stone and stepped up to the line. He selected four others and set them down as Rok had done. He drew in a deep breath and threw the stones one after another. Two exploded, and three were past the third line but off target. Zack ran down to fetch those.

The gray dragon bowed to Porter, picked up a stone, and handed it to him. Grinning, Porter selected his five, set them on the line, and waited for Zack to return. When he did, the boy's eyes met Porter's and he grinned. Porter took a moment to draw his power around him and threw one stone after another without bothering to see where the last stone landed. When they looked, all five were intact and past the third line, and three were on target.

Naturally those results sparked a competition. The green-and-gray dragon wanted to see if he could beat Porter, and the gray was eyeing Zack. As the games continued, the cheers and groans drew in small groups of humans and dragons to watch. Some were even drawn in to try. When Zack lost, he was able to keep grinning. He was happy to have gotten one stone on target past the third line. The gray was thrilled to have gotten two on target.

As the crowd thinned, the green-and-gray dragon returned, looked around and snorted, spewing spit and snot on Porter. Brom walked in laughing.

"He's disgusted that all our games are noncombative. Lif would prefer to see his power set against yours." Brom kept his mental voice mild and amused. *"You offended his sense of dragon superiority by beating him throwing stones."*

Lif picked up one of the stones and eyed Zack.

"Zack, shield now!" Porter yelled at the boy, who stared at the dragon in astonishment as he complied.

Brom shook his head slowly, spoke in low rumbling Dragon, and looked at the sky. Grabon was circling slowly overhead. He spiraled down, and Heron jumped off his shoulders when they were a good distance from the ground and landed at Lif's feet in a threatening stance. Grabon settled by Zack, keeping one wing extended over the boy in a clear gesture of protection.

Heron eyed Lif and spoke in Dragon, his tone harsh as he slowly came out of a defensive crouch. Lif answered, his tone full of appeasement. Zack imagined he was trying to explain that he had intended no real harm. Grabon then provided him and Porter with a translation. It had only been a passing thought, just to provoke a response. He was attempting to incite Porter, a mere human, to accept a power challenge. It was not meant as a challenge to Grabon or his companion.

As Heron spoke in Human, Brom translated to Dragon. "These games were offered to avoid combat, not goad it. If Lif wanted to challenge Porter to throw stones, Grabon himself would be pleased to stand as witness. If he wanted a different human to test his power against, Heron, companion to Grabon, would be happy to accept Lif's challenge in any of the games the market had to offer."

Porter swallowed nervously, sensing the power that surrounded Heron. Lif bowed and spoke to Heron directly, declining his invitation but glancing at Porter from the corner of his eye. Amused now, Heron looked at Porter. "He wants a rematch. Are you willing to accept?"

"I would be pleased to beat him a second time," Porter answered with a grin as Brom translated. Heron laughed and watched Lif as they moved to select the stones. Porter was feeling generous, so he motioned that the green-and-gray dragon could go first. Heron nodded in approval and stepped back to watch.

Lif sent his five stones flying one at a time. Two landed within the target zone, and the rest went past the third line. He stomped in frustration twice and stepped back. Porter set out his stones and took a moment to collect himself. Then he launched the five in quick succession. All went past the third line and three were within the target zone.

Grabon chuckled and ruffled Zack's hair as he chortled in approval. Lif muttered something to Brom as he took to the sky. Brom looked immediately to Grabon, who waved a hand.

"It is not important. His words pass as hot air over excrement. Let him stew in his own discontent. As long as he does not aim his ire at our youngsters or my boy Zack, I am willing to overlook his attitude."

"Would he have really thrown that stone?" Zack asked curiously.

"No, he was merely trying to cause a problem with Porter. Only he underestimated how provoking such a gesture would be; he now understands," Grabon explained.

"Zack did a good job at shielding on command,"

Heron pointed out. "He can be proud of that."

"Yes, he can. Porter did well in advising him. If I had chosen to blast Lif from the sky, my boy would have avoided injury, even from that. I chose well in assigning Porter to protect you." He grinned at Zack and ruffled his hair one last time. Heron vaulted on Grabon's back and they took off, spiraling upward.

"Keep practicing with the stones. It will help you coordinate power and muscle for other lessons you must learn."

When they flew out of sight, Zack let out a harsh sigh. "He really thought about blasting Lif."

"Lif is a fool to have provoked Grabon. He knew you were a territory youth in his nest, but assumed Grabon valued you less because you were human. It is not a mistake another dragon will make." Brom walked down to collect the stones. *"I will practice with Zack for a game if you want to get some tea,"* he told Porter.

"That's not a bad idea." He could use a few minutes. In his current state of mind, he was more likely to blast the stones to pieces. He went to the nearest tea stand and saw Tad leaning against a tree.

The other Dragonman pushed off with his shoulders and came to join him. "Now that you've gotten to know Grabon a little better, has your opinion changed from this morning?"

Porter shook his head, chuckling as he collected his

tea and sat with Tad. "My opinion has changed so many times through the day it's going to take hours to put my thoughts together. Do you know what just happened with Lif?"

"Only that Heron and Grabon arrived and wanted shields to keep everyone out of the play area."

"Lif threatened to throw a stone at Zack, trying to provoke me."

Tad sat up straighter. "Do we need to clean up a mess?"

Porter smiled. "No, violence was avoided. Grabon let Heron handle it. I think because he knew he would not be completely reasonable."

Tad nodded thoughtfully. "I wonder where Lif thinks he's staying tonight? I doubt Brom or Griss would give him perch with their own youngsters running lose in their nests."

"You think Grabon is going to kick him out?" Porter questioned, surprised.

"I can't imagine him letting Lif stay that close to his boy after he threatened him." Tad grinned at the sky. "It's going to rain this evening, sometime after sundown. I'll make sure the others know not to give perch to Lif. He can't be trusted around youngsters."

"What are his options?" Porter asked curiously.

Tad grinned. "He's going to have a cold, wet night. Even if he flies to another territory, he's going to be caught in the rain. Our dragons take that sort of thing much better than most. Besides, they all have enough power to generate shielding around their own area. Lif doesn't; it's why he's a permanent visitor. He relies on the shields of others."

"Then he is one stupid dragon," Porter admitted.

"This certainly hasn't been one of his brighter days. I'll walk back with you. I'm curious to see how Zack is doing."

They brought Zack and Brom each a cup of tea. When they arrived, Zack was deep into his fourth round with Brom. His shirt was soaked with sweat and he was grinning. They finished their fifth and final round and Zack took the tea with a word of thanks. Brom did the same and they sat down to enjoy it.

"You're looking pretty good, Zack. A couple more days and you'll be ready for some of those other games Grabon is planning on showing you."

"I've learned so much today," Zack commented, rubbing his arm muscles.

"He is going to be hurting tomorrow," Brom predicted.

"Griss sold him some liniment and brews for sore muscles. If he's smart he'll use those before he goes to bed," Porter said.

"I heard Grabon has been working all afternoon with Heron setting up other training games for tonight and tomorrow. I hope his boy is up to the task." Tad grinned and headed back toward the rest of the market. "If you think he's earned it, Mia has one last story before closing."

Porter looked at Zack and nodded. "I think he's earned a break before he has to go home. Come on, Zack. You're going to love story time. What story is she telling?"

Tad turned and smiled at Porter. "The forming of our clan, from the beginning."

Mia's booth was packed, and Thane and Pit were up front watching the crowd, which included Lif and his friend and all the youngsters including Golly. Rok stood over them with Redseth on his arm. Another group of dragons came in and settled to one side, sitting comfortably on their tails.

Mia began telling them all about Grabon's first days of awandering and how after his first year he unexpectedly met a human drowning in grief from the loss of his own family in a great fire. As she projected in Human, Pit gave the translation in Dragon. As she described them learning to communicate and the exchange of language, pictures flashed of them learning to hunt and fly together.

"They made many friends along the way, and Heron chose to awander with the young territory dragon," Mia explained. *"They shared their lessons and Heron added his own human wisdom to the young dragon's perspective, just as the dragon added to the man's understanding. They became companions and wandered for thirty years, going places dragons and humans had never shared."* Images of territories close and far flashed through their minds along with those

of human towns, colonies, and farms.

"*The day arrived when Grabon finally knew himself to be mature.*" Mia's posture changed, and her voice became more intense, more mature. "*They returned to a land that had captured both of their imaginations. It was the home of Heron's human friend, the Farmer Gordon. He had recently claimed his mate, Hanna, a talented gold crafter who, through no fault of her own, was alone in the world.*

"*Grabon and Heron claimed this territory and with the aid of Gordon, Hanna, and cousins Tad and Hess, they built the great nest Grabon lives in today. Heron's mate arrived after wandering for two years, bringing a youngster named Jenny, a sister to Trissy whose family had died of a terrible sickness. Heron claimed not only his mate, but her sister as his child. A clan was formed to ensure the security of this youngster, and the Dragonmen were born.*"

There was a smattering of applause, but Mia held up her hand.

"*Not too much later, Brom, Griss, Rok, Pit, and Thane, dragons known for their loyalty and courage as well as intelligence and ingenuity, traveled to see their friend Grabon. They had heard he had finally reached maturity and had claimed a territory of his own. The idea of merging human and dragon customs fascinated them, and they applied for clan status shortly after their arrival. Grabon gave them each a task to perform that would not only benefit the clan, but the territory. They had only a single cycle to see it through.*

"The sisters, Jamie and Janie, who had befriended Hanna and also Trissy were accepted. Grabon and Heron recognized their hidden talents and skills and they became the official designers and makers of the clan garb. They are treasured for their compassion and skills." Mia paused to grin at the sisters. *"Matti, born a Farmer youngster, was first befriended by young Jenny and later claimed and accepted by Trissy and Heron as one of their own. She left behind her old family and stepped into the position of the oldest youngster of Heron and Trissy's nest."* Mia gave a small wave to Matti, who returned the gesture with a grin.

"Tad and Hess returned to Grabon's territory to join the Dragonmen, bringing their many contacts in business and trade. After Brom and Griss completed their tasks and earned full clan status, they planned a combined human-and-dragon mission. They ransomed Brom and Griss's youngsters from a distant territory and successfully transported them home in the middle of winter. Brom and Griss earned the right to raise their own youngsters with full support from Grabon. During that journey, Tad found his mate, Dotty, and brought her home to be included and treasured by the clan. Pit claimed his mate shortly after, and Hanna and Trissy grew round with child."

The crowd collectively gave a sigh and Mia grinned.

"Certain members of the clan decided to open a market. We believe that alliances and understanding often begin with an exchange of foods and goods. On the day the market opened, Hess found his mate, LeeAnn, a gifted healer who helped to rescue Golly, a giant youngster who was in need of help. Everyone

welcomed LeeAnn and Golly to the clan with a special meal." Golly waved his hand, shouting that he was the Golly in the story. Several members of the audience chuckled.

"Hanna's child, Kenseth, was born and a new naming tradition was started. Now we have three new applicants to the Dragonmen clan being considered: one human and two dragons. Porter, born a Woodsman, is well on his way to earning his clan status. Dane and Nat came together to see the market. They seem fascinated by the workings of the clan and have announced their intent to earn acceptance. Last and accepted just this morning as a territory youth, was Grabon's boy, Zack. Half-mature and in need of guidance and training, he is just beginning to find his place, but he is welcome." Mia paused for emphasis and met the eyes of many visitors in the audience.

"This is our beginning. Our plan is to develop a shared culture and customs between humans and dragons. We inhabit the same planet and share in her bounty of power. It behooves us to find the means to get along. We act in honor of the old customs of dragons and the newer customs of humans, following the rules set by our planet, council, and territory. We are Dragonmen and we defend and protect, sell and trade in peace here in Grabon's great territory. We are people of power, strength, and skill and we demand respect."

As she finished there was applause and foot stomping. LeeAnn and Hess grinned at one another as they stood with hands clasped in the back of the crowd. They had slipped in unnoticed because Tad had warned them Mia was going to tell this tale. It seemed that every time she told it, it grew. The youngsters were always thrilled to hear their names.

As the visitors left, the Dragonmen remained and smiled at one another.

"In the next telling," Brom began, speaking gently to Mia, *"you may name Starseth. I know it goes against dragon customs, but it would mean much to her to hear her name as part of our story."*

Griss shifted on his feet. *"You may include Redseth as well."*

Mia grinned and nodded. *"I will be pleased to include their names in the next telling of the story. Have you changed your mind that youngsters should be sheltered, so their names are never to be included in a story told in public?"*

"I find my mind changing all the time as to what should and should not be," Brom admitted. *"The blending of two cultures is not easy, but without that, my youngster would be completely blocked from my influence."*

"I do not think it is supposed to be easy or convenient," Griss added. *"Tradition is difficult to surrender; it is locked in with our memories and our concept of self. I seem to be changing only one piece at a time."*

Mia patted their shoulders. *"If it is any comfort, I do*

not think it is any easier for the humans. They are changing too."

Hess put his arm around LeeAnn, and Golly came over to join them, filled with excitement over the day's events. Zack watched from beside Porter as LeeAnn adjusted his clothes and brushed his hair off his forehead.

"Why doesn't Golly live with LeeAnn and Hess?" Zack asked Porter quietly.

Tad put a hand on each of their shoulders. "Come with me and I'll explain," he invited softly. They followed him back into the market and found a bench beside a large old tree.

"Grabon made the decision that Golly should stay with him. Aside from Hess and LeeAnn needing time alone to secure their bond, Grabon felt our healer needed some distance from her own trauma, as did Golly. It has worked out well so far."

Porter, who knew far too much about LeeAnn's trauma, nodded. Any distance they could give her would be a help. How she had managed to establish a bond with Hess after so recently being rescued was beyond his understanding.

Tad grinned as their newest couple moved toward them, Golly close on their heels. "I had wondered whether you would manage to hear that."

"It was close, but we arrived just as Mia started. I liked Pit doing the dragon translation at the same time, at least for this story. So tell me, brother, would you like me to do the closing announcement? You did literally drag me out of bed to get me here." He bent over in a whoosh when LeeAnn hit him in the belly.

Zack stared at them wide-eyed. "She just hit him," he whispered to Porter.

"He deserved it," LeeAnn whispered back with a grin for the boy.

"She doesn't hit me," Golly told them.

"That's because you don't embarrass her, Golly. You're a good boy and she loves you. I was teasing her and I shouldn't have. Are you ready for closing?"

Golly thought about it for a minute. "Do you think Hanna made any cookies?"

"I think you'll have to stop by on your way home and ask. You might even ask Rok if you could go with Zack and meet them up in the nest."

Golly looked at Zack. "Do you like cookies too?"

Zack looked over at Porter for a second until Porter nodded permission. "I think everyone likes cookies. Let's ask Rok and see what he says?" The boys went off and Porter looked at LeeAnn, then Hess.

"You both look in much better shape than you did this morning."

"We've been growing the bond all day, so I'm not feeling quite as feral. Where is Josiah?" Hess asked.

Tad snorted and motioned with his head. "He's been in the vegetable stands or the garden all afternoon. I think he's got some plan going to create some new vegetables and thinks our garden setup would work perfectly."

"You did remind him that it's a public garden and if he wants to experiment he needs to create his own, right?" Hess asked.

"Of course. He said he'd talk to Grabon about a little piece of land. I have a feeling we're not getting rid of Josiah anytime soon."

Golly and Zack came back, both looking pleased. "Rok agrees that Golly can walk home with us and we can stop and see if Hanna has any cookies. Come on, Porter, he said you have to go with us," Zack urged.

Porter waved as he let the two boys drag him off.

***

"I really wasn't sure about him at first," Hess confessed.

"Porter or Zack?" Tad asked, grinning as Dotty joined them and took her mate's hand.

"Porter. He seemed too reserved, but something happened."

"He simply needed time to drop that civilized veneer he's worn his whole life and get rid of a few human notions that don't belong here."

"Which notions are those?" LeeAnn asked.

"Human superiority," Hess and his brother answered at the same time.

"What does that mean?" Dotty asked, frowning.

"He couldn't understand why Gordon or Heron wasn't the territory leader and wondered why we had chosen Grabon." Tad explained with a shrug.

All four of them chuckled and looked over the market. "He finally got it," Tad finished.

"It took him long enough," Hess grumbled.

LeeAnn poked him in the stomach. "How long did it take you and Tad?"

The brothers looked at one another and shrugged. "Not that long," Tad answered.

"It took me longer to claim my mate," Hess confessed sheepishly.

Tad grinned and pulled Dotty close. "We always knew it would, despite your many protests. It's a whole different thing when your heart is involved."

"That's the truth," Hess answered, grinning at LeeAnn.

***

A nip of cool broke the heat as the second sun began to set. Summer was coming to a reluctant end. The Farmers visiting the territory had helped plan and witness the latest bonding ceremonies and everyone was drowsy and content. Grabon tucked Golly into his bed, knowing the end was closer than most people knew. The large boy had been experiencing shortness of breath and weakness for some time. LeeAnn had done everything she could.

Tria frowned at him before stepping closer with tears running down her nose. *"He is not ready to meet the planet's strength with his own."*

"It is not a choice I make, Tria. When his heart stops, he will join his power to the planet, just as I will and you will at the end of our lives."

"I am not ready to say goodbye."

He took a deep breath and had to blink back tears from his eyes. *"None of us are ready, but it is Golly's task, his purpose, and we must help him if we can."*

"There is nothing more LeeAnn can do?"

Grabon shook his head.

Tria settled on the headboard watching Golly sleep. A little at a time his heart slowed, but his eyes never opened again. Rok and Thane came and sat with them along with Zack, who called out to Porter. The visitors on the walls turned their backs to give them privacy as the clan slowly began to assemble. By the time they called LeeAnn up to the nest, Golly lingered only a few moments more, but he never woke.

***

As they had with the bonding ceremonies, they combined traditions for Golly's farewell, walking him in a wagon through the village, market, and town, so everyone could wish him well before they buried his remains so he could nourish the planet and grow a very tall tree.

Afterward, LeeAnn knelt at his grave, holding on to Hess's hand crying inconsolably. After a time, Hess pulled out a red button and showed her and she sniffed back tears and tried to smile.

"He loved that game."

"It was a favorite." Hess nodded, blinking to keep his vision clear.

"Do you know how many times he checked inside my shoes?"

"You never hid a button there?" Hess asked in disbelief.

"Never."

Hess helped LeeAnn to her feet. "Let's go home."

"Your family and relatives...."

"They understand. Besides, Tad will keep them away. It's just us and we'll get through this together."

"Should I say something to Grabon?"

"I do not think it is needed. He has Zack, Tria, Rok, and Thane to keep him company. Let the bond ease our pain together. Most days I am most grateful for the love and passion of the bond. Today I am grateful for the ability to heal heartache and grief."

She turned into his arms and laid her ear upon his chest over his beating heart. "I will miss him."

"We will *all* miss him." Hess gently stroked her hair as their combined energy sealed them together in a healing cocoon of warmth, love, and compassion.

Dear Readers,

I am so excited to bring out Healing NewEarth 4. It is one of my favorites because so much happens. Now that readers know something about my world, the opportunities are endless to create side stories and build up other characters. I am sure that given enough time, I will probably do that, but I am fascinated by Grabon and his commitment to Heron and their drive to find a way for dragons and humans to coexist in more than a superficial level.

This story more than any of the others so far, shows how willing Grabon is to listen to someone else's good ideas. He allows Pit, Thane, Hess and Tad to build their market and bring crowds of strangers into his territory. I would bet money he knew some of those visitors were going to cause problems, but he also knew his people needed to contribute to the cause and be a part of something larger. Grabon is a wise dragon and he knows how to keep his people busy and happy.

I hope you enjoy this book as much as I have and please, leave a review on Amazon. Feel free to contact me at JuliaSchmeelk.com. I love to hear from readers. Be on the lookout for Grabon's Nest NewEarth5 coming out in July.

Happy Reading,
Julia

Made in the USA
Lexington, KY
04 May 2018